MW00931459

Forbidden
Book Three in the Kindred Series

By Nicola Claire

ISBN-13: 978-1482537000
ISBN-10: 1482537001

nicolaclairebooks.com

Cover Art by LA LA
Image credit: 123RF Stock Photo
Image #12942160 & #25634698

1

More books by Nicola Claire:

Kindred Series

Kindred
Blood Life Seeker
Forbidden Drink
Giver of Light
Dancing Dragon
Shadow's Light
Entwined With The Dark
Kiss Of The Dragon
Dreaming Of A Blood Red Christmas (Novella)

Mixed Blessing Mystery Series

Mixed Blessing
Dark Shadow (Coming Soon)

Sweet Seduction Series

Sweet Seduction Sacrifice
Sweet Seduction Serenade
Sweet Seduction Shadow

Sweet Seduction Surrender
Sweet Seduction Shield
Sweet Seduction Sabotage
Sweet Seduction Stripped
Sweet Seduction Secrets (Coming Soon)

Elemental Awakening Series

The Tempting Touch Of Fire
The Soothing Scent Of Earth
The Chilling Change Of Air
The Tantalising Taste Of Water (Coming Soon)

H.E.A.T. Series

A Flare Of Heat
A Touch Of Heat
A Twist Of Heat (Novella)
A Lick Of Heat (Coming Soon)

Citizen Saga

Elite
Cardinal
Citizen

Scarlet Suffragette

Fearless
Breathless (Coming Soon)

For: You, the Reader.
Remember you are more.

Definitions

Accord – A blood binding agreement, often between two parties of equal power; cannot be broken.

Alliance – A word of honour agreement; has varying degrees of binding, some alliances cannot be broken.

Blood Bond – A binding connection between master and servant, requiring the exchange of blood to seal. It can only be broken by someone more powerful than the master who created it. A blood bond establishes a close relationship between the blood bonded. The master provides safety and protection, the servant offers obedience and loyalty.

Bond – The connection between joined kindred Nosferatu and Nosferatin; reflects the emotional and psychological relationship. Enables both parties to find each other over distance; to perform whatever is required to get to that person, overcoming any obstacle; to direct thoughts to each other; to feed off the life force of each other. It is always an equal exchange.

Command – A directive given by a Master vampire to one of his line. It requires *Sanguis Vitam* in order to enforce obedience. It cannot be ignored.

Dream Walk – A Nosferatin power, enabling the Nosferatin to appear in a different location. The Dream Walker is invisible, cannot be sensed or smelled, and only heard if they talk when in this realm. They can, however, interact and be harmed. The only exception to a Dream Walker's invisibility is another Nosferatin. Two Dream Walks in a 24 hour period results in prolonged unconsciousness once the Dream Walker returns to their body. A very rare power.

Final death – The true death of a Nosferatu. There can be no survival from the final death.

Glaze – The ability to influence another. It requires direct eye contact and *Sanguis Vitam* to insert the influence. Usually a Nosferatu skill, allowing a vampire to influence a human.

Herald – The Nosferatin who recognises the Prophesy. It is the Herald's responsibility to acknowledge the *Sanguis Vitam Cupitor* and thereby initiate the Prophesy.

Hapū – (Maori) Tribe; sub-tribe – e.g. the Westside Hapū of Taniwha is the local Auckland sub-tribe of New Zealand Taniwha.

Iunctio – (Latin). The Nosferatu connection and governing power. All vampires are connected to one another via this supernatural information exchange highway; enabling sharing of rules, locations of safe havens and hot spots to avoid. It is powered by both Nosferatu and Nosferatin *Sanguis Vitam*, but is operated by the Nosferatu in Paris. There are twelve members of the *Iunctio* council, headed by the Champion. The *Iunctio* is tasked with policing all supernaturals throughout the world.

Joining – The marriage of a kindred Nosferatu with a kindred Nosferatin. Upon joining the Nosferatu will double their *Sanguis Vitam* and the Nosferatin will come into their powers, but for the Nosferatin, their powers will only manifest after reaching maturity; the age of 25. The joining will also make the Nosferatin immortal. A symbiotic relationship, should one member of the joining die, the other will too. Without a joining, the Nosferatin would die one month past their 25th birthday. The joining also increases the power of the *Iunctio* and Nosferatu as a whole.

Kaitiaki – (Maori) New Zealand Shape Shifter (Taniwha) name for Nosferatin. Meaning protective guardian of people and places.

Kindred – A Nosferatu or Nosferatin sacred match, a suitable partner for a joining. To be a kindred there must exist a connection between the Nosferatu and Nosferatin; only those suitably compatible will be kindred to the other.

Line – The family of a Master Vampire, all members of which have been turned by the master, or accepted via blood bond into the fold.

Lux Lucis Tribuo – (Latin) The Giver of Light. The third part of the Prophesy. The *Lux Lucis Tribuo* is charged with balancing out the Dark in vampires, with the Prophesy's Light.

Master – A Nosferatu with the highest level of *Sanguis Vitam*. There are five levels of Master, from level five – the lowest on the *Sanguis Vitam* scale, to level one – the highest on the *Sanguis Vitam* scale. Only level one Masters can head a line of their own. Some Nosferatu may never become Masters.

Master of the City – A level one Master in control of a territory; a city.

Norm – A human unaware of the supernaturals who walk the Earth. They also do not have any supernatural abilities themselves.

Nosferatin – (*Nosferat–een)* - A vampire hunter by birth. Nosferatin were once of the same ilk as Nosferatu, descendants from the same ancestors, or a God. The Nosferatin broke off and turned towards the Light. Their sole purpose is to bring the Nosferatu back from the Dark, this can include dispatching them, bringing them the final death, when they cannot be saved. They are now a mix of human and Nosferatin genetics.

Nosferatu – A vampire. The Nosferatu turned towards the Dark, when their kin, the Nosferatin turned towards the Light. They require blood to survive and can be harmed by UV exposure and silver. They do not need to breathe or have a heartbeat. They are considered the undead.

Prohibitum Bibere – (Latin) The Forbidden Drink. The second part of the Prophesy. The *Prohibitum Bibere* is a siren to the Dark vampires throughout the world, calling their Darkness towards the Light.

Pull – The Nosferatin sense of evil. Guides a hunter to a Dark vampire; sometimes, but not always a rogue, who is about to feed off an innocent.

Rākaunui – (Maori) Full Moon.

Rogue – A vampire no longer controlled by a master, full of evil and Darkness, feeding indiscriminately and uncontrolled.

Sanguis Vitam – (Latin) The Blood Life or life force of a Nosferatu. It represents the power they possess. There are varying degrees of *Sanguis Vitam*.

Sanguis Vitam Cupitor – (Latin) The Blood Life Seeker. The first part of the Prophesy. The *Sanguis Vitam Cupitor* can sense and find all Dark vampires throughout the world.

Sigillum – (Latin) A permanent mark of possession.

Taniwha – (Maori) New Zealand Shape Shifter. Dangerous, predatory beings. The Taniwha have an alliance with the Nosferatins.

Turned – The action of changing a human into a

vampire.

Vampyre – Old term for vampire; used rarely in modern language.

Never show fear.
Never give an inch.
Always stay on guard.
Nosferatin Mantra

Chapter 1
Full Moon

I hadn't planned on being here, I didn't really want to be. I had hoped things would be a little different, that was for sure. Jerome *had* made it quite clear, that being on Hapū land tonight could prove fatal. Besides it being Rākaunui, which is never a good time of the month if you're visiting shape shifters, it was also the night of the challenge.

But then of course, that was why I *was* here.

Since returning from Paris one week ago, I'd been trying to get my former best friend Rick to agree to a meeting, but he'd been evasive. Hell, he'd been missing in action. I had visited *Tony's Gym*, where he works as a kick-boxing instructor, twice daily for the past seven days, but he'd just been a no-show. No explanation to his boss, no idea what he was up to, just vanished.

Not to be out-done, I'd phoned continuously, leaving messages on his home phone as well as his cellphone. And when that didn't work, trying Celeste, his fiancée and also a good friend of mine. But she'd either been turned against me by Rick's absolute hatred of vampires and anything to do with them, or she simply didn't want to be in the middle anymore.

Fine. I could take a hint, but then I am also extremely stubborn when I set my mind to something and stopping Rick from making this fundamental, idiotic, absolutely ridiculous mistake was at the top of my shit list right now. And trust me, to be at the top, it's gotta be big. My shit list is long and complicated and includes two master vampires fighting for my affections, the vampire governing body, the

Iunctio, breathing down my neck waiting for me to screw up, and oh, the latest, the entire world population of Darkened vampires homing in on me and heading my way. And that's not even mentioning the Prophesy.

But, one thing at a time. Shape shifters and shape shifter politics.

Rick used to be my best bud, we did almost everything together. He was my kick-boxing instructor, my bar hopping mate and someone I could talk to about all the supernatural crap that invaded my life. Being a shape shifter he was privy to that world, being my friend he didn't judge, just lent an ear. But, then things changed.

The shape shifters helped me fight a particularly nasty master vampire named Max and in the process one of their young Taniwhas, Rocky, died. I'll never forget Rocky, he was so full of life. And I'll never forget watching him die. It's just something that will stay with me forever. Since then, Rick has changed. I'm not entirely sure that some of what he has become wasn't lurking in the background before and I never saw it, or if Rocky's death was what did it. But since that battle, since the Taniwhas came to my aid, honouring a centuries old alliance they had with my kind, Rick has changed.

Now he wants to hunt the creatures of the night, he wants them all dead. Not that I don't sympathise with some of that desire. I'm a vampire hunter, it's in my blood to hunt and kill the Darkest of the creatures of the night, but they are not all bad. In fact, I'm joined to a fairly decent one. Well, most of the time he's decent and some of the time he's a manipulative son of a bitch, but he has Light in him, as well as Dark. But, because of that Light, he does not deserve to die. Rick disagrees. He thinks I've gone soft, or been glazed by vampires into believing something that is not true. But Rick's the one who's had his mind messed with. I don't know if it's the grief or years of pent up anger, but he's not thinking straight and I've got to do something about it.

He challenged Jerome, the Hapū master and a really nice, down to earth, kind of guy. And as an alpha in training, Rick's challenge is for that top spot, Alpha. A challenge like that can only have one outcome, one winner. To win, someone has to die and Jerome has told me, it will be him. He can't bring himself to kill Rick. Although not his biological son, Rick is like a son to Jerome all the same and Jerome just can't end his life that way.

So, here I am. Hiding out on Hapū land, trying to stay downwind of those super sensitive noses. Trying not to make a sound as I approached the central area, where all the houses are and the cars park and they have *Hangis* and gatherings and live their communal lives with such love. And where they will watch their Alpha fight their Beta and someone die. It is ludicrous, but they are not entirely human, are they? They're Hapū and as much as I don't understand what's happening tonight, I cannot stand by and not do something. I just can't.

It had taken me a good twenty minutes to make it on foot through the woods that surround their homes, not to mention having to cut through the barbed wire fence that surrounds the land, keeping Norms out and allowing the Hapū to run free on Rākaunui. But I finally made it to a decent spot, still hidden, but able to take in most of the scene before me.

13

I could feel the tension, I could smell the fear. If you don't know already, I'm also not entirely human too. I'm a kindred Nosferatin, a descendant from a long line of vampire hunters, but more than that, I'm from the same line that vampires, or Nosferatu, descend from as well. So, I've got a little bit of them in me too. I don't need blood to survive, but I'm fast, strong and have heightened senses, such as smell. I've also got a little bag of Nosferatin powers to call on, but I'm seriously hoping none of that would be necessary tonight. Not that I'm sure any of it would work against Taniwhas, my powers seem to be specifically related to the undead, but you never know.

In the few minutes I'd been sitting there, hiding behind a bush, more and more of the Hapū had come out and positioned themselves around the clearing, in a big, uncomfortable, feet shuffling circle. Some of them had blocked my vision, but they were all too riled to stand still, so the shuffling from foot to foot was a help. At least I could see through the gaps and get a glimpse of what was about to happen in the glow of all the tall lamps of fire that rimmed its edge. The flicker of the flames lighting the area leant an eerie cast to the setting, making goosebumps rise on my bare arms. At least it wasn't cold, summer was making an early appearance, thank God.

Just what did I plan to do when Rick and Jerome came out? I didn't really know, but if I could stop this I would and to hell with the consequences. I would not stand by and watch a friend die right in front of me again and do nothing to prevent it.

Finally they both came out at the same time, as though it had been agreed upon, or they had just simply felt the

14

other emerge from their home and came out too. The silence was all-encompassing. I couldn't even hear any insects in the undergrowth anymore, nor birds in the trees. Everything was holding its breath.

Part of me still thought this would stop, this wouldn't happen. Rick would come to his senses or Jerome would say something that would appease Rick and it would all be over. Hugs and kisses all round. But, I've seen how bad people can be, how bad creatures can be. Sometimes there is only Dark and even the Light can't be seen.

The rich, deep timbre of Jerome's voice filled the night air, making my heart thump in my throat and my hands clasp over my mouth to stifle a gasp.

"You have been called here tonight to witness a challenge." He turned in a circle, looking at each of his Hapū members. Taking his time, making sure to see them, I guess, one more time before he died. How could he face this and be so strong? "Your Beta wishes a different path for you, than I can condone. Tonight will decide which path you take. I ask only this, as your current Alpha, think wisely before you follow blindly, do not walk into temptation without a second glance. We may not be a democracy in a Hapū, but we have honour. Do not forget that *kairakau*, do not forget your honour."

"Enough." Rick spat the word at Jerome, the look on his face so alien, so not right. I had never seen him look at Jerome with anything but love and respect before, this was so wrong, so not Rick. "You are a weak Alpha. You don't have the strength it takes to keep us proud, to keep us strong."

Jerome just shook his head sadly. "You think pride

15

equals prowess, you think strength equals dominance. Have I not taught you anything, *tama?*"

"I am not your son." Rick's fists were clenched, his face grimaced. Jerome just sighed.

"You called the challenge, Rick, what limitations will you have?" Jerome just sounded tired now, like he'd given up, he wanted this to be over.

"No changing, we fight as men and the victor leads the hunt on the Rākaunui in our true forms."

There were howls from the crowd, human voices raised in inhuman sounds. Whether they agreed with what Rick proclaimed, or didn't, or just were too excited being a Rākaunui and couldn't wait to change form with the victor, I couldn't tell. But there was a noticeable hitch in power through the clearing, enough to make me sit back on my butt, blown over by the force of it.

Taniwhas are supernatural creatures too, they have their own power to call on when they change and right now, they all wanted to change. I could hardly draw a breath, the force of that combined otherworldly power washing over me, making my body tingle, my chest tight and my head pound. Even getting up and walking into that circle suddenly felt impossible. I couldn't move.

I fell silently onto my side, drawing a short breath in and then another and another. All I could see was a sideways view of the clearing, through the brush, through the legs of the excited crowd, to Jerome and Rick, a few feet apart facing off at each other. I tried to open my mouth, to say something, to scream *stop*, but my mouth wouldn't move, couldn't move. The slow realisation that I was about to watch my ex-best friend kill another person, someone I think I can also call a friend, and do nothing about it, dawning in my mind. Like a cancer I wanted rid of, but knew it had passed that point of no return, no longer possible to be stopped, no longer possible to be excised. Just like Rocky, I would stand by and watch this happen and do nothing to stop it.

I'm not usually one for tears. I was raised on a farm. Every Spring I would fall in love with the lambs only to have them taken by a truck at the end of Summer to the slaughter house. When I was very young, my parents, my Aunt and Uncle actually, would make a story up, so I wouldn't know what was about to happen to them. But when I turned five, my Uncle decided I was old enough to know the truth. I cried that Summer, like I had never cried before, but it didn't stop them from herding up the lambs, from loading the truck and from the truck driving away to the abattoir. My Aunt cooked lamb for dinner that night. I don't think she was trying to be cruel, I think it was just what she had it in the freezer and that was what dinner was that night, but I didn't want to eat it. I swore I'd never eat lamb again.

But, then I smelt the roast from my bedroom, the succulent smell of rosemary and garlic, roast lamb and potatoes wafting toward my room. I'd been crying all afternoon, unable to face my Uncle, but the smell of that delicious meal pulled me out of my bedroom and into the dining room. My Aunt and Uncle didn't say anything when I sat down at the table and started eating my meal. They didn't apologise for taking the lambs away to be killed, they didn't ask if I was OK, they just nodded, as though I had done a brave thing and went on with their meal.

I learnt a valuable lesson that day. Some things you can change, some things you just can't and others you just have to accept for what they are. Tears didn't help. Reality doesn't answer to a sob. So, I try not to cry, whenever I'm faced with something that is too much to bear. I try not to, but sometimes there are some things you just have to cry over. And lately, I seemed to be having that issue more and more.

I felt the hot wet flow of tears down my cheeks into the dirt and dust of the underbrush beneath my face. My vision became blurry, my breathing more of a hiccup than a shallow gasp. I was still unable to move, the Taniwhas' power escalating to such a level that I felt frozen in time, but I could see everything. Although distorted, I could tell what I was looking at. Man on man, beast on beast, it's all the same when you're fighting to the death. Taniwhas are strong, even in their human form, they can rip a man's arm off, use their human teeth to tear flesh from bone. Their nails are not claws, but the marks left behind can be just as deadly.

Jerome fought for a while. I think it's instinct to fight back. You either give in to the flight response immediately, or you fight. He didn't have a choice to flee, he was only ever going to have to face this and not run, but initially he fought back. He landed a few blows, he made Rick's job harder, but then he settled into it, like an old familiar coat, he accepted its weight. And when Rick had least expected it, when he had resigned himself to a battle to the end, Jerome simply stepped forward at the right time, angled himself towards Rick's fist at the right moment and let physics take over.

He went down like a dead weight, because that's what he was.

I held my breath, just as those gathered held theirs and Rick slowly stepped forward and knelt by his mentor, his Alpha, his enemy, confirming he was dead with a howl from his thrown back head. Letting it carry away on the wind under the gaze of a Full Moon.

The rest of the Hapū began taking up the howl. At first so fierce and then so sad, like a lament on the night air, they mourned their leader, they cried through their howls and they said their goodbyes.

I still couldn't move. I knew the predicament I was in. If someone found me here, it would not be pretty. Not only had I witnessed a private sacred Hapū rite, I had witnessed murder and on top of that, they were about to change and nothing could stop them now.

I felt the power shift slightly around me, like a heatwave, shimmering in front of my eyes. Through the haze of power I saw Rick change; swift, smooth, nothing like they have you believe on TV. It's almost magical, something to marvel at, not be afraid of. But I knew I needed to be afraid, because as soon as they changed, they'd find me. In their Taniwha forms their sense of smell is so much greater and I'd been lying here for a while, sweating, crying, snivelling any number of smells they'd instantly home in on. I was a perfect prey to the predator awakening.

One by one the Hapū followed suit, like a set of dominoes, unable to stop the force that topples the next. Just going with the flow from that first dominant push, from their now new Alpha, they began to change. Scales and claws, jaws full of serrated teeth, greys and whites flashed throughout the clearing before me. Although all basically the same shape and colour combination, each one looking distinctly different in their Taniwha skin. No two humans are ever the same, likewise no two Taniwhas.

When the final member of the Hapū had changed I felt the power lift and I could move. The magic that had made them what they now were, dissipating into the night. I took a deep breath in, the first in over half an hour and I carefully sat myself up.

That shift of my body was enough. Heads swivelled to where I had been lying hidden, noses sniffed the air, muzzles drew back exposing impossibly long Taniwha fangs and a low growl came from the closest of the Hapū, flowing out towards the rest until it reached Rick. His eyes bore into me, even though I knew he couldn't really see me through the thick foliage I was behind, but he knew it was me.

I had a second to comprehend this. And then I ran.

I'm faster than Taniwhas, since I joined with my kindred vampire and matured at the age of 25, I have come into some nifty powers, speed being one of them. But, this was rough terrain and I didn't know it. I'd only ever driven right up to the clearing where the houses are at, along a dirt road, I had never gone for walkies in their woods. All of it was unfamiliar, but to them, it was their home, they knew it blind.

I fell over fallen logs, I scraped my knees on barely hidden rocks and smashed into low branches, scraping my cheeks, nearly piercing my eyes and still I could feel them on my heels. Their snapping and snarling and growling and baying to the moon. The hunt was on and I was the prey. My heart was in my throat, my breathing ragged. I'd been in tight situations before, some may even say I thrive on them, but having a Hapū of angry, hungry Taniwhas chasing you over rough and uneven, unfamiliar ground on the night of the Rākaunui is not my idea of a cup of tea.

I thought I was heading in the right direction, back to the car on the other side of the fence, where I had cut a very small gap in the chain-link there. If I was wrong, things were going to get bad. I only had a silver knife on me, my stakes were still in the car, but a knife against one Taniwha could be useful, they don't do silver well, but against fifty, maybe more? I wasn't hopeful.

I could tell they were flanking me, I could hear them fanning out around me, moving ahead and circling round. If they made a complete circle before I reached the fence, I was in trouble. I can't fly like a vampire, I can jump pretty high given the right circumstances, but not a 10 foot chain-link fence topped with barbed wire. Even I can't do that.

So, I just ran faster.

Faster meant more branches, more scratches, but strangely enough less tripping, less falling, somehow making me skim the undergrowth and hidden hazards, almost flying across the terrain. If I wasn't shit scared right now, I'd be revelling in this new found freedom. Speed, but more speed than I had ever used before in my life. I have had to run fast since joining and Bonding with Michel, but I'd never managed this type of speed before.

I made it to the fence before the Taniwhas, but not quite at the right spot. I recognised the area, so it wasn't far away. I had to scan quickly, slowing my speed a fraction,

21

but I spotted the gap and made for it, closer to the Taniwhas coming from the right than I wanted. But I knew now, I could make it. I knew I could get there before them.

I slid to the ground, feet first towards the gap. Don't ask me why, I think most people would have thrown their arms forward and let their bodies follow, but I have skidded through tighter spots feet first before, so I knew it was a move I could pull off. My feet slid through the gap, followed by my body, then my head. I landed crouched down on the grass on the other side of the fence and turned my head in time to see a claw slice through the gap towards me.

One of the most nifty new things to happen when I joined with my kindred, was an increase in reflex action. I thanked my luck stars tonight for that.

I rolled back from where I had been crouched, doing a complete reverse somersault away from that claw; head over back, feet flicking out behind and over, just managing to stay out of its reach. I landed with a thud against the Land Rover Discovery I'd driven tonight. One of Michel's pool vehicles, but mine to use when I needed it. At least I could be grateful it wasn't the BMW Series 1 Convertible Michel had presented me with. I gave that one back. This was our compromise. I *borrowed* the Discovery when I needed a car. That way Michel knew I was driving something suitably safe and I didn't feel like a kept woman. The Discovery never came home with me, it stayed at Michel's. I was adamant about that.

I sat there stunned, trying to catch my breath and make myself move, but unable to pull my gaze away from the muddy brown Taniwha eyes that watched me. I knew those eyes, even in Taniwha form, I still recognised them.

"Congratulations." My voice was even, if just a little breathless. "On your promotion in the Hapū."

He just growled, low and long.

We stared at each other for a moment. Him unable to get through the small gap, me catching my breath, then I stood shakily and opened the door to the Land Rover, slid in and turned the key.

I guess, at least, I knew where I stood.

Rick was Alpha of the Westside Hapū. And I was at the top of his shit list too.

Chapter 2
Laying Down The Law

I'd made it about a kilometre down the road. I knew the Taniwhas wouldn't leave their land in Taniwha form, too dangerous out in the country like this, they'd be shot on sight by some well meaning farmer who just happens to carry his shotgun in the back of his Ute. They couldn't risk discovery, even if I was the one that got away.

Despite that knowledge though, I was still pretty much a wreck. I had scrapes and bruises and cuts all over me, but that wasn't the worst of it. No, the worst was the image of Jerome falling to the ground. The worst was the knowledge that Rick had killed him. Rough, tough, gruff Jerome, who had a heart of gold and a bear hug to rival the best of them. He'd welcomed me on pack lands, he'd opened up his world to the lost Nosferatin and been there when I needed to call on old ties.

My depth of respect for Jerome was bottomless. And now he was dead, because of Rick. I stifled a sob and tried to brush the tears away so I could focus on the road. I really didn't want to pull over, I was still too close to Hapū land to feel entirely safe, so I was risking an accident just to get away, but it was getting harder and harder.

Suddenly, out of nowhere, a figure appeared on the road ahead. I slammed on the brakes and made the four-by-four screech to a stop before hitting him. Thank God for ABS brakes. He was at my driver's side door in a flash, pulling it open and pulling me to him, crushing me to his chest.

"*Ma douce, ma douce*, what have you been doing now?"

I didn't reply, just let him hold me, just let his warm arms encase me and took shaking breath after shaking breath in, letting the clean smell of his scent wash over me, salty sea spray and freshly clean cut grass, washing away the images. I felt his gentle touch against my mind and automatically lowered my shields. His healing power rushed in and took away all the pain, healed the cuts and scrapes and bruises, but couldn't touch one ache. No amount of vampire *Sanguis Vitam* could fix that one. That one I'd wear in my heart for eternity.

Michel drove us back to *Sensations*, his club and daytime retreat. He didn't ask any questions, just let me cry silently in the passenger seat. He parked in the underground parking, it's only for his staff and vampires of his line, many of which stay on the premises too. *Sensations* is a large old brick building, Michel owns all of it, some he rents out as offices up above, but the club and living quarters and garage underneath are all his.

He sat silently next to me once he'd switched the car off and said nothing, just waited. I think I'd managed to cry myself out and now I just felt exhausted and frustrated and the beginnings of being really pissed off. Always a good sign, an indication I was getting *me* back and not some fragile weeping girl unable to hold her own against the baddies and monsters of the night.

I opened the door and turned to slide down to the ground. Land Rover Discovery's have a high wheel base and at 5'4" tall, it's a long way down for me. Michel had made it around the car to me before my feet had touched the concrete, offering me his hand. He's old school. Michel is 500 years old so it's not surprising, but the thought of a woman not requiring a hand out of a vehicle, or not have a door opened when they walked up to it, was just not his bag. I was having a hard time bringing him into the 21st century, but then again, I've never entirely been a women's libber anyway. I let him take my hand and help me out of the car.

He pulled me to him again and kissed my forehead.

"I felt your pull, your need tonight, *ma douce*. I felt the Bond call for some of my powers. It has never done that before. Will you tell me what happened?"

Well, that covered the faster speed than usual thing, didn't it? Here I was thinking I'd just received a ramp up in power levels, when it was actually just on loan from Michel. Bugger.

"Can I have a shower first, then let's talk."

That received the obligatory raised eyebrows, head cocked to the side, smirky grin. You know the one, the one that says *by all means, as long as I get to come too*. I just smiled and shook my head. Even in emotional crises Michel could think of sex.

I turned towards the the door that led to the club and stopped. The BMW was back, sitting sleekly in the corner, shiny black exterior, red leather seats.

"I thought you got rid of that," I said stiffly.

"I live in perpetual hope that you will see reason, *ma douce*."

I just humphed and punched in the code to the internal door before Michel got to it. I could feel the weight of his gaze on my back. Michel wanted to look after me, hell he wanted me to be ensconced in his world without any chance of an independent thought or action. Sometimes, it was cute and sometimes, just so damn annoying. The man could smother. And yet, a part of me couldn't help feeling he had no right. I still had trouble forgetting Paris. Forgetting the images of him in another's embrace.

We didn't have to go into the club proper, the access from the garage led to part of the private quarters of the club. Michel had recently had to take on more vampires under his line. An accord with a master vampire named Jock, who had died fighting beside Michel, had led Michel to extend hospitality to those under his line. In a short amount of time, he had almost doubled his entourage. There were still some teething problems and he had settled many of them in Wellington, under the care of Jett, a level two master vampire from Jock's line. Serious sort of dude, lots of curly long black hair and a crooked nose that managed to add to his appeal, not detract. From the brief interactions I'd had with Jett, I liked him. He took his role seriously and despite only a new addition to Michel's line, I think Michel trusted him.

But, because the *Iunctio* had all but turfed Michel out of Wellington - there should only be one city per Master of the City - all of his vampires had to return. A new section of the club had been made over and plans were in motion to convert the rest of the building into accommodation as well. Just one big vampire Frat House, I guess. The garage came out into the newly renovated section, half way between Michel's private quarters and those of his existing line.

We took the right hand branch of the plushly carpeted hallway towards Michel's area. I walked straight past his office and into his chamber. It was extravagantly decorated.

27

Michel liked to surround himself with beauty and more so here, in his private retreat, than anywhere else. Although *Sensations*, the club part of this building, was rather well done too, here in his chambers, you got to see a bit more of Michel.

Lush fabrics in rich colours, dark wood, solid modern furniture with an antique twist, comfort and design at its best. It had surprised me the first time I had come here, no coffin, nothing like that, all elegance and extravagance and beautifully put together furnishings. It could have been a room out of a luxury resort, or a top notch hotel, *The Ritz* or *The Regent Beverly Wilshire,* but here and there was Michel. A sculpture in the corner from Italy, a small trinket on the bedside table from his childhood, books accumulated over centuries, mementoes and memories in little pockets around the room. It was, for all intents and purposes, his home. He owned other houses around Auckland and New Zealand, but this was where he lived.

I walked straight into the bathroom and flicked on the light. I had to admit, Michel's bathroom outshone mine to an alarming degree. I had a bath and a shower, everything a girl could need, but Michel had a rain shower with multi head massaging jets, big enough for a nest of vampires, not just the two of us, beautiful cream tiles and gold fixtures and a plethora of expensive shampoos and creams and soaps and smelly delights, all provided for me.

He was trying to entice me, to make me spend more and more time here, away from my small but convenient apartment. I think he thought, the more desirable things he dotted around the place, the more likely I was to capitulate. I, on the other hand, had picked up a thing or two from the master manipulator Michel and I was playing him, like a card shark; *bring it on maestro, let's see how far you take it.* Unfortunately, he'd gone for the BMW. I hadn't quite recovered from that one yet.

I turned the taps on in the shower and proceeded to strip. Michel had followed me in and was leaning against the vanity, arms folded over his chest, legs stretched out and crossed at his ankles. He was in his usual night time business wear. Made-to-measure Armani suit, Italian leather loafers, gold cuff links on his crisp white Pierre Cardin shirt and tonight, a sky blue silk tie. He'd long ago forgone other coloured ties, somehow picking up on the fact that I adored blue, the way it matched his eyes, complemented or enhanced the indigo swirls within.

Michel has had a long time to practice his wiles on members of the fairer sex and he'd spent the first two years of our platonic relationship assessing me, figuring out what made me tick. I'd just spent it surviving his charms and staying on my side of the line. Consequently, he knew how to push my buttons far better than I did his.

I wasn't affected by him being in the bathroom with me though, we'd long ago passed that awkward stage, so I just let him watch as I stepped inside the shower and let the water fall around me, luxuriating in its warmth. I adjusted a few of the nozzles to get the best effect, massaging away the heinous start to the night and reached up for my currently favourite shampoo. It smelt of cherries and vanilla and made my slightly longer than shoulder length dead straight brown hair, shine like I'd spent three hours at a hair salon. It felt gooood.

I was just reaching for the conditioner when I heard the

shower stall door open and Michel stepped in. I turned and gave him a look. He cocked an eyebrow at me and reached for the conditioner, taking it from my hand and turning me away from him. He massaged my hair, letting his fingers ease more of the tension and letting the smell of cherries and vanilla fill the room. His touch always had an effect on me. I knew, logically, that it was the Joining and Bond we shared. As kindred, we needed to have that touch; physically, emotionally, mentally, it made us stronger, but I couldn't help responding to it even if my brain was saying: *slow down tiger, it's not all you.*

I had tried to stay away for a while, to sort out how I really felt. But after Paris, when we had almost died, when things had got a little kooky, what with gods and extraordinary powers and all that madness, I hadn't been able to make the break from him again. He was my drug, but not by choice. And because of that, I swore daily I would find a way to be me and not just the kindred Nosferatin of perhaps the most powerful vampire in the world.

"What happened at Whenuapai?" His voice was soft, but he still managed to surprise me. In the shower and he's all business? This was new.

I sighed, I knew what I was about to say would not be well received. "I went to see if I could stop it." He knew what *stop it* meant, he knew the challenge was on tonight, he'd made me promise to stay away. Oops.

"I gather that didn't work out how you planned." Now his voice was flat, even, but he still massaged my head, fingers moving deftly, making it hard to concentrate, hard to ignore the feel of him naked behind me, his breath

30

against my neck. I closed my eyes and took a deep breath in to steady myself.

"No. I saw Rick kill him."

He stiffened slightly, paused from his massaging, but only a moment, then pulled me towards the shower of water to rinse my hair clean. "Close your eyes," he whispered, turning me towards him now and helping the suds out of my hair. When he was satisfied I was squeaky clean, he pulled me closer, until I felt the wet slickness of water on his skin against mine, his arms going around me as we stood under the spray together.

"How close did you get, Lucinda?"

The fact that he was no longer using his pet name, *ma douce,* for me anymore, was a sure indicator of just how angry he was.

"Enough to be paralysed by their power," I answered.

I felt his *Sanguis Vitam* climb then, but he reined it back in immediately. Just a brief loss of control, enough to make me realise how much danger I was actually in. An angry vampire in the close confines of a shower stall, not the best place to be.

"Is there a reason you insist on defying me and endangering yourself, Lucinda? Do you wish yourself harm?"

"Firstly, I am not yours to control." I pushed away from him and scowled. "Secondly, he was my friend, Michel, I had to try."

"But it was futile, was it not? You were unable to do a thing but stand by and watch."

And there you have it, Michel knows me so well. Right now he's angry, furious even and he's lashing out. Part of

31

me knew it was because he was scared that I had almost got killed tonight, part of it though, was because I had gone against his wishes and he wanted me to pay for that defiance. He is a vampire, it's how they operate. I disobeyed him tonight, so he was punishing me. And saying I had to watch another friend die, saying that that's *all* I could do, was a little too close to home. I had watched Rocky die and did nothing to stop it. It haunted me and Michel knew it.

"Damn you, Michel." I pushed past him into the bathroom and grabbed a towel. He didn't stop me, probably knew he'd hit his target, there was no need to continue. He'd made his point, or so he thought. He'd hurt me, but would that stop me from defying him again in the future? Not on your Nellie.

I dressed quickly, not wanting to face him in a wrapped towel. He, however, was quite happy to stand there and watch me. He'd dried off, but not bothered to cover up. He wore nudity like a fashion statement, wielded it like a weapon, displaying it whenever it suited his needs. Right now, I gathered, he hadn't finished chastising me and his body on display was a sure-fire way to put me off balance.

"How am I to protect you, if you refuse to let me?" he said, a little too reasonably for my liking.

"I don't need your protection, Michel. I'm more than capable of taking care of myself."

"Like you did tonight?" he asked incredulously.

"I was doing fine, I'd got away. I was getting away."

"You did not look fine, Lucinda, you looked close to having an accident in fact. Had I not turned up, would you have ended upside down in a ditch on the side of the road?"

32

"Is that what you're worried about? Me crashing your car?"

He barked out a sound full of anger. "You know damn well it is not! Lucinda, you are precious to me, I will not have you in danger."

I doubted the *precious to me* part, but I let it go. "My life is full of danger, Michel. Would you wrap me up in cotton wool and place me on a shelf for safe keeping?"

"If I have to, yes."

We just stared at each other for a while. He would do it too. His damn stubborn ideas of protecting and providing for me were insufferable. He might be a centuries old vampire from a different time, where things were done differently than today, but I'm a modern girl, I don't give up that easily.

"Get used to it, Michel. I am what I am and I will not change for you."

"Oh, I am well aware of what you are, my dear." Michel was always good at sarcasm.

I shook my head and went out the door. If he wanted to continue this, he could either follow me buck naked into the club, or get himself dressed and chase me out the door. Either way, I was leaving.

Of course, I hadn't counted on Bruno, Michel's second. Nor on that telepathic communication Michel has with his vamps.

I started across the clubroom floor, weaving through the usual Friday night revellers. The club usually making me feel at home, with its plush surroundings, dark wood and sleek furnishings, all in deep reds and golds. But I was not even registering it tonight, I'd almost made it to the door too, but then he pounced.

"Going somewhere, Luce?" His evil smile making the piercing blues of his eyes shine fiercely in the club's lights.

"Yeah, Bruno, I am." I tried to step around him, to get to the door, but Bruno's big and I mean brick out-house size big. He just crossed his arms and sighed.

"Now you know I could just block your way, or glaze you into staying, but I'm giving you the benefit of the doubt, because I like you. And offering you a chance to behave yourself."

I just glared at him, crossing my arms in front of my chest in a mirror of his stance and almost stomping my foot. I stopped myself though, just in time. He just smiled knowingly.

"How about we have a drink?" He nodded towards the bar.

I know I could have just given in, just gone with the flow. It was Bruno and he is fast and strong and can amazingly glaze me when he wants to - not many vampires can - but I was mad. Spitting fire out my nostrils mad. So I smiled sweetly and nodded. He looked momentarily surprised and then suspicious, but I turned towards the bar and he came with me. We took a few steps, he relaxed a little, I could feel it. And then I bolted for the door.

I'm fast, faster than a human and as there were humans in the bar tonight, I was kind of breaking the rules, but shit. I was mad. So, I high tailed it at top speed, but then Bruno's older and faster and just that much more vindictively nastier than me.

Before I'd gone a few feet I was airborne, over his shoulder, whacking my head down on his big broad back as he swung me around and headed back towards the bar, holding firmly to my thighs in front of him. There were catcalls and whistles and many jokes being passed around the room, but the vampires in amongst the humans had stilled. They knew me. They knew what I was capable of and if they'd been paying attention since I walked in the room, then they damn well knew how pissed off I actually was.

I let my Light build up inside me. The vampires would have felt the power grow, would have sensed my magic, if you can call it that, they all knew what was coming. I held it tightly coiled, but if Bruno could sense it he was ignoring it, or choosing to let me fall completely into the hole I was creating, because he just kept carrying me towards the bar. When I couldn't contain the Light any longer, I started to open up, about to unleash it on him, make him fall to his knees in blindingly bright white Light. And then I breathed, letting it all out towards him.

It would have been so easy, he would have been awash in my Light and unable to do a thing about it. I hadn't made it sensual like I have been known to in the past, I was angry, so it probably would have hurt, hurt like a bitch. A bit like a full fight bruising in one hit, but it didn't go to Bruno, because suddenly Michel was there, touching my arm, opening up his mind to me and the Light recognised him and flew straight for him, bypassing Bruno and smashing into Michel's chest.

He gasped and collapsed to his knees; white, ashen and in pain. Bruno dropped me to my feet and turned to his master and all of a sudden I had a three foot long sword thrust at my neck, pricking my skin ever so slightly, by a

35

short and very angry blonde female vampire.
   Damn.

Chapter 3
The Call to Come Home

"Pull it back." Blondie had an American accent.

"You first," I replied evenly.

My hand had already gone for my stake, inside my jacket pocket, but how I thought I was going to land a blow when she was still over three feet away, at the other end of her wickedly sharp looking sword, I don't know. But a vampire hunter can live in hope, can't she?

Michel was still gasping on the floor, Bruno hovering. The rest of the vampires had secured the room, stopped any Norms from leaving or entering and had started to glaze up a storm. The usual, Obi Wan routine; *these are not the droids you are looking for.*

Blondie and I just stood still, staring off at each other. She looked about my age and was pretty, of course, they all are. A little taller than me, maybe an inch, with pale perfect skin, long blonde straight hair and brightly blue eyes, almost electric blue. She had a red tank top on, displaying well toned arms and low hipster dark blue denim skin tight jeans, tucked into red leather knee high boots. No heels. I don't think her lack of height had given her a complex, she carried herself with an assured confidence, completely unaffected by the taller people milling around us. I had a sudden liking for her.

I felt down the link or connection that joined me to Michel, just to see how he was doing and I stifled my own gasp. I had obviously been angrier than I realised, because he was in real pain. I almost went to call the Light back straight away, but with Blondie's sword to my neck, I knew that wasn't an option. It's not that I wanted to prove a point, but giving in to a vampire was not a good political move. I could occasionally give in to Michel, if it suited me of course, but an unknown vamp was a totally different thing altogether. Never show fear. Never give an inch. Always stay on guard. They were mantras, Nero my Nosferatin trainer, had instilled in me. Repeatedly. So, I wasn't backing down right now.

"Luce," Bruno said, from the side, tentatively. "Michel's hurting, you don't want to do this."

"You don't know what the fuck I want to do, Bruno, so shut it."

I was starting to shake with controlling the Light for so long and I was angry, still, more so than before. Not just at Michel and his insistence that he control me, not just because I am still haunted by unwanted images of him in Paris, but also because of Bruno for throwing me over his shoulder in front of everyone, like I was a sack of potatoes. And now this foreign vamp who had taken it upon her blonde self to protect my kindred vampire. He was mine to protect or otherwise, not hers. I suddenly realised how bad that actually sounded. Not good.

I shook my head to clear the thought. "Get the Norms out of here." My voice was surprisingly steady, but quiet.

"Now, why would we do that, Luce? With them here, you might behave yourself." Bruno again.

"Does it look like I'm behaving myself, Bruno? Get them out of here, now!"

I had shifted my gaze to his when I spoke the last and followed it up with a glaze. It was a relatively new Nosferatin power I had come into, being able to glaze vampires. They, of course, can glaze humans and me sometimes, but anyone ever being able to glaze a vampire is new. And very scary for the sunshine challenged. I don't like that vamps glaze, having influence over another's mind is not right, so I had sworn I would only do it when in a life or death situation.

I didn't think I was in one now, but it was too late. A little bit of the Dark that I constantly feared had seeped in and was setting up home right inside me.

Bruno commanded the vampires to clear the room of Norms, much to the protest of Blondie. They didn't hesitate, Bruno may not be their master, but he was second in command, so they knew how to obey his orders. Vampires are nothing if not military in their hierarchy. I just smiled sweetly at the blonde at the end of the sword and raised my eyebrows. She frowned.

"Now what, Luce?" Bruno asked, almost begging for a further command. Yuck, I hated glazing. How had I got myself into this mess? Too late to stop now.

"Lower the sword." I tried to catch Blondie's eyes, but she'd cottoned on to my game and refused to make eye contact.

"Pull back your power," she replied, looking at a spot over my shoulder.

"You know, this could go on all night," I said conversationally.

"Or not," she replied, pushing the sword a little deeper into my flesh.

I didn't pull away, that would have been showing fear and she was only threatening, not yet following through on the action, so I felt the trickle of blood as it escaped the tip of the sword, where she had breached my skin.

39

But, it wasn't just that she could impale me, slit my throat, kill me, it was holding the Light that was taking its toll. I'd got good at it recently, having spent a lot of time using it for defensive purposes and also in training with Nero. He had made it our number one training session over the past week, since returning from Paris. It was a tool and a powerful one, but I needed to be in control and sometimes, just sometimes, when faced with a particularly Dark vampire, the Light just took over. I never wanted to stand by and watch it do its thing again, without having the ability to pull it back. But, despite all of that training, this was a lengthy piece of time and I had put an awful lot of emotion into that Light, so I was waning, tiring. I only had a few minutes left in me before it became obvious to those vampires around me and they took their chance.

Even though I was Michel's kindred Nosferatin and they were all sworn to protect me, his life and health would always prevail. I was a threat right now and they wouldn't hesitate to deal with me if the opportunity arose. So, what to do?

The Norms had all been bundled out onto the street, so it was just us left in the club. Fifty odd vampires - who had suddenly appeared out of thin air more than doubling the original number in the club when I had first arrived - and one Nosferatin. Not great odds, but there you go. I took a hold of the Light again, I wanted to change it from pain, but the concentration required was too great, if I paused to alter its effect now, I could lose it and lose this battle. Even if I had begun to realise how wrong this all was, I was stubborn, I would not give in to a vampire. It's not in my blood.

I grabbed the Light roughly from Michel and threw it out into the room before he could stop me, making every vampire there fall to their knees in pain, including Blondie. It was horrendous, so *not* what I would normally do, so wrong, so not me. It made me sick to the stomach, but I had won.

Michel just looked at me, as the Light slowly dissipated into the room, releasing the vampires, I'm not quite sure what the look said. It wasn't fear, it wasn't anger, it wasn't pride, I think it was calculation. He was deciding how best to use this new powerful tool in his arsenal. He was deciding how to use me.

"Fuck you, Michel." It was all I could manage before sinking to the floor in exhaustion.

He smiled. "Always so eloquent, my dear."

All of us had ended up on the floor, trying to recover. The vampires would manage it faster than me, they had only been awash with pain, it would pass, but me? I was exhausted and angry and more than a little ill at what I had just done.

I felt the vampires moving to their feet, in that languid otherworldly movement they have, all grace and smooth motions, like a puppet on a string. I couldn't move, just sat in an undignified heap on the polished concrete floor of the club.

"Do we move her?" Bruno asked. I guess he was talking about me.

"I am tempted to say no, but she is my kindred Nosferatin, so I shall have to bow to centuries of protocol and aid her in her hour of need." Oh, Michel was loving this, wasn't he?

41

Rub it in a little more why don't you.

Now, now. You know I adore you when you are angry, ma douce, lets not fan the flames any more than completely necessary.

He'd answered my thought in my mind. We can project thoughts to each other, I hadn't realised I'd projected that last one.

I just glared at him as he bent to pull me to my feet and into his arms. We stared at each other for a long moment, he'd wrapped his arm around my waist and pulled me close, unable to look away. The thing with vampires is, they love confrontation. I'm not so good at it, I run whenever I can, but vampires, they love it. They also love shows of power and strength, and I had not only confronted all the vampires in this room, but shown them just how much mojo I really had. Michel was in heaven right now, luxuriating in my actions, like a cat rolling in the sun.

Blondie coughed into her hand. It wasn't uncomfortable, just a sound to bring us out from the bubble Michel had created.

"Ah yes, Erika. So good to see you made it." Michel turned me in his arms to face the petite vampire. "Erika Anders, my kindred Nosferatin, Lucinda Monk."

Erika bowed at the waist, her fisted hand across her chest, the formal bow a vampire makes to their master, or another of equal standing.

"I pledge my undying allegiance to my master's kindred Nosferatin." Oh, here we go, I'd heard this one before. All of Michel's vampires had made the same proclamation when I joined with Michel, but I hadn't met Erika before, she was new to me. And the thought that she

42

was one of Michel's made a small flutter of anxiety, no maybe jealousy, settle in the pit of my stomach. "But, if you ever pull a stunt like that again, Nosferatin, I will impale you. Not kill you, mind you, but maim. Definitely maim."

My mouth dropped open in utter surprise and I felt Michel begin to laugh, his body shaking as he held me against him.

"Oh I have missed you, Erika. Welcome home."

"It's a pleasure to be here master."

Michel huffed. "Since when have you called me master?"

"Since you joined with a powerful Nosferatin."

"Oh, am I finally worthy of your respect, little one?"

She laughed and it was delicate but strong, a full throat laugh, that made the other male vampires in the club turn to watch her.

Dangerous this one, I thought.

Indeed, replied Michel. I just elbowed him in his solar plexus as a returning answer, receiving a satisfying grunt in reply.

Erika smiled. I think she liked that I held my own with the master, clearly she wasn't one for conventional vampire hierarchy. Maybe we could get along after all.

Michel led us over to a private booth, the club had opened up again, Norms returning none the wiser. The vampires peeling off into the night, only a handful remaining, socialising, guarding, whatever the hell they were meant to be doing. Doug, Michel's vampire barman, brought a tray of drinks over and surprisingly a plate of cheese and crackers for me. He just winked as he placed

43

them in front of me, no words, he's a vamp of little words. And then he headed back to his station at the bar.

I wasn't so sure I could stomach food after that little incident, my mind was still reeling from what I had done. Michel simply placed his arm over the back of our bench seat and gently stroked the back of my neck. The motion alone calming me, settling my stomach and allowing me to breathe.

He can feel my emotions through the connection we have. He would have been able to tell what I was experiencing, the pain I was putting myself through, he was simply doing his part as my kindred and grounding me again. I picked up a cracker and began to nibble the edge.

"So, how fares the Land of the Free and the Home of the Brave?" Michel began to sip his Merlot, still stroking my neck, still giving me that connection to his calmer self.

"Well, it's definitely brave, but for vampires, I'm not so sure of the free," Erika replied, she flicked a glance at me and then continued. "But, nothing new to tell since my last report."

"You can speak freely in front of Lucinda, she is well aware of our relationship difficulties with the American Families," Michel offered.

I nodded. "I met a representative of the Council of Families once, we had a disagreement." He'd appeared in Michel's bar one night when there was a private vampire function on, the type where the humans in attendance are all either part of the menu or part of the entertainment. I hadn't realised and walked right into it. He'd assumed I was dinner. I didn't much go for that.

"Oh, that would be Jonathan." Erika laughed, another

one of those delicate but throaty peals. "That would also explain why he is fixated with you."

"Fixated with me?" I looked at Michel, he just did one of his shrugs that always seemed to be so elegant on him.

"What is there not to be fixated with, *ma douce*?"

I rolled my eyes at Erika, she chortled.

"So, you live in America?" I asked her, realising I was about to chomp into my fourth cracker and cheese. So much for my conscience having an effect on my appetite.

"Lived. I guess I'm setting up home here now."

I frowned. "Why?"

Erika looked pointedly at Michel. "You haven't told her?"

Michel didn't look uncomfortable when I glanced at him, just relaxed, sipping his wine. "Why don't you, little one."

I don't know what sort of relationship Michel and Erika had, but the fact that he had a pet name for her said something. I hadn't decided if it was something worthy of my jealousy or not yet, I was tending towards not. I liked her, I figured the pet name was more of a tease than an endearment and I felt her struggling not to rise to the bait.

"I'm to be your trainer." Erika smiled at me as she said it, as though this should have been the best news I'd had all week. Not hard, considering the week I'd had, but still.

"I already have a trainer."

"A Nosferatin trainer who can teach you how to kill vampires. I think your troubles have increased a little from just the solitary night time fanged variety. Or so I hear."

"You mean the Taniwhas?"

She nodded. "Silver will harm them, but getting a stake

45

anywhere near them may prove fatal to you. Somehow I don't think Michel would go for that." She flicked a smile at Michel and winked. Actually winked. I don't think I'd seen anyone wink at Michel before.

He shook his head in admonishment and turned more towards me. "Erika is my Sword, among other things, but she has been recalled here to me to help train you. I think it is time for you to expand your weapon base. A sword will have a far greater chance against the Taniwhas, than your usual arsenal and let us not forget the multitudes of vampires currently on their way now."

No, how could we forget those? As we were flying back from Paris last week I received another Nosferatin power. Although calling this a power would mean it would help me in some way, but from what I can tell so far, it's not going to help, but hinder. I am the *Sanguis Vitam Cupitor* or Blood Life Seeker, which basically means I can *seek* out all the Dark or evil vampires in the world and see where they are, what they're doing and how many there happen to be. Now, with this new power, they can suddenly *see* me. And the sense I got when they realised this, was that they wanted to meet me in person, fang to face.

Nero has not been helpful in unravelling this new mystery. At first he seemed surprised, shocked even, but now he just avoids talking about it at all cost. I don't know what he's hiding, but I trust Nero implicitly. I'll wait until he's ready to divulge, but in the meantime, I keep a constant tab on those Dark vampires, almost *seeking* every few hours or so, just to see how close they have come. Right now, they're reticent, unsure what will happen when they do come, but I feel their need, I feel their hunger. They *will* come. It's just a matter of time. And when they do, I need to be ready. Maybe carrying a sword would not be a bad thing after all.

"So, you just gave up your life in America and came *home* to your master?" I'd turned back to Erika. I wanted to know how happy she was about this new environmental change in her life. How happy she was to be training me.

She shrugged, another elegant movement that only vampires can seem to master. "He calls, I come running. It's just how it is."

"It doesn't bother you?" Michel was staying very quiet through all of this, just sipping his wine, stroking my neck. Damn, but if he couldn't be casual when the shit might be hitting the fan.

"I would rather be serving here than in America. They are different from us, they are fiercer and yet more controlled. The families are run like an American gangster movie. The punishment for disobedience, of any kind, is fatal."

"Not something our Erika can tolerate with ease," Michel decided to add.

She smiled crookedly at him. "No. I have trouble with toe-ing the line sometimes, but I know my place." Then she shook her head. "But America, it's different. Even I was scared."

"How long had you been there?" Me again.

"Ten years."

Wow. Ten years and just like that she's called home and comes running. I shook my head, I just didn't get vampires sometimes.

Erika leaned forward over the table towards me,

47

registering my confusion. "It's not just that he commands, Lucinda, it's that we *want* to serve him. It's the blood bond, there is nowhere I would rather be than near my master and serving a purpose he needs."

I turned to Michel. "And this doesn't seem creepy to you? Not allowing them to have a choice?"

He stopped stroking my neck and just looked at me. "We are vampyre, my dear."

Nothing else, just that.

Even after all of this time, even after practically living with him for the past two months, I still didn't really understand them.

I suppressed a shiver. "Well, I'm glad I'm not a vampire then."

"So am I," Michel whispered.

Chapter 4
Shall We Dance?

That did it for my appetite though, I pushed the remaining crackers and cheese aside and folded my arms across my chest. OK. So, it might have been a bit petulant, but still, *call and come running* just didn't sit well with me. Especially for this vivacious, smart mouthed blonde vamp, who seemed to be able to tease Michel and hold her own on equal footing. I suddenly felt like she needed protection from him. Somehow, I think she would have disagreed.

Michel laughed quietly, he could read me like a book.

"I think it might be time to demonstrate to my kindred just how capable you are, Erika and therefore how important you are to me." He paused long enough for me to unfold my arms and turn to look at him

"Shall we dance, little one?" He was looking at Erika.

My head shot towards her to see her response. She just slowly smiled. "It has been a while since I kicked your butt, Michel. Let's see if you've forgotten any of what I've taught you."

He laughed out loud at that, obviously thinking it was riotously funny, but slid out of the bench seat we were on and offered me his hand, still laughing, chuckling. This was going to be entertaining, whatever the hell it was going to be.

We walked towards the second private area to branch off *Sensations* main club rooms, this was where the bar had a storeroom and the sleeping quarters for some of Michel's vampires could be found. It also had a very large room which had been turned into a daytime retreat for the vamps. Complete with private bar facilities, couches and at the

49

moment a big expanse of nothing. I think the plan was to bring in a pool table, some other entertainment, maybe a large flat screen T.V. Even vampires need something to do during the day. But I was guessing we were heading there for the large expanse of nothing and not to play poker on the little table in the corner.

There were a couple of vamps in the room when we entered, but they just nodded and left as soon as we arrived. No doubt Michel had given them direction through that telepathic link he has with all of his vampires. So, it was just Michel, me and Erika with a large long bag. She dropped the bag on the floor and proceeded to pull out wrapped lengths, which on closer inspection turned out to be swords. Wickedly sharp, shiny swords.

She pulled one from its sheath, or scabbard and brandished it in the air, twisting it one way then the other, catching the light in the room every now and then. It was a little longer than the one she had used on me earlier, with a diamond shape at the base of its hilt and a curved cross bar separating hilt from blade. The hilt was wrapped in a bronze type covering, very plain and simple, almost utilitarian. Both hilt and blade together were about four feet long, the blade about two inches wide, tapering to a tip at the end. It looked like it would be heavy, but she brandished it like it weighed mere ounces.

"This," she said looking at me, "is a Svante Sword. The sword of the viceroy. It is from my ancestral home. Not an original, I've had it altered slightly; better materials, lighter weight, but its design is original Svante. It is a good, strong weapon. One that calls on the history of the warrior diplomat who first wielded it. I won't train you with this one exactly, but one based on its design. But, for tonight's demonstration," - She turned and smiled at Michel. - "it will do nicely."

Michel had stripped off his Armani jacket and crisp white shirt while Erika had been talking and now stood opposite her on the bare mat that had been placed on the large rec room floor. He was naked from waist up, making it hard for me to look anywhere else but his deep cream coloured torso. I licked my lips self-consciously and willed myself to behave.

Erika pulled a second Svante Sword from her bag and walked towards Michel, handing him one with both hands on either end of the sword, bending at the waist, like you'd expect a Japanese swordsman to hand over a Katana. He accepted the blade with two hands and the same bow at the waist. She returned to her other sword and lifted it, then settled herself into a fighting stance, legs scissored, sword raised only slightly in front. Michel mimicked her pose.

"Let's dance," she whispered. Michel nodded his head slowly in agreement.

I don't know what I had expected to see, the swords looked large and slightly cumbersome, even though they both wielded them with such ease, but it was a dance of sorts. It was beautiful and graceful and the only sounds initially were the clanging of the blades, that ringed around the room. Their bodies glistened in the lights, Erika had stripped to just her jeans and tank top, she had removed her boots and socks and was in bare feet. Michel still had his shoes on, but his body shone in the glow of the bulbs overhead, almost luminous. They moved like dancers, swirling and turning, ducking and diving, but all of it was exquisite, elegant, surreal and fast. Very fast. Vampire fast.

They blurred here and there, then stilled to parry a blow, thrust the sword, block a strike. The clanging of the blades got faster, more rhythmic in nature, as if they were both giving themselves over to the moment and dancing to their own combined beat. It was beautiful. It was mesmerizing. It was a dangerous dance for devils alone. Neither landing a blow, making that first cut and although they were only demonstrating the captivating beauty of swordsmanship, I knew they were also playing for keeps.

I'd been watching both of them as a unit, one moving forward the other retreating, then counter attacking, the to and fro between them dazzling, but my natural pull towards my kindred meant my gaze somehow shifted there of its own accord. I found myself unable to look away from his body as it flexed and twisted, stretched and moved in a motion that was simply hypnotic. His bare torso showing every minute muscular movement, the ripple of his upper chest, the curve of his waist, the flight of his body in full battle. It was obvious Michel knew how to wield a sword, second nature, something he had done for centuries and he was breathtaking.

"You're being cruel Michel." Erika spoke between warding off a strike and returning with another thrust of her sword towards his abdomen. He dodged it easily and repositioned for further contact.

"Whatever do you mean, Erika?" he casually replied.

"Her heartbeat has trebled, she can't take much more of watching you like this."

"I am well aware of what my kindred's heartbeat is doing." His voice was level, but held a slight amusement.

I felt the blush creep up my face and was unable to stop it. I willed my heartbeat to lower, even closed my eyes to stop looking at the magnificent male in front of me, but the damage had already been done. Great. Does everyone know I lust after him?

Erika laughed, no doubt at my discomfort, but Michel took advantage of her lowered guard and sliced a line from the neck of her tank top to her waist, making the fabric gape in the front. She flashed electric blue eyes, threaded with shades of cyan and turquoise, at him.

"Now look whose heartbeat has climbed?" Michel quietly offered.

She rallied and increased her speed and all of a sudden what had seemed a fast and furious, but friendly fight, turned into a maelstrom of slashes and parries and clanging metal against metal, in a whirlwind of colour that was blinding. I held my breath, unable to tell who was landing blows and who wasn't, until finally Erika's sword went flying through the air, arcing across the expanse of space, glinting in the lights, to clatter against the far wall. Michel held his sword to her neck, just as she had held hers earlier against mine in the club.

"Do you concede, little one?" he asked, barely out of breath.

She glared at him briefly then nodded. He removed his sword and bowed towards her slowly. She followed suit rubbing her neck, where he had pricked her skin, as she stood up.

"So, have I passed the test?" Michel asked as he walked over to the fridge in the corner and pulled out a bottle of water, taking a long drink.

"You always do, Michel, but one day, one day I'll win."
She said it with such defiance, he laughed. A low rumble in
his chest.

"I would expect nothing less."

His eyes flicked to me. I still hadn't managed to get my
breathing entirely under control, but my heart rate had
quieted.

"Your turn," he said, holding my gaze and smiling
wickedly. Then he went to sit down on the couch, settling
in to watch.

"Wh..what?" I stammered. You have got to be joking, I
couldn't wield a sword at this woman to save myself.

"It's all right, *chica*, you can use your stake. I just want
to get a feel for what I'm working with, that's all."

Erika had replaced her sword in its scabbard and had
ripped her ruined tank top off and stood in a sports bra and
jeans. Not in the least bit self-conscious. She looked me
over. I was wearing my usual evening hunter gear; short
black mini skirt, black tights and boots, fitted black Tee and
a custom made black jacket. Custom made to hide two
silver stakes and a silver knife. You wouldn't even know
they were there unless you knew me. I never went
anywhere without my stakes. I even slept with one under
my pillow, although Michel had refused that notion when I
shared his bed. I couldn't blame him, even I would have
baulked at that, had I been a vampire.

"Take the jacket off." She nodded towards me.

"I always fight in my jacket." I'd feel a bit bare in my
skin-tight top. It's one thing to wear skin-tight under my
jacket, another to flash my body when I fight.

"I need to see how your body moves, which muscles

you use. Preferably, I'd suggest stripping to your underwear, so I could get a better look, but I'm picking you'd refuse. So, jacket. Off."

Michel chuckled in the corner, finding it highly amusing no doubt. I glared at him and he just shrugged. "You heard her, *ma douce*. I would have insisted on stripping, but she is the teacher."

I sighed, what did it matter? She made sense and he was Michel, he'd seen me in less, but I don't know, the way he was watching me now made me think of a predator watching his prey. Normally, that should have made me scared, even with Michel that look can be terrifying, but it didn't. I felt a thrill of adrenaline skip through me, making my heartbeat increase all over again. He smiled that knowing smile he so often wore around me and just kept watching.

Bugger this, if he wanted a show he could have one. I stripped my jacket off and slipped out of my boots and tights, grabbing a stake and returning to the mat. I felt a little under dressed, standing in my short skirt and top, baring way more flesh than I would normally do when fighting a vamp, but I wasn't going to let them see my discomfort. Never show fear. Never give an inch. Always stay on guard.

I was ready.

I rolled my head from side to side and said softly, "Shall we dance then, vampire?"

Erika laughed. "Oh, I like her already, Michel." And then pounced.

Vampires tend to fall into two categories. The over confident and the extremely over confident. I placed Erika in the latter. She had no doubt heard all about my moves, she'd even seen a bit of my power in the club, but she was fierce and experienced, a level two master vampire herself, by the feel of all that *Sanguis Vitam* she couldn't hide when about to do battle. But she didn't know me. Not really. I've spent my younger years working on my parents' farm, hard labour on the weekends and school holidays, interspersed with one martial art obsession after another. Then more recently, when I moved to Auckland, I picked up kick-boxing and had an untold number of play fights with the Taniwhas, picking up their street fighting techniques and quickly mastering them too. Even without my Nosferatin mojo, I am formidable. I can switch from one form of fighting to another, mid stride, if an opponent thinks they can find my style easily, they are mistaken. The best part about being able to master so many different forms of fighting, is mixing it up a bit.

So, her first pounce was met with a lightning fast roundhouse kick, which she dodged but which also made her forgo her attack and move to defence. And I followed that with a front kick and an overhand punch, landing the first blow. I quickly rolled out of the way of the responding swipe of her arm, ending crouched some distance away facing her.

She paused, seemed to consider the last and nodded. I guess the test was over and we were onto the real deal now. She wouldn't hold back.

We circled for a moment, trying to find a weakness, but I knew from experience that finding a weakness on a vampire was damn near impossible. It was just a waste of time and only good if I needed a delay tactic, to catch my breath or something like that. I wasn't puffed yet, so I didn't give her time to consider my next move and just came at her with a jab, which she countered and then I followed it with a foot sweep, which she nimbly jumped. So far, she had been on the defensive, but I knew that wouldn't last.

I fingered my stake, letting the weight and feel of it settle me, centre me, bring me further into the zone. I don't know what she saw in my eyes, but she picked up on the change in my mood, she knew I was taking this seriously and her eyes flashed briefly, turquoise in amongst the blue. The next time she came at full vampire speed and there was nothing I could do stop her. I managed to raise the stake, but only partly and it just grazed the side of her arm as her fist landed a punch on my cheek, spinning me away from her body and her arms wrapped around me, crushing my back to her chest.

"Too easy," she breathed against me, only to feel me twist against her, obviously stronger than she had anticipated and manoeuvre in for a body drop, literally throwing her over my shoulder onto her back. See, cocky vampires equal flat-on-their-back vampires. Never lower your guard.

She was on her feet in an instant, but I had moved and countered her blow with my stake, scraping again, this time more deeply into her forearm. She growled, that nasty vampire growl they do when getting a little hot under the collar and didn't hesitate to come at me, this time her fangs were down and her eyes were glowing. She'd shifted from that sassy smart ass vampire I'd seen in the club upstairs, to a deadly accurate predator and my inner monologue chose that moment to pipe up and say, *oh fuck!*

I couldn't stop the body hit, there was simply no time to brace or block, so instead I let my body go with the force of her momentum and we went head over heels in a Nosferatu-Nosferatin jumble of legs and arms and long brown and blonde hair. By luck, hers not mine, she had ended up on top of me, pinning me to the floor. Her goal was my throat, her fangs glinting in the light, her eyes only for my jugular. She didn't expect me to come towards her, she expected me to pull away, to shift to the side, anything to get away from those sharp and menacing incisors, so when I thrust my head against her nose, putting myself so close to those fangs, so close to losing the battle, to giving her the victory she desired, she didn't fight me. She just let me come full force against her face, smashing my forehead into the bridge of her nose and breaking it instantly. I never said I'd play nice.

Blood poured out all over me and her and she screeched, loosening her hold, pulling back slightly and allowing me to raise my stake and press it against her chest, just above the thumping of her heart.

Breathless, I said, "Do you concede, Blondie?"

She froze, looking down at me, then slowly lifted her gaze to Michel. There was shame in her eyes then, mixed with a little fear. I couldn't see Michel's face, what his returning look to her would have been, but she seemed to relax slightly. Maybe he'd said something telepathically to ease her worry. And then she stood up, vampire puppet-on-a-string up and offered me a hand.

When I was standing in front of her finally, I felt Michel move, a stirring in the air, a warmth at my back. Without even turning around I knew he was behind me, close.

"Leave," he said over my shoulder.

I knew it was for Erika, because she instantly dropped my hand, winked at me and walked away toward the door. When I heard it click closed behind her, I took a deep breath in and turned slowly to face Michel. This would be interesting. I'd just kicked the butt of his favourite fighting vamp, the *Sword* in his arsenal, he was either going to shout at me or punish me. I had no idea which.

I hadn't expected the look I received though. Hunger, longing, utter desire.

"My turn," he said in a low, growl.

Oh shit.

Chapter 5
Try Harder

I swallowed. Michel watched every movement like the hungry predator he was.

"What did you have in mind?" Yay for me, my voice was steady, if not a little lower than usual.

"You land the stake, you get to pick the prize. I land my fangs, I choose."

I just stood and stared at him. He was serious, this was definitely a game, but he wanted it to feel real. He wouldn't hold back and fighting Erika was one thing, but fighting Michel, that was a whole different ball game right there. I knew I couldn't win, I knew he was stronger, faster, sneakier than me, but could I say no? Never show fear.

I smiled and I think it might just have been as wicked as those he tends to give me. He blinked slowly and wet his lips.

"Let's dance," he whispered, eyes never leaving my mouth.

I've fought Michel before, I've even had a stake to his chest on occasion, but that was when he'd really pissed me off and our relationship has stabilised a little since then, so my heart wasn't really, truly, committed to the task at hand. And let's face it, even if he did get fang to neck, it was going to be pleasurable. I guess a part of me secretly wanted that outcome anyway. So, the fact that it took him mere seconds to breach my meek and extremely pathetic defences and place his lips on my skin above my pulse at my neck, was not surprising. But, the fact that he didn't extend his fangs at all, was.

"You are not even trying," he growled against me.

I laughed a little nervously, I couldn't help it. Part of me was amused by his actions, longing for his bite and part of me couldn't help feeling just a little scared at the power that was rolling off him, the strength of his grip on my body.

"I think we should change the rules," he whispered against me. "There is obviously not enough incentive to make you commit to this enterprise."

We were standing in the middle of the mat, he had my body crushed up against his, hands gripping my arms, just below my shoulders, face still buried against my neck.

"I land my fangs and you move in with me, permanently."

"Oh no." I pulled away from him, he let me, his eyes shining in the light of the room, his smile wicked. "I am not playing this game with you, Michel."

"It is only fair, *ma douce*. You have accepted a challenge, of sorts, but are not committed enough to honour it appropriately. Perhaps a higher risk is required to get you to play? Your apartment, for your failure to land the stake."

I knew how vampires worked, on the whole anyway. Once a challenge had been made there was no going back and this, although a game of a fashion, it was still a challenge and I had accepted it. The fact that Michel would not let me just give up on the challenge and let him win, was just all him. I guess nobody likes to have their meal handed to them on a plate, it's so much more fun if you have to work for it.

"OK," I said slowly. "But, not my apartment, not that." I couldn't face giving up my sanctuary. It was what kept me connected to me.

He nodded. "But, it needs to be worth your while, *ma douce.*"

I couldn't argue there, I just didn't have it in me to fight him, when all he was going to do was bite me. I shook my head at that thought. Two months ago that would have been enough, more than enough, to make me want to stake him, now I craved it. Shit. I was an addict after all.

He smiled knowingly, he'd either heard my thoughts, felt my emotions, or just knew me pretty damn well.

"The car," he finally offered.

"What about it?"

"I land my fangs and you accept my gift, completely. You land the stake and I get rid of it, no more car in the garage waiting."

Huh. He had me there. I so did not want to accept that car. Sure it was sexy and divine and would no doubt be unreal to drive, but it was a gift of unparalleled proportions. It would signal to everyone that I was a kept woman and I mean, come on! Bank tellers just don't drive around in BMW Series 1 Convertibles, even if they are dating the Master of the City. And, even if the car wasn't part of this deal, he'd leave it there, in the garage, bringing it up every now and then, finding another way to manipulate me into driving it. At least this way I had a chance, albeit a minute one, of winning this battle of wills.

I nodded. He laughed. Somehow, I think he had this planned all along.

We circled for a moment, just watching the other, me not really wanting to take that first step, him devouring every line of my body. I really didn't think his full attention was on the fight, part of him was already undressing me, but still, this was Michel and his concentration wasn't necessary to win.

He took the decision to strike out of my hands and lunged. If I had thought I wouldn't fully commit to the battle, then I hadn't taken into consideration my Nosferatin instincts. They kicked in big time and I danced out of his grasp, spinning to face him again, stake out and ready to go.

"That's better," he said softly and then struck out again.

This time he came in low, so I took a flying leap towards him, intending to flip over the top of him and land the stake on his back as I flew past. It has worked before, but it's probably one of my more signature moves and Michel had seen this one and was prepared. Almost in slow motion, but no doubt just a blur, I watched him twist in the air, so he now faced me as I sailed over. I saw his hands come up in my peripheral vision, ready to pull me down on top of him. I struggled to think of an out, to think of a move that would work, a way to put my stake between me and him, but he was too fast. His fingers gripped my sides and I felt myself falling down towards him, but he hadn't grabbed my arms, they were still free.

I let him pull me down, he'd stopped my motion forward and almost slowed his, so we were heading for the floor, rather than skimming it now, but when his back hit the mat, I was ready. I used the rebound that impact created, along with my hands on either side of his body, to force myself up and over his head, in a somersault. Twisting as I made the move, making his grip loosen and my body fly away from his grasp. I landed in a crouch behind him, but he was up and in a crouch facing me in an

63

instant. A low appreciative growl escaping his lips. His eyes were flashing all shades of blue and amethyst and magenta, swirling and sparkling around the room. Michel's eyes are one of the most extraordinary things about him, usually when magenta enters the mix, it means he's about to explode in an uncontrolled rage of some sort, but at times like this, it can also mean he is extremely turned on.

I was betting it was the turned on this time. I was hoping, even praying, that I was right on that one.

We looked at each other for a moment and I couldn't help it, it just slipped out.

"You're not even trying." My voice was breathy, but the response it created was perfect.

His mouth dropped open. "You are paying for that, *ma douce.*"

"Prove it."

He smiled and flew through the air towards me, but I was ready and so 'in the zone'. I danced out of his reach, leaping into the air like a ballerina, twisting my body into a spin, bringing my arms in against my chest, crossing my legs as I flew and spinning away from where I had moments before been standing. I heard his body hit the wall behind where I had been and then the grunt of air escaping him. Spin fighting is still new to me, but it's something Nero has been making me practise for weeks now. When it works it's great, when it doesn't, it can cause more problems than it's worth. Tonight it worked, but I still hadn't been able to land my stake. For that, simply escaping Michel was not going to cut it, I would have to get close.

I carried my spin on around the room, ramping up the speed, so that when I was back near Michel, I was just a blur. Most vampires are in awe of this move, usually allowing a small window of opportunity to land the stake. Michel has seen this manoeuvre before, but every time he has stood stunned while I executed it, I had planned on that being the case again. But, maybe he wanted me to drive that damn car more than I had realised, because he came towards me, rather than standing stock still. And the resulting crash of our bodies against each other stole my breath and rattled my brain, so when he pinned me to the floor, my arms both held firmly above my head, by just one of his hands, I was seeing stars and unable to do a thing about it.

"You are amazing," he breathed against me, his own chest rising and falling on top of me with such speed. I struggled, trying to buck free of his body on top of mine, I even tried to throw my head against him, but he held firm and just kept his face out of reach.

A simple twist of his hand and a soft thump of my wrists against the mat on the floor beneath us and my stake fell away. I was disarmed and unless I could move him and get to my stake this was over. His free hand came up and stroked my hair out of my face, I refused to look at him, to admit defeat. He knew I wouldn't concede, so he didn't ask. He just gripped my hair tightly, almost painfully and turned my head to the side, exposing my neck. I fought him, I pushed against his hold, almost as though he *was* my enemy and his intentions weren't carnal but murderous. I would not give up. I would not show fear. I would never give an inch.

I tried to wriggle my body beneath him, to get a leg free to maybe knee him in the groin, but he just growled

65

and manoeuvred himself between my legs, pushing against me, flattening me, stilling me. He held me there for a full minute, my heart in my throat, tears stinging my eyes. I don't know why they were there, I just guess I don't like losing.

When he sensed I had settled, he slowly lowered his mouth to my neck, softly kissing my pulse, licking over the top of its rapid beat, grazing his teeth against my skin. I wanted his bite, I wanted it with every fibre of my body, but this was a battle and I *would not give in.*

I twisted my arms and rolled my body at the same time, almost managing to upset him and throw him off me. I'm stronger than I used to be and I think I caught him momentarily off guard. For a second, just a split second, I thought I had him. His body weight shifted, I felt my back leave the floor and my foot gained purchase so I could use my leg to further push against his hold and then he rallied, growled, gripped my hair tightly, pulling me back to the ground and twisting me painfully on my side and his fangs pierced my skin.

The bite was excruciating. I don't think he realised he had not tempered it all. Usually the sting lasts only a split second, but this time he was too caught up in the fight to think and he let me feel the force of his dominance, the right of his win, through the pain at my neck. I whimpered, managing not to scream, although perhaps a scream would have broken him from his moment sooner, but I did struggle against his hold, making my neck move under his mouth, forcing him to grip me tighter, firmer, to stop his fangs from tearing at my skin. Then, maybe because I was fighting and making it hard and he wanted me more compliant, or maybe he just woke up a little from his battle crazed bubble, but his desire washed through me in a tsunami of a wave, forcing my breath from my lungs and my body to still, only to be replaced by a hunger for him so raw that it made me ache.

I breathily whispered, "Michel." And received a purr from the back of his throat in reply.

He still gripped my hands, but now I was pushing my body up towards him, wrapping my legs around his waist and holding him tight. He groaned against me, removing his hand from my hair, tracing down my side, down past my breast, over my hip, to my short skirt, which he somehow managed to rip off me, with a small lift of his hips and a flick of his wrist and a smattering of *Sanguis Vitam*. Before I'd even realised he'd gotten rid of it, his body was against me again, his erection obvious through his trousers, pushing against my underwear. His hand returning to my top, feeling his way slowly up my stomach, finding my breast and taking his time tweaking it, stroking it, kneading it.

I moaned and he shuddered in response. Removing his fangs and licking where he had bit me. He still gripped my hands, seemingly reluctant to let them go just yet; a small ache had started in my shoulders, unable to shift them only making it worse.

"My arms," I whispered.

He lifted his head and looked at me, amethyst and indigo swirling in his eyes.

"I don't think so. You are still mine," he breathed against me before his mouth met mine in a rough crush of lips and teeth and tongue, almost trying to climb inside me, to get closer to me, to eat me.

He pulled away to let me breathe and I took my chance. "You've won, Michel. The car stays, but this wasn't part of the deal."

He didn't let me go, just ground against me, circling his hips in a little dance, body to body.

"You don't want me?" His eyebrows raised in mock shock. He knew damn well I wanted him. I would always want him, regardless of any negative emotions I may harbour, as soon as he touched me all thoughts of elsewhere were always lost.

"Let me have my arms and I'll show you how much." I held his gaze.

"Not tonight, *ma petite lumière*. Not this time. You have made the game too sweet, to end it just yet."

I stared at him. "What are you playing now?"

"My game, my rules. I'm taking my prize." And his hand came up under my top, grabbing it at the neckline and tearing it slowly down the front, baring my chest to him, save for my bra.

Oh dear God, he meant it.

His head came down and he kissed the crease between my breasts, nibbling a little, until he found the edge of the bra and began to worry at it, bite it and I knew what would come next; his fangs to rip it.

"Not the bra, they cost a fortune." But my voice wasn't all that convincing.

"I'll buy you more. I promise," he growled between his teeth and bit harder. The bra snapped open and his mouth didn't pause, wrapping around a nipple and lavishing it with licks and nibbles and kisses. The pull of his mouth making me rise up towards him.

I thought he'd just stop there, kissing me, sucking me, licking me, but he was obviously on a whole new level than I had ever been, because I felt his fangs scrape either side of my areola and then pierce the sensitive skin on my breast.

I'd always thought vampires needed larger veins to feed: arteries in the neck, upper thigh, arm, wrist. And I'm not even sure if what he was doing was feeding right now, maybe he was marking me. He'd already marked me at my neck, his signature that any other vampire could read with a glance, marking me as his own. But here, on my breast, so much more intimate, so much more private, I had no idea what he was doing, but he was enjoying it. And so was I, so maybe it was because I had accepted it, this moment of surprise, that I didn't stop him, didn't say anything and just let him feed, mark, have his way with me. But I didn't stop him. I just said his name, almost a plea, not to stop.

Without even realising it - I must have lost a few minutes there - he had removed my underwear and somehow unsheathed himself from his trousers and he was now pressing at my entrance, so hot and firm, just there, no further. He licked where his fangs had been on my breast and studied the mark he had left, smiling. I vaguely thought, so mark not feed then, before he thrust slowly against my entrance taking away any intelligent thought I may have had. He was big and hard and so damn good. Sometimes, he felt almost too big. But, I moaned and arched my back and welcomed him greedily inside me.

"You are so wet, *ma douce*," he groaned against me, pulling out, almost completely and then slowly, tortuously thrusting back inside. Then he repeated it all over again.

I whimpered, wanting more of him. Wanting a faster pace. Harder thrusts. But he continued to deny me, slowing his movements down even further. Refusing to enter me all the way. "Michel," I begged. He chuckled. "Please. Oh God! Please!"

With that he thrust inside me with a cry of need until he was as deep as he could go. It took me by surprise, I had expected him to play the game a little longer and not give in to my demands. But those thoughts were lost in amongst the beauty of the moment and I let myself luxuriate in the feel of him. All of him. He pulled out slowly again and entered with more control, but I bucked beneath him, calling out his name and he caved and started moving more forcefully, pushing me wide, stretching me uncomfortably, but making his way faster and faster, in and out, in and out, inch by inch further. Until I was drowning in the feel of him.

His mouth claimed mine, his hips thrusting against me. My hands still held firmly in one of his above my head, the other stroking my side, fondling my breast. And the flutter in my stomach turned to a tightness and heat, spreading its warmth up my body, down to my core and lifting me up on a wave I couldn't fight - didn't want to fight - until we both came crashing down the other side. Michel calling out in victory as he slammed into me one final time and at last released my hands and collapsed against the floor beside me, pulling my body to him, wrapping one of his arms around my waist and the other under my head.

We lay there quietly for a while, just the feel of our sweat-soaked bodies against each other, listening to the thumping of our hearts and trying to catch our runaway breaths.

Finally, my head cleared and my heart settled and I found I could actually form a string of words into a sentence after all.

"You marked me again, didn't you?"

His hand went to my breast, tracing his mark. "Yes," he whispered against me.

I didn't know what to say. Michel had wanted me to mark him, to give him my *Sigillum*, for a long time, but I had been tricked into sharing *Sigillum* with Gregor, a master vampire and member of the vampire council, the *Iunctio*. I hadn't realised what I was doing at the time and how precious it was. And now I shared a connection to Gregor that was hard to fight. I never wanted to give my *Sigillum* away again, unless I truly meant it. And here Michel was, marking me with his *Sigillum* for a second time. What do you say to that? Thanks. You shouldn't have. But, here's the thing, you can't be marked unless you accept it and I know I wasn't thinking straight at the time, but I had accepted Michel biting me there, I'd even thought he may be marking me and not feeding from me, so in essence, I had acquiesced.

At least I could cover this one up more easily than the neck. I would always have two marks on my neck, one from Michel and one from Gregor, visible to any vampire who cares to see. Somehow, I kind of liked that this mark was just between me and Michel, no one else. No one else at all.

"Thank you." It just came out.

"I would give you the world, *ma douce*, this" - his

71

fingers still tracing his mark - "is only my heart."

Chapter 6
Lambton Quay

We managed to make it back to Michel's chamber without coming across any wayward vamps - well, aside from Erika, who had been guarding the door, unbeknown to me. I had covered myself up in Michel's white shirt - it was almost long enough to be a dress - all of my clothes were ruined. Michel really did owe me a new wardrobe. So, I was at least clothed, but even that couldn't stop the blush flowing up my cheeks when she smirked at us as we passed.

At least she'd managed to grab another top, but she was still barefoot and the blood had dried on her face from our fight. The nose did look healed though.

"Sorry about your nose," I mumbled when I spotted her.

"Don't worry, *chica*, I'll take it out of your hide at first training tomorrow. That is of course, if you're feeling up to it. It sounded like quite a sparring session in there. You must be real tired." She exaggerated the *tired*.

Michel just growled, but it wasn't his usual scare tactics, more for my benefit than hers and it just made Erika smile more.

Back in his chambers I realised I *was* tired. Once again, it had been a long night. First Rick and Jerome, followed by exerting my Light all over the club. Then the faux fighting of Erika and Michel, and of course the rest, you know, the horizontal mumbo jumbo, so I was yawning by the time we'd shut the door. It was only 2am, according to the bedside clock, normally I would have stayed up longer on a Friday. You never know when I'd feel the pull, that evil-lurks-in-my-city pull, but I was shattered.

Michel kissed me on the forehead and suggested a bath and early night. I would have gone back to my place, but that would have meant taking *the* car and considering how tired I was, I just couldn't face that hurdle. I would honour our deal, he had won fair and square, the car was now mine, but despite that mental acknowledgement, I wasn't quite ready to physically drive it. That seemed to be the final step in accepting Michel and I had more than just a *joined* kindred relationship.

So, Michel left me to it and I dutifully ran a mandarin bubble overload bath and settled in to soak away the aches and pains and bumps and bruises. Normally, Michel would have healed me, but we both seemed to just forget at that moment, I was sure he'd be able to attend to it later, when he also retired for the day.

I must have fallen asleep, not a good thing to do whilst in the bath, but my head was resting back on one of those padded pillows on the edge of the bath and I was floating so comfortably, that I managed to relax enough, to feel safe enough, to fall asleep, because the next thing I knew, I was Dream Walking.

Usually when I Dream Walk it's a conscious thing, a controlled thing. I lay myself down with the intention of Dream Walking to someone or something and I allow my mind to fall into that black nothingness I seem to be able to find and I simply appear where ever it is I am wanting to be. I appear as I lay myself down, so usually in hunter gear with stake in hand, but I am invisible to those around me. They can't see me or sense me or even hear me, unless I talk, so it's a nifty little power, one I have utilised when

74

needed to take out the bad guys and hit them totally unawares.

I don't abuse it, it's usually for a life and death type situation and the bad guys are usually reeking evil, so my conscience is clear on the *they can't see me* front. They are vampires and they are evil. It's a war. End of story.

But, there has been a couple of occasions where I have not been in control of the Dream Walk. Those times have been controlled by another. Gregor. He had sworn he would not call me in a Dream Walk again, for fear I had already *Walked* once that night. Two Dream Walks in one night will leave me unconscious for three days. Not a good thing. So, Gregor had been behaving himself. But not tonight it would seem.

I woke to the cold air of a Wellington evening/early morning and the sounds of a nearby fight. The first thing I realised, after figuring out I had Dream Walked unintentionally, was I didn't have a stake. I hadn't had one nearby when I fell asleep, so I didn't have one now. The second thing I realised, was that I was buck naked and dripping in mandarin smelling bubbles and foam.

Oh, for the love of Christ, how do I end up in these situations!

"Lucinda?" It was a whisper, nearby, interspersed with a grunt and the sounds of a fist hitting something solid.

I spun around to see where Gregor was when he'd said my name and spotted him and about three other vampires and alarmingly a fair bit of vampire dust floating around their feet, fighting for their lives with about a dozen humans, all armed with rudimentary silver stakes. What the hell?

You called? I sent my thoughts with sarcasm towards him. Gregor can read my thoughts, but only if I send them or shout them in my head. He can't talk back, only Michel can do that, but trust me, reading my thoughts is more than enough trouble.

I heard Gregor mutter, "Shit!" My foul mouth attitude was rubbing off on him lately. He was just as suave and eloquent as Michel, swearing was a relatively new language skill, courtesy of me. But, it did tell me one thing, he hadn't realised he'd called me to him.

Well, I was here now, despite being inconveniently naked, they couldn't see me - well Gregor could, kind of. But it was really just a sense of my aura, a sense of me, not really visible, but quite unfortunate all the same - but they needed my help. They were outnumbered and it looked like they'd lost some of their group. Not good.

I wasn't armed, but then I don't tend to stake humans anyway and I am much stronger than they are, so a little hand to hand combat was called for. I could still kick their butts with my bare - that's very bare - hands and only my sparkling wit and attitude.

I came up behind one at the back, he was doubled over having obviously felt the cold hard strength of a master vampire and was trying to recover while his friends covered for him. They had cornered Gregor and his kin at the end of a dark brick alley, ironic don't you think? The first time I met Gregor he'd had a Nosferatin cornered at the end of an alley and was tucking in to dinner by the time I arrived. And here he was on the receiving end. I love Karma.

I tapped the human guy on the shoulder and he spun

76

around to look at who was there. Of course, he couldn't see me, but he could hear me if I talked, so I leaned forward and whispered, loud enough to be heard over the battle raging behind him.

"It's a bit late to be out brawling, isn't it?"

"What? Who said that?" His head was scanning the alley back towards Lambton Quay, his eyes wide with fear and uncertainty.

I'd figured we were in vamp central as soon as I arrived, not far in fact from the club Michel had established recently, to house and occupy his Wellington based vampires. He had been compensated for his investment when the *Iunctio* threw him out of this city. It was just his ego that had suffered, not his wallet.

"Look. I'll give you the benefit of the doubt, you are human after all," I said conversationally. "Grab your buds and get outta here. This isn't your fight."

He seemed to think about that for a moment, then his whole demeanour changed, a snarl appearing on his somewhat handsome face, ruining the effect of his looks completely.

"I don't know who the fuck you are, or where the fuck you are, but this is our fight. No vampires in Wellington!" He spat the last, thankfully I was far enough away not to wear it.

Oh boy. I guess I was meeting the humans against vampire portion of the Windy City's population. Vampires are not known to the larger public, but here and there you have sympathisers, those willing to aid and offer their blood up for food. But, lately, Wellington has had a run of humans killing vampires. It was part of the reason Michel

77

had been chucked out by the *Iunctio*. They were not happy it had not been solved, so they had sent in their Enforcer, Gregor, to investigate and clean up. Do whatever it took to cover this up from the general public, before it got further out of hand. I'm guessing, so far, Gregor was having the same troubles Michel had, little success at all.

Well, I couldn't leave this as it was. Gregor and his vampires were in trouble and whether these humans had a right to fight or not, they couldn't just kill vampires willy-nilly. No, that was my job and those of my kind.

"Sorry mate, but this has to stop." I struck out before he had a chance to answer with a simple front kick to his face, making his head snap back and his eyes roll up in his skull and forcing him backwards onto his back on the ground. Bugger. I forget my own strength sometimes. I quickly leaned down and checked his pulse; still strong, still regular, just out cold.

I jumped out of the way as one of his mates ran to check him and then the shit hit the proverbial fan. Panic ensued, the humans going batshit crazy, slashing out at the vampires, because they thought it was their super speed that had allowed them to get to their man and they hadn't even been able to see it to stop it. Their anger fuelling their actions, making them equally dangerous and reckless at the same time. Stakes were slashing, landing here and there, but not full heart strikes, just deep gouges and tears in vampire flesh. The vamps were taking a beating and even with their combined supernatural strength, they were unable to stop this number of crazed humans on a rampage.

Time for plan B.

I danced up behind the back of the humans, sucked in a

deep breath and spun. I usually reserve this move for vampires and I usually have a stake in hand. This time no stake and definitely no vampires, but the result was just as effective. I landed next to one human and flicked out a roundhouse kick, followed by a sweep of their legs and then a straight jab at their nose. Then in a spilt second, after making those moves in a blur, I was off to the next. Repeating my actions all over again. I managed to take out five before they realised they were in serious trouble. They also realised it wasn't the vamps in front of them doing the damage, but something altogether never heretofore seen.

It's a little scary when you first realise there are actually monsters of the night. We've all read the Fairy-tales, read the urban fantasy novels, we've heard of Bram Stoker and Dracula, we're almost prepared for all of that. But, something that strikes with a speed you can't even comprehend and is also invisible, can make a grown man whimper. They couldn't see me, they couldn't hear me, I just took one out after the other in little more than ten seconds flat. I only stopped, because they had stopped. No longer fighting the vamps, but turning their backs to them and facing the new, bigger, more evil threat behind them.

I could have laughed, but I was too damn weary and too damn disillusioned to do it. I was supposed to be the good guy, the one who protected the human innocents from the creatures of the night and here I was beating on their fragile human butts, to save the Nosferatu. What a screwed up little world I created for myself.

The humans finally got the message, those still standing grabbing their mates and hauling arse out of the alley and back towards the safety of the late night pub crawlers and the lights of Lambton Quay.

The vampires were all standing stock still.

Gregor was the first to make a move, slowly raising his hands and clapping, a huge grin across his handsome face. I hardly ever noticed the scar any more, his beautiful grey eyes, now laced with silver and platinum swirls, plus the recent addition of my *Sigillum*, an ethereal shine or light around said eyes, distracted from the 8cm jagged pink line that graced his right hand cheek. He was beautiful, not surprisingly, but it was my *Sigillum*, my mark and the fact that I wore his, that called to me. I fought it even now, not to rush into his strong arms.

"Ha. Ha," I muttered sarcastically. "What the hell, Gregor? How did you get cornered by a bunch of humans?" I asked.

"*Ma cherie*, how is it that you always find me in such compromising positions?"

Like I said, the first time I Walked to Gregor he was munching on a Nosferatin in Rome. The second was to his private chambers, his boudoir he called it, where he tried to have his wicked way with me. And the third, he was with a vampire named Alessandra, a supposed ally of Michel's. All three times, he was not behaving as a member of the *Iunctio* should. But that was Gregor. Bad boy, through and through. Why is it we all have a soft spot for at least one bad boy in our lives?

I stifled a sigh. "Well, if you guys are all sorted, I gotta go."

I was cold and shivery, not to mention standing in the buff in front of three well dressed and equally well preserved handsome men and even if they couldn't see me,

I was naked for God's sake! There's only so much a girl can get away with before she's caught out. I did not want Gregor to cotton on to my current predicament.

"We need to talk." Gregor's voice reached out and wrapped around me, trying to pull me closer. I resisted, just. And suddenly, the two remaining vamps left us, vanishing into the shadows and leaving me with Gregor. Alone.

I took a deep breath in. "Can this wait? I'm kinda cold." I could admit to that at least, he probably could hear my teeth chattering right now anyway.

He cocked his head to the side and smiled, his wicked boy smile, lighting up his eyes, making me cringe at what he might say next. Both in fear and mild excitement. Damn.

"Are you dressed in lingerie again, *ma petite chasseuse?*"

You see, the first time I Dream Walked to Gregor, I'd been asleep in a shortie slinky nightie. He'd loved it, of course. But, before I could formulate a reply to throw him off the scent, he was in front of me. Poof. Out of thin air. I didn't even see him move. They can really book it when they want to, vamps.

His hands ran over my shoulders, down my arms and back up my sides, sending shockwaves and tingles from the magical touch of his fingers against my flesh. He took a sudden step back, the look on his face, one of utter shock, almost making me smile.

"You're not dressed. And you smell of... mandarins." He recovered himself slightly. "Were you bathing? Did you fall asleep in the bath, *ma cherie?*" And then he started

81

laughing, really laughing, his whole body shaking with the delight of it.

I sighed, again, I was doing a lot of that lately. "I'm glad you find it amusing, Gregor, but I am cold."

He tried to stop laughing, to pull himself together again, but I could see he was having a hard time and enjoying himself just a wee bit too much. Finally, he shook himself out of his dinner jacket and handed it to me. I gratefully slipped it on, wrapping it around me, as close as I could get it. It smelled of him. Chocolate coated ice cream and cherry trees in Spring. I couldn't stop myself from inhaling deeply.

He noticed and just smiled. I don't know exactly what I looked like in a Dream Walk to him. He sees my aura, my shape if you will, but I'm still not there. Just a haze of colours wrapped up in his jacket. Surreal. That's my life. But still he just kept smiling at me.

"So, you wanted to talk?" Best to get on with things, God knows if my body would suddenly sink under the water in the tub and snuff me out.

"I met your cousin," he said, matter of factly.

"My cousin?"

"Timothy, I believe."

Oh, my cousin. I've only recently been introduced to someone on my biological father's side of the family tree. Before then, I knew they existed, in a non-specific kind of way, but they had never come to seek me out before. My Aunt and Uncle decided, for whatever reasons, to cut off all contact with them. They are the Nosferatin side of my genealogy, my Aunt and Uncle have absolutely no idea what I am or what I do. I intend to keep it that way. But,

Tim turned up on my doorstep a couple of weeks ago, wanting to get know me and wanting to know about being a Nosferatin.

Nosferatin is in the blood. The first born is the vampire hunter, or Nosferatin, the second carries the gene and knowledge, passing on the hunter instincts to their first born and the carrier gene and knowledge to their second. I was an only child, I don't have a younger brother or sister to carry on the gene. My biological parents died when I was just a baby. So, there is no other gene carrier to pass on the genetics required to be like me. I'm the last of my line. Tim is the son of my father's younger brother. No gene, no Nosferatin mojo. Just a normal human related to a freaky supernatural. I wasn't surprised at his curiosity, but I was still cautious about the guy.

A friend of mine, well an acquaintance actually, warned me about Tim. A gut instinct, which may or may not be right, but I'd take Pete's gut instinct over anyone else's any day. It's just that, Tim seems so normal, so nice. The kind of cousin you could easily get along with. I guess, the jury is still out on this one.

"How did you meet Tim?" I asked, getting my mind back on the present.

"He came into the club, asked for me. Introduced himself as your Nosferatin cousin. He is not a Nosferatin."

"No. He's not. What did he want?" What was Tim up to?

"He asked if I needed a vampire hunter in my city, to keep the peace. He offered himself"

To keep the peace. "Were those his exact words?"

"Yes."

Gregor was watching me, not that I'm sure of what it is he actually sees when I'm Dream Walking, but I got the impression he was trying to see my reaction. To gauge just what my involvement here was.

"I don't know what to say, Gregor. I've not known him long and I knew he was curious about what I am, but to ask this? To want to be a vampire hunter when he hasn't even got the gene? I don't know what he's playing at. Really."

Without the gene, Tim would just be a vigilante, roaming the streets hoping to find his prey. I, on the other hand, am born to do this. Natural vampire repelling skills, the evil-lurks-in-my-city pull and now of course, a bag full of Nosferatin joined to Nosferatu mojo. He couldn't possibly do what I do. But, here's the thing. Wellington did need a Nosferatin. Vampires were on the loose and humans were interfering. This was a recipe for disaster.

"You do need a Nosferatin though, Gregor. Things are getting out of hand."

"Not him."

No not him. I could agree with Gregor there. I needed to speak to Tim, but this also needed to be done face to face. I think a little sojourn to Wellington was on the cards.

"I'll deal with it. I'll come and speak to him."

Gregor perked up then, picking up on the I'll come and speak to him part, not just an: I'll call him and speak to him line.

"You would be most welcome in my city. At any time. I insist, however, on providing your accommodation."

"That won't be necessary, Gregor, I'm sure I can find a hotel."

"If you are in my city, Hunter, then it is very

necessary."

"I won't be here to hunt." And then I stopped myself saying anything else. If Wellington didn't have a Nosferatin and things were getting out of hand, then maybe I should be visiting more often.

There's not many of us left. A few centuries ago my ancestors decided to leave the creatures of the night to themselves, hiding us away, denying them our powers and in the process, condemning their first borns to death. Without a joining, I would have died. Thank God I got that transfer to Auckland. But, it has meant far fewer Nosferatin alive today, than previously. And therefore, far greater Nosferatu.

"You have decided something." How is it that Gregor can read me when I'm just a haze of colour?

"Until we find you a Nosferatin, I think I should make regular visits. Weekends only, I've got a job that I won't let suffer because of this. But, you do need someone here to at least send a message to your rogues. Maybe that will be enough to help dampen the human interest as well." You never know, you can always live in hope anyway. Keeping the *Iunctio* away from our shores was a top priority. Gregor was OK, but the whole force of the *Iunctio?* No way thanks.

I thought Gregor would argue, I thought he wouldn't want me interfering in his city, but he just smiled, that damn knowing smile he and Michel seem to share.

"Anything you say, *ma cherie*. Anything at all."

Aw damn. I had so heard that before and it never bode well.

"Well, I really have to go now. I'm asleep in a bath full

of water, not really a good combination." There was no point denying it, Gregor already knew my predicament.

"Of Course, *ma cherie*. I would not wish you harm. But, perhaps... a goodbye kiss to tide me over?" He cocked his head to the side and gave me an endearing, if not wicked, smile.

I laughed at him then. "Not on your life, Romeo." And then I let myself fade into the black of nothingness and return to my body before he could change my mind.

I woke up feeling heavy in the cooling bath water, realising I had shifted back to my body wearing Gregor's jacket. Anything minor that I have on me, be it clothing or scratches and bruises, comes back when I Dream Walk. I caught myself before I went completely under, spluttering the small amount of bath water I had swallowed out of my mouth, cussing a few choice words in the process and brushing my damp hair from my face.

When my eyes finally did adjust to the new lighting around me, they were unfortunately greeted with the face of a very pissed off master vampire, sitting above me on the side of my bath.

"Is there something you wish to tell me, Lucinda?" Michel said as he plucked at the wet fabric of Gregor's dinner jacket.

Oh, and here we go again.

Chapter 7
It's Not How It Looks

There was no point denying it. And Michel didn't look in the mood for half truths, so yet again another sigh and I prepared to face the music.

"I fell asleep. Gregor called me to him. I don't think he meant to. He and a couple of his line were fighting a group of humans, they were outnumbered, he must have just thought of me while they battled and I ended up in the middle of it."

Michel slowly raised a single eyebrow at me. "I take it he survived?"

Yeah, that's just what Michel would like. Gregor to be taken care of once and for all. I just nodded.

"And you were naked?" His voice was flat.

Now we were getting to the pissed off part of the equation. Michel knew Gregor wanted me for himself, he had even kind of accepted that as par for the course, but me appearing in front of another vampire buck naked was not going to sit well. Even if said vampire couldn't really see me when I Dream Walked. Too much temptation methinks for vampires of any kind.

"He gave me his jacket." I kind of thought that would cover Gregor's chivalrous side.

"Yes. I can see that." He paused and looked at me, taking all of me in, in a sweep of his eyes; dripping wet, jacket clinging to my small frame, mandarin bubbles sitting in my hair. "How close did he get?" He gritted his teeth when he said that.

Michel may have acted like it was all OK for Gregor to *try* to seduce me, but underneath it all he was seething. He did not share what was his well. And unfortunately, I was his; a possession, nothing more. Sometimes, I really hated being reminded of that.

I tried to get up out of the bath water, but the jacket was surprisingly heavy and Michel just pushed me back down, with a firm hand on my shoulder.

"Answer me."

Michel could be a real prick sometimes. He knew I didn't go for this *you are mine Lucinda* crap, but he still couldn't stop himself. It was a part of him that was so deeply ingrained he had no chance of stopping it when it started. Michel was just along for the ride, his jealousy and possessiveness took him on.

"Not close. He just handed me the jacket when I said I was cold."

Michel's eyes flashed magenta. Ah oh. He knew I was lying, or at the very least not telling the full truth. This was just going from bad to worse, wasn't it?

"Why is it that I don't believe you, my dear? Did he touch you?"

I blew a puff of breath out in frustration. Michel was going to drive me crazy with all this ownership and controlling that he was lately exhibiting.

"Nothing happened, Michel, just drop it." And I pushed up out of the bath splashing as much water as I could muster over his super-expensive Armani suit. *I hope it goes in your shoes.*

He stood up and back quickly. "Childish, Lucinda."

That's it, I'd had enough of this crap. "No, Michel. I'll tell you what is so damn childish. *You* thinking you own me. *You* thinking you can control me. *You* thinking you can

88

demand explanations from me and make me feel guilty for something that did not happen at all. Why don't *you* grow up for once?"

He looked a little shocked at that. I don't think he was used to someone challenging his authority. Michel tended to get his own way a little too often. So, for the real hammer blow.

"I'm heading to Wellington tomorrow. I need to sort out my cousin who thinks he can be a quasi-Nosferatin and the humans are getting a little hot under the collar. Gregor lost vampires tonight. This is going to reach the *Iunctio's* ears, we can't just sit back and let that happen. I need to get down there and help make the vampires step back in line, there's no other Nosferatin available, so it's up to me. I don't want the Champion anywhere near our shores."

The Champion was the head of the *Iunctio's* council. She was formidable, scary as Hell and really wanted me dead. The good thing though, was that she couldn't outright kill me, my goddess of a mother Nut - we're descended from her apparently - made sure the Champion and I were connected to each other and she was now unable to snuff me out. A positive to be sure, but still, I had no intention of the plight of Wellington registering on her radar any time soon.

Of course, I expected Michel to argue. Going to Wellington was not something he would normally condone, it put me within Gregor's grasp. But, I was angry enough to push for this if needed. Michel had to learn I was not his to control. So, I was surprised he stepped back and leaned against the vanity with a look of thoughtful consideration on his face.

"I cannot go with you. I am not welcome in Wellington while a master is setting up his base. It would be considered a challenge."

Huh. "But you agree with me, that I should go?"

He raised his eyes to mine, the magenta had gone, just traces of indigo and amethyst now in amongst the deep blue.

"I agree Wellington is a problem and that there is no other Nosferatin available to stand stead, but I am not in the least bit happy about you going." I could tell that quite easily. "I shall advise our pilot that you will fly out tomorrow evening." Michel owned a *Gulfstream G650*, handy for personal flights around the country and when summoned to the *Iunctio* in Paris.

"I was thinking of heading out at first light."

He shook his head. "Erika can not travel to the airport in daylight. She will be going with you as your guard." More like chaperone, but I couldn't argue. At least I knew she could hold her own in a fight.

I nodded. At least I wouldn't have to drive, even if the BMW could have handled the ten hour drive effortlessly.

He suddenly reached up and stroked my cheek with the back of his hands, his face softening. "*Ma douce*, do have any idea how much you put me through?" I smiled and leaned into his hand. There goes that Karma again, I thought, making sure to keep the words well contained in my mind.

"But," he added, "I would very much prefer it if you removed this monstrosity immediately and had it burned." He threw Gregor's jacket off my shoulders and hurled it into the corner. "Now that, " he said, his eyes flashing

90

wickedly, "is more like it."

His hand went to the back of my neck and he pulled me towards him. "I'll get your suit wet," I offered meekly.

"It's already ruined." This was whispered against my mouth, just before his lips met mine and his arm crushed me against him. I didn't fight him, I let him have his wicked way with me, some battles are just not worth the effort. And besides, this was a battle I preferred to fight willingly, wanted to fight with every fibre of my body. Have I mentioned how hard it is to say no Michel's charms?

Damn hard.

I fell asleep in his arms some time later. I had no idea if the night had ended and he needed to rest to, or if he just decided it was better to stay close to me, skin to skin, to keep me out of trouble. Or maybe, the thought of me heading off to Gregor's territory tomorrow was just a bit too much for him to bear and he craved the closeness just as much as I did.

I woke to Michel stroking my hair out of my eyes and realised he was no longer wrapped around me, but sitting on the side of the bed fully clothed. I rubbed the remnants of sleep away from my eyes and glanced at the clock. It was midday.

"Rise and shine, sleepy head," he said and leaned in to kiss me on my forehead. "As you will miss the opportunity to train with Erika this evening, she has agreed to an early session during daylight hours and is waiting for you in the rec room." Vampires don't actually need to sleep during the day, just to rest for a while and avoid the harsh light of the sun. So the fact that Erika was prepared to bust my arse didn't surprise me one little bit. Although I admit, I had hoped to skip it all together.

I decided on trying a delaying tactic instead and ran my fingers up Michel's arm, letting my hand rest above his pulse in his neck. A vampire finds that spot very intimate and Michel's eyes flashed a small amount of amethyst at my suggestion. He swallowed and I watched his Adam's apple bob up and down, then shifted my gaze to his mouth.

"You are not playing fair, *ma douce.*" He licked his lips.

"I never said I'd play fair, Michel."

He chuckled. "But, you are trying to distract me, I think."

I just shrugged, he knew me well.

"It will not work." I raised my eyebrows at that. Since when did Michel turn down an offer like this?

"Your training is too important to me. Besides, once Erika has worn you down, you will be that much more compliant to my desires."

"Is that how you like me, Michel? Docile, compliant, cooperative?" I said it with a hint of a smile. I knew Michel pretty well too.

He growled softly. "This will have to wait, as much as it pains me, but be assured, my dear, there will come a time when the tables are turned and *that* will be my reward for such control now." I didn't doubt him, he would now make sure I paid for this momentary distraction and slight on his commands.

"Bring it," I said smiling more broadly.

He couldn't resist forever and the challenge was enough to make his eyes sparkle a brief flash of magenta and then his mouth was on mine, his arms around me, pulling me up off the bed and into his lap. He kissed me like a man possessed, all teeth and tongue and lips and hands, eating me, climbing inside me, taking my breath away, making my heartbeat stutter and my fingers dig into his shirt, pulling him closer and giving as good as I got. I felt him harden beneath me and knew I had him. He couldn't fight this, neither of us could, so I moved against him, encouraging him and moaned a demand against his lips.

He laughed, registering my desire and need, knowing he had me at the point of no return, begging with my body, my hands, my mouth and tongue. Begging with the little whimpers of need spilling from my lips and then he simply slid me off his lap and stood up with a smile as he walked away.

"Hey!" I shouted at him.

He stopped at the door and looked over his shoulder, a satisfied smile playing on his face. His eyes raked over my naked body, from the flush on my face, to the pout on my lips, to the taut tight readiness of my nipples.

"Round one to me, *ma douce*. Now get dressed, you'll have an audience, my kin are very keen to see Erika *kick your butt*, as you say." And then he walked from the room without a second glance.

Son of a bitch!

I heard that, he replied in my mind letting his laughter fill my head as he walked down the hall outside and away from me.

Damn, but if the man couldn't play the game well.

I got myself dressed and resigned to the fact that I

couldn't get out of this, so within twenty minutes - no way was I not showering after last night's escapades - I was on my way via the fully functional kitchen belonging to the bar, swiping a sandwich Michel's human day staff had sitting waiting for me at the ready. And after a brief thanks and a wave, set out to face just what Erika the Sword had in store for me today. It couldn't be that bad, could it? I was, after all, her master's kindred Nosferatin.

I was not at all prepared for what faced me. The rec room had been transformed into a legitimate sparring room. All evidence of the casual day resting place of Michel's vampires was gone, instead a padded floor area had been prepared for sparring and various paraphernalia relating, no doubt to sword fighting, dotted the room. Erika had shifted in.

But, that wasn't the worst of it. Some twenty of Michel's vampires were dotted around the room in various forms of relaxing poses, on chairs and stools and bean bags, waiting for the show to start. I knew most of them too. Bruno smiled at me with a shake of his head, it said everything: you're in deep shit girlie. Shane Smith was there, he's one of Michel's lesser vampires, only 30 vampire years old, or there about, no master status and never would have, but he was usually on my side. Plus Jett, the highest ranking master to join from Jock's line. Dillon Malone was too, Michel's roaming level two master that I think he used as some sort of spy across the country, tracking any of his vampires who travel and those of other lines that frequent our land. Even Doug the barman was here, handing out bottles of beer to the crowd like a bloody drinks vendor at a rugby match. They were certainly gearing up for a spectacle, weren't they?

I paused on the threshold of the room, mouth full of uneaten sandwich, as I took in the scene before me. I slowly chewed my meal and swallowed, not at all liking the feel of it sliding down my suddenly dry throat. Hmm. This required some serious Nosferatin guts and moxie. Never show fear. Never give an inch. Always stay on guard.

"So, anyone for poker?"

I few of the vamps laughed, the rest just shook their heads.

"No takers, huh? I guess we'd better just get on with this then."

I turned to Erika, who was already kneeling on the floor of the padded mat, two swords lying out in front of her.

"You're late, Nosferatin. That will cost you dearly."

Oh great, Erika was one of *those* task masters then. Just flippin' great.

"Kind of got held up by the master. You know how he is...." I let that trail off, it also provided a few more knowing chuckles around the room. Maybe I could at least dazzle them with my wit. It was my usual fall back when uncomfortable.

Erika just looked me up and down, taking in my tight fitting yoga pants and tight fitting T-Shirt. I really thought she'd have little to complain about, you could definitely see my muscles move in this outfit, so I had to force myself not to bite when she finished assessing my outfit and said, "Take the top off, leave the pants, but I need to see your arms, your abdomen, your back. I can't with the T-Shirt on." Her tone brokered no argument, it was a command, one I think she had used on others she had trained in the past. I was getting the feeling that Erika was a warrior first and foremost, a well trained, highly experienced and highly ranked warrior. I would not show fear.

I had a sports bra on underneath, that covered me quite adequately, so much to the surprise of several vamps nearby I just did what she asked, without complaint. They all knew me better. Had Michel demanded, I would have thrown a hissy fit. Erika just smiled and it wasn't a knowing smile, just a you go girl smile. We may have been still sizing each other up, but I think Erika might just have had a little respect for me already, like I did her.

I came and knelt down next to her on the mat, mirroring her stance.

"We will use bokken when we spar each other, but for starters I want you to practice the Weapon Dance, so as we won't be sparring off against each other, the real deal will do."

"Weapon Dance?" It sounded something like a performance, not too hands on at all. That I could handle.

"We are using traditional Swedish style swords, but a combination of Swedish fighting methods and Japanese kendo moves. When practised repeatedly, your body begins to memorise the muscles needed, the motions required, to carry out the actions of brandishing a sword. Eventually, they will become second nature, you will not even have to think of the action itself when fighting, just follow your muscles' memories to combat your enemy."

OK, so pretend moves repeated. How bad could it be?

I will never ask that question again in my entire long

eternal life. Erika had me practising the same moves over and over and over again for more than four hours straight. She barely let me take a breather to rehydrate, only allowing a marathon runner swig from a bottle between one set move and the next. My muscles ached, still not having been healed by Michel since yesterday, my limbs were fatigued, my head pounded and still she kept shouting, "Again!"

Most of the vampires had given up after an hour or so, some of the more staunch supporters - or sadists, I'm not sure which - stuck around a lot longer. Shane Smith offering me sips from water bottles every now and then, bless him. And Bruno playing poker with Jett and a couple of others quietly in the corner. Occasionally slipping a glance my way. I guessed he was there on Michel's orders, making sure Erika toed the line.

When I thought I couldn't possibly last another second she called a halt to the proceeding and took away the sword. Re-sheathing it while I stood shaking and swaying on the mat. I was so relieved I could almost have cried. Finally I could go take a soak in the bath.

I went to walk off the mat and she growled. Vampire growl.

"Not yet, Lucinda." I almost went to say, you can call me Luce, but I am so, so glad I held my tongue, because this woman did not deserve to call me by my nick name. "Now, we spar."

Oh fuck!

Chapter 8
Never Give An Inch

"I don't think I have it in me, Erika." I couldn't deny it any longer, I could almost feel myself sinking into sleep.

She grinned menacingly. "You giving up on me, Nosferatin?"

I didn't want to agree with her, but I was knackered, and that's KNACKERED in capital letters. But just then, out to the side of the room, in a gap left by the recently deserting vampires, a flicker of light started and then within seconds the form of my other trainer, - the Nosferatin one - Nero, appeared. Nero can Dream Walk, that's how he trains me from all the way over in Cairo where he lives.

He took a slow look around the room, taking in the training arena, the few vamps sitting wearily in the corner and the sight of my sweat soaked, slowly swaying self on the centre of the mat and smiled.

Nero's gorgeous. He's my trainer and I have a completely professional relationship with him, but I still can't help noticing his thick short black hair, the fine lines on his chiselled face, his deep golden brown skin flashing from beneath his cream coloured linen top, his well-toned muscles under his rolled up sleeves and long, lithe physique. But best of all, Nero's eyes shine like a vampires, with coffee coloured swirls and cinnamon flecks in a deep brown well of sheer brilliance. He's the only other human, well half human-half Nosferatin, who has eyes like a vampire. It could be to do with the fact that he is as old as Michel. Immortality must have its perks after 500 years or so.

He didn't say a word, just took a seat and crossed his

legs at his ankles, put his hands behind his head - the usual Nero comfortable sitting position - and inclined his head. So, here's the thing. I could quite possibly have let Erika get the better of me and caved due to fatigue, but with Nero now watching. Not a bloody chance.

I rolled my shoulders and shook out my limbs, limbering up as best I could.

"All right, Blondie, bring it on!"

I think she was momentarily surprised. I think she really thought she had me, but she recovered quickly enough and went and got what I guessed were the bokken; two wooden swords in the same shape as the Svante replicas we had been using for the Weapon Dance and when I hefted one, about the same weight too. I did a few of the practice moves and was surprised at how realistic it felt. So similar, but not quite as deadly. I'm sure though, that a well placed whack from one of these wooden ones would still smart. Here's hoping I could avoid that.

Of course, I wasn't as smooth as Erika and I was quite sure she was holding back, letting me get the feel of sword on sword, but I kind of held my own. The dance moves she had instilled in me over the past four hours had actually sunk in. Possibly not to the point of intrinsic movements, but, with a focused determination, I could pull them off when needed. Changing my way of thought from repetitive movements, to utilising the strokes I had practised on the fly. Choosing the best action to counter whatever move Erika made.

She started out making a move and instructing me at the same time on what Weapon Dance action was needed to counter it, but within twenty minutes, she had stopped directing and just let me get on with it. Somehow, I was a natural. I have never picked up a sword before in my life, this was my first training session with a blade or bokken, but it felt like I had done this for years, decades even. I was a bit jerky to start with and the aches were distracting, but I found my groove, I sunk into the rhythm and I began to move with more and more grace. Our combined speed increased with each minute that passed and I vaguely realised that more and more vampires were returning to the room to watch.

I couldn't better her, there was no chance of that right now, but I knew, just knew, with practice that was not going to always be the case. I'm not sure if this new found skill with a blade was a natural balance, sporting confidence or hard fought from fitness. Or if it was just because of genetics, my Nosferatin fighting skills, blending with those of the traditional Nosferatu. I could tell Erika was surprised, but she was also holding back and when the room was back to capacity, she'd had enough of entertaining me. Quite frankly, I'm amazed she lasted that long. Vampires don't like being shown up. They are natural predators, they crave confrontation and they are always ready to fight.

She started landing the odd whack of the wooden blade against my side and when that didn't deter me or slow me, she began to jab me with its point. I, on the other hand, hadn't landed a single blow, just managed to stave off most of the attacks, holding my own and no doubt looking good for the part, but not actually closing the deal. The more whacks Erika got in, the more determined she was to make me beg for release, to beg to stop the spectacle it was becoming.

I noticed Nero now standing at the edge of the mat, I could tell he wasn't happy. I've fought a lot with Nero, side by side against the bad guys of the night and together sparring like I was right now with Erika. And I can tell a lot by the way he holds himself. His arms were now crossed over his chest, his legs spread shoulder length apart, his gaze intense and following every move Erika made. He was sizing her up, looking for a weakness and not impressed she was pushing me to this level. Not impressed at all, that she was using the opportunity to beat me to a pulp.

For me, there was no going back. I had committed to this to the end. I was not going to show fear. I was not going to give an inch. I would fight this to the bitter conclusion, which I was becoming more and more aware, was going to be me unconscious on the mat.

Finally, Nero must have had enough, because I caught the glint of his silver stake as it appeared in his hand and watched out of the corner of my eyes as he stepped onto the mat.

"No," I breathed out between clenched teeth. "Stand down."

Erika cocked her head. "Stand down? Why would I do that, Nosferatin, when I am winning?" Of course, she couldn't see Nero Dream Walking, she had no idea who I was talking to. I just shook my head and kept focusing on warding off her blows. Nero had heard though and reluctantly nodded his head and stepped back off the mat. This was my battle, he would let me fight it how I saw fit.

He did however make sure I could see him from where

I was battling across the mat and he raised an eyebrow and mouthed, "Spin."

I had been battling this like a vampire, using strength and speed, agility and endurance as my only weapons. I had not even considered calling on my Nosferatin powers to aid in the battle, it had somehow felt like cheating. But now I realised that that was not the case. Erika had been a swordsman for centuries, I'd had five or six hours training, there was no way I could win a battle against her with that limited amount of experience, so what was I doing? Holding my own, just, but content to let her wear me down until she won and I capitulated in a heap of jelly-like mess on the floor? I don't think so. I never enter a fight unless I intend on winning. What would be the point of that?

It took me several more minutes to centre myself sufficiently to attempt the move, in the meantime Erika had managed a few more choice bruises to my shins - and fuck doesn't that hurt? - and back. And Michel had decided to join the show. He did not look impressed at all. I have no idea if that was because I was failing miserably and I didn't have time to consider the ramifications of that thought just then, because I'd found my zone. Erika came at me with an overhead swing, which I anticipated might have been her killing, or at least knocking unconscious, move and I spun.

I danced up in my Nosferatin spin away from her bokken, away from the bruising glance of her strike, around the back of her and landed with the sword at her neck, coming in from an angle, showing the intent was clear: a decapitation with one blow.

"Bang, bang, you're dead." Wrong weapon, but hell I was spent.

A round of raucous applause and hoots and cries of *Well done, Luce! Knew you could do it!* Yeah right, on that last one. And Erika dropped her sword in defeat.

I slowly sunk to my knees in utter exhaustion and glanced up at Nero to mouth, "Thank you". He smiled, nodded his head and flickered out of sight. My hero, come to add support and guidance even when I didn't realise I needed him. Nero and I are connected, not like Michel and I, or even Gregor and I, Nero is my Nosferatin Herald. He is part of the Prophesy I am also part of. I am the *Sanguis Vitam Cupitor*, the first key to the Prophesy and he is the one to unlock it, pulling all the relevant parts together to complete its task. So far, I'm the only one to appear, we're still waiting on the rest of them, but in the meantime, he comes when I call, even if I don't realise I've called.

"Well, you took your time, Lucinda." Erika said turning to look at me. She was breathless and covered in as much sweat as me, but she was smiling. "I wondered when you'd realise you had more in your arsenal than just guts."

Bugger me! Even Erika had expected me to use my Nosferatin skills. I was still trying to catch my breath, so it took a couple of efforts before I could counter her statement.

"I was trying to go easy on you."

She laughed and stepped forward to hold out her hand. I took it and we shook. Hers firm and commanding, but not so firm she was trying to make a point. She leaned in and said, "You are amazing, you know?" Then winked.

Michel stepped onto the mat then and came to stand next to me.

"Well, if you have finished completely exhausting my

Nosferatin, I will now try and make her recovered enough for your trip in a few hours." His voice was not at all pleasant. I don't think he liked how far Erika had taken this training session.

She just straightened her shoulders and raised her chin towards him. "She is not as fragile or delicate as you suspect, Michel. She is more than capable of holding her own."

I appreciated the vote of confidence, really I did, but right now I couldn't move a muscle and Michel kind of had a point. Still, Erika, the evil task master that she undoubtedly is, and I, were going to get along quite fine. Quite fine indeed. Somehow, I just knew, she had my back. And in that moment I knew also, that I had hers. I looked up at her and smiled, it was all I was capable of, but it was enough to let her know I'd heard her defence of me and I liked it.

Michel's fists, however, were clenched and I'm betting there was a fair amount of magenta in his eyes, although I couldn't turn my head enough to see right then. His voice when he did speak again was all icy chill. "You will remember your place, vampyre, or I will teach you it."

The atmosphere in the room had shifted in that instant. The vampires watching almost pulling in on themselves, trying to vanish from sight, to not get noticed by their now reeking *Sanguis Vitam* master. Michel, unfortunately, had a bit of Dark in him too and when threatened or pushed to the limit, it crept out of whatever corner it usually hid in and started to play. My job as his kindred, was to temper that Dark, to call him back to the Light, but I also knew shows of power, strength and dominance were all part of the political game of a master of a line. Most ruled by fear and strength alone, Michel had also earned respect, but he was still a vampire and would always revert to one when angry.

I was guessing, right now, his anger was because of the state I was in. Regardless of whether I sometimes wondered if Michel cared for me, loved me even, moments like this made me realise if nothing else, I was precious to him, important enough to him, to get so riled up over such a stupid event. I was tired and a little bruised, sure, but I was generally OK. But, part of me also acknowledged that I was a tool in his arsenal and his concern could also have been for the damage of a valuable asset. I sighed. I couldn't very well make a move publicly in front of his vampires, I don't think he'd listen to thoughts projected to him right now either - sometimes even he is too far gone - but what I could do was send him my emotions.

So, I concentrated on what I felt and it was a combination of exhaustion, but the type of exhaustion you get after a really good, really hard workout and pride at what I had achieved in such a short amount of training time. And elation at having succeeded to land the end blow and gratefulness to Erika for letting me do it under truly just circumstances, for not holding any punches, for making me work for it - something a vampire could understand. And then I sent it out towards him with my love and appreciation for his standing up for me, for his caring enough for me - for whatever reason, be it true affection or political gain - to confront his kin with such strength on my behalf.

He turned slowly towards me, looked down at where I sat, still crumpled on the floor and looked at me with such amazement on his face, such utter respect and understanding. And for a brief moment there, I saw love; unadulterated love for me. And it stilled my heart.

He suddenly came to his knees at my side and reached up to cup my face in his, looking at the surprise that must have graced my features. His fingers running along my jaw, his eyes taking in every part of me, a thumb stroking my cheek.

"You still do not accept what I feel for you, *ma douce*. You do not believe it possible. Look at me and tell me I do not love you."

I couldn't believe he was saying this in front of his line. I felt a little uncomfortable, but the vampires had all, including Erika, gone still; that preternatural calm they do, sinking into themselves, no breathing, no blinking, no heartbeat. I'm sure they continue to be very aware of their surroundings, but they were offering up what privacy they could, given the circumstances.

Michel just sat and waited for me to answer. He was serious, he wanted me to consider his question, so I did. I looked at him, really looked at him and he let himself be open and bare, to show everything he felt and more. I could see his determination to win, whatever he set his mind to. His desire for power, which was not a new characteristic, I was well familiar with what Michel craved. I could also see his pride at the life he had made for himself and his line here in New Zealand, his affection for the vampires under him, his commitment to their safety and health. I could see all of this, right there, but I could also see his love. He did love me and it wasn't just words to placate, it wasn't just a means to an end, to get me to stay with him, to make me feel safe in our relationship. It was the type of love you would die for. The type of love that you would always put first before all else.

If I had ever thought that Michel just saw me as a way to feather his nest, a way to further his power base, then it was no longer true. He loved me.

He actually loved me.

And he would do *anything* to keep me safe and to keep me as his.

Wanting it and having it are two different things altogether. This level of love was frightening. He would keep me safe at any cost, his determination to have me to himself unfathomable. And I couldn't afford that. I had a job to do, I had a responsibility to my Nosferatin ancestors, to Nut, to Nero, to the Prophesy, to the innocent humans of the world. I couldn't let him cosset me, I couldn't let him smother me, I couldn't let him lock me away so I never came to any harm.

So, I did the only thing I could think of to do, I let him see that I didn't feel the same way. I let it all show in my eyes, in my face, that I loved him, in my own way, but that it was not the same as his love of me. That it was only physical, only there because of our joining, only there because of our Bond. And that it really didn't mean a thing, in the end.

I watched as he comprehended what it was that he saw on my face, in my eyes and I watched as a part of him shut down, locked away from me forever. And I hid the fact that my heart was breaking even as I lied to him, even as I broke his and I swore I would never let him know otherwise, or I would truly be lost and the war would be over.

The Dark would win and the Light would cease to exist forever, for everyone.

In every war there are sacrifices. This just happened to be mine.

Chapter 9
Blood Lust

The next few hours were a blur. It was Erika who helped me to Michel's chamber. Erika who ran a bath and packed my bags. She rustled up some food, which I pecked at, but mainly ignored. Erika who massaged my aching body, trying to ease the pain and make the bruises heal.

Michel had simply stood and walked out the door of the sparring room, leaving me there on the floor without a further word. No one knew where he was, what he was doing. He wasn't answering their calls, cell phone or telepathic, he'd taken a Land Rover from the garage and he'd simply disappeared.

Bruno swung by his chamber while I was resting and Erika was getting herself packed and ready to head to the airport. He didn't chastise me, he didn't frown at what I had so obviously done to his master. They had seen in my face what Michel had, they had heard what he had admitted to me; his unadulterated love, but still Bruno said nothing.

He just told me Gregor was expecting both Erika and myself and he wished me luck.

"Anything you need, just call and I'll arrange it, Luce."

I nodded. "He's gone to Taupo," I said, I could feel where Michel was headed through the Bond and what he was feeling. Hurt, betrayal, despair. He'd gone to the only place that settled him, to the only people who would offer the type of support he needed, human support. Kathleen and Matthew are his human servants who look after his holiday home in Taupo. They have a close bond with Michel, more than just master and servant. I realised in that moment, that he saw them as family. His human family long lost to him due to time.

Bruno nodded. "I thought as much, but thanks. I'll have some guards sent down to protect him. I don't think he's quite himself right now."

I tried not to let the tear that had been threatening slide down my cheek, but it was too late. Bruno saw it and sighed, but he didn't say a word, he just patted me on the shoulder and walked out of the room.

Erika got to test drive the BMW. I couldn't have concentrated on the roads to save myself. She'd been to Auckland before, over a decade before, but she was fairly familiar with the layout. If not the multitude of topographical changes and population explosion that had occurred during that time, she could still find her way to the airport without my direction. I just got to lean my forehead against the cool glass of my window and stare blindly at the lights passing by.

I knew I needed to get out of this depression I had pushed myself into, but the guilt and loss and heartache was too strong. My cellphone went off and I jumped, instantly thinking it was Michel. I fumbled as I picked it up and felt my stomach drop in disappointment at the name on the screen. Nero. I took a deep breath and flipped it open, holding it up to my ear.

"Kiwi? What is wrong? I sense your Darkness, what has happened?" Of course he couldn't Dream Walk to me again, it was too soon, but the connection we shared let him know where I was heading emotionally. And it wasn't good. The last time this had happened, Michel had been unable to break me from the Dark's hold. Nero had risked himself to Dream Walk twice in one night and had to resort to extreme measures to get Light back into me and save me from the Dark. I could still feel his lips against the skin of mine now, weeks later.

I placed a hand on my mouth at the memory of it.

"I've hurt Michel," I whispered down the line. "I've really hurt him, but I had no choice, Nero. I had to do it. He would have smothered me. He wouldn't have let go." I didn't care that Erika could hear me, I didn't care what she would think. I was lost to the Darkness already.

I heard Nero's sigh down the line. "Kiwi. He will understand. He is your kindred."

"You didn't see him, Nero, you didn't see the hurt and pain in his eyes. I'm not supposed to do that to my kindred. I'm not supposed to be the one that causes hurt."

"Meaning he is? We all have Dark in us, Kiwi, not just the Nosferatu. *Where there is Dark, there is always Light. And where there is Light, there is always Dark.*"

Another Nosferatin mantra. It didn't seem to make me feel better.

"I don't know if I'll be able to ever fix this, Nero, but I do know that I shouldn't. I have a job to do and he would protect me to the detriment of that job. I had to do it."

"If I could take the burden of the Prophesy from you, I would, you know that. But, you are right. You did the right thing."

"Then why do I feel so bad? Why does it feel so wrong?" I couldn't stop the tears from falling. I know I had sworn off them, but I allowed them this once. Nero couldn't see me crying.

There was a pause for a while and then when Nero spoke again he sounded pained. "I don't know, Kiwi, but sometimes the right thing to do, can be the most painful, the most heartbreaking." It sounded like he was speaking from experience, the weight of his words so heavy.

"How do I live with my decision, Nero? My choice?"

"You take one day at a time, you remember to breathe and you surround yourself with people who care. Have you got someone with you now, Kiwi? Someone who cares?"

I flicked a glance at Erika, she had no doubt heard the entire conversation, both my side and Nero's, vampire hearing and all. She locked gazes with me, nodded briefly, an understanding passing between us in that instant.

"Yeah. Yeah, I do," I whispered into the phone.

"Good. Then relinquish some of that hard fought for control and let them take care of you for a while."

"OK." I nodded and then realised he couldn't see me, so said it again. "OK."

"And know this, Kiwi. I will always be there for you. Always."

"Thanks, Nero."

"I sense more Light in you. My work here is done."

I smiled.

"That's my girl," he whispered and then the line went dead.

Thank God for friends.

I slept on the couch on the plane, the one Michel normally sat on, where his scent still lingered from a couple of weeks ago. Clean cut grass and fresh sea spray.

I missed him already.

Erika didn't talk the whole trip, just let me sleep fretfully and when we landed she gently shook me awake.

"We're here, *chica*. Better put on your game face, I see

112

we've got someone to meet us."

Typical. Gregor couldn't just let us come to him, he'd have to pre-empt the entire stay. I really wasn't sure if I was up to Gregor, but we were here now and I was damned if I was going to let him see me upset, it would only provide fuel for his fire. I slipped into the on-board bathroom, despite not being allowed to wander around when the plane is taxiing. Michel's manservant wasn't on-board with us this time, the co-pilot had shut the door before take off, so no one was there to tell me off.

Like the rest of the plane the bathroom is exquisite; faux granite bench tops, ceramic tiles and gold fixtures, a dancing dragon etched delicately here and there. I splashed some water on my face, brushed my teeth with the little travel kits provided and combed my hair. Done. A vampire hunter doesn't need much more than that, oh and her stakes. I checked the pockets of my jacket, all accounted for. I was ready.

"Let's do this," I said to Erika as we came to a stop next to a private hangar and the co-pilot, a human, opened the door and saluted us off.

Waiting next to a Mercedes-Benz CLS-Class in silver - with the obligatory vampire tinted windows and 19 inch alloy wheels making it a bold statement against the black tarmac next to the hangar - was Gregor. Dark grey Armani suit, hands in pockets, long legs crossed at the ankles, leaning against the front door. Of course, he couldn't just drive a normal car, it had to be an uber-expensive, stand-out-in-a-crowd one.

Erika let out a low whistle. "Nice car." But I knew she was looking at Gregor, her eyes hadn't even strayed to the

Merc.

"Have you not met the Enforcer before?" I asked as we came down the plane's steps.

"Nah. I avoid Paris as much as possible, just not my bag."

Gregor pushed off from the car and strode towards us, with a little Nosferatu glide thrown in for good measure. I'm picking that was for me, Erika could glide herself, it wouldn't have impressed her.

"*Ma cherie*, you look well." So, the spruce up in the bathroom had done the trick, thankfully.

"Gregor, this is Erika Anders, Erika, Gregor... ah, the Enforcer." I finished lamely, thinking: *what is your last name?*

He smiled at me, having heard the question in my mind. He thrust out his hand to Erika and said, "Gregor Morel." But winked at me.

OK, Gregor Morel, good to know.

"So, a personal pick up by the boss, huh?" I frowned at that, it hadn't quite come out the way I had intended.

Of course, Gregor couldn't leave it. "You know, I am always keen to pick you up, *ma petite chasseuse*." I let him have that one, I had left myself wide open after all.

Gregor stowed our bags in the boot and opened the front passenger door, I think for me, but I stepped behind him and opened the rear, sliding in before he could protest. Let Erika ride shotgun.

I couldn't see his face, but I was betting he was smiling. The game was on and I had just walked straight into it. Shit.

Gregor drove us straight to his club on Lambton Quay,

Desire de Sang. Even I could translate that French: Blood Lust. I had no idea if that was what it had been called when Michel owned it, I had never come to Wellington with him back then. I presumed it was much the same as he left it, he'd only handed it over to the *Iunctio* two weeks ago, that hardly left any time for Gregor to stamp his mark.

"A little close to the truth, isn't it?" I asked as we drove past the black and red façade, where a queue of people was winding down the footpath away from the vinyl clad vampire manning the door. I mean, vampires aren't out of the coffin yet, so to speak and this just screamed Nosferatu.

He just shrugged, that elegant shift of his shoulders that means everything and nothing and parked in a reserved spot round the side by a door that was marked private. He didn't get a chance to open my door, but then again, I think he wasn't even going to try, I'm sure he smirked as I swung it open as soon as the car came to a stop.

The club itself had a little more verve than *Sensations*. Where *Sensations* was all sleek and elegant with a little extravagance thrown in for good measure, *Desire de Sang* was playing the vampire vibe loud and proud. The staff were recognisable, not just because of their *Sanguis Vitam* running rampant around the room, but because of the amount of skin on display and the small, but very prominently placed strips of leather or vinyl. Everything straight out of a fantasy horror novel. Next they'd be serving up blood in bottles. The décor redolent of sinful deeds, dark shadows and hidden secrets, every item that graced the room chosen for its lush fabrics, sensual style and striking colours. Red and black only, nothing else.

It was almost too much. Tacky was the word that came

115

to mind, but also not. Maybe I was being overly harsh due to the fact that, although a piss-take, it was actually pretty close to the truth. Not that vampires go around in leather, flashing skin all the time, but the atmosphere was definitely vampire lust on steroids. I shivered as we crossed the packed floor, recognising the power that floated around the room unchecked. They weren't even trying to hide it. The Norms were all but lost to the whims of the fanged amongst them.

This was wrong on so many levels. Against every rule the *Iunctio* would have, especially about keeping the Nosferatu hidden from the humans. This was an outing waiting to happen. What on Earth was Gregor thinking?

Gregor opened the door to an area marked private, leading us through to a plushly carpeted hallway and towards the back of the building. He pushed another door open and stood to the side, to allow Erika to pass. As I walked through the gap he had left, between himself and the door jam, his fingers brushed against mine, in an almost unconscious movement, unplanned but unavoidable. The moment his skin touched mine my breath was stolen, my heartbeat scattered and I stumbled against his chest.

His arms came up to steady me, increasing the sensation of warmth that had rocketed though my body at the already too close proximity to him and to my *Sigillum,* and I found myself turning in his hold to look up into his eyes, unable to stop myself, despite every thought in my head shouting, *No!*

His eyes locked on mine and platinum shot through the granite, a low growl escaping his lips.

"It has been too long, *ma cherie,*" he whispered and his

116

head bent down towards me, his eyes shifting to my lips, my mouth already parting for him. I was so lost.

I'm not sure if she had only just realised what was happening, or that she had been shocked at what was unfolding in front of her, but Erika only now entered the moment. Somehow locked out of it, by the power that connected Gregor to me. When the tip of her Svante sword slid through the small gap between me and Gregor to rest on the pulse point at the base of his neck, I was finally able to breathe and blinked in surprise.

"No wonder Michel wanted me to come along," she drawled in her American accent. "Back up, beautiful, she's taken."

Gregor's response was an even lower growl.

"I have no qualms at all," she said calmly, "shedding your blood, Enforcer. It has been a long time since the *Iunctio* and I last saw eye to eye, one more mark against my record won't matter." The sword tip didn't waver.

Slowly, as though he was fighting every impulse to not do it, Gregor released his grip on me, finger by finger, until I was standing so close, but no longer touching. His eyes, however, had not left mine.

I wanted to say something, to do something, but I was trapped, not by Gregor's glaze, or his *Sanguis Vitam*, but by my own desire to not move, my own desire to stay as close to him as I could. He smiled slowly.

"Later," he promised, his eyes sweeping my body, then returning to my face.

Erika sighed and lowered her sword as she grabbed my jacket and hauled me into the room and away from Gregor. The look she gave me said everything. I was in deep

117

trouble. What else is new?

I shook my head to clear the tumble of thoughts pouring through them and feigned interest in my surroundings, taking in Gregor's office. Here, I could imagine Gregor being. Fine antiques, priceless artworks and delicate furnishings, much like his quarters in Rome and his chamber at the *Palais*, the *Iunctio*'s headquarters in Paris. This was so much more Gregor's style than the gaudiness of the club outside.

I allowed myself a minute to completely pull my Nosferatin shell back on and when I finally had myself in order, turned to face him. Erika was sitting in the corner on what looked like a Louis XV chair, cream upholstery and gold frame. I couldn't imagine it was extremely comfortable, but she had one leg over the arm rest, was leaning back in a relaxed pose, spinning her Svante sword vertically in her hand. I had to smile. Dressed in her skin tight jeans, red leather boots and fitting red leather jacket, she could do the whole relaxed threatening pose quite well.

Gregor was equally relaxed behind his large partner's desk, ignoring Erika's presence entirely and concentrating on me. When he knew I was looking at him again, he let his gaze trace over me, taking in my normal hunter gear, black on black, short skirt, jacket, boots. My usual style. And just smiled.

"I forget how stunning you are in person, my little Hunter. Dream Walking, although a pleasure, does not do you justice. You were made to be gazed upon unhindered by distance or realm."

I didn't know what to say to that. Gregor could be a pain in the arse when he wanted to and right now I knew he was trying to put Erika off balance, as much as me. I didn't need to answer however, because Erika simply let her sword land blade tip down into the carpet with a twang, shattering the silence and making a rather obvious threat.

Gregor just smiled and turned to look at her.

"You are here, vampyre, on my sufferance. Hospitality can be revoked at any time."

They glared at each other for a minute, neither prepared to back down. Great, we were never going to get anything done at this rate.

I decided I'd start out with something easy, something obvious. I knew if I didn't say anything about it, Gregor would take that as my acceptance of the situation. I couldn't on all conscience not step up to the mark

"What's with the *Sanguis Vitam* pouring through your club, Gregor? Those humans are trapped in a potential vampire blood-lust fest. You know it's not right."

"Are you here to question my club's techniques, Hunter?"

"I'm a Nosferatin, Gregor, you know I can't just walk past humans being subjected to that sort of power over them."

"Would you notify the *Iunctio*? Bring their attention to your shores?"

Bastard. He knew damn well, I didn't want the *Iunctio* here, that's why I'd come to Wellington, wasn't it? To try to settle things down so they wouldn't come running, guns blazing, into my land. Gregor may still be a member of the vampire council, but he had recently mentally cut all ties, he was simply playing the role, no longer bound by the rules they had previously inflicted.

119

"You know this is wrong, Gregor. Why are you doing it?"

His own *Sanguis Vitam* came out towards me then, wrapping around my waist, brushing up my stomach, fingering over my breasts. I felt my knees go weak and a heat wash up my body from my core, setting my senses on fire and making me draw in a sharp breath.

"Is it not pleasurable? Do you wish for me to stop?" Even his voice was coating me with desire, pulling me towards him, telling me to give in to the sensation, to ride the wave, to seek release. It was an overpowering suggestion and it occurred to me, that he shouldn't be able to affect me quite like that. Sure, I'd always had trouble brushing Gregor's *Sanguis Vitam* aside, but I do have natural anti-Nosferatu repelling skills. The humans, or Norms, however, do not. The thought that they couldn't fight this made me fume.

Michel can feel my emotions, it's easy for me to send them towards him, but unnecessary, he has a constant tap on what I am feeling, even from a distance. He blocks me out most of the time, but the negative emotions are harder. Right now if he was paying attention, he'd know I was angry at something and about to lash out. Gregor, on the other hand, doesn't have that ability to read my emotions, but I can, when really pushed, make him or any other vampire in the vicinity, suffer them. So, I grabbed that anger and hurled it at him, like I would at Michel if I was really wound up at something he had done.

The instant it hit him his hold over me snapped free. He held his ground and didn't blanch, just a small widening of his eyes and a slight flush to his face.

"Do it again," he finally whispered hoarsely. So, more affected than he seemed, then.

"This is not why I am here, Gregor. I'm not interested in fighting with you."

"I am glad to hear that, little Hunter, you would undoubtedly lose, but the exchange would be... invigorating."

He held my gaze, daring me to answer.

I could pick my battles and what was happening in the club was not top of my list right now. I wasn't going to let it drop completely, but now was not the time to expend unnecessary energy on something that so obviously played to Gregor's hedonist nature. I wasn't a fool, for all the times Gregor had been a gentleman to me, for all the times he had swept me off my feet - and I will admit, he has done that on occasion - he was also a self serving hedonistic playboy. He loved the dance and was trying to get me to sway to his beat.

I shook my head at him and threw the thought, *this is not over and you know it*. Meaning of course, the issue with his vampires influencing so many people in his club.

Gregor, on the other hand, decided to take it differently. "I wait with baited breath for your invitation to Tango, *ma cherie*."

Sometimes, just sometimes, I felt like I couldn't win a battle with Gregor, that he would simply never stop until he got what he wanted.

And he wanted me.

Chapter 10
Evil-Lurks-In-My-Country

I pretended I hadn't heard that last comment, denial is a wonderful thing and went to a seat opposite his desk and sat down.

"So, tell me about the attacks on the vampires."

As soon as I had asked the question Gregor's demeanour changed. We were on professional terms and his vampires were being culled by an uncontrolled mob of humans, he was taking this part very seriously.

"Since we arrived, I have lost six of my line and we have encountered at least ten episodes. We have had word that several Rogues have gone missing too. They are persistent, and although not obviously Nosferatin trained, their numbers alone have aided their success. They are an undeniable threat. It will not be long before I will be forced to notify the *Iunctio*, as it is, my reports have been more than just misleading. I risk exposure and death every time I omit information."

This was graver than I had thought, things were escalating. I knew Michel had lost about three of his line prior to the the *Iunctio* taking over the city and that maybe three more Rogue vampires were also unaccounted for. Those numbers were big and they were obviously hitting Gregor where it hurt. To lose a vampire from your line, was to lose a member of your family. It was personal.

"Any ideas on who they are? Where they're from?"

"None, that we have been able to ascertain. Even when we have been able to capture one alive, they fall unconscious as soon as it's evident they are captured, followed not long after by death."

Shit. "Suicide?"

He nodded. "It would seem the case. They are hard core, committed to whatever warped crusade they have started." He paused and pushed a large hand through his long black hair, making it come loose from the clip at the base of his head. "There's more. We've heard there have been similar events in Christchurch."

"There are vampires in Christchurch?" Michel's vampires have really been the only ones in New Zealand for more than a century, recently a few Rogues have strayed our way, but most have centred themselves around Auckland and certainly not as far south as the South Island. The population density was too thin, why hunt for food in the meagre offerings of Christchurch, when you had Auckland at your beck and call?

Gregor smiled indulgently at me. "New Zealand is a popular country since word the *Sanguis Vitam Cupitor* was to be discovered here."

I let a huff of air out at that. "If I was so damn popular, why aren't they now coming to Auckland to see me?"

"Why should they, when you will eventually come to them?"

I stared at him. Just what did he mean?

"You are here, are you not, Lucinda? Those vampires in Wellington wishing to tread the fine line of life and final death, have you in their back yard to play with, as it were. You have come to them. We are, if nothing, predators, but being a predator does not always mean we chase our prey. Sometimes, we also lure it to us."

Oh, and this wasn't at all a little creepy.

"Are these humans attacking vampires part of your

lure."

He smiled a little sinfully at me. "I am not luring you, Hunter, you come to me willingly." I rolled my eyes and he continued. "The humans act alone, they are not part of the vampire psyche."

So, now, not only did I have to keep evil-reeking vampires in line, my Nosferatin day job so to speak, but I also had to calm a group of red-necked human vampire hunters down from exterminating all the Nosferatu. But then also ward off a bunch of vampires trying to lure me into their wicked webs. Oh, and lets not forget the hordes of vampires watching me right now. Watching from across the waves, watching and waiting for some signal to march forth.

And the icing on the cake? Shape shifters at home wanting to join in on the fun.

And all of this I have to keep from the all powerful, all knowing vampire council, the *Iunctio*.

Easy, huh?

I ran a hand through my own hair. First things, first.

"Where have they been striking?"

Gregor looked at me for a moment, sensing, no doubt, the weight that had settled on my shoulders. He didn't look sad for me, he didn't look pleased about it either, he just assessed me, with sparkling grey eyes, taking me all in.

"Mainly around Lambton Quay, various side streets down to the wharves, but nothing further afield. Purely vampire central, they know our habits well."

"*How* do they know your habits well?" That's just the thing, humans aren't even meant to be aware of vampires and all of a sudden they are hunting them en masse. Michel has only had a base in Wellington for a month or two, nothing more and the killings really only started about that time, maybe slightly before. So why, all of a sudden, did humans know about our world?

Gregor sat back in his seat and looked off into the distance. After a while he spoke, still not quite back in the room with us.

"There has been no reported incidents elsewhere in the world. New Zealand was always going to be a difficult location for us to keep quiet. Too many Ley Lines, too much Nosferatin power." - I guess that would be me - "Too many vampires wishing to be here. It was always going to be a hot spot. That's why the *Iunctio* was pleased when Michel made the move to come here. Why the Champion did not stop him."

Well, that was news to me. Michel had told me Gregor had never understood why he left Paris, it has been a bone of contention between them since, so I had assumed the council felt the same way. Obviously not. The Champion trusted Michel to be strong enough to control here. No wonder she's got a bee in her bonnet about him now. He's kind of failed her on that one.

Gregor went on. "But, I sense more than fortuitous location and opportunity from this group of humans. They are not Nosferatin, but... I don't know..." He shook his head. "There is also something very familiar about them. Something that I can't quite put my finger on, but it calls to me."

Vampires talk freely about what calls to them. It is considered as much a power as glazing or reading minds. I guess humans would call it a gut instinct, but for vampires,

125

everything is always so much more significant, so much more supernatural. A gut instinct to them is a call. Both Michel and Gregor have said I called to them, Gregor has admitted that Nosferatin blood calls to him too. If he feels like he's called towards this group of people, then I believe him. But why?

"Have they struck again since last night?" Maybe there was a pattern we could work out, maybe they strike only on certain evenings, at certain times of the month.

"No, but I wouldn't be surprised if they did again tonight. They have increased their activity tenfold this past week."

"So, no pattern?"

"None that I can determine. No."

Well, waiting for them to strike just wasn't going to cut it. The only thing to do was to bait them. Walking the streets aimlessly didn't make me feel confident, but strategically placing a few vampires in the hit zone may just do it.

"We don't have much time to spare and I'm only here tonight, so this is what I suggest. We assume they will hunt again tonight and we lay a trap. They trigger the trap, we deal with them." I wasn't quite sure what dealing with them would entail, I couldn't make myself complete that thought. Killing humans to keep the vampires safe just didn't seem right. If I could talk to them, as a born vampire hunter, if we could glaze them into forgetting, if we could do anything that didn't make me feel like a traitorous Nosferatin, then all good.

It was at times like this that I wished I could pick up the hotline and talk to Nut. Just what did she expect me to do in situations like this? Who are the bad guys and who are the good?

"So be it." Gregor stood and came around the front of the desk, leaning his well-buffed body against it, so he was directly in front of me, only a foot between us. I could feel the warmth of him from where I sat. I could also see Erika fingering her sword out of the corner of my eye.

"I have organised two of my line to wait as bait, just down the street. Not too obvious, but close enough to human bars to raise suspicion should any human hunters stroll by. They will signal, when something is amiss." He reached forward and before I could stop him, took hold of my hand in his, rubbing his thumb over the back of it. Erika stood up. "Have you eaten, *ma cherie*? Perhaps, something from our kitchens? We may have based the look of our club on the more overtly seductive side of our natures, but we have not failed to include enticements on the menu. I believe there is a delectable blood red wine risotto, or maybe the lady would like a piece of our sinful chocolate cake with freshly ground and brewed coffee, topped with cream, on the side?"

Oh, he knew how to pull my strings, didn't he? How could I say no to coffee and chocolate?

He smiled, having either seen the look of hunger on my face or read my thoughts. "Chocolate cake and coffee it is." He helped me to my feet, but was very careful not to pull me too close, Erika had taken a couple of steps closer, Svante sword still out in her hand.

The table he led me to was small and intimate, privately situated behind a wall of foliage. There was not enough room for Erika and she was immediately waylaid by members of Gregor's line, not threatening at all, but rather trying to flatter, to flirt, to get her attention away from me. I knew what Gregor was playing at, but I also knew I could handle myself. I didn't need Erika to keep things in line, I'd managed before on my own and I could do it again. Besides, her being here was just another Michel controlling tactic. So, I just shook my head at her and mouthed, it's OK. She gave a short stiff nod and went and positioned herself by the bar where she could not exactly see us, but was close enough should I call if needed.

Gregor pulled my chair out and once I was settled slid gracefully into his own. Intimate, was a phrase for the setting, practically snug against my side, was another. His presence almost engulfed me in the small area we were in. I tried in vain, to block out the smell of him, chocolate covered ice cream and cherry trees in Spring. The sounds of the club permeating the greenery before us, but not quite reaching the sanctuary the spot provided.

"So, you have a *Hemvarnet* now, little Hunter?"

"A what?"

"A Swedish Guard. Erika was one of the best, she originally worked as a *Hogvakten*, a Royal Guard to the Swedish Royal Palace, I believe, before Michel found her. And now, he has her guarding you. Poetic, no?"

Ignoring the dig at Michel guarding me. "She said she hadn't met you before." How did he know so much about her?

"No, we have not met, but I am aware of her reputation. She is formidable. The Champion wished for her services at one time, she was most put out that Michel would not share. But, that's Michel for you, he doesn't

128

share his precious toys willingly."

"I am not a toy." I knew what he was insinuating.

"But, you warrant a guard all the same. A guard that he has not shared with any other. Perhaps, you and Erika are well suited, both pawns in the game he plays."

OK, so I may have just pushed Michel away and made him believe that what I felt for him was not true love, but I didn't have to pretend with Gregor. There was no chance that he would tattle on me and let Michel know I had been lying. So, I didn't hold back.

"I am not a pawn in Michel's game, Gregor. You talk of me coming willingly to you, you know nothing of willingness. My love for Michel transcends all else in my world." Liar, liar, pants on fire.

"*Touché, ma cherie.*" He sipped some of the wine that had been waiting at the table and just watched me through hooded eyes.

My coffee and I admit, delectable looking, chocolate cake arrived just then, saving me from meeting his gaze and giving too much of the turmoil I was in away.

I concentrated on the tantalising taste of cocoa and caffeine, a finer mix could not have been invented and felt my body relax for the first time in hours. Caffeine has that effect on me, where normally people feel a little geared up drinking a coffee, I can feel a range of emotions, from invigorated to relaxed. Whatever my body needs, I seem to get it at the bottom of a coffee cup.

"Where are we staying when dawn comes?" I decided to get back onto business, our accommodation sounded as good as anything.

"My apartment."

"You have an apartment? Don't you have chambers here at the club?"

"There are chambers for my line here, but I am accustomed to something a little more refined. My apartment is not far, just down the end of Lambton Quay. There is ample space for yourself and your guard."

He wasn't going to just drop the guard thing was he? But, at least she would be staying with us and not expected to stay here at the club. Even I wasn't sure how to handle Gregor alone in his apartment.

I just nodded and continued to work on my chocolate cake and to be honest, it wasn't hard to get transfixed by it. It was rich and smooth and coated the roof of my mouth with succulent tasting cocoa, making my mouth water and my tongue dart out and grab any wayward chocolate from the edges of my lips. I couldn't bear the thought of missing some.

Gregor suddenly laughed, his little huff of a laugh he does, as though he's trying to hold it in, stay professional, not let himself go, but unable to hold back completely. I flicked a glance at him and his eyes were sparkling silver and platinum in the grey.

"You are delight to watch, *ma cherie*. Do you think it sinful?" He nodded towards the cake, his voice low.

I shook my head. "You're just jealous you can't have any."

"Oh, I could have some. I could have some right now." He shifted closer to me, bringing his upper body within inches of mine. I had a sudden flashback to Paris, where Gregor had bought me a coffee and a piece of Opera Cake. He told me he could taste whatever I ate through a kiss, or through drinking my blood, both thoughts erotic on their own. And then he proceeded to show me.

His proximity now making me flush with heat and embarrassment at how close we had come to overstepping the mark, to passing that point of no return. And I had wanted it too. God I had wanted it. The fact that I had been under a member of the *Iunctio's* influence at the time, is all that keeps me from falling into a pit of guilt over that interlude. I swallowed now, as I watched him move closer and closer, the predator taking over the man. His eyes were on my lips, maybe I had a stray bit of chocolate there I had missed. I stupidly licked them just in case, before I could stop myself and it was enough. He pounced.

His hand came behind my head, softly cradling me, his other came up and tipped my chin up, making my mouth line up to his. I raised my hands to his chest to push back and he whispered against my lips, "Don't fight it, *ma cherie*. You want this too."

I started shaking my head and he closed the distance between us in a flash, before I could gain any traction, push for any space between us, or turn away.

His mouth was warm and soft, his tongue sure and confident as it flicked along my bottom lip and darted inside. I find it difficult to resist the connection between Gregor and me, logically I know it's the *Sigillums*, but he doesn't make it easy. He can kiss like no other. I think it's the temptation, the fact that he is something I should not want, that makes it so much better. He is the bad boy I shouldn't chase, the forbidden drink I shouldn't taste. He calls to me, as though I were a vampire, my body hums in response to his pull.

He groaned against me, my body now flush against his chest, his hand up in my hair, pressing me close. "You are a drug to me, a fine wine, an exquisite perfume. I will have you in my bed, Lucinda. I will have you by my side."

I shivered at his words hot against my skin, so sure, so confident, so final. This was something I could not let happen. I loved Michel, even if I had pushed him away, I could not go into the arms of another and burn my bridges so comprehensively. Part of me knew this war, between the Dark and the Light, would not last forever and when it did end, I would get my Michel back. This was not a path I could afford to tread.

But, oh how hard it was to turn away. His arms around me, his hands all over me, sending shockwaves of pleasure down my spine, his mouth against mine, moving across my jaw, down my neck, hovering over my pulse, gently suckling the spot, teasing my body, reminding it what it felt like to have him drink from me. I convulsed at the memory, gripping him tighter. I was drowning, where was Erika? I needed help, now.

It wasn't Erika who came to my rescue, maybe it was Nut, although the thought of Nut placing an innocent in danger to rescue me from my flagging morals did not sound right. But for whatever reason, I thanked every god I could think of when I felt my pull. Not the pull towards Gregor, but the evil-lurks-in-my-city pull. The pull that overrides anything my body could be feeling at that time. It is so deeply ingrained in me, it is simply part of my soul. I cannot deny it.

A vampire was about to strike, sinking his fangs into the neck of an innocent human and it would not be the

fantasy I had just been living.
It would be hell.

Chapter 11
Be Careful What You Wish For

I pushed back against Gregor with a strength I think both he and I had not expected. Don't underestimate the power of the pull. His eyes searched my face and immediately realised what was happening. You can say what you like about master vampires, but they are very astute when it comes to their environment and survival.

"Where?" he asked.

"Down the road, one of the side streets. Just one, she's about to strike."

He just nodded. If he was frustrated at the interruption, he didn't show it. I knew then, that the lives or more precisely, recent deaths, of vampires of his line had affected him. His city was acting out of line. And now, a vampire in his city was about to break his rules, again, a slight on his control. No vampire likes to be disobeyed and no vampire likes to feel that they are losing control of something they own. Gregor owned Wellington, everything in it was his.

We didn't waste time, heading for the main doors of the club in an instant. I flicked a glance at Erika and nodded towards the exit. She was on our tails immediately, no sword drawn yet, there were too many Norms in the bar to witness that kind of fighting power. I quickly brought her up-to-date on the situation. I didn't want her thinking this was the humans and she was about to face off against a dozen. I could just imagine her fingers itching to draw that sword from its hidden sheath down her back.

Once outside they followed my lead. I just followed that pull, allowing it to direct me, like water down a chute, I just followed the path that it set. My evil-lurks-in-the-city pull is undeniable and fail safe, it's never proved wrong. Like a magnet I'm sucked towards that evil, it's what makes me a born vampire hunter, a Nosferatin. The humans who were attacking vampires in Wellington have no such radar, no such beacon calling them to their target. They are aimless, set adrift in a sea of humanity and plethora of creatures of the night. The dangers that face them are phenomenal, but the chance of success is even less. I had to stop them from taking this any further, I had to stop them from getting themselves killed.

It was at that moment, as I ran full speed towards the evil with two vampires at my back, that I knew Nut was sending me my answer. I wasn't to kill the humans, I was to save them from themselves. I sent a silent prayer of thanks towards my metaphysical mother, I needed to know I was on the side of good. If I questioned that at all, I'd never be able to complete my task, never be able to fulfil my destiny. I am the Light to the Dark. I just needed to be reminded of that from time to time.

We came to the street I could feel the evil in, it was powerful. This was no baby vampire and if it was Rogue, then it was a free ranging master, something that was not common at all. My guess was it wasn't Rogue, it belonged somewhere. I just hoped it wasn't under Gregor's line. Even I didn't know how Gregor would take that.

I stopped at the entrance to the side street and just breathed. Erika had her sword out, Gregor was all tension, radiating fury already. I didn't look at them when I spoke, but my voice was even and firm. I would not argue this with them and they needed to know.

"You will not interfere. You will stand back, unless I

135

ask for your help."

Neither acknowledged my words.

"Do you understand?" My voice was lower than usual.

"Yes, mistress." Erika answered. I shook my head at her words, but put it down to the fact that she is of Michel's line and I am his Nosferatin. Perhaps, it was simply required of her to obey when I ordered and this was a vampire traditional response. I'd have to deal with that later, right now evil wanted to eat.

I glanced at Gregor. "You need to let me do my job, Gregor. I'll take care of this." My concern wasn't so much relinquishing some of my role as the vampire hunter, but more the fact that if I let them barge in there, nothing would be left of the scene. Maybe even the human who was being held captive would suffer too. There's a fine line between punishing the evil and avoiding collateral damage. I couldn't risk the life of the innocent to the rage of vampires. There is a reason why they don't have their own core of vampire hunters.

I have fought beside Gregor before, against evil vampires and he is astounding and well controlled, but that was in Paris, not here. And I had picked up an altogether surprising signal from him since we arrived. He'd do anything to protect this city. He wasn't just a caretaker, he was in fact its master. The connection was undeniable. And a little frightening.

If he was Wellington's Master, then he was here to stay. To relinquish one's position as Master of a City, is to die. It is seldom done without that closure. The fact that Michel was able to relinquish Wellington so easily was partly because he was already Master of a City elsewhere and partly because he hadn't connected in the same way as he has to Auckland.

Gregor still hadn't answered me and the delay was making me twitch. The vampire hadn't struck yet, she was still playing with her meal, but any further delay could prove fatal for the human she held.

"Gregor."

He flicked his eyes to me and nodded, reluctantly by the looks of it. It was the best I could hope for.

I started down the street quietly, I knew exactly where the vampire was. We'd made it about about three metres when Gregor took in a sharp breath beside me. I stopped immediately and looked at him. He look pained, conflicted.

"What is it?" I asked quietly.

"The bait has been taken, my vampires are in trouble."

"Then go, I don't need you here. As soon as I finish, I'll come to you." And then I thought of something else. "How many humans are there?"

Gregor was a little wild eyed as he looked at me. I couldn't tell if it was the thought of leaving me to do my job without his support, or the fact that his vampires were under threat, but he looked slightly alarmed at the situation unravelling before him.

"At least twenty."

Shit. That's a mob.

"Go!" I said to him and he nodded and disappeared. I shivered at the fact that he had almost dematerialised in front of me and turned to Erika. "You go too."

"No," she said, stepping up beside me. "I have my orders and they are to watch your back."

Yeah, I bet you do.

137

"Was it a command?"

She looked at me strangely, obviously not expecting me to question an order from Michel. If it had been a command, I would have to glaze her out of it, not something I take to lightly, but I needed her to help Gregor. "Well?"

"No, but I will not leave you."

I sighed, I didn't have time for this. "Erika, this is what I do, this is who I am. But, what's happening down the street is out of my league and firmly in yours. Gregor needs your help more than I do and you know it." I hated admitting this, I hated voicing it aloud, because to say it, to acknowledge it, was to give it power and I just didn't know if I was ready for that. "I don't want to lose him, he's important to me."

She baulked at what I was saying, to outrightly admit another master vampire meant so much to me was to lessen my connection to Michel, her master. I had thought pushing Michel away was a technicality, as I had counted on the fact that at least Erika and Bruno were aware of how cut up I still was, allowing me a connection to Michel still. But now, to openly admit such a connection to another, was the final blow. I may as well have been getting a dagger out and stabbing it through Michel's heart in front of her.

Her face hardened, just slightly, before returning to its mask. The mask vampires wear when they truly don't want you to know what they are thinking or feeling. It was too late, I knew what she thought and there was nothing I could do to change that. I had spent a lot of time trying to figure out what I felt for Gregor and now I had just gone and tipped the scales. And I hadn't even thought the action through. It had been natural, instinctive and it scared the hell out of me.

She didn't say anything for a moment and then just flashed away towards Gregor. Maybe she thought I deserved to get hurt, maybe she just couldn't stand to be near me right now, either way, she had done what I asked and I quietly thanked her.

My attention was returned to the vampire down the street as I felt its hunger peak and the need to sink fangs into flesh overwhelm it. I sprinted towards that evil without a second's pause, no longer heeding my environment, just determined to get there in time before it was too late. I'd been delayed enough, now was time for action.

The vampire, a female, had her captive human by the throat, holding him a few feet off the ground against the window of a clothes shop. His feet were making pitiful attempts to kick her, but only managing to move enough to make the window behind him threaten to crack. The whole façade of the store rattling as his heels kept gently pounding back against the glass. He was having trouble breathing and had turned a little blue around the lips, which looked ghastly against the ghostly white of his face. He knew what held him and he was terrified. She hadn't even bothered to glaze him, to convince him he was elsewhere, with something remotely human, normal, not some monster of his nightmares. Not something that shouldn't even exist. What was she playing at? Even blood crazed vampires knew enough to hide their tracks, but then again, she probably had no intention of this one surviving, so maybe the not glazing thing was understandable. Why bother if you intend on wiping not only their mind, but their existence from this world?

She'd had more than enough time to sink her fangs into his neck, I had been slower than usual to get here - a few distractions along the way, you might say - so she was clearly getting off on his fear and enjoying herself. That just made me sick.

"You know, you really shouldn't play with your food. It's bad manners," I said evenly as I came to a halt a few feet away.

She whirled around to face me, keeping the human, her meal, still held firmly in her grasp, but now clutched to her chest like a prize, or a shield, I vaguely thought. She took in my outfit, from my black on black ensemble, to the shining silver stake in my hand, perfectly shaped, honed to the exact right size for a vampire kill. I was no mere human playing vampire slayer, I was the real deal and she knew it.

She was well dressed; fine expensive clothes, a tailored pants suit in navy blue, a paler blue blouse underneath, exquisite jewellery at her neck and wrists, her hair immaculately coiffured, her make-up subtle, but definitely there. This was no Rogue to be sure, this was a vampire straight out of the upper echelons of vampire society, even Paris maybe. What the hell?

"The *Sanguis Vitam Cupitor* I presume?" Her accent was French, so that narrowed her heritage down at least, but what was she doing in New Zealand? In Wellington?

"You have me at a disadvantage, vampire, I don't believe I know you."

She laughed, a harsh tinkle in the narrow side street, bouncing off the windows of the high street shops, making the human in her arms whimper ever so slightly. *Hang in there mate, just hang in there.*

"We have not met, Nosferatin, but I know who you are. My mistress knows who you are."

OK. So she was of a line headed by a female vampire, that would cut it down by at least 50%.

We just stared at each other for a while. Why wasn't she doing anything? Why wasn't she dropping the male and fighting me? Biting the male in front of me? Snapping his neck and waiting for me to go ballistic? She was just watching me, waiting. I got a very creepy chilling feeling up my back at that moment. She was waiting, watching, just like all the vampires overseas who could sense me now. But, waiting for what?

"So, are you going to eat him?" I just had to ask.

"Are you going to fight me?"

"Yes."

"Then I shall eat him." And her fangs came out and down in a flash. Huh, she hadn't had them out before, such control. And her head bent to his neck, her eyes still on me, daring me to do something to stop her. That was why I was here after all.

She probably expected me to come at her, to get within staking distance, or to try to pull the male out of her hands, but I'd been practising throwing my knife recently. A silver knife can't kill a vampire, only the perfect shape of a silver stake through their heart, but the knife will get their attention, that's for sure.

She still had the human in front of her, but she had turned slightly to the side, to get better access to his neck. I feinted a move one way, making her turn further to use his body as a block, but flicked out my knife the other way,

141

sending it flying towards her side so quickly, even she, a powerful level two or three master couldn't beat. The knife landed in her side and she screeched, releasing her hold on the human and spinning away to grasp her upper chest, under her armpit.

I didn't waste my time, leaping forward, grabbing the male who was already slumping to the pavement and simply tossing him several feet down the street. I couldn't worry about him getting more hurt, I needed him away from her fangs. They were the greater danger right now.

She had already removed the knife and thrown it away. Stupid. If I had been her, I would have kept it and used it against me. I don't recover as quickly as a vampire from a knife in my side. She was already healing it would seem.

"That wasn't playing nicely, Nosferatin." Her voice was dripping acid.

"Who said I played nicely, vampire? They lied." Mine was low and even, the voice I adopt when I am in the zone, ready for the kill. This vampire had no redeeming qualities, whatever game she was playing, it was to the death and I had to get there first.

"My mistress will be pleased with my efforts tonight. I go unto the *Elysium* willingly. My reward awaits me there."

And before I could even think about what she was saying, that she was talking about the vampires' version of the afterlife, she came at me in a flash, arms wide, chest bared, a small smile of release upon her face. And I had no choice but to raise my stake in front of me and aim for her heart. She didn't swerve, she didn't protect herself, she just ran onto my stake at exactly the right spot and and turned into dust all around me.

What. The. Fuck?

I choked back the dust that had entered my gaping mouth and spat a fair bit of black gunk out onto the footpath. Damn vampire dust, it just got everywhere.

I glanced over at the human, now curled in a ball, but watching me, watching what had just happened, with large fearful eyes. Shit. I can glaze vampires, but I can't glaze humans and this human needed his memory wiped. I couldn't shout out to Gregor in my mind, he was probably knee deep in shit right now and didn't need the distraction, nor could he have come to my aid. What to do?

I walked over to him slowly, returning my stake to its pocket out of sight, opening my hands in a peaceful movement, *I mean you no harm* type of thing. He looked like he was going to scamper. The vampire wasn't the only thing that freaked him out right now.

"Hey, you OK?" My voice was soft, quiet. I was trying not to scare him, but he just yelped and crab walked backwards away from me.

"Look, I'm not going to hurt you and she's gone, she won't either. You're safe now, OK?"

"Wh...wh...what the hell are you?"

I took a deep breath, this was what I feared most, humans knowing too much about my world. Hell, even I could easily do with not knowing half the shit I do now.

"You need to forget what you saw here, it didn't happen. You just got caught up in someone else's war. It's not yours and as long as you stay off the streets at night, stick to crowds if you have to go out, you'll be OK. You'll be fine. But, what happened here, is not for you to worry about. It's nothing. Don't think about it again."

He looked at me as though I was mad and I had to admit, he had a point. How could he forget this evening, how could he not be afraid of what happened and not want to know more? Everyone has a little morbid fascination with their death, he'd just looked his in the face and survived, he wouldn't drop this. And I had no idea how to wipe it from his mind.

I racked my brain for a solution. Nut obviously hadn't thought of this outcome, if the vampire I just toasted thought *I* was not playing nice, then she most definitely was breaking the rules. Vampires always glaze their meals. They never leave anything to chance. So, why had she? Nut hadn't provided me with a power that countered this. I was on my own.

"OK, look, you can either do what I say, which by the way, is actually the *only* thing you should be doing if you want to survive this world, or you can go to *Desire de Sang* and ask for Gregor. He'll tell you everything you need to know, but, be careful what you wish for my friend, sometimes getting it is not the solution to your problems that you think it will be."

That little speech made me think of Michel, I knew now he loved me, loved me so much he would protect me from myself, he would prevent me from my task, but although it was something I had wanted to know for so long now, it was also a curse. And me sending this human to Gregor was as much a curse as that. I hoped Gregor would understand my outing him. I hoped he'd be able to glaze the human retrospectively, removing him from harm. But, hoping and receiving are two different things entirely.

I should know, I'd had my prayers answered and look

where it had got me?

Alone. Again. Naturally.

Chapter 12
Dockside

I left the human getting into a taxi back on Lambton Quay. I wanted to make sure he was going to be safe, that female vampire may not be able to come back from the final death, but there could be others around. Once he was safely on his way home I allowed myself to feel what I had been holding back for the past ten minutes. Fear. Fear of what had just happened. I have never had a vampire commit Hara-kiri on my stake before, it had stunned me. Vampires didn't give up eternal life that easily. Why had she?

And it was that question that left me cold, chilled to the bone. What was worse than the final death to a vampire? Facing their master's wrath?

If only she had told me her mistress's name, given me something to go on. She was beautiful, like all vampires tend to be, but there was nothing to her that was any different from thousands of other vampires in this world. Even describing her to Gregor would do me no good. But, I knew, I needed to find out who her mistress was. I had that awful gut instinct that this was more important than it seemed to be right now, that this was the key or missing piece to a puzzle. But, was it a puzzle I really needed to concentrate on now?

I blew out a long breath and centred myself. Best to find out where Gregor and Erika were and lend a hand. I sunk into the black nothingness that allowed me to *seek* and sent my senses out all around me. They weren't too far away and they were no longer alone. Gregor had called in reinforcements. Although I couldn't see how many humans

146

were there, there was now close to twenty vampires. If there'd been twenty humans attacking before, they were now well and truly toast. Shit. I did not want those humans killed.

I shifted into Nosferatin gear and sped towards the scene. It only took seconds, but I knew I was too late when I rounded the corner of a side street and was met with a scene from *Underworld*.

There were four or five humans on the ground and a whole lot of blood. The vampires, bar none, had blood coating them; their bodies, their faces, their mouths. Holy shit. This had been a massacre. But I couldn't equate the number of bodies with the blood, where had all the human corpses gone?

Gregor glanced up as I arrived and took in the shock and horror on my face. He took a step towards me, away from the tightly coiled vampires surrounding him and the last humans remaining visible at the scene.

"What have you done?" My voice was quiet and uneven, I hadn't realised I was shaking until I heard how quaky it was.

He was in front of me in an instant, holding me by my arms, trying to get me to focus on him and not the diabolical scene before me.

"Lucinda. Lucinda! Look at me."

I dragged my gaze away from the lifeless forms on the ground and looked into his silver and platinum eyes. They were ablaze, swirling with blood lust and hunger and something else, I couldn't quite determine, but made me shudder at the same time.

"We had no choice, they were too organised, we

147

couldn't hold them off without fighting back."

I let a small breath out. "And you couldn't stop once you started, is that right? You had to keep going until they were all gone?"

He closed his eyes for a long moment and then when he opened them again I saw bright yellow flames flickering inside. I blanched, I couldn't help it. I'd only ever seen those flames once before and I was sure they were not a good thing at all. He growled, low, his fingers now digging into my upper arms, his hold going rock solid. I lifted my stake as though in slow motion and placed it against his chest, right above his now thumping heart.

"Don't make me do it, Gregor. Please."

"You know you have to. Do it, *ma cherie*, end it now."

And here we were, back where it all started. Gregor wanting me to end his existence, me unable to do so.

The flames in his eyes had vanished, replaced with a pain that rocked my soul.

"Did they all die?"

He shook his head. "Most escaped, but they are harmed, some will not survive this night."

Shit. I wanted to rejoice that some had escaped, that only those five bodies on the ground were the total of it, but *some will not survive this night* seemed to put a dampener on it for me.

"You realise what you've done," I said still in shock. "You've given them purpose. You've given them the fire they needed. They will be determined now, they will be unstoppable."

He looked at me strangely, as though he didn't believe a word I said. For intelligent, cunning and manipulative

148

creatures they had a woefully poor understanding of human nature.

I looked him firmly in the eyes, only partially aware my stake had dropped to my side. "Humans are survivors too, Gregor. You threaten their world, the safety of their young, they will hunt you down and they will not stop from fear. Not now. Not after this."

I saw a flicker of understanding cross his face and then he growled, so loud I covered my ears, but I could still hear it and I could still hear the accompanying growl of his vampires around him, as though it was a call to fight, a call to do battle. The humans may have started this, but the vampires were prepared to finish it.

I had never felt so removed from their world than I did right then. The thought that I loved one of these creatures, that I slept with him, allowed him so close to me unguarded, froze me in that spot. Oh dear God, how do I escape this? How do I survive this? How do I save the humans from this?

Lucinda. It was a whisper in my mind. A plea. Michel begging me not to pull further away. I held onto the sob that was rising and clamped my shields shut, barring him and anyone else from my mind.

I waited for Gregor and his vampires to calm and then I simply turned away from his now looser grasp and walked towards the lights of Lambton Quay.

No one followed, well none that I could tell and I was beyond *seeking*, although not sinking into the Dark. I was awash in Light; Nut trying to comfort no doubt, but I was hollow, empty, a void of emotions, just a shell. I wandered the still busy street of downtown Wellington, club and bar central, watching humans interacting with each other, watching life spill out around me and unable to connect.

I found myself down by the waterfront, at Queens Wharf, under a canopy of sun shades, blocking out the stars, but giving me a sense of protection. I walked on automatic towards a bench seat and sat down numbly to watch the late night pub crawlers cross the paved expanse before me. All dressed up for a night on the town, all safe in their perfectly normal worlds, with their perfectly normal beliefs and their perfectly normal expectations of life. I envied them that normal perfection, I so envied them tonight.

I'm not much one for regrets, for second guessing the path you're on in life. So, I didn't have much say in where my world had taken me, I didn't have a choice to be a part of this Nosferatin-Nosferatu world, but I am a part of it now. The decision to join with a vampire may have been made on my behalf, but I could have allowed myself to die. Not many people can play those odds and get away with it. My ancestors had, but I was not them, I could not throw away life so easily. It is precious.

So, here I was slap bang in the middle of a war and it was getting complicated. Not only was I battling the Dark, but now the vampires were battling the humans too. What side was I on?

What side was I on?

I didn't realise I'd leaned forward and placed my head in my hands, closed my eyes and given in to the moment. Hell, I was so deep in that moment, not crying mind you, but consumed by thought, that I didn't even hear him walk up. He could have been a vampire hell bent on taking out

150

the *Sanguis Vitam Cupitor*, he could have been a human against vampire activist wanting to take out the vampires' key Nosferatin asset, he could have been a bloody shape shifter taking advantage of my lowered guard and ridding opposition to their genocidal plans back in Auckland.

But it wasn't. It was Tim.

He sat down quietly next to me on the seat and sighed. "You don't seem well, cousin."

My hand was on my stake and my body turned and braced in an instant. I may have been distracted, but my reflexes never failed to kick in when needed.

"Tim? What are you doing here?"

He looked startled at my hand in my jacket and the flash of silver now glinting in the lights of the mall. I quickly re-pocketed it and tried to ease the tension in my shoulders.

"I recognised you from across the way. I'm with some friends at a bar over there. I didn't know you were in Wellington, why didn't you phone?"

"It was a last minute trip and I planned on phoning you tomorrow, getting together for a coffee and chat."

I was a little uneasy that Tim just happened to be here at this exact moment and that he happened to see me too. I don't believe in fate. I don't trust it. But, he did seem surprised and he did seem genuinely concerned. And he had been startled by my stake. So, maybe, just maybe, I was over reacting.

"Great. That would be cool. But, I'm here now, how about a drink?"

I wanted to say no, I wanted to say just leave me alone. I needed to think, but his face was so open, so friendly and

151

the thought of going back to the vampires right now scared me shitless I guess, so an open and friendly cousin was perhaps the exact thing I needed. So, I just nodded.

He beamed at me, like a little boy on Christmas morning, grabbed my hand and led me towards a bar across the way.

Dockside was a bar and restaurant, brightly lit, with moss green weatherboard sidings and white painted window frames, copious amounts of outdoor tables and white canopies, people milling around drinking, shouting, laughing. It was a beacon of light and life on a dark night at sea. Inside was a warm combination of wooden panels, bright lights and loud music, the warmth of so many bodies making the chill in mine ease. I needed to be around humans, I needed to feel that combined beat of their hearts.

Tim asked what I wanted to drink, then he left me with a couple of his friends and dashed off to the bar to grab it. His mates looked about his age, maybe older and were casually dressed in black jeans and shirts. They were quiet and just kept flicking glances at me, but they seemed OK. I didn't bother to talk to them, if they wanted to chat, they could have, but I also wasn't in the mood to make conversation for the sake of it. So, I just continued to take in the life around me, relishing the sounds and feel of humanity.

Tim returned and one of his mates stood and said something in his ear that I couldn't pick out. They all three shook hands, unusual for young guys and then his mates just nodded at me and left.

"Is it something I said?" I joked to Tim.

He just shook his head. "They've got work tomorrow,

they're not up for a bender."

Neither am I, I thought, but gratefully accepted my *Bacardi and Coke* anyway.

"So, what brings you to Wellington?" Tim asked while he nursed a *Heineken Beer*.

"Oh, just some business that needed attention."

"For your bank?"

Tim knew I worked in a bank, he also knew I was a Nosferatin, but he didn't know how entrenched in the Nosferatu world I was and I planned on keeping it that way.

"Actually, on behalf of a friend who couldn't travel. I also wanted to talk to you about a certain visit you made to a vampire in this city." I had lowered my voice and leaned across the table towards him, he had copied my stance and we were now almost head to head over the table top. I'm sure none of the patrons in the bar could have heard our conversation over the noise, but you had to play it safe and we just looked like two friends having a chat in a rowdy room.

"Oh, that." He actually look abashed. Hmm, maybe my job here was going to be easier than I had thought.

"You know that wasn't wise, don't you, Tim?" I prodded gently.

"Yeah, he was one scary bugger, that was for sure. I just... I don't know... I just wanted to help."

"Help the humans?" I could understand. Tim had recently found out about his family heritage, although not a Nosferatin, he is descended from them, he is related to me. He may not have the vampire hunter mojo, but he was close enough on the family tree to feel hard done by it. If you coveted that sort of thing, that is.

153

"Yeah. I know you help them in Auckland and now the vampires are here and I don't know of any Nosferatins in Wellington. Certainly, no one left in my family, um, our family, has the gene, so I guess we're on our own."

Aw damn, I didn't want to get into this with Tim, I wanted him to stay apart from the nightmare that is the reality of my life.

"This isn't your fight, Tim." He bristled at that slightly, trying I think to hide it, but I could tell, he didn't want to be brushed aside, who does? "I'm going to be keeping an eye on things here for a while and as soon as I can, I'll find a Nosferatin willing to move here, to take on the mantle of responsibility."

I thought he would be pleased with that. I'm going to be visiting and helping to keep the vamps in line and eventually there'd be a permanent solution, a Nosferatin protecting the humans every night. It was a win-win situation as far as I could tell.

But he obviously didn't like it. Didn't like it at all, because his fists clenched on the table top where they had been resting, but as soon as he noticed what he was doing he hurriedly placed them out of sight on his lap and took a deep steadying breath in.

"That's good to know, Luce. Good to know."

I studied him for a moment. I wasn't quite sure what I was looking for, what I was looking at in fact, but my inner monologue was humming, no words, just a constant sound of warning. Strange.

I decided to give him the benefit of the doubt. Tim had always appeared to me as an over-enthusiastic puppy. Incorrigible but mainly harmless, I wasn't about to go all paranoid on him because of someone else's gut instinct and even if my inner monologue was humming, he was my cousin, he needed a break.

"Promise me you'll stay away from them, Tim." He didn't answer, just kept looking at the wooden table top between us. "Tim. Promise me."

His eyes came up to meet mine and they just looked normal, normal brown eyes. "OK. I promise. I promise I'll stay away from them from now on."

I don't know why, but that seemed to take an enormous weight off my shoulders and I finally relaxed. He seemed to sense it too and smiled.

We spent the next couple of hours chatting about inconsequential things. His apprenticeship, my bank teller job, Auckland versus Wellington. The Blues versus The Hurricanes, rugby not being my main focus, I was kinda outdone there. But, it was a pleasant couple of hours, a break from reality, an oasis in the desert. I welcomed it and enjoyed it and finally accepted that I had found my family at last.

When the crowd had well and truly thinned out, I knew it was time to face my night time job and re-enter the world of Nos. Nosferatu that is. So, I said goodbye to Tim and we went our separate ways. He had, of course, insisted on walking me to my hotel, no way I could tell him I was staying with the Master vampire of the City though, but I did manage to convince him I could take care of myself. I am a Nosferatin after all. Even if he didn't fully know what that actually meant for me, how deeply entrenched in that world I had become.

I was half way back towards *Desire de Sang* when I

sensed it, *Sanguis Vitam*. Not hidden, but slowly becoming more obvious the more steps I took. I recognised it of course, she'd meant me to.

I stopped next to a souvenir shop and waited for her to catch up.

"Erika."

"Lucinda."

"You've been following me all along, haven't you?"

"You've not been out of my sight once."

I hadn't even been aware. It didn't surprise me though, just made me feel sad. Even out of Auckland, so far away from Michel, he had eyes and ears telling him what I did.

I had to ask. "He knows I met my cousin, that I've been having drinks with him for the past hour or so, doesn't he?"

"Yes."

"You tell him everything." It was a statement, a fact, I didn't need her to answer and she didn't.

I stood there for a moment and let that sink in. I may have pushed Michel away intentionally, for the greater good and not because I didn't love him, but this, this right here, was why I had to do it. He owned me and I would never be free again, unless I cut the ties. Unless I severed the connection between us completely. I knew I couldn't battle the joining or the Bond, but I could battle the emotional and physical hold he had over me. That was still within my powers to do. That was still mine.

My heart wept at that thought.

Oh Nut, why have you laid this at my feet?

Chapter 13
The Challenge

We walked silently back to Gregor's bar, dawn was approaching now, so I wasn't surprised to see him leaning against his Merc, casually waiting for us to arrive. He'd probably had vampire eyes on me too and knew exactly when I would come back. His reasoning though, no doubt, because I was a Nosferatin in his city and any master worth their salt would have kept tabs on me. His invasion of my privacy I kind of understood.

He didn't say anything just opened the front passenger door, I didn't argue this time, I kind of felt defeated, so just slipped in and let him close it. The ride to his apartment was short, it really was just down the road. He parked in the underground car park and carried both our bags in, even Erika didn't argue, but then Erika was in full guard mode, scanning for threats, shoulders rigid, back straight. I was silently glad she hadn't drawn the Svante yet, but I could tell her fingers were itching.

Gregor placed a swipe card in a small slot and hit the button for the penthouse. Surprise, surprise, the penthouse. The trip up the 30 odd floors was smooth and quiet. None of us talked.

The elevator opened up on a hallway, plush cream coloured carpet, cream walls and lots of autumnal shades in the furnishings. Scatter cushions on a couple of antique looking chairs, gilt framed mirrors and artwork, everything positioned just so, beautiful, priceless no doubt and so Gregor. He hadn't taken long to make this home *his* home.

The hall opened up to a large open plan lounge, with multiple sitting areas and an expansive view of the harbour.

It was still dark, but the electronic shades would be lowering soon, so I took the opportunity to appreciate the view. I wandered over to the windows and just let the scene roll over me.

I heard quiet words behind me, not raised nor argumentative, but firm and that's when I felt *Sanguis Vitam* fill the room suddenly, peaking, then vanishing just as quickly. I cast a glance over my shoulder and saw Erika nodding at Gregor and walking down another hallway out of sight. I turned back to the view. I knew what Gregor had done and I was just too damn tired and disillusioned to complain.

Well, maybe not completely. He came to stand next to me, not touching but close, looking at the view.

"You shouldn't have done that."

"Done what, *ma petite chasseuse?*"

"To what end would getting Erika to retire for the day serve you, Gregor? You think a guard is the only thing between you getting me?"

"Such confident words, but they are wasted, *ma cherie.* You want me as much as I want you. I can feel it, sense it, smell it."

I closed my eyes in an effort to deny his words. Suddenly, images invaded my mind, corrupted my emotions. They were unwanted. Uninvited. Yet I could do nothing to prevent their assault. Usually, they came when I was alone, thinking of nothing and no one, when it was most unexpected they struck. In the shower, making a sandwich, walking to the car. Now. Michel wrapped in French Pretty's arms. Sweat-soaked, lust-sated, flush with her blood.

158

I hated him.

I loved him.

I wanted him to feel something of what he had made me suffer. I wanted him to feel pain.

And here was Gregor.

A small, unfamiliar voice whispered in my mind, *use him*.

I didn't know that voice, it was not mine. Yet I felt compelled to listen to it. I was afraid of that voice. I was blinded to it, blinded to this moment. Like an unrelenting, undeniable force it welled inside me urging me on. But there must still have been some of me present, because I knew if I was to do this, it would be entirely by my hand and none other's.

I should stop this. I should be stronger. I should deny the images purchase. But, I can't.

And not when that sweet, seductive, unfamiliar voice murmurs in my ear, *seek your revenge, take back your control. Do it now.*

Before I even realised what I was doing a whimper of pain - or was that regret? - escaped my lips. But it was too late for Gregor to stop this, there would be no retreat. I had already taken that fateful step along this path. I owned it now.

I pushed Gregor against a column next to us, forcing the air out his lungs, showing him just how strong I could be, just how much in control of *my* life I could be. And proceeded to kiss him with all of my body, not holding anything back, trying my darnedest to climb right down his throat.

He groaned against me, placing his hand on my rear,

159

lifting one of my legs to wrap around his thigh, kissing me back as though there was no tomorrow, as though this was his one and only chance to have me and he wasn't stopping, not for anyone, not for anything. He was a runaway train on a collision course he had no desire to shy away from. And I let him come towards me, come closer than I had ever let him before.

"Lucinda. Lucinda. Lucinda. Say yes, please say yes." His mouth had left mine and was tracing kisses across my cheeks, over my eyelids, down to my jaw, so light and delicate, barely touching but searing me with each brush of his lips, each stroke of his tongue, each hot breath against my skin. I melted under his touch, I caved against his desire and I felt my own building, uncontrolled, unstoppable, undeniable. I wanted him and I wanted this now.

"Bedroom. Now," I managed breathlessly against him.

He didn't hesitate, lifting me in his arms and claiming my mouth again. I have no idea how we made it to the bedroom, how he had been able to see where we were going at all. I lost seconds or minutes, I don't know, I was just floating in his voice, soft murmurs of gratitude, love, desire, against my skin. I was lost in the onslaught of his hands, his fingers so deftly stroking, probing, finding every conceivable spot that sent further shockwaves through my body.

Before I even realised what was happening, we were both naked on his bed, arms around each other, legs intertwined, lips locked together. His tongue darting in and out, claiming me, making me his. My fingernails in his back, scratching, marking, making him growl against me, rub his hard body along the length of mine. Things were moving so fast, there was no time to think or second guess, the flood gates had been sprung and were now wide open and even if I wanted to, I couldn't have stopped this.

But I didn't want to, I wanted to feel Gregor, all of him, to hold him close, to have him inside me, closer than he had ever been before. I wanted my revenge. And it helped that Gregor wore my *Sigillum*, we were connected in a way I didn't quite understand, but it was easy to not fight this, to just let it happen. And I almost watched it unfold from a distance, detached and not there, but feeling everything, enjoying everything, savouring everything. Relishing the moment I took back control of my life. The moment I sought my vengeance on Michel.

Part of me cried out in alarm at those thoughts. I knew that this was not me, but the unfamiliar voice inside my head joined mine, *yes, yes* it whispered, it urged. Gregor's mouth started trailing kisses down my body, leaving my face, covering my neck, pausing only briefly above his mark, then slowly creeping down towards my breasts. He took his time discovering, finally able to follow his desires and whims, no longer fighting to convince me, no longer playing the gentleman saviour. I was his tonight and he knew it. And he wasn't going to miss a thing.

His mouth found one of my nipples, already hard and taut, his tongue lapping around it, his teeth gently nibbling, teasing, sucking, making my back arch up against his chest, my body start to writhe and things deep down inside start to stir and warm. He shifted his attention to my other breast and paused, long enough for me to notice and raise my head. It took a moment for me to realise what he was seeing and for my world to crash in on me again.

Michel's second mark, the one I wanted no one else to see.

He closed his eyes slowly and held his breath. He knew already what had happened, I'd stiffened, I'd put up the wall. His head came down against my stomach, his lips lightly caressing, but not seeking to thrill, just comforting. His last chance to touch me before the inevitable, before I pulled away.

But I didn't pull away. I listened to that unfamiliar voice and I lowered the wall and gave myself over completely to this moment. To this decision. To sensations Gregor washed my body with, blocking out all unwanted images and replacing them with only here and now. I reached out to him, putting my hand in his hair, pulling his face back up towards mine, laying a kiss against his cheek, his mouth, his eyelids, then gently pushing him over onto his back and starting the process in reverse. Kissing my way down his beautiful body, across his broad chest, following the line of soft curly hair as it trailed the length of him, down to his hard stomach. I paused at his navel, licking, kissing, biting around its edge, making him moan beneath me, even whimper when I blew a breath across the wet trail left by my tongue. I moved to his hips, so firm and strong, so hard and masculine, I couldn't get enough of him. I allowed my teeth to mark him there, harder than I would normally, leaving a perfect impression of my mouth, making him cry out in ecstasy.

"Oh God, Lucinda. Oh God." He started to push up from the bed, but I placed one hand against his chest, firmly shoving him back on his back and let my other trace

162

the mark I had left. It would fade, it wasn't permanent, but I liked it all the same and I wished for a moment that it would stay forever against his perfect, perfect skin.

My attention was drawn elsewhere however, as the sight of him naked before me set in, his hard length bobbing up towards his stomach. He was so large, so hard and thick and long and I couldn't stop myself from touching him, holding him, squeezing him, just a little, getting a pleasing groan from him as I fondled his sac below.

My mouth kissed its proud head, my tongue lapping around the tip, he shuddered beneath me as my fingers formed a tight circle around its base, slowly stroking up and down as my mouth took more and more of him in. I stopped when I could fit no more and slowly withdrew, letting my teeth scrape along the sides and being rewarded with a hiss of pleasure. His fists clasping at the bedspread, his head thrown back, eyes closed in bliss.

"Did you want me stop?" I said breathlessly against him, my eyes rolled up to catch his response.

"Oh dear God, you are amazing." He raised his head to look at me, the silver and platinum swirling intensely, dazzling me in their shine.

"I'll take that as a no." And I began moving more quickly, my hand up and down at the base, my mouth and tongue in sync from the tip, meeting in the middle, then pulling apart, then back again and apart, over and over. Until he was writhing and lifting his hips to meet me, forcing as much as he could in my mouth as fast as he could.

I thought he wouldn't be able to stop, it had been my

intention to push him over the edge, to prove my control, but you don't get to his age, 400 odd years old, without some measure of discipline. And suddenly I found myself on my back with my legs being pushed up and apart as his head lowered towards my sweet centre, his eyes now on mine, the roles reversed.

"My turn," he whispered and then lapped at my wet folds, making me close my eyes and suck in a breath.

He was ruthless in his pursuit of my pleasure; licking, sucking, biting, nibbling. His tongue darting in and out as surely as if it was something else, some other part of him he so desperately wanted inside. He found that beautiful nub, that spot that made me toss back and forth and lavished his entire attention there, bringing me close and closer to the edge. Making me start to pant and grasp the headboard above me, my hips already raised off the bed by his hands, my body arching to meet his mouth, my heart thumping in my chest like a beat of drums. Until finally I had no choice but to submit to the release, to allow it to engulf me, wash over me, making me scream out in euphoria and then collapse against the bed.

He rose up above me slowly, crawling up my body, wiping me from his mouth with the back of his hand, only to turn it over and lick me from there too, his eyes on me the whole time. I had a sudden image of a predator about to catch his prey, but he'd caught me already, I'd let him, this was just part of the dance.

I felt his hard length against my centre, my legs spreading wider to accommodate his hips, he pushed slightly, then shifted his hips sideways, in a circle, then back against my entrance; teasing, testing, stroking me.

164

Until I felt the heat build again and my own hips started to rise and fall with his rhythm.

"I intend to take this slowly, *ma cherie*. I am in no hurry. Will you last?" His eyebrows lifted and a wicked smile graced his face.

"I'm tougher than you think," I said evenly, smiling back at him.

"We'll see." And then he started moving those hips in a circle again, slowly, so slowly. One stroke passing my most sensitive spot, then moving away, only to come back again and grip me further towards a luxurious kind of heat, then deny me as he moved away. With every brush of that sensitive part of me he sent more shivers down my spine, the more he did it, the more fierce the reaction. My breathing was uneven, a fine layer of sweat now covered my skin and my heart was rocketing along at an alarming pace. My mind had gone to welcomed mush. My hips had a will of their own, trying to entice him closer, trying to manoeuvre themselves into just the right spot so he would be forced to enter, forced to plunge inside me.

"Now?" he said and I was so happy to hear his voice crack slightly, his restraint beginning to weaken.

"I'm fine," I breathed out.

"You are impossible," he replied equally as breathless.

"Then take me, you know you want to. Take me now."

He closed his eyes to fight it, but the invitation was too good, the words too long desired. He thrust his hard length inside me, making us both shout out at the sensation, I was still tight, but wet and he was so big and long. I felt him fill me up in that one swift movement, to come right to the end of me, there was simply no more room and then he moved his hips in a circle and I screamed as an orgasm took me completely by surprise.

"God," I managed, as he held me up against his chest with one arm wrapped around my back. "That was unexpected."

He laughed, his chest rumbling with the sound, so deep and attractive.

"Does that mean I win?" he whispered against my hair and then gently lay me back down on the bed, starting to move against me, almost subconsciously, his hips rubbing back and forward, his length sliding in and out. My body shuddering in an overload of sensations that just didn't seem to want to stop.

I wanted to answer him, to make him pause so I could catch my breath, but he had found his rhythm and he just pulled me along with him, making all thought escape my head and my hands start to grab him, my fingers digging in as another orgasm built inside me and his pace picked up and his breathing became ragged. And then we both came at the same time, calling out in joy, clasping each other closely and collapsing back against the bed.

"Oh God," he said in a rush of air against my neck. "I had not intended to stop things just yet, but you seem to have caught me unaware."

I laughed, as his arm came over my chest, his face buried in my neck and he pulled me close. "Does that mean *I* win?"

He shook his head. "Oh no, *ma cherie*, not on this. The challenge has been met and I am most decidedly the winner."

I let his words wash over me. I kept my breathing even,

166

concentrated on my heartbeat, so it would not hitch and willed my body not to stiffen.

The challenge. I had forgotten the challenge. I had even stupidly thought that the challenge no longer existed. But to Gregor, someone who has never lost a challenge in his long, long life, it would always have existed. He tricked me into the challenge. My escape from his chambers in Rome when I Dream Walked there, him calling off the *Iunctio* who were hot on my tail, for his right to court me, to seduce me.

He had won all right and I had been a fool. And now I had more than the uninvited images of Michel swirling around in my head. Now, I had to contend with my revenge being manipulated by another too.

Could nothing be because *I* designed it? Was I forever to be the pawn in someone else's game?

Chapter 14
Broken Hearts and Apple Tea

Gregor fell asleep some time later, the covers pulled over us and the sun now, no doubt, high in the sky, but I couldn't sleep. I couldn't relax. I could hardly breathe.

I silently slipped out of the bed, from under his arm and grabbed his shirt - the quickest thing available to cover my naked body - doing up the buttons automatically, while I watched him sleep so soundly, so peacefully in his bed. He was beautiful, that was no lie and I rarely spare time on regrets. I'd chosen to sleep with him, to feel his hard body against mine, to have him inside me, on top of me. For whatever reason, it had been a conscious, adult choice. I could blame no other but me.

But, as I quietly stepped into the lounge, noticing the shutters were down tight and the room was awash in an unnatural dark, I also felt an overwhelming sense of confusion. For so long now, I've felt like my life was tumbling out of control. First, there was the whole vampires exist thing. The creatures under your bed, in your closet, when you were five years old, actually friggin' exist. There's loss of control right there, your universe turned upside down. Then there was the fact that I am not human. Not totally, anyway. But, on top of that, I would have died if I hadn't have joined with one of those creatures from under my bed, from inside my closet. I would have died if I didn't spend the rest of my now very long life tied to one. Some choice that. There was no choice. There was no control. It just was.

Then of course, there's the whole vampire trying to control me issue. Michel always has, right from the start.

But now, now that he loves me, it's worse. Sometimes, I can hardly breathe for the noose around my neck. It is what he is. Vampires spend their entire existence controlling others. Gregor did it too, tricking me into sharing *Sigillum* with him was a type of control. I had no choice. And now he has proven, yet again, that he is in control. Manipulating me through the challenge, taking away my revenge at Michel. Making it no longer just mine.

Images flashed through my mind, taunting me. But no longer just images of Michel in French Pretty's arms, now they were overlaid with images of me in Gregor's. I had set out to achieve revenge, to take back control, but now I just felt at a loss.

I rarely spare time on regrets, but I think I might just regret what had happened now.

I let the nausea of that realisation wash over me until it started to fade and I was left shivering in a curled up ball on the couch. If there had been no challenge and I hadn't been so desperately trying to take control of my life, if those images hadn't invaded my mind uninvited, would I have slept with Gregor? And with that thought came the others, the ones I'd been denying myself feeling, the ones that allowed me to crumble, to admit a weakness, to really, truly, regret. Michel.

What have I done? I am not a vampire. A vampire will do anything to survive. Anything at all. Michel fed off French Pretty because I denied him my blood. Denied him sustenance when he needed it most. And feeding is sensual to a vampire. Coupled with a powerful spell placed on him by the Nemesis, how could Michel have behaved otherwise? But me? I am better than this, I am not a

169

vampire. I do not have an excuse, other than revenge.

I didn't realise I had started crying, those damn sneaky tears. I didn't realise I was moaning, a soft whimpering sound, so awful, so not me. I let it all come out, every emotion, every chastisement, every curse for the stupidity I had committed and then when I thought I could not take it any more, I felt him. He hadn't been there before, he'd only just come to me now, sensing my pain, hearing my curses, cursing myself to hell and back, feeling my regret.

Michel's power rushed through the Bond to me, trying to comfort me, trying to take away the pain, but he didn't know why I was feeling this way, he didn't know what I had done. If he knew he wouldn't have tried to help me, to take care of me. He needed to know before he offered that unconditional support. So, I opened my mind to him, not showing what I had done, that would have been cruel, but letting him see my thoughts, the reason behind my grief and anguish.

His power fluctuated briefly, as he realised what it was that I had done and then I felt the backlash of his pain and despair and anger, and before he could strike out I shut the door. I deserved his anger, I deserved everything he threw at me, but I simply was not brave enough to take it. I was a coward and a cheat and an absolute useless piece of crap who couldn't even take control back over her life without screwing it up some more. I wanted the floor to open up and swallow me straight down into hell.

I heard a sound at the door and glanced over. Erika came and knelt down beside me, brushing my hair from my eyes, shushing my sobs, rubbing my back. I couldn't hear what she was saying at first, too hung up in my misery to listen, but finally I quieted enough to catch her words.

"He still loves you. He forgives you. Let's go home."

I sat up slowly and looked at her, shaking my head. "I don't deserve his forgiveness. I will not except it."

"He has offered it, *chica*. He will not take it back. You need never think of what happened here today again, it is forgotten."

I stared at her, incredulously. "How can he forgive me? I can barely forgive him." She opened her mouth to say something, but I pushed her away with a wave of my hand and a shake of my head. "No. He can't forgive me. I did this to hurt him. To teach him a lesson. I did it intentionally. He should be in pain. I *know* he is in pain, I felt it. He can't have forgiven me. Not that easily. That makes no sense."

Erika shrugged her shoulders as if to say, *but he has* and I just felt angrier. The fury rolling around inside me like a caged tiger. It wanted out. First Gregor steals my moment of revenge, taking my control away. Now Michel has the gall to forgive me for something that should not be forgiven so easily. Hell, he had a reason for betraying my trust in Paris and I still find it hard to forgive. There was no way he should be forgiving me this transgression at all.

"No, Erika. No." My head was shaking from side to side, my fists were clenched and my heartbeat racing in preparation for some battle that seemed just out of my reach. "Why?" I said it almost to myself, but Erika snorted. Just softly, I don't even think she realised she had reacted to my words. But, I reacted to her.

I spun around on my seat and grabbed her shoulders, staring her hard in the eyes. "Why would Michel forgive my infidelity so easily. Why, Erika, why?"

She replied woodenly, automatically, compulsively. "He set you up to fail. He wanted the balance back between you. He was unfaithful, he wanted you to see how easy it was to make that mistake."

I think I had stopped breathing. I had stopped moving, my fingers a permanent addition to Erika's shoulders. My grip rock solid, my knuckles turned to white. I vaguely acknowledged I had glazed Erika without even being aware of what I was doing. But, it was too late now. I'd opened up Pandora's Box and created an evil that could not be undone.

"He wanted me to sleep with Gregor?" I said it slowly and more to myself than her, but whatever glaze I had given before was still in effect. Or Erika felt a need to divulge more, because she answered.

"He didn't think you would follow through. He just wanted you to see how easy it would be to fail. How easy it was for him to fail. He wanted balance."

I couldn't take this in. "I need a shower," I whispered, pushing past her and going to find my bag.

It had been placed in a spare room, so I used the bathroom there to scrub myself raw, scrubbing away my mistakes. Scrubbing away the foul stench of Michel's manipulation. But it didn't make me feel better, the pain of the rough loofah against my skin was a distraction, but as soon as I stopped, the guilt and confusion was back. I stayed under the spray of the shower for a long time, trying to sort my feelings out, trying to organise my thoughts. Why had I done it? Why had I been so determined to seek revenge? That was not me, I am not like that. Petty, vengeful, evil. If I had allowed myself to see what Michel had done without emotion, I would have accepted it eventually. But I didn't allow myself, I clung to those unwanted images, I let them fester and grow. And then I acted like a vampire and struck out.

And Michel? Oh God, Michel. He had let me come to Wellington, he had planned for me to be tempted by Gregor. He had manipulated me, controlled me. Set me up to fail. I let a huff of indignant air out. He had not expected me to follow through. That's what Erika had said. He wanted to open my eyes, he thought he knew me. He thought that would be enough to even the balance out in our relationship. He didn't know me well. Neither did I, it would seem.

I dressed in a haze in the bathroom, but felt more in control of myself when I was fully clothed in my familiar hunter gear. My jacket was out in the lounge, so I could grab that and head out the door as soon as night fell. With any luck, Gregor was a sound and long sleeper and I could escape without a confrontation, my worst nightmare after last night.

I shouldn't have been shocked or surprised when I exited the bathroom. I had been in there quite a while and this was Gregor, but I jumped when I noticed him sitting on the bed, waiting. His elbows on his knees, his head forward staring at the floor. He sat up straighter when the door clicked shut behind me, his face carefully neutral, but his shoulders slightly tight.

"I woke and you were gone, *ma cherie*. The bed was colder without you there. I missed you."

I just started at him. He would have seen it on my face: regret. My usual rigid control of my facial features simply lost to me right now. Loss of control, very familiar pattern

173

in my life right now.

"Do not regret this, Lucinda, please." He didn't stand up, just kept looking at me, willing me to agree. I couldn't.

"I love Michel. I shouldn't have done this. This was not me." I was a fucking idiot.

He ran a hand through his dark hair in obvious frustration. Then stood and walked toward me.

He stopped a foot away, no closer and just watched me. So tall and dark and handsome, taking up more space than he had any right to take. I kept my eyes on the blue bedspread to the side and behind him, determined not to look him in the face.

His hand reached up and fingers cupped my chin, bringing my eyes reluctantly to his.

"Do not regret what we just shared, it was beautiful. It was a gift and one I have every intention of sharing with you again, my sweet little Hunter."

"You won't feel that way once you've slept on it. This time tomorrow you'll realise, it was just the challenge. You've won, Gregor, it's over. You can let me go."

"To a vampyre there can be no greater thrill than the pursuit of one's desire. I desire you, Lucinda. You desire me. What is so wrong with fulfilling one's desires?"

I stood there silently, unable to form a sentence. In a nutshell, Gregor had summed himself up. I had always known he was a hedonist. Michel had warned me and now I had irrefutable proof. Gregor didn't love me, not really. I think perhaps he loved the game, the challenge I represented. But it wasn't love for *me*.

I had cheated on my relationship - a relationship with someone who *did* love me - with someone who only

174

wanted to win me. To win the game. I have forsaken all that I am for this?

"I have to go, Gregor."

"The sun has not yet set. Erika cannot go out."

I didn't really give a damn. I had to leave, now. I know it was running. I know it was leaving the horrible mess I had created piled high and still tangled, but I had get away from him.

I had to get away from me.

"Leave me please. I'll just sleep in here until the sun sets. I need to be alone."

He stood up, his hands running up my sides, from my hips to my upper arms as he rose. He didn't say anything, just leaned down and kissed the top of my head and left the room, closing the door quietly behind him.

I laid myself down on the bed and stared up at the ceiling. I must have laid like that for half an hour, finally allowing my body to relax, then closing my eyes and doing the only thing I could think of that would get me out of this sun kissed prison. I needed guidance. I needed a friend. So, I Dream Walked to Nero.

I came to standing in the corner of his training room, he was fighting Amisi, demonstrating moves, correcting her posture. She was good, at only 19 she had the skills I only recently acquired at 25. Amisi was one of Nero's extended family, an immature Nosferatin. She could fight, hold her own against the vampires, but she wouldn't come into her Nosferatin powers until she was 25 and joined with a vampire. She was going to be formidable.

Recently, she had been kidnapped by some very nasty vampires intent on taking over the world. Nero and I had rescued her, I almost died doing it, since then she's been a fan. I've even had the odd training session with her, she can't Dream Walk, but I come to Cairo occasionally when I Walk. It's nice for a change of scene.

They hadn't noticed me appearing, something of a novelty, usually I poof into existence right in the middle of the mat, almost getting bowled over by whatever move they are currently practising, so this was a nice surprise. I sat down cross legged on the floor, quietly, and settled in to watch the show. I could take a moment to enjoy Nero move and Amisi dazzle and then I would sort my chaotic thoughts out.

They had maybe been going for another fifteen minutes before Amisi tripped whilst trying to execute and Crescent Kick, falling flat on her stomach and looking at me. She went red in the face and jumped to her feet.

"No fair, Lucinda! How long have you been watching him kicking my butt?" Amisi has a lovely thick Egyptian accent, but speaks English to perfection, recently improving it even further with my choice word selection and carefully scripted guidance. There's just no point speaking a second language if you don't know the slang.

I laughed - surprising myself with the sound - at her outrage, knowing she'd calm in a moment, nothing riles Amisi for long. I flicked a glance at Nero, standing still, so intense, watching me.

"You honour us with your presence, Kiwi. Have you come to train?"

I attempted a smile back at him, trying to elicit a grin out of that strictly set face. It worked, his lips twitched slightly at the corners, but his brow furrowed in direct

176

contrast to the action.

"I needed a distraction and what better way to be distracted than by my two favourite Nosferatins."

Amisi jumped up and down, she was still so young, but looked so much older. The world she had grown up in was not safe, was not always kind. She was surrounded by love of course, but evil lurks out there and she knew her nightmares were real.

"I'll grab some apple tea. We were going to break now anyway, weren't we, Nero?"

Nero just sighed at her and shot me a pointed glance. Disrupting his training sessions was not something he tolerated lightly.

"All right, Amisi, you know how much Kiwi loves our apple tea."

She scooted off and Nero headed to the other corner where a pile of cushions were scattered on the floor. I got up and joined him. I'd only recently learned the knack of falling gracefully onto Egyptian cushions. Prior to mastering the move, I had been an embarrassment to my sex. Short skirts are just not lounging wear. Not that I would wear this outfit if I was actually in Egypt, I know not to offend, but when Dream Walking it's only Nero and Amisi who can see me. She doesn't care and Nero has never complained, often glancing at me right when I sit, trying no doubt to cop a flash. He is a man after all.

"So, what is on your mind, Kiwi?" he said as he settled back against the brightly coloured cushions, his white linen top making the dark colour of his skin simply gorgeous. I have always wanted to reach out and touch his skin, to make sure it didn't rub off, to make sure it wasn't fake, but I had enough boy problems right now, overstepping the boundaries with Nero was not one of them.

"Nothing. I just fancied a visit."

He huffed at me. "I know you too well, Lucinda. You seek a distraction because you are running from a problem."

I frowned at him. What the hell? Why am I such an easy book to read.?

"I like that I can read you so well, Kiwi. I like knowing you."

I held my breath while I digested that. One, how had he used the exact same words I had been thinking and two, he liked knowing me? He said the knowing as though it meant more than just the word. Huh.

I sighed and swallowed past the lump in my throat. "You don't need to know about all my pathetic problems, that's not why I came. I need to get away from it for an hour or so, until the sun sets and I can actually get my butt away too."

He looked at me with that intense look he often wore, like he could see right through me.

"I am your friend, Lucinda. You know you can talk to me."

I dropped my eyes from his. Usually that coffee and cinnamon gaze could centre me, could bring me back to Earth. But right now, I knew it saw more than I wanted it to. I knew Nero could see my pain. He didn't say anything, just waited patiently. I wanted to change the subject, I wanted to forget for a moment my woes, but hadn't I come here for some guidance? I could hardly seek guidance if I didn't open my mouth.

I took a deep breath in. "I've done something. Something that is foreign to who I am. I don't know why and it scares me." Not to mention breaks my heart in two.

Nero leaned forward and placed a warm hand gently on my arm, making me raise my eyes to his. I saw compassion there, understanding. And surprisingly, forgiveness.

"Do you remember when I told you, that you would have to battle the Dark? More now than ever. We are Nut's Light, Kiwi, but that does not mean we can't be led occasionally, by the Dark. For *where there is Light, there is always Dark. And where there is Dark, there is always Light.*"

I didn't want what he was saying to make sense. Strange, but true. I had wanted answers, guidance, an explanation for what I had done. But I did not want absolution. Those images, those unwanted images, they had been from my memory, but I was not in control of them at all. Had they been controlled by the Dark?

Nero leaned back, releasing his hold on my arm. "Just because we can succumb to the Dark, does not mean we should." I flicked an uncertain gaze at Nero, he held mine without reproach, but with a steadfastness that said I wouldn't like what he was about to say. I lifted my chin to face his chastisement head on. I deserved it. He sighed and ran a hand through his spiky, short black hair. "You are so young, Kiwi. So new to all of this. Sometimes I forget. You show such maturity with what you have had to face. With the responsibilities that rest on your shoulders. It is unfortunate that this has happened, but maybe it is for the best. To truly face what lies ahead you will need to master the Dark. To be aware of it, but to not let it fully in."

179

I let his words slowly sink in. He was right. I had screwed up, I had let the Dark lead me astray. I had forgotten what I was. But I could face this hurdle one of two ways. I could let it drown me in guilt and regret and sorrow. I could let it win. Or, I could learn from my mistake. I could use it as a lesson and I could make sure it never happens again.

"Am I strong enough?" I said whisper-quiet to myself.

"Without a doubt," Nero replied, just as quietly.

I held his gaze then, saw the swirls of cinnamon and copper deep within the brown. Nero's eyes did ground me, did bring me back to Earth. But his words, his guidance, they were what settled my mind, helped create order in chaos. I had made a mistake, I knew this, I would not forget. But, I would not let it rule me. Michel may not be able to forgive my actions that easily, despite Erika saying he already had, but I would try to learn from this, to not let it steal any more of my Light.

But what of what Michel had done? "Michel set me up to fail." God, even saying those words aloud left me almost gagging with distaste.

"He is closer to the Dark than you, Kiwi. Without you leading him back towards the Light, he will find it easier to succumb." Then obviously seeing the look of incredulous disbelief on my face, he added, "Even your Michel is capable of mistakes. Of losing control of the Dark within. He is vampyre, Kiwi. He is the Dark."

How many times have I thought of vampires just like that? And how many times had I forgotten that Michel was one too? I had placed human conceptions on Michel. I had expected him to behave as I would want him to. But a

180

vampire will do anything to survive, to retain their power. To Michel I am essential to his survival, I am the core of his power. His vampire-within would do anything to keep me close and maybe it saw the balancing of our relationship as essential to that end.

I wasn't sure if I had realigned my worries, sorted out the mess of my mind, but I did feel closer to acceptance. Of what I had done and why. Of what Michel had done in Paris and why. Even, if I am honest with myself, of what Michel had done sending me to Wellington and why he seeks to control my life. I may not like it, but I was beginning to understand it and with that, maybe accept it. I don't know, accepting control from Michel was still entirely too foreign. But, I was one step closer to the Light and that much further from the Dark after talking it through with Nero. I offered him the first genuine smile I had given since arriving in this Dream Walk. His returning smile was almost blinding.

Just then Amisi came back in the room, her arrival lifting the moment from the heaviness of Nero's and my conversation and placing it firmly back in the familiar territory of a friendly gathering. She was carrying a tray and the sweet smell of apple tea wafted towards me. I can't eat, when I'm Dream Walking, but I can drink. I'd only just realised this recently when I'd Dream Walked to Nero and found him having a cup of apple tea. It was just so divine smelling, that I had to try it when his back was turned and what do you know? I can drink tea when my body is asleep on the other side of the world. Go figure!

Amisi handed me a glass cup with no handle and sank into the cushions with practised ease. Amisi is all legs and long body, she's tall, way taller than me. Has long gorgeously black shiny hair and the sweetest smile, it just lights up her face and makes the brown of her eyes sparkle. She's a real sweetie, I wish I could see more of her.

Which made me think of something, the last vestiges of my current worries dissipating into the air. "Nero, have you got any spare Nosferatins around who would like a stint in Wellington? We've got a burgeoning population of vampires and no one to keep them in line. With that sort of action, humans are starting to notice."

Picking up on the change of mood, Nero relaxed further into his cushions and answered, "That is not good, Kiwi. How have they been managing?"

"They haven't. But, I'm there right now, did a little hunting, tried to get things settled. It's going to take a certain amount of to-ing and fro-ing and the more I'm away from Auckland, the more chance of a vampire striking and getting away with it. I can't be in two places at once, I need to send the word out there's a new city on the books."

"Yes, you need to advertise." Yeah. If only we had a gazette or something, that would be grand.

"What about me?" That was from Amisi. I turned to look at her, but picked up the rigid set of Nero's shoulders. He wasn't happy with that suggestion.

"Not yet, Amisi."

"I'm ready. You said so yourself. It's time for me to spread my wings." She looked at me pointedly and said, "His words, not mine."

I glanced at Nero, he cringed.

"Well?" she said, not dropping it. I had the feeling Amisi could be quite determined when she wanted to be. I

182

wondered how Nero handled that.

He flicked a glance at me. "She is cast in the same mould as you, Kiwi. Both of you are impossible to deal with."

I smiled, so did Amisi. I could handle impossible.

"You know..." I said before sipping my tea to add emphasis. "If Amisi wants to branch out a bit, she could come visit me in Auckland. Kind of like a vampire hunter sabbatical. If she handles the culture shock well, then you know she's ready and if she doesn't..." I shrugged, took another sip. "No harm, no foul."

Nero just glared at me, I got the distinct impression he wished to tan my hide right at that moment, it almost made me blink. But Amisi was jumping up and down on the cushions, like an over excited little puppy.

"Please, Nero, please. Please let me go to Lucinda's, she'll take care of me, you know she will and I can prove to you both I am ready."

Nero looked like a man drowning, being ganged up on by the two most determined Nosferatins in his life.

He sighed. "I will talk to Nafrini." He raised his hand at Amisi's squeal and my fist punch. "But, this does not mean you can move to Wellington and become their Nosferatin. That, is a decision only your parents can make."

"She's nineteen, Nero, surely she gets some say."

Nero just looked at me, head cocked slightly to the side. "This is Egypt, Kiwi, the land of Nut. Amisi is a precious child of our mother goddess, her parents would have to be involved in the decision, at least until she is 25."

Whoa doggy. Culture shock, here she comes.

And just like that, I felt myself back on an even keel. Family doesn't have to be blood, it's where your heart is. I loved these two Nosferatins very much. They held my heart, soothed my soul and settled my mind.

Chapter 15
Welcome Home

I stayed another hour, talking, laughing, forgetting my worries in the closeness of friends. I don't know what I'd do without Nero. Not only has he become my Nosferatin trainer, the source of all knowledge when it comes to Nosferatin mumbo jumbo, but he has also become a friend. A very close friend. Sometimes I think he knows me better than I know myself. He is my lighthouse on a stormy sea-tossed night, my rock. He grounds me, he brings me focus, he guides me home.

The fact that I can visit him when I need to is more priceless than anything else in this world. Right now I needed his strength, his support. I would have to ultimately deal with this myself, in my own time, but without Nero's guidance I don't think it would have been possible at all.

I hugged them both goodbye once the apple tea had been well and truly consumed and fell back through the nothingness to my body at Gregor's. I half expected to see him hovering, watching me, but he had left me alone as promised and I let a breath out in relief. I could feel the night approaching. Like a vampire, I have a sense of its closeness. Maybe because of the time I spend with them, maybe because I'm a Nosferatin and the sense I get when nightfall comes is a little foreboding. The creatures of the night are about to stir, my work may well begin before long. Either way, I knew I had about half an hour before the shutters would raise and the stars would be out.

I quickly freshened up in the bathroom, made sure my bag was packed and took a deep breath in before facing the two vampires I could feel in the lounge. This was not going to be fun.

Erika was sitting in a chair, spinning her sword, hilt in her palm, blade straight up in the air, the lights of the room glinting on the steel as it danced on her hand. Gregor was sitting on a chair reading a book. It momentarily shocked me, I didn't picture him as a book reader, but there you go. I couldn't pick out the title, he placed the book face down, with a bookmark, on the table next to him as soon as I entered the room and just watched me for a while.

"Are you hungry? Would you like something to eat, *ma cherie?*"

I shook my head, food was the last thing on my mind. Damn, I wished those shutters would rise up already. I should have stayed in the bedroom a little longer, waited until I heard that blissful sound of freedom as they whirred away to reveal the night.

"I have called more of my line to me, they will arrive over the next few days. I think we will have to take a proactive stance against the humans, this is escalating too quickly and needs to be shut down." He seemed to want to talk business, keeping things professional. I could handle that. I wondered briefly, if he was doing it for my benefit.

"Proactive? Just what do you consider to be proactive, Gregor?" I couldn't stand the thought of more humans dying, even if they were way out of line and trying to kill the vampires, it still didn't feel right. I had walked to a chair near him without realising and once there couldn't think of a casual way to move away, so just sat down, crossed my legs and braced myself as I met his eyes.

He was wearing his vampire mask, no emotions visible, his grey eyes only showing a hint of silver, nothing

186

more. He was doing his best not to scare me. I couldn't help feeling thankful. Gregor was a lot of things, but occasionally he could play the gentleman well. I just wished I could tell what was real and what was an act.

"I will not stand by and watch my vampires die because of some misguided human fear and anarchy." He spoke the words softly, no obvious anger or threat, simply a statement of fact.

I understood what he was saying, how could a vampire not retaliate? How could they not do everything in their power to protect those they are honour bound, blood bound, to protect?

"Will you promise me one thing?" I looked him directly in the eye, this request required courage, it deserved respect. He deserved respect when I asked it of him, as Master of the City.

"Ask and I will answer honestly."

I sat there for a moment and just breathed. Vampires are not known for their ability to pull punches, they live for confrontation, for the chance to dominate, but if there was any chance of this not becoming a human massacre, I needed to ask.

"Will you try to find a solution that does not involve death? Will you try to negotiate an understanding?"

He looked at me for a moment, no emotions on his face, just vampire neutral.

"I will promise you this, little Hunter, I will endeavour to avoid bloodshed as much as is possible without endangering my kin, but I will not negotiate with humans."

He said it like humans didn't deserve that right of equality. After the way humans had been acting in this city,

I really couldn't blame him for that response, but it didn't feel like he was just referring to the humans who had attacked his line, but to *all* humans. The reminder that vampires are at the top of the food chain hit me like a slap in the face.

Why is it that I always lower my guard around them and fall into the trap of believing them capable of coexisting with humans on an equal footing? You'd think I'd know better by now.

I didn't say anything in reply, just then the shutters whirred into action and rose up and away out of sight, displaying a beautiful clear starry night out of the windows of Gregor's apartment. I was on my feet and walking to the door in an instant.

"Lucinda."

Gregor's voice was soft, but commanding. I didn't want to turn around, I didn't want to hear what he had to say, but I was trying to be an adult and ignoring him just didn't feel very grown up at all. I turned slowly willing my face not to show any emotions.

"Would you mind leaving us for a moment, Erika?" That surprised me, him asking her, not glazing, not commanding as the Master of the City. I flicked a glance at Erika, she raised her eyebrows at me, looking for consent. I just nodded and she grabbed her bag and walked out the front door, no doubt to stand on the other side and wait.

Gregor didn't say anything for a few seconds, just looked at me, his implacable mask on his face.

"What do you want, Gregor?" I just sounded tired, not strong and capable, but tired. Tired of this mess, tired of my inability to do the right thing, tired of the mistakes. I forced myself to stand straighter, taller. If I was to learn from any of this, I had to step up to the plate and accept what had happened with broad shoulders.

"I do not regret today, I will treasure it, hold it close to my heart for eternity. And I will not stop pursuing you either. You know what I want and I always get what I want, Lucinda."

I let a long breath out that I had been holding and just looked at him. We were right back at square one, just as I had suspected. The challenge may be over, it may have been met, Gregor the victor, but he did not consider himself a winner, not yet, not until he had all of me. Controlled all of me. I didn't want this man before me. I didn't want to want him either. But I was still unsure if I was strong enough to ignore the pull of the *Sigillums*. I did want Michel though. Despite what he had done, despite how close to the Dark he is. I still wanted him, but should I give in to him?

To give in would be physically easy, natural even, but it would be mentally and emotionally suicidal. Michel would hide me away, making it impossible to fight. He was potentially dangerous to the outcome of the war. I couldn't afford to let him distract me from my path.

All of this was fairly moot though really. Even if I had managed to come to some tentative understanding and acceptance of Michel's Dark within, of what has made him act the way he has, he would surely not be able to forgive me. I forced myself to focus on the vampire in front of me and push all thoughts of the complicated relationship I had with the vampire in my heart away.

"I would ask you to back off, for me, but I don't think

189

you would comply."

He just shook his head, a small measure of pain and sadness now reaching the corner of his eyes. "I am unable to, *ma cherie*."

"Then, you do what you have to do, Gregor, and I will do what I have to do. And may God forgive us, for whatever happens."

I turned and walked out the front door, heading straight for his car. Erika and I stood next to it quietly for five minutes, before Gregor finally joined us, opening the car with the press of his electronic key and slipping in the driver's side. I smiled, at least I had stopped him from opening the door for me, but I knew it was only a temporary reprieve, Gregor didn't give up that easily.

He drove directly to the airport, but didn't wait for us to board. He said a simple goodbye, only briefly catching my eyes and then sped away. I didn't feel sad, I didn't feel regret, I just felt relieved. I felt a little of me returning, a little of the fighter coming back. So, I had fucked up royally in the past twenty four hours, sue me, I'm only human and I'm about to take part in a war. I deserve a few mistakes along the way, but I wasn't going to let any more happen. I'd learned my lesson, I'd let the Dark in when I should have been strong enough to say no. But it was time to move on.

The flight home was quiet, we watched a couple of old episodes of *True Blood*. Can't help laughing at the entertainment industry's interpretation of the fanged. It always lifts your spirits. Both Erika and I hurling insults at the flat screen. It was cathartic, I have to admit.

I drove us back to *Sensations* after we landed and

although it was the first time I had driven the BMW, it felt like home. Michel had chosen well, the car fitted like a glove and brought out the inner hunter in me. I gunned it along the Southern Motorway, managing to avoid a speeding ticket and made it to the city in record time. I dropped Erika at the front of the club, a queue already lining the pavement.

"You not coming in, *chica?*"

"No, need some home time. Washing, you know, domestic crap."

She nodded, she knew I was avoiding Michel, but she didn't push.

"You need anything, another *True Blood* fest, just call, OK?"

I smiled and nodded in return and then pulled the car into the K Road traffic, heading towards St. Mary's Bay and my sanctuary. I couldn't wait to get home. It felt like an eternity since I had been alone there. I was craving a coffee, not only the taste of my current Arabica obsession, but the routine of filling the bean hopper, watching the beans grind and smelling the infusion of caffeine through the air as thick, dark, liquid gold poured into a cup. Then topping it with the fluffiest, whitest milk. Perfection awaited, so I didn't delay.

I parked in a free parking space on the property. Our building was lucky, we had off-street car parking, but not garaging. I momentarily paused by my car, hoping my new baby would be safe out in the cold. I shook my head, I was becoming attached to a bloody car after only one drive.

The place seemed quieter than usual, but it was fairly late, after midnight, so maybe my neighbours were all having early Sunday nights, back to work tomorrow, gotta be prepared.

I had just made it past Mrs Cumberland's, her curtains drawn, light shining through from behind, but no T.V. to be heard, which was a little strange, when I sensed it. I don't know what, but the hair on the back of my neck lifted, like hackles and I immediately slipped my stake out of its pocket. It wasn't vampires, so the stake would probably be a waste of time, but it was something that set my internal warning bells off. And they were clanging.

I glanced around at the bushes that bordered our property, but nothing seemed amiss. I even sniffed the air, which until recently had made me shiver in discomfort whenever I felt the urge to smell, but it didn't faze me now. Determining what was making me jumpy was more important. I couldn't tell what it was so I continued on to my apartment.

I noticed the door first, it was hanging off its hinges, no lights were on inside, but the external sensor lights, which had flicked on as I approached, shone through the shattered windows illuminating the room within. I took a sharp breath in at the destruction and then was instantly surrounded by vampires.

"It has only just happened," Michel said quietly behind me. "Secure the building and land," he commanded his vampires and they flashed to various places around the property. Bruno streaking inside my apartment to assess the threat.

I stood still while the movement of the vampires swirled around the periphery, numbed by the violation to my home, my sanctuary, my refuge. Bruno came out and announced it was all clear and I shot inside to inspect the damage.

Nothing was left to salvage. My cream sofa was a ripped-stuffing explosion of broken pieces, my dining suite just tinder. My coffee machine, oh hell, my *Saeco Royal Professional* cost-me-a-month's-salary coffee machine was in pieces on the bench, as though someone had taken delight in dismantling it and crushing each individual piece. I couldn't even cry. I turned numbly to my bedroom, noticing Michel was watching me quietly from the door, just inside the threshold, but not daring to come closer. My bedroom was just as bad, the bedding shredded, the frame destroyed and my laptop; little teeny tiny pieces of electronics scattered on the floor. Above my bedhead was a long series of slashes. Claw marks, definitely claw marks.

The coffee machine had already given me a clue. Rick and I had enjoyed many coffees at that bench, savouring the perfect brew that it created, but this mark, this gash against my wall, sealed the deal. The shape shifter had left me a welcome home message. Bastard.

"You can stay at *Sensations*, it will be safe there." Michel was behind me, close, closer than I wanted him to be.

I took a step further into my room and turned to face him, crossing my arms over my chest.

"I don't want to stay at *Sensations*." I hadn't said it petulantly, just an even flow of words.

"You are not safe here, *ma douce*."

I looked around the mess, fractured glass from the windows littering the floor and letting in a late night breeze, swishing the torn curtains as it passed. There was nowhere to sleep or sit, he was right of course, but I would not stay at *Sensations*.

"Can I stay at your house in St. Helier's?"

Michel's eyes widened slightly, then returned to their normal neutral mask. "Of course. But you would be safer at *Sensations*." He held a hand up as I opened my mouth to argue. "I would stay at the house and give you the chamber, if you would agree."

"I'm not turfing you out of your home, Michel. And I know *Sensations* is a home to you."

He looked at me for a while. "Would you allow Erika to stay with you at the house?"

I really wanted to be alone for a while, I knew Erika would be quiet, but she'd relay everything that I did to Michel. I just couldn't face that type of scrutiny right now.

"Maybe later, but not tonight. I need to be alone tonight. The house is well warded and Rick doesn't even know it exists, so I should be safe. You can..." I sighed, I guess I would have to meet him half way on this one. "...you can have some vampires guard it if you like, but not inside."

He smiled slowly. "Thank you... Lucinda."

I shook my head, we were reduced to formality. Shit.

I walked over to the bed and tried to lift the frame, it was heavy, even with my Nosferatin strength, or I was tired and beaten. Definitely beaten. Michel was beside me in an instant lifting the frame away from my chest beneath. The chest had survived, thankfully. Obviously missed in the chaos that had reigned. I opened it up and took in the stash. Four perfect silver stakes, along with four brand new silver knives, all nestled safely in their fitted slots. I shut the lid and turned to my wardrobe.

They hadn't missed in there, much to my disgust. My clothes were all ruined, even my Bank Teller uniform, but hidden in the back of the closest was another box. I hauled it out and checked to make sure my satellite phone was OK. All good. A gift from Nero and an occasional Nosferatin necessity. Sometimes you just need a means of communicating that can't be traced or overheard.

I placed the satellite phone on the chest and looked around. I had some clothes and my toiletries already packed in my bag outside, there really was nothing else I needed.

Bruno entered then and took the chest and box out, no doubt to my car. I didn't argue, Michel would have called him and I couldn't be naffed carrying the things anyway.

Silence stretched between Michel and me, standing in the mess that was my room, a sure representation of my life. I wanted to say something, to apologise maybe, to ask him why? But I couldn't even do that, it was too soon and I was too tired. He noticed and just smiled, I think he was as tired as I.

"I am pleased you are home, *ma douce*. I am pleased you are well."

Yeah, as far as welcome homes went, it pretty much sucked.

Chapter 16
Changes

Michel walked me to my car and just stood there with his hands in his trouser pockets, his Armani jacket open and pushed back. I forced myself to look away from him, it hurt to just glance upon his face, his body, his beauty. What a fucking idiot I was.

What a fucking idiot he was.

I straightened my shoulders, refusing to address the issue. If I just kept it at bay, I could do what I needed to do and right now that was getting into the car and driving away from the man I loved and had hurt so much. From the man who kept hurting me.

"I will arrange for the apartment to be refurbished," Michel said quietly, dark blue eyes watching me closely. "But, until this issue with the Taniwhas has been resolved, it would not be safe for you to return. I cannot ward against shifters."

"I guess I'll have to let my landlord know." I'd never spoken to my landlord, just dealt with a letting agency, the middle man. Michel hadn't said anything, so I chanced a glance at him. His smile was rueful. Oh shit. "You're my landlord, aren't you?"

He shrugged, that elegant shift of his shoulders. "It seemed the best way to ensure your safety."

I took in a slow breath. "Have you owned it since I moved here?"

"Yes."

"How did you know I would choose this one?"

"I had the real estate agent only show you my properties."

I laughed out loud at that. The man was simply incorrigible.

Then a horrible thought dawned on me. "Did you arrange the transfer too?" My voice had gone whisper quiet. My transfer to Auckland from the BNZ bank in Cambridge had been a big coup for me. Country Bank Teller stepping into the Big Smoke worker's shoes. I lifted my head up to meet his eyes. I'd been looking at the ground as I asked that, too scared to see his reaction, but I needed to know this, I needed to know the truth.

"Would it be better if I lied?"

I didn't want to hear those words, I didn't want to know what I had already figured out in my head. I didn't want it. At all.

Loss of control. Manipulation. I had only just begun to accept his recent actions to some degree, now I felt all the anger and frustration well up again as though no progress had been made on my part at all.

My inner monologue whispered *vampire is as vampire does.* I told it to shut the fuck up and opened my car door to slide inside. Starting the engine in a flash and reversing out of the car park without a backward glance. Michel didn't try to stop me, he didn't say a word. And I didn't look back at him, as I sped down the street and away from the heart of my messed up, fucked up, totally screwed up, life.

I made a brief stop at a supermarket along Quay Street to grab some food and supplies, I didn't want to brave the night again when I got to St. Helier's. It was further out of the city than I really would have liked, if I felt my evil-lurks-in-the-city pull, it would undoubtedly take me longer to get to the problem and neutralise it before damage was done, but I did have a fast car now. I was sure I could just manage to meet my previous on-foot speed, just.

The lights were on at the house as I approached along the cliff top, that didn't surprise me, Michel would have sent some vampires ahead to make sure it was safe and probably make me feel welcome. I parked the car in the open garage, flicking the automatic door switch on the wall at the internal door and grabbing the remote to place in my car. I took my bags and chest and box in and dumped them on the floor in the kitchen.

A quick glance around and I took in two things. One, there was a *Royal Saeco Professional* coffee machine on the bench that hadn't been there the last time I came here and two, there was a long wrapped item on the breakfast bar. A small card leaning against it. It never failed to amaze me at how quickly Michel could work. Part of me wondered if he had suspected, even engineered, me into moving in here, I wouldn't put it past him. But I pushed that thought aside. I had been the one to suggest it, he just has telepathic mojo and a multitude of vamps at his disposal to get the items he wanted, when he wanted, to the place he wanted them to be, with ease. Vampires.

I walked over to the machine and switched it on. First things first. I needed coffee. It would take a couple of minutes for the behemoth coffee magic maker to stir to life, so I turned to the long item on the bench, picking up the card. In Michel's old-style flowing writing it read: *I had hoped to present this to you in person, ma douce. Please honour me and accept this gift as it is intended. M.*

I stared at the card. He knew I wouldn't want to accept anything from him right now, I didn't deserve a gift, he didn't deserve to give me one, but asking me to *honour him by accepting it*, well that just made my rejection of it childish, didn't it? I sighed and unwrapped the parcel.

As soon as I lifted it I knew what it would be. A shorter Svante sword, in a beautifully intricate scabbard, inlaid with with tiny bees and flowers, only noticeable when you ran your fingers over the leather. Perfectly made, precisely created, it was beautiful. I ran my hand over the sheath, noticing something else dropping out of the wrapping as I lifted it closer to my eyes. I glanced at what had fallen out, trying to figure out exactly what it is. Finally, I put the sword down to look at the strips of soft leather, almost suede and shook it out. It was a holder of some sort, designed to secure the blade and scabbard to me. I had seen Erika wearing something like this, it allowed the sword to hang down her back, under her jacket out of sight, the hilt covered by her hair. She had little difficulty removing the blade from its sheath when required. I looked at the contraption and realised I'd need to practice that move a bit before I was anywhere near her proficiency.

I pushed that thought aside and returned my attention to the sword. The hilt was breathtaking. I'd practised with swords of Erika's, all of which seemed to be rudimentary, utilitarian in their ornaments. Plain bronze or copper wire surrounding the handle above a simple curved cross bar. But this, this was truly something else. The hilt was awash with different colours, woven together to make a pattern of sorts. At first I thought it was geometrical or just random, but then as I turned it slowly in the lights of the room I began to get a picture of what it was. A dancing dragon. The entire hilt was one colourful dancing dragon.

I had seen this dragon before, at Michel's chamber in *Sensations*, on-board his private jet and now here. It meant something to him and he had now given me one too. I sat down in the stool next to the bench, unable to hold my own weight anymore. Of course, he'd had this commissioned before I was unfaithful, before I had pulled away. Perhaps he regretted it now, but then, he could have just not given it to me and had another made in its stead. He'd chosen to carry through with the gift, unchanged, despite what had happened.

There was no denying, it was beautiful. I stood again and practised a few moves, a few Weapon Dance motions, getting the feel for the sword. It was perfect. Like the car, Michel had given me something that felt like home.

I spent a few minutes just swinging the thing, but kitchens really aren't conducive to swordsmanship, so I re-sheathed it carefully and laid it down on the bench with reverence. A weapon like this deserved respect.

I made quick work of my groceries, stacking them away, downed a well deserved and fantastic coffee and then switched all the downstairs lights off and headed to bed. I had stayed here once before, while recovering from the first time I had Dream Walked twice in one night. I was out cold for a week then and didn't stay much longer than that, so I spent a little time getting familiar with the layout. The room I had stayed in before was not the master, it was large enough and had a view of the sea, but I didn't fancy sleeping in there. I almost walked on past the master suite, thinking it just wouldn't be right, but something caught my eye from the door.

The light was on in the ensuite bathroom and as I

walked towards it, intending to switch it off and go in hunt of another place to sleep, I smelt it. Mandarins. I pushed the door open and swore softly. He'd run a bath for me, copious amounts of mandarin smelling bubbles waiting for my submission. I stood still at the door for a moment trying to decide, but tiredness and mandarins won, and within minutes I was soaking in the still warm luxury of an oversized jacuzzi tub, trying not to sigh.

Once I exited the bath, after twenty minutes of sheer bliss, I was simply way too tired to venture elsewhere, so climbed between the crisp cotton sheets, not even bothering with a nightdress and fell instantly asleep.

I slept soundly, the only dream I remembered was a dragon dancing around my bed.

I headed in to work early the next morning after a wonderful coffee wake-up, not sure where I would park, but on the way along Tamaki Drive I noticed a parking permit on the dash of the car. I had no idea if it had been there before, but if it had, I just hadn't noticed. I picked it up and registered it was for one of the parking garages in the CBD, not far from the bank. I was guessing it hadn't been there before. I could have just parked at *Sensations* for free, but that would have been too close for comfort. A little petty part of me was angry at Michel, angry that he was trying to think of everything to make this easier on me, to allow me to keep my distance but not be inconvenienced by exorbitant car parking prices in downtown Auckland. He was making my life too easy and I just didn't quite know how to deal with that. Damn him for being so reasonable and nice.

I took in a deep breath and parked in the garage

anyway. I'd have to spend my lunch hour shopping for clothes, I really wasn't in a position to be fussy about money saving gifts. Luckily, I had a spare uniform at work, so dressed appropriately, I put in a request for more supplies and started my day. There is just something about my daytime job that settles me. The repetition of counting coins soothes my soul. One morning of that routine and I was more clear headed than I had been in days. I zoomed around shops in my lunch hour, managing to spend a month's salary in one manic shopping spree, but believe me, with lingerie and necessities, as well as a few mix and match items, you'd be surprised at how much a closet full of clothes will cost you. If I wasn't already so pissed off at Rick about the whole killing Jerome and coming after me part, I would have killed the prick right then and there for destroying my wardrobe. You never go after a woman's clothes, never.

The afternoon passed as swiftly and before I knew it, I was in rush hour traffic, crawling out of the CBD towards my new temporary home. I knew there was a reason I liked to live in St. Mary's Bay, fifteen minute walks home and no honking drivers getting pissed off at the expensive BMW cutting in front of them before the lane finished. Merge like a zip people!

Finally back at my new haven, I changed into workout gear and headed to the downstairs gym. Not being able to workout at *Tony's Gym* had made me twitchy, right now I was on a one-way road to self satisfaction, getting my Nosferatin mojo back on and that included an intense two hour long workout in Michel's well appointed home gym. It could hardly be called a home gym really, every conceivable gym machine was in attendance, plus a most awesome sounding *Bang & Olufsen* stereo system. I was lost in an exercise endorphin-released, thumping music workout when I noticed Nero standing quietly in the corner.

I didn't jump off the treadmill immediately, but went through my usual warm down routine, slowly coming to a stop ten minutes after noticing him there. His eyes hadn't left me the entire time, sparkling a little cinnamon and copper in their depths.

"Hi," I said as I reached for a towel and wiped my face clear of sweat.

"Hi yourself, Kiwi." He looked around the room. "Where are we?"

"My new temporary digs." His eyebrow raised in a question. "It's a long story, but it involves Taniwhas, destruction, my apartment and worst of all my coffee machine. This is one of Michel's homes, I'm borrowing it until my place is remodelled." At least, that's my plan, I'm not entirely sure what Michel's is. "Come on, let's go upstairs, I'll make you a coffee."

Nero took in the coffee machine on the bench, but didn't say anything, I could tell the little cogs in his head were whirring, but bless him, he kept his mouth firmly shut. He settled into a seat at the breakfast table, relaxing back, legs crossed at his ankles, hands clasped behind his head. Nero's signature pose.

"So, what's up? I wasn't expecting you today was I?"

"No, but I thought I would visit in person to advise Nafrini and Amisi's parents have agreed to her visiting with you for a while. Perhaps, in light of your current housing situation, this is not a good time though."

"Oh heck yes, I've got this entire house to myself, I could do with a roomie."

"A roomie?"

"A flatmate, someone to share the place with. I think Erika will probably be thrust upon me at some stage, it's inevitable that Michel will want one of his line near me as he can't be right now, but she's cool, Amisi will like her."

"He can't be near you right now?" Trust Nero to pick up on that.

I concentrated on finishing off his coffee and didn't offer a reply.

"Kiwi? I knew you were worried you had hurt him, but that should not keep your kindred away."

I passed him his coffee over the table and as I went to pull away he grabbed my wrist, not too hard, but firmly, so I couldn't move. I just looked down at his dark skin against my pale arm and struggled to think of something to say.

"Talk to me, my Kiwi."

He released my hand slowly, when I didn't say anything straight away and I reached for my own coffee, then sat down next to him at the table, taking a fortifying sip.

"I'm still a bit of a mess, Nero. You know, what we talked about in Cairo yesterday? Well, I've really fucked things up, one gigantic mistake after another. And so has Michel. But it's done now and we just have to live with it. My current solution is to avoid men altogether and that includes my *kindred*."

He sat quietly for a while, sipping his coffee, watching me no doubt, but I couldn't be sure, I was looking at my hands in my lap.

204

"You are strong, Lucinda, you will get through this and you will do what is needed to survive, but consider this, your kindred is also a tool, something to give you power, to give you support. If you cannot be with him intimately and that is not always necessary as you are aware, then at least allow him some contact platonically. The longer you are both apart, the weaker you will become."

I knew this, I had always known this. Nero and Nafrini, his kindred vampire, are like brother and sister, their relationship is not intimate in the slightest, but they maintain physical contact all the same. A brush of hands here, a touch there, all casual, all brief, nothing remotely sexual, but necessary in keeping their connection strong, their powers full.

But, Michel - I just wasn't sure I could have him that close and not get confused, or worse, cave in and make it intimate. It was too much to ask.

"What happens if I can't do that? What happens if we don't have that contact for some time?"

"You compromise yourselves, both of you, your strength, your power, your ability to focus, your Light. The joining is more than just a sharing of power, it allows both of you to balance the Light and the Dark within, without it one will prevail over the other." He sighed when he saw the look of mortification and fear on my face. "Kiwi, you think by being separated from him you can do your task properly, fulfil your role in the Prophesy, but by *not* being near him, you weaken yourself to such a point that the Light may no longer be able to shine and then we have already lost." He ran a hand through his hair, making it stand up in spikes heading in all different directions. "I realise he is over protective, so some distance is necessary for you to be able to move freely when needed, if you are unable to come to a compromise, an understanding, that is. But, don't shut him out completely, you mustn't. Have that contact in neutral territory, or with whomever around you that you trust to keep you safe, but do not deny it. Ensure it continues, guard it as fiercely as you guard your independence."

Well, didn't that just suck. Somehow the words *rock and hard place* sprang to mind.

We drank the rest of our coffee in silence.

"Amisi will be flying out tomorrow, she should be here your time Tuesday evening. I'll send the details of her flight through."

Man, those Egyptians didn't muck around when they made their minds up, or maybe Nero knew how much I could do with a friend right now, either way, I'd have to let Michel know, I hadn't even run it past him yet. Shit.

"Text it for now, I haven't sorted out a new computer yet."

"They smashed your computer?"

"They smashed everything apart from my stakes and my satellite phone, only because I hid those two."

He nodded, as though that was exactly what he would have expected me to do. It was just lucky the chest fitted under my bed and the box the phone was in was at the back of my wardrobe. I hadn't planned on getting my flat trashed, so I was bloody lucky on those counts.

"How long can she stay?" I asked.

"We'll assess that after she has been here a week or two. She does require a new scene. She has only known Cairo and we already have three fully matured Nosferatin, it was always understood that she would have to move away. I just have trouble admitting she is old enough to do it."

I smiled at him, he really did care for her like she was his own daughter or younger sister. It was nice to see this caring, selfless side of him, instead of the intense warrior that he so often portrayed.

"What about the shape shifters, are you worried about my current dangerous predicament?"

"I have discussed it with her and Nafrini and we all agree, this is something she would have to face elsewhere and maybe on her own, it is best she have you to help her and I will also visit when I can."

I nodded and stood to remove the empty cups and rinse them in the sink.

"I am sorry if I have been harsh towards you, Kiwi."

I spun to look at him and found he was standing right behind me, I hadn't even heard him move. As a Nosferatin I should have been able to, just because he's Dream Walking, doesn't mean he is invisible to me.

"What do you mean?"

He reached up and pushed a lock of my hair behind my ear, resting his hand against my cheek. "Forcing you to be near your kindred when you so obviously do not wish it."

"I know it's for the good of the Prophesy. I understand."

His eyes flashed cinnamon and gold, I hadn't seen the gold before, only coffee, cinnamon and copper. The gold was mesmerising.

"It is for the good of you, Lucinda. My only thoughts are for you."

I didn't know what to say, I felt trapped under the weight of his stare, the intense shine to his eyes, the feel of his thumb stroking my cheek. And then just as quickly as he had touched me, he smiled sadly, kissed my forehead and flickered out of sight.

Why was it I felt like things were changing, like quicksand all around me, I was just along for the ride.

Loss of friggin' control.

Chapter 17
Love Hurts

I had a quick shower and once dressed in hunter gear, tried to decide whether a phone call to Michel would suffice. Shit. Platonic contact and all that. The best solution was a trip to *Sensations* and a meeting in his crowded bar. It was the only solution, albeit one that made my stomach flip and butterflies take up residence in my belly.

The sun had set by the time I hit the road and headed into town. I had my stereo up as loud as my ears could take it and sang along to *Fergie's Big Girls Don't Cry* trying to bolster myself up with some musical therapy. Fifteen minutes later I pulled into the underground carpark at the club and after a fortifying deep breath in, went through the coded doors and straight towards the bar. Ignoring the corridors to either side; one towards the vampires quarters, the other to Michel's.

I couldn't spot Michel at his usual table, maybe it was too early and he was still in his office. There was no way I was going there, so I headed over to the bar and waited for Doug to finish serving his customer.

"Good to see you, Luce," he said sliding me a *Bacardi and Coke* across the bar. "It's been quiet without you here."

"I was gone one night Doug and it was a Saturday, I'm sure the regular crowd made up for it."

"Not the same," he said and turned toward another customer at the other end of the long bar. Nice to feel wanted, I supposed.

"You are wanted, *ma douce*. You are always wanted." I turned at the sound of his voice, it was instinct, a habit, I almost uttered a curse as soon as I looked at him.

Irresistible, gorgeous, perfect. I clamped my mouth shut and booted my inner monologue the hell out of my head before I embarrassed myself further.

He just smiled, hands in pockets, all perfectly at ease. When I didn't say anything he stepped towards the chair beside me.

"May I?" he asked, indicating the seat.

I actually hated that he was being so formal, so careful, I hated the false sense of unfamiliarity, the distance it created. I hated myself for creating it. But I sucked it up, it was for the best. I had chosen this path.

"Sure," I managed without giving my inner turmoil away.

He slid in next to me and Doug immediately placed a glass of red wine in front of him, before heading back to paying customers.

"I trust everything is to your liking at the house. You are comfortable? Do you need anything else?"

I sighed, this was just crap.

"Is something wrong?" He had heard the sigh, of course.

Yes. Hell yes. Abso-fucking-lutely yes.

"No. I'm fine, everything's fine."

He took another sip of his drink and watched me, so still, so quiet. I felt nothing coming from him, no predator hunger, no male desire, not even curiosity, he was locked down tighter than Fort Knox.

"Amisi is coming to stay for a while. Kind of like a Nosferatin student exchange, except there'll be no student heading over there, just her, here, with me. So, a one way student exchange, not two." Bugger, now I had verbal

210

diarrhoea. "Um, is that OK, if she stays with me at the house?" Drink, alcohol, that will make it all so much better. I downed most of my glass in one hit.

"Nafrini has been in touch, I have extended our heartfelt welcome towards Amisi." Of course Nafrini had been in touch. How silly of me, any excuse for Nafrini to phone Michel. Being old friends and all that.

"Good. Well, that was all I had to say." I finished the last of my drink with a slight grimace, I don't even think that took sixty seconds. Not healthy.

"Are you in a hurry to rush off? Would you care to drink your next drink and actually savour it, *ma douce,* rather than inhale it?"

Ha. Ha. Very funny, but there really was no point in staying longer, just stand up, touch his hand or something briefly, get the contact thing out of the way and leave.

I sat still, unmoving. Doug slid another drink in front of me, I forced myself not to reach for it.

Michel sighed. "Come sit with me and have a meal, my dear. You have lost weight, you are fading away. I do worry you are not taking care of yourself. Let my chefs prepare something you will like. We need not talk, being close would do for contact to start with, we can worry about touch another time."

I looked at him then. "Have you been reading my mind?" Or was he spying on me at his house, had he heard the conversation I had with Nero.

"You forget, *ma douce,* I know you well. You could have picked up a phone to ask me about Amisi's visit, but instead you have willingly entered the lion's den and with such courage, yet such fear. Doing what is right has always

211

been your greatest character trait and your greatest downfall."

He stood then and picked up both our drinks, heading to his favourite spot in the corner. It allowed him to watch the club floor, but not have anyone at his back. I dutifully followed, I really wanted that drink.

We sat opposite each other, but despite a fervent desire to *inhale* that *Bacardi and Coke* I made damn sure I didn't touch it. I decided one alcoholic drink would be my new standard, I did have to drive now. Before, when two was my limit, I relied on my own steam to get around. Now, with a six cylinder twin turbo 225 KW engine at my control, I thought a little reserve would go a long way. I drummed my fingers on the top of the table for a while and then couldn't stop myself.

"I'm just going to go ask Doug for a *Coke*." I started sliding out of the booth.

"He is already bringing you one." I glanced towards the bar and sure enough, Doug was coming over with a tall glass of *Coke*. He plopped it down in front of me and took the *Bacardi* away. Bless him. Bless him most dearly. I sipped the *Coke*.

You know how you're supposed to feel comfortable sitting with the one you love in silence, how there shouldn't be any awkward moments, long stretches of discomfort? Well, it's a lie. A big fat what-a-crock-of-shit lie. My legs were bouncing up and down, just small movements, nothing monumental, but it made my fingers drum restlessly on the table top and my heart start to pick up speed. Where was that dinner? Because, sure as eggs, Michel would have telepathically placed the order even before he suggested the meal. So, why was it taking an eternity to get here?

That's it. I'd had enough. I could eat at home, grab McD's on the way back. I know I have a full container of *Kapiti White Chocolate Raspberry Ice Cream* in the freezer at the house. That could prove the answer to all my prayers. I'd just placed my palm flat down on the table to make the statement that I was off, when Michel reached forward and covered it with his own. I stopped breathing and slowly looked up at his eyes.

"Don't run," he whispered, his eyes deep pools of blue, pleading with me not to move, not to make the shift that would bring me to my feet and pull me from his grasp.

I slowly let the air I was holding out and he took his hand away, sitting back against the seat and just looked at me, his chest rising and falling slightly, just as breathless as I was. We stared at each other for a moment and then his chef arrived with a plate of roast lamb shanks in mint sauce, baby potatoes and carrots on the side. Simple, Kiwi fare and not what they normally serve in the club. I glanced up at the white-frocked guy, he was a human, they all are in the kitchen, can't blame the vampires for avoiding that job.

"It's special order, just for you." He smiled, nodded to Michel and walked away. I stared at the food and tried to blink the tears away.

"Why are you being so nice?" My voice was tiny, I couldn't help it. "Do you think it will change things?" OK, that was a bit stronger, a bit more like me.

"Not at all, you are too stubborn for that." He paused, considering his words carefully. "I need to provide for you, Lucinda. I need to make you happy." He sighed. "It is

213

difficult for me to step back, but I am trying, please believe me. I am trying."

"And I suppose it wouldn't hurt to smooth over your own mistakes?" I asked a little bitterly.

He stared at me, I couldn't tell what he was thinking, but he didn't say a word.

The smell of the lamb had permeated the space in front of me, I was tempted to push it away, but I was so damn hungry. I hadn't realised I'd been skipping so many meals and it was lamb. Lamb! I can't resist lamb.

"This is not consent of your actions, I'm just hungry," I said, picking up my knife and fork and starting in on the meal.

"And it is lamb," Michel added drily.

I just shot him a glare and then forgot about what we were discussing altogether as the succulent and delicious taste of mint, rosemary and lamb met my taste buds. I let a little moan out and then realised what I was doing.

Michel just laughed. "The chef will be pleased you like it, *ma douce*."

I couldn't answer, my mouth was full with a second bite. Before I even realised, I'd polished off the entire meal. I hadn't felt this full in ages. Someone came and took the plate away, I just leaned back in my chair, tempted to loosen the button on my skirt, so my distended belly could relax too, but a girl's gotta have some pride. However, *Coke* just wasn't cutting it with lamb and without even thinking I reached over and took a sip of Michel's Merlot, to wash the lamb away. An easy slip, I'd often drunk from his glass, but now it just felt wrong.

"Oh God, I'm sorry. How rude of me." I quickly

pushed the glass back towards him. He probably didn't want it now though, considering it was full of my saliva, but he just kept his eyes on me and slowly lifted the glass to his lips, turning it in his fingers so the rim, where I had drunk from, was now facing him. He touched his lips to the exact same spot as mine, closed his eyes - I think he might have inhaled - and then tipped the drink back and finished it. When his eyes opened again they were aglow with indigo and amethyst swirls.

Okey dokey, not concerned about sharing glasses then. I had trouble pulling my gaze away from his though, but finally managed it when a plate of *Kapiti White Chocolate Raspberry Ice Cream* was placed in front of me. I glanced back up at Michel.

"I may have cheated a little on that one," he said with a wicked smile. "Your thoughts were rather loud, I don't think you realised you were projecting." He shrugged his shoulders as if to say, *what else would I have done?*

I just looked at him, now I was really confused. He was being so kind, so thoughtful. Was it because he wanted to make me feel forgiven? Was it because he couldn't help providing for me as he had suggested? Or was it because he wanted to wash away my anger at his manipulation?

"Why are you being so nice?" I asked for the second time.

He cocked his head at me in puzzlement. "Because I love you."

I shook my head back at him. "Michel, I slept with someone else." I was going to add something to that, but the flash of magenta in his eyes and the look of pain that fluttered over his face made me pause. He may have been acting like he had forgiven me, but he was hurting all the same. I closed my eyes. Then shook my head again and took a deep breath in. He had forgiven me because he had made what happened possible. He felt responsible. "You set me up," I said as I opened my eyes to look at him.

"I... what?" Michel didn't usually have trouble forming sentences. I'd caught him off guard.

"You only let me go to Wellington so I would be faced with how easy it would be to make such a mistake. Like the mistake you made in Paris." He looked mortified, shocked. He was utterly speechless that I had figured it out. Of course, I'd had help; glazing Erika, Nero's guidance. "You should know, I understand," I went on. "I've accepted what happened in Paris." Well, sort of. "I even understand why you sent me to Wellington to fail. I don't like it." I shook my head and frowned at my hands clasped on my lap. "But, it didn't go the way you intended, did it?" I looked back up at him then. "I *did* fail, I didn't just come close and then realise how easy it would have been for you when you made the same mistake. I actually fucked up." I squared my shoulders and straightened my back, then looked him in the eyes. "So, I ask again, why are you being so nice?"

Michel had stopped breathing, blinking, but I was sure he had not stopped thinking. If I could have read his mind right then, I think it would have contained a few expletives. We sat like that, in silence, for several minutes, then he slowly began to relax. First his shoulders, then his back, then forehead, lips, eyes and lastly he began to breathe again.

"I owe you an apology." I hadn't expected that. "I forget how well you know me." He sighed. "When I am with you, it is not so Dark. I hurt you in Paris and even though I was fighting a spell, I knew you expected better of me." Had I? Yeah, I guess I had. Michel is the Master of Control. Add to that, the Master of Manipulation. But, I had expected more from him back then and I guess, I hadn't been hiding that fact.

But really, whose problem was this? Mine or his? Yes, he made the mistake, under duress, but a mistake all the same. But I have been the one to not let it go.

"It's the Dark," I said suddenly.

He held my gaze and slowly nodded. That one simple movement said so much. I wasn't sure if he was in my head right then, if he understood exactly what I had meant by blaming the Dark. The Dark was responsible for so much of what he did, but it was also responsible for me not letting it go. Not moving on. Not accepting he had been under a spell and capable of making a mistake regardless of his formidable control.

The Dark was also responsible for him trying to manipulate me by sending me to Gregor.

I hated the Dark, I detested it. I subconsciously pulled my Light around me as I pushed those thoughts away.

Michel cleared his throat softly, then said quietly nodding towards the melting ice cream, "Are you going to eat that, *ma douce*?

I was pretty full, I did *not* think it was a good idea to eat more, but I took the lifeline he offered, the chance to return to normal ground and said, "Yeah, I am," and took a small spoonful in my mouth.

Michel watched every movement like a hawk. Savouring the moment. Maybe banishing his thoughts with

217

images of me eating, I don't know. But his gaze was intense. And it wasn't that I was trying to seduce him, I swear, it's just the ice cream was divine and I couldn't help it if I closed my eyes when I tasted it, or licked the spoon to get every last drop, then my lips to make sure I didn't miss some. By the time I finished the plate - a miracle in itself because I have absolutely no idea where I managed to stow that extra dollop of calories - Michel's mouth was slightly open, his hand was gripping the table top and his pulse was racing at his neck. Oops. How had we gone from such treacherous ground to such a dangerous one?

"You have no idea." He practically breathed the words out.

I bit my lip, suddenly feeling really awful, really pathetically awful. He just shook his head and seemed to be unable to look away from my mouth.

"I think I should leave," I said tearing my gaze away from his face. "Yeah. I should go."

I slipped out of the booth, Michel didn't move, I think a conscious choice, standing now may have been a little too revealing even with a suit jacket on. Part of me was in wonder that I could still do this to him, part of me was hating myself for being able to at all.

I turned half towards him, before I walked away. "I'm sorry," I whispered and when he didn't answer I started to move. His hand came out and clasped around my wrist stopping my motion forward. The shot of desire charging from his fingers to my skin almost made me collapse, my knees buckling slightly. He was standing in a second, his arm around my waist, the other up in my hair, his body pressed to mine, his face nestled in my neck, inhaling,

218

crushing me to him. *Oh God, Michel, I'm so sorry.*

He didn't let me go, just held me for a minute, maybe two. It was so tender, but also completely possessive. I think Michel was as mixed up as me right now too. Then slowly he relaxed his hold, creating a little space between us, moving his head from my neck to rest forehead to forehead. His breath hot against my face.

"However long you need, I will wait, but know this, I am yours, completely and utterly yours." His voice was low and husky.

He spun away in an instant and flashed out of sight. The door to his private quarters clicking quietly shut, just to the side of where we had been sitting, even though I hadn't seen him move through it. I was struck dumb, I couldn't move, just a statue in amongst the noise of the club, swaying slightly, trying to breathe. Oh dear God, I loved him. I loved him so much it hurt.

I don't know how long I stood there or if the Norms in the room noticed, I didn't care. The first thing I became aware of was a hand on my shoulder and a voice in my ear.

"I've got the first season of *Moonlight* with as much popcorn and chocolate a girl could ever want, plus a bottle of *Baileys* to boot. What do ya say, *chica*? Fancy a girl's night in?"

I breathed out a long breath and relaxed into Erika's touch.

Suddenly I didn't really fancy being alone with my thoughts, the happy ministrations of a sexy vampire detective and his ditzy blonde human sidekick, could just about manage to drown out the white noise that had taken residence in my head.

That and a bottle of *Baileys*.

Chapter 17
Knocking on the Door

I really think there is only so many calories you can consume in one night. A full dinner, followed by ice cream and then chased with chocolate and *Baileys*, several *Baileys*, is about the limit. Trust me.

The popcorn didn't even get a look in.

But, it was a good way to spend the evening. Erika ended up staying over. She said it was because she'd had too many *Baileys* to high tail it back to *Sensations* and I had definitely had too many *Baileys* to argue with her. So, when morning came around, the house did its little vampire in the dark thing, all the shutters coming down and banishing the sunshine for the day.

Erika would stay put while I went to work, although that was a mission in itself. I know, my own fault, right? But still, not pleasant. And the day did drag. The only consolation? Amisi was landing at Auckland International Airport at 7pm. Just enough time for me to get from work to the Airport to greet her.

I spent the day thinking about my new flatmate and just what sort of mischief I could get her into and by the time closing came around I was back to myself, hangover over, never to be repeated again and setting out for Manukau and the Airport.

Of course, Amisi landed in a private jet and taxied to Michel's hangar. I don't think any of the Nosferatu world travelled economy, it's personal comfort all the way. I made it with ample time to spare, so was soaking up the last of the sun's rays as I watched the plane come to a stop.

I was so hyped up about seeing Amisi, having another

Nosferatin to work with, to bounce ideas off, to hunt with, that I was totally caught unprepared for her to have had a chaperone with her. Of course, Amisi wouldn't have called him that, he was just company on the flight over.

Amisi bounded down the stairs with all the grace of a nearly six foot tall teenager come Nosferatin star student, followed by the more measured, but equally graceful Nero. I couldn't help smiling, not only at Amisi's frantic hand waving, but at the sight of him. He was a sight for sore eyes, that was for sure.

Dressed in casual black trousers and a black shirt, not his usual Middle Eastern attire, much more suited to New Zealand. He was obviously more than capable of blending in when required, but God! He did look good in black.

I hugged Amisi and although Nero had been standing back, intense look on his handsome dark face, hands thrust deep in his pockets, once she released me, I threw myself at him too. Nero was startled for a second and then gave in to the moment and hugged me back.

"Are you staying long?" I asked as we stepped apart.

"No, Kiwi. We will return to Cairo immediately, I only wished to accompany Amisi, to ensure she arrived safely."

"That's one hell of a round trip, Nero. No break at all? It'll take the pilots a while to refuel and they probably need a break, I'm sure there's some union out there that insists on it, so how about a couple of hours in the City of Sails?"

I couldn't let him just get back on board that plane as soon as he arrived. This was his first visit to Auckland. The first time I'd had my Nosferatin trainer in my city, there was no way in hell I was letting him climb back aboard that plane straight away.

He looked at me and slowly smiled.

"You would not let me, even if I insisted, would you, Kiwi?"

I smiled back. "Just a couple of hours, that's all. The pilots can use the facilities here at Michel's hangar to rest. I promise to have you back here by 11pm, you'll be outta here by midnight."

He shook his head slowly, but he was smiling, so I knew I had him. I helped Amisi put her bags in the boot of my car, while Nero spoke to the pilots and then we were ready. Amisi managed to curl herself into the back-seat and Nero rode shotgun. There was no point taking them into town, so I shot across to St. Helier's Bay and my new home away from home.

Luckily traffic was light, so it only took thirty minutes to get there and we talked all the way. Catching up on what had been happening in Cairo, where Amisi was at with her training and what Nero expected her to gain from being here with me. Basically, she was ready to hit the world, so minimal guidance was required, other than helping her get used to Kiwi ways.

When we made it home, the shutters were well and truly tucked up in bed and Erika was working out in the gym. I had a sneaky feeling I wasn't going to get rid of her now that she had stayed one night, but as far as room mates go, she wasn't too bad. Good taste in kitschy T.V. series aside.

I'd just shown Amisi to her room when the phone rang. Nero had been waiting in the lounge, so I used the phone in there, rather than go to the kitchen.

"*Ma douce*, your guest has arrived?"

Even his voice made me sigh. Despite everything that had happened, everything we had addressed - or not - last night, he still stole my breath with simple words. I leaned against the door jam and flicked a glance over my shoulder at Nero. He and Amisi had moved to the windows to take in the view.

"Yeah, she's just getting settled now."

"You will bring her to me, yes? I should like to meet your Amisi in person, I did not have time in Cairo to become acquainted."

We had left Cairo in a hurry, I was hurt and Michel had only been concerned for my wellbeing, so we hadn't stayed long after we had destroyed what was left of the *Cadre of Eternal Knights* and rescued Amisi.

"Sure. It won't be until later though, close to midnight."

I would have to drop Nero off at the airport first.

"Certainly, I will await most eagerly your company."

"Whatever will you do with yourself until then, Michel?" I couldn't help it, he was being so facetious. This was the old Michel back, the one I knew so well. It made me relax, lower that brick wall I had surrounded myself with. It allowed a little of the familiar back and banished that stiff atmosphere of earlier last night. It allowed us both to breathe.

He chuckled, the sound of it sending a shudder down my spine. I almost asked if he was using his powers on me, but he can't, not since we had been joined. I would have to lower my shields to let that happen and a quick internal scan of those particular walls showed me all were functioning at full strength. So, it was pure me, just my response to hearing him. I shook my head to clear the thought.

"It will be a long night, *ma belle*, I shall have to keep myself busy."

"You do that. I'll see you later."

There was silence on the other end of the line, as though he wanted to say something, but had thought better of it.

Finally a reply came in a soft voice. "Until later." The line went dead before I had pulled the handset away from my ear.

The thought was in my head before I could stop it and I'm not sure if I had projected it or not, it felt so powerful, it had a strength all of its own, I don't think I was in complete control.

I love you.

I cursed under my breath when I realised how stupid that had been and clamped my shields down tight around my thoughts again, bound them with chains and shoved a padlock on just to be sure. I was a friggin' yo-yo right now, one minute letting him back in, the next slamming the door in his face. Could I be any more screwed up than this?

When I turned back towards Amisi and Nero, he was watching me, a haunted look on his face. He quickly reschooled his features and came to the couch to sit down.

"Any progress with your shape shifter situation, Kiwi?"

Since Sunday night, I had been constantly thinking about when I would have to face the Taniwhas. The thought of an impending fight or battle hanging over my head had been terrible. I knew in my heart that there was no going back, that there was no way to make Rick see reason, not

225

now, not ever. But the idea that it may come down to a me versus him, life versus death situation, did not sit well. My stomach churned again, for the hundredth time and I realised that was why I had not been eating lately. The thought of food just made me want to vomit.

I shook my head at Nero. "I know it will happen soon, but I have no idea what I will do when it does."

"You are strong, Lucinda, you will get through this and do what needs to be done."

"You think I will have to fight him, don't you? Kill him?"

Nero sat forward on his seat and looked me in the eye. "You are the *Sanguis Vitam Cupitor*, your role in our world is far more important than your friendship with a shifter. Do not let sentimentality unsettle you when the moment comes. Your survival above all else is imperative. You must not forget this."

"So, I am more important than him." My voice was flat, unemotional, but inside I was screaming.

"Yes, but you are also not the one determined for this conflict. He seeks you, to kill you, I merely ask that you don't allow that to happen."

I laughed abruptly, a short huff of breath. "Self defence then?"

"Self defence, self preservation, your duty to Nut, all of the above. He has started this, not you, but if the only way for you to carry on being the *Sanguis Vitam Cupitor* is to end this once and for all, then do it. Do not hesitate when given the chance. End this and get on with what our goddess has chosen for you."

"Never show fear. Never give an inch. Always stay on

guard," I muttered.

"Precisely, Kiwi. Precisely."

Well shit, it's not like I hadn't known that was going to be the case, but actually saying the words aloud sure did sound final, didn't it?

Amisi chose to join the conversation at that point, probably thinking a change in topic would be well received by me. If that was the case, she and I were going to get along just fine.

"How far are we from the VC?" VC, is the term we give Vampire Central, the area where vampires congregate in a city for hunting purposes. As I have no doubt mentioned before, vampires tend to stay in the centre of a city, they like to be entrenched in humanity, not for the company mind you, but for the benefits of food choice. The city centre is densely populated, it's easy to find accommodating food, or just fast food if you're a Rogue.

I was just about to answer when I felt a sudden slamming against my shields in my mind. An attack was my immediate thought, it took my breath away and it may have even made me gasp out loud, I'm not sure, I was too busy hastily building yet more walls in my mind whilst trying to figure out who the attacker was. I'd never experienced anything like it before, it was frightening. Not just because it was unusual, but also because I knew whoever, or whatever it was, wanted to get at me.

The overriding sensation I got from the thing that was battering me was a need so strong, a desire so powerful, that it would do anything to get to me. I couldn't tell what it wanted when it did get to me, all I could feel was its urgent cry *to* get to me.

I realised Nero was kneeling on the floor in front of me, his hands on either side of my face, trying to get me to look at him, to talk to him, to even acknowledge him, but I was too busy fighting whatever the hell it was. It was strong and determined, like a dying man trying to get his last breath, the sense of desperation was astounding. This thing had to get to me. Now.

It must have taken only minutes, but it felt like hours, when I was sure my shields were holding enough for me to try to figure out who or where this thing was coming from. I decided to try the who first, so allowed my senses to flow out and *seek* it. I was surprised, although in retrospect I'm not sure why, that it was evil. It was very evil, like one of the evil vampires I can seek using my *Sanguis Vitam Cupitor* powers. In fact, I had no doubt sought this thing before. But, the surprise was how close he was, how determined he was to get to me and then something small fell into place, like a piece of a jigsaw puzzle. It had been there all along, but I'd overlooked it and now it was staring me in the face I couldn't see anything else.

The power that I recently received on the way back from Paris felt like a door opening in my mind and when it was wide open and hinged back, I could feel all the evil vampires throughout the world turning towards me and wanting to come to me. None of them had taken that first step, they had been too scared, too unsure of what they felt, but now, this vampire, this thing attacking me, was doing more than just watching and waiting He had taken that first step.

If I had been scared of the power before, now I was petrified. I knew, without even thinking about it, that this was the first of many to take that step. And once they started, would it be like dominoes? One tipping over the next and then the next and then the next, until they all landed on top of me.

I was panting by this stage, with fear and effort. I vaguely heard Erika come in the room, Amisi saying something in reply to her query, but all my concentration was now on determining where this creature was, because if he was as close as he felt, then I was going to be in trouble. Deep trouble.

I had to work hard on calming myself enough to sink further into the black nothingness, to let myself not only *seek* what he was but precisely where he was, but I got there in the end. Sweat staring to trickle down my temple, my fists bunched so tightly I could feel my nails digging into my palms. He was in Auckland, he was in the CBD and he knew the only way to get me to come out and play, was to call me using my pull.

As soon as he sensed my understanding of the situation, he ceased his attack and I felt like I had been released from a great height and had suddenly fallen back down to earth with a crash. I ached all over, I was trembling from head to foot, but I could breathe. And talk and focus on my surroundings again.

"Kiwi? What was that?"

My breath was still rapid and I had to swallow a couple of times before my dry throat would allow me to make any sounds.

"That new power, it just got a wake up call. One of those vampires watching me, has finally realised he doesn't need to wait."

Nero looked really strange, a little pale and quite confused. I understood, it sounded kooky to me too, but there was more to it than that. He was looking at me as though I had sprouted two heads. And he was shaking his back and forth at an alarmingly fast rate.

"It can't be. This is not right. Nothing has indicated that this would happen. It is not right." He was almost saying it under his breath, just to himself, but we could all hear it.

I glanced at Amisi and she was awash with concern, but when she noticed me looking at her she just shook her head and shrugged. She had no idea what he was talking about either.

Erika handed me a glass of water. I hadn't realised how thirsty I was until it was right in front of my nose. Man, she was taking this looking after the master's Nosferatin seriously, wasn't she? I just smiled weakly and downed the whole glass in one.

That felt a hell of a lot better. If every time one of those nasty vamps knocked on my metaphysical door and I reacted like this, then Nut help me. It was sudden, unexpected and I had absolutely no chance to prepare for it. Had I been driving or fighting at the time, I would have been toast. Shit. It didn't bear thinking about.

Finally, Nero seemed to have gotten himself back under control and he lifted his face to mine. The confusion from before was gone, now there was just resolve and as his hand came up to cup my chin. I also saw surprise and awe. He looked at all of me, my face, my neck, my arms, my body. His gaze travelling everywhere, intense and sure. I wasn't certain what the hell he was doing, where this was going, but I was starting to get a little uncomfortable under all the scrutiny. Erika had also started shifting uneasily at my side, having stepped closer, maybe within a foot now and looming over both me and Nero, who was still on his knees in front of me.

"Nero?" I asked, wanting to bring him back to reality before he did something really embarrassing in front of Amisi and Erika.

He laughed and brought his gaze back to my eyes. His own were a blaze of cooper and cinnamon, dancing before me in hypnotic waves.

"You are truly Nut's child, Kiwi." Well duh, I knew that, but what the hell?

"You are more. You are the *Prohibitum Bibere*."

Chapter 19
You Called?

"The what?" That was Erika, no longer shifting uneasily next to me, but standing stock still, glaring down at Nero.

Amisi had her hands up to her mouth and her beautiful chocolate brown eyes were big and wide.

Nero was just smiling.

"Yeah, the what?" I said for emphasis, as he hadn't bothered to answer Erika yet.

"The *Prohibitum Bibere* or the Forbidden Drink. I didn't think it was possible, none of the scrolls have indicated that one Nosferatin could be two of the Prophesy components, but here we are. Here you are and it's obvious," - he indicated the length of my body with a swish of his hand, - "your glow when you felt the vampire answer your call, it's obvious."

OK. It might have been obvious to Nero, but I was still at a loss.

My head was spinning, my body ached from the recent attack and nothing made sense at all. I had a million questions swirling around inside my skull, all of them tumbling over each other, none of them making any sense at all. I took a deep breath in and then another, then another and organised my thoughts. I was sure I had myself sorted, but when I opened my mouth it all came spilling out one after the other in a torrent of questions.

"How come you haven't been able to see this before? I've told you about this power. And what is the Forbidden Drink? And, by the way, how many parts to this Prophesy is there? Am I to expect some more Nosferatin juice in the near future? Am I going to get every god-damn bit of this Prophesy to myself? Is it *all* to be on my shoulders? Where's the support you spoke of, Nero? Where are the other Nosferatins who are meant to lend a hand?"

I had stood up and started pacing and wringing my hands at the same time, not a good combination. The electricity in the air had become tangible, I hadn't realised I was letting off such energy, but the room did seem an awful lot brighter than it had before. As though my Light was building inside me, the more agitated I got.

Nero stood and raised both hands in a placating manner. "Calm down, Kiwi. Nut has a plan."

Oh God. If he mentioned the goddess one more time I would scream. I was so sick of this crap. I had barely got my head around being a Nosferatin, having to join with a Nosferatu - hell the truth is, I haven't got my head around it at all, evidence of that is back in Wellington - when I was landed with the first key to the Prophesy, the *Sanguis Vitam Cupitor* or Blood Life Seeker. And now this? *Prohibitum Bibere*, bloody Forbidden Drink. What the fuck was that all about? How much more did Nut want to test me, how much more did Nut want to push me? Was she insane? I was only one girl, I couldn't do this.

I'd been counting on the other Nosferatins with Prophesy related powers to come forward and take up some of the slack, but now? Now I was getting a sinking feeling that there would be no other Nosferatin, that I would be it. That made me stop pacing and just stand there.

Holy shit. Crap. Crap. Crap. This was not happening.

"Kiwi?"

I looked over at where Nero was still standing, still

233

holding his hands out in front as though trying to calm a jumper down off the balcony railing. Not a bad analogy, I really did feel like I was about to fall a long, long way, but it wasn't intentional. I sure as hell did not want to jump. Loss of friggin' control.

"First of all, how many Prophesy components are there?" My voice was even, well controlled.

"Three. The *Sanguis Vitam Cupitor*, the *Prohibitum Bibere* and the *Lux Lucis Tribuo* or the Giver of Light."

I sank to my knees on the floor and just stared at him. He smiled ruefully and came over to kneel down in front of me.

"We can assume you will be all three. You have already more Light in you than any other Nosferatin I have ever met. Plus you can do things with Light I have never heard nor read of before. I had just assumed it was part of who you were; your strength of power, the combination of you and Michel joined. But it would be foolish to think it is not related to the Prophesy now." He took a long deep breath in and I just thought, don't say it, please don't say it. "You are the Prophesied, Kiwi. *The Light will capture the Dark and will hold it dear.*"

I felt numb, totally removed from the situation. This was surreal, not happening, not to me. Farm girl, turned business banker, come vampire hunter. And now the Prophesied.

I ran a hand over my face hoping to wipe away some of the fog that had descended. So many thoughts running through my mind. I rifled through them, trying to get some order, trying to make sense of the chaos inside. Michel, I needed Michel. It was the one thought that kept repeating

234

in my mind. I wasn't surprised. I was about to have a little conniption, my Bond was calling for Michel to calm me down. But, I had made my choice to battle this without him by my side. I would be strong.

I would be strong.

I was taking deep breaths in and not even realising it, almost hyperventilating. Nero had stood again and looked like he wanted to reach out to me, but I just raised my hands to ward him off. I couldn't bear anyone touching me right now, I couldn't stand the distraction. I needed to think this through. There had to be a reasonable explanation, a loophole in the contract, we'd made a mistake. Why would Nut put all of her eggs in one basket? It just didn't make sense.

Start at the beginning, or near enough. "What does the *Prohibitum Bibere* do?"

Nero relaxed a little, this was familiar ground for him, he knew the Prophesy through and through and although it had thrown him tonight, defining the titles was old news, easy to do.

"The *Prohibitum Bibere* is another name for a Siren."

I raised my eyebrows at him, you're shitting me?

He just smiled, his Nero-light-up-the-world smile. "In this case, Kiwi, you are not luring the sailors onto rocks, you are luring vampires to the Light. That is why you are called the Forbidden Drink. To drink of your Light would be to allow the Dark to fail, therefore you are forbidden to them, by the Dark itself."

I let another long breath out. "You've talked about the Dark as though it is a sentient being before, just who is the Dark, Nero?"

235

"We do not know for sure, there are no records of where the Nosferatu has come from. We, of course, are Children of Nut, we know our heritage. We are born of the Lord of the Light. But, is it not feasible that the Nosferatu are born of a Lord of the Dark? And if so, who is their God? Who directs their lives as Nut directs ours?"

"OK. How come you didn't see this before? I told you about this power and you just clammed up. Why?" I wasn't being demanding, or trying to rub it in, I just needed to understand. Really.

Nero looked a little sad. "It's not that I didn't believe you, Kiwi, I just couldn't make that leap of faith. Everything and I mean *everything* I have read, indicated three Prophesied, not one. I did not want to believe it. I did not want you to bear this burden alone. But, seeing is believing, so they say and having witnessed you receiving a caller, a vampire seeking the Drink, I cannot fail to see that this is so. I am sorry, if I have disappointed you."

I wanted to tell him it was OK, he was just trying to protect me, but dammit, he is my Herald, he recognises the keys and starts the Prophesy in motion. It was his job to recognise this and he had chosen not to. I did feel a little let down.

But, what difference would it have made? More time to digest it maybe?

"So, what do I do with this? I am what I am, I guess, what now?"

Nero didn't say anything for a moment, he just stood there watching me, as if he had expected me to forgive him and now that I hadn't, he didn't quite know how to go on.

He cleared his throat slightly. "You can seek the evil,

tell where they are, how much evil resides in each one. You can also call them to you, although they need to take the step that brings them closer. And, if we are correct in our assumption, you can give them Light. You can banish the Dark and flood them with Light."

Sounds easy, doesn't it? But, I know what my Light is capable of. Sure, it can make you have a fantastically orgasmic experience, or it can kill. I'm not sure if there is a spot in-between. I'm not sure that I have the ability to control it like that. So what? I kill all those vampires coming towards me? *Or,* I flush them with my desire and lust. Stuff that, I'm not that free living.

And that brings us back to kill, then, doesn't it? I am a vampire hunter, killing the bad creatures of the night is what I do, but I've met a lot more vampires since I started down this road. I've befriended a lot more vampires and not all of them are Dark or evil, or deserve to die. And even those I have met who seemed so very evil, have turned out to be OK. Gregor, when I first met him was reeking evil, but now? Not so much. So, do I kill them straight up, because they are evil and that is all I have ever killed? Or do I try to find a way to bring them more Light, to allow them the choice to live?

I kind of liked the idea of allowing them a choice. No loss of control. Not like me.

So, that would be my plan, my big modus operandi. I could even start my own mantra with that one: Bring them more Light. Let them choose Life.

Or maybe I could flog one: *I am the Light to the Dark. You call to me as I call to you. I will always hold you dear.* Another Nosferatin saying, specifically relating to the

Prophesy.

Well I'll be buggered. Nut had been telling me all along what I was. But now that I knew, how did I carry out my goal? My Light can kill or it can pleasure, I had to find a way to the middle ground between those two. I had to learn to control my Light.

"Well, this has been very educational, hasn't it? I need to process this, but in the meantime we've got a vampire wanting a drink from the fountain of Light and for some reason he doesn't want to come to me here at St. Helier's. So, I'm going to have to go to him in the CBD. He hasn't done anything yet, but the impression I got, was if I didn't get there soon he would, just to tick me off."

I stood up and dusted my uniform down. I hadn't had a chance to change and I thought I could just quickly slip into some hunter gear now and then we'd all head into the city. I was about to voice that as I headed towards the door and my bedroom, when I felt it. We all did. Well, everyone except Erika. The evil-lurks-in-my-city pull called to me, it called to Amisi and it called to Nero. We all stopped what we were doing and just stared at each other.

"I guess he's got tired of waiting," I said into the silence and reached over to the couch to pick up my hunting jacket, already laden with stakes and a knife. I slipped it on over my uniform, watched as both Amisi and Nero checked their own gear and then led the way back out to the car.

"You coming, Erika?" I called over my shoulder.

"Oh, I wouldn't miss this for the world, *chica*," she said fingering her Svante sword in its sheath at the back of her neck.

The trip in was quick, traffic was light, maybe coincidence, maybe a higher power at work making our job that much smoother. But the road was clear and there were no cop cars to be seen. The BMW made it into town in less than ten minutes. A definite record from St. Helier's Bay. I wasn't complaining, the more time it took, the stronger the pull. Nero and Amisi were quiet, riding the sensation, biting their lips, wanting above all else to be near that vampire before he struck.

I knew exactly where he was: Fort Street, at the bottom of the main CBD thoroughfare, Queen Street. A popular location for massage parlours and all sorts of nefarious deeds. The vampire had chosen well. It was easy to get to him, park the car and be on foot, without further delay.

I don't usually think of a plan of attack when about to face evil vampires fanging an innocent. My Nosferatin hunter skills just take over. But, there was three of us tonight, so not wanting to waste the numbers, I directed Nero and Amisi to come in from the other end of the road, Queen Street side. And Erika and I came at him from Customs Street. We had him cornered, bar a couple of minor side streets, but I got the distinct impression that this one wouldn't run, he wanted me there, he was waiting, eagerly.

Bizarre did not cover the sensation at all.

Erika and I slowed down our approach, she had her Svante sword out, I had my stake. Anyone watching from the shadows would have copped an eye full, we weren't trying to hide ourselves or our weapons and the energy in the area was off the scale, making us both jumpy and unable to hide it. This vampire was evil, but there was something more.

I tried to calm myself to sense the area. I managed to determine we were alone, he was on his own, no other Nosferatu nearby, but he was sending confusing signals. *Sanguis Vitam* fluctuations and a buzzing that just didn't sound right. Vampires always buzz to me, or hum, it's just a sound in the background you get used to. The bad ones have a more annoying noise, the OK or good ones, a kind of musical accompaniment, kinda nice, but this chap, he sounded like an orchestra tuning up in the pit at the Aotea Theatre. It was all wrong and yet in amongst the strings, woodwinds, brass and percussion, there was the odd note of beauty, a straining chord trying to break free. The potential for wonder existed, but it was drowning in the cacophony of clashing noises, unable to be heard clearly, washed away and lost forever.

I paused, trying to catch that note again, that beautiful sound, but the rushing noise of opposing notes just kept hammering away. It almost made me cry, I wanted that note, I wanted it badly.

While I was standing there trying to sort out the noises, the vampire slowly stepped out of the shadows, a human woman, dressed for the nocturnal pursuits of Fort Street's finest, hanging from his arm. She wasn't struggling, she was clearly unmoving. I ran my eyes over her neck and body, trying to see bite marks, but nothing obvious stood out. Her breasts were heaving under the restriction of her hot pink bra and black fishnet top - so, unconscious it definitely was, not dead.

The vampire just looked at me. Erika had taken up a stance behind me and farther back, almost in the shadows

240

herself. She knew this was my game, she was here to watch my back, to keep me safe, not to interfere. I was really liking how Erika operated. She did not tend to crowd, not when I was hunting anyway.

It was a male, about 300 years old, not a baby, a level four master at least, but he looked about twenty, so young, so untouched, an almost baby-like face framed with wispy light brown hair down past his shoulders. He was dressed well, clean jeans and an un-tucked dress shirt in black. Simple for a vampire, but not Rogue, he belonged to someone, so why was he here?

"You called?" I always seem to be the one to start the dialogue, the vampires do either one of two things. They attack as soon as they see me or they stand there and just watch. Either one is perturbing, but for very different reasons.

"You seem smaller than I thought you would be." He was American, his strong southern accent appealing, almost a drawl. I flicked a glance at Erika over my shoulder. She shook her head. She didn't know him. I guess it's kind of a huge assumption to think she'd know every American vampire that exists.

"Why are you here?" I might as well cut to the chase.

"I couldn't stay away. I tried, but I wanted to see you. I had to see you." He seemed pained, I'm not sure if it was because he couldn't stop himself coming to see me, or because he had been dying to see me for so long it hurt.

"Well, here I am. Now what?" He wasn't exactly doing anything to the human. I don't think he had bitten her, just glazed her asleep, so pouncing on him with my stake didn't seem right somehow.

241

His hand came up towards me, he was still over two metres away, so he couldn't reach me, but he was obviously thinking about it. I didn't move. Never show fear. That's me. A vampire craning his hand out to touch, with a look of such longing on his face, but reeking evil, just doesn't make you feel safe, but you never show fear. Rule number one.

"What is it you want from me?" I just wasn't getting any of this. None of it made sense.

"I...I don't know." He looked down at the woman under his arm, blinked slowly, as if it was the first time he realised she was there, but didn't drop her, just stood there, shaking his head.

Well, this was awkward, what now?

"Did you intend to feed on her?"

"Yes. No. I suppose so."

I blew a breath of air out. "You don't seem convinced."

"I would normally feed off her, right?"

He's asking me? How the hell should I know? This was crazy stuff right here. Weird. Bizarre. Surreal.

"Why don't you put her down and we'll just talk."

He looked back up at me and for a moment, I really thought he'd do it. That he wanted direction, he wanted to be told what to do, that he was so confused, but so in need of whatever it is he thought I would give him, that he would just put the human down and talk.

But, that's when Nero and Amisi turned up, having made it down the block to Queen Street and back up Fort to us. I understood they wanted to help. I knew they had been concerned that I had approached the vampire alone, not that it isn't something I do on a regular basis, but they had just seen me have a mini breakdown because of a metaphysical

242

attack from this vamp, so they were on high alert.

Unfortunately, they came at a run, no quiet approach, no stealthy assessment of the scene. They just ran towards us, stakes out, eyes flashing, ready to jump into the fray.

But there had been no fray, just talk, however the moment the vampire sensed them he stiffened, flashed angry red eyes at me and bit the woman before I could even get a breath in to scream.

Shit!

Chapter 20
Revelations

It was actually Nero who staked him. I was still too shocked and angry to move, and anyway, Nero is fast. He didn't hesitate, he just spun out towards the vamp, pulled the woman from his arms and placed the stake above his heart, following it through with a small grunt of effort.

Done and dusted in under two seconds flat.

Amisi went to the woman to staunch the flow of blood at her neck and Nero offered direction. I just watched.

"Are you all right, *chica?*" Erika's voice was soft at my side.

"He was going to put her down. He didn't deserve to die."

"You don't know that and he did bite her."

"Why are you defending them? They just killed one of your kind."

"He broke the rules, even I obey them, Lucinda. He bit an unwilling donor. He wasn't just biting to feed either, he wanted to drain, he was lashing out. That is not good for business."

Everything she said made sense, but I still felt hollow. I still felt like I had let the vampire down. Death is not always the answer. It can't be the only answer. It just can't. I couldn't stand myself if it was. I am not the grim reaper, I am not God, I have a part to play and no more. This could have been avoided, but it wasn't.

I slowly raised my eyes from the dust mark on the ground and found Nero staring at me. I quickly looked away. I couldn't meet his gaze, I couldn't face him right now. My mentor, the one Nosferatin I believed was above all others and I... hated him right now. I really despised his speed and efficiency, his utter conviction to the cause. His inability to think outside the square. Damn him for for being what he was. Damn me for not being able to accept it.

A car's headlights flashed down the street and we all jumped to the shadows, ensuring the woman was hidden while she came around.

"It's all right," Erika said, stepping back out into the headlight's beam. "It's one of ours."

I recognised the vehicle then, one of Michel's Land Rover Discoveries, all sleek black and tinted windows. Shane Smith was at the wheel. His shock of blonde curly hair standing out against the dark of the night. The car came to a stop beside us and he stepped out.

"Luce." He nodded at me and smiled his shy smile.

"Are you here for the woman?" I had no idea why he'd turn up otherwise.

He shook his head and looked at Nero. "For him. I'm his ride to the Airport. Michel wants to see you. Now."

It had been a long time since Michel had summoned me like this. Well, really, the last time was before I even knew what I was and Michel had just been the Master of the City, something to be scared of, but stand up to. I bristled at the return to master and servant status I had fought so hard to break from before.

No one said anything for a while. I guess they were waiting for me, but I really didn't want to speak to Nero right now, let alone drive him all the way back to Manukau and the plane. So, Shane's offer seemed to sound OK actually.

"You better go with him," I said, not really making eye contact, but kind of turning Nero's way.

He stepped toward me. "Kiwi?"

I sucked it up and looked him in the eyes. Despite my feelings right now, he deserved at least that.

"Just go, Nero. Michel doesn't like to be left waiting."

"What have I done to offend you? Please tell me so I can make amends."

I just looked at him for a moment, as though I was seeing him for the very first time. He was still Nero; handsome, regal, omnipresent, very easy on the eyes, but now I felt like I didn't know him at all. Like so much of my life right now, he was just another piece controlling me, but out of my control. I was his *Sanguis Vitam Cupitor*, his *Prohibitum Bibere* and his *Lux Lucis Tribuo*. I was no longer Lucinda Monk to him, I was more.

I didn't want to be more. I wanted to be me and right now Nero represented the loss of me.

"Please, Nero, just go."

I might as well have hit him in the stomach, the look of pain and disbelief was so pure. I felt a little bad then. How many people would I take down with my anger and pain at being controlled? But, I took a shaky breath in and held it, forcing myself to strengthen under his gaze, to stand up for what I believed was right. Never show fear. Never give an inch. Always stay on guard.

I just hadn't thought I'd use that mantra against Nero.

Nero's path in this war was different from mine and I couldn't afford to let it sway me. I couldn't afford to become like him. I always thought Nero was so full of Light, but right now, I couldn't see it. I couldn't see the

Dark either, but just because I was temporarily blind to it, didn't mean it wasn't still there.

We stood looking at each other for another minute, then I turned my back to him and started walking toward my car.

"Can you take care of the human?" I asked Erika briefly as I passed her. She nodded and walked to where the woman lay.

"Come on, Amisi. Time to meet the Master of Auckland City," I said loudly over my shoulder, not stopping my progress away from the scene.

I made it to the car before her, of course, she didn't show for another few minutes. No doubt saying goodbye to Nero, I didn't mind. I switched the stereo on and listened to *Fergie*, she was still in the CD player. This time I went for *Losing My Ground*.

When Amisi slid into the passenger seat I could tell she was angry, but I ignored it as I pulled the vehicle out into the main flow of traffic. The song finished part way up Queen Street, so I switched the stereo off and listened to the strained silence between us. I've never had a problem with silence, but Amisi needed to calm down before she met Michel. Meeting the Master of a City when you're in a foul mood was not a good move. So before I reached K Road, I pulled over and switched the engine off.

"I know you think I was harsh on him back there and you're probably right, but it was either that or lose it altogether. We can't afford to be distracted like that Amisi. We can't let emotions get in the way of why we are here. He means a lot to you, I know that, he does to me too, but that does not mean he is always right." I sighed and turned to face her, sitting sideways in my seat. She had her head down and hands clasped in her lap, her face was set in a grim frown, eyebrows down, forehead furrowed. She still looked beautiful.

I watched her for a moment, trying to think of what else I could say to make her see why I behaved the way I did. To make her at least understand, if not agree, but enable her to lose some of this anger before she met Michel.

"He loves you, you know." She surprised me with that. I hadn't seen it coming, maybe a scolding of some sort, but not soft words of love.

"I know he cares, I do too."

"No. He's *in love* with you." She looked at me now and I could see unshed tears in the corner of her eyes.

"I don't think..." I paused and reconsidered what I was about to say. "He loves me like a sister, Amisi. He's just that sort of guy."

She smiled sadly at me, as though I had lost a precious treasure and didn't even know it.

"I asked him out once, or at least from where I come from, I asked him if he'd court me. It's not normal for women to do that in Egypt, but I'm a bit forward for my time."

I wasn't sure I wanted to hear any more of this confession, but it was like watching a train wreck happen before your eyes. You're horrified at what might eventuate, but you can't seem to shift your gaze.

"Needless to say," she went on, "he turned me down, gently, nicely, but it still hurt. I demanded to know why. Was it my age? Was it something I had done? He refused to

248

elaborate further, just told me it was inappropriate."

That made sense, he was her teacher, but from the look on Amisi's face, I was gathering she didn't see it that way.

"Eventually, I figured it out. By watching him." She laughed a little mirthlessly then. "I practically stalked him. But, when I understood it, I confronted him. He didn't deny it. He just said it was irrelevant, it was his burden to bear."

I didn't want to ask, I didn't want to know really, but my mouth had other ideas. "What was irrelevant?" My voice was quiet in the space between us.

"The fact that he loves you."

I sat there numbed by what she said. At first, my immediate reaction was to say no. That's untrue. But, then I thought back over all the things he'd said to me in the past, all the actions he'd made. The moments he'd stopped himself midway between reaching for me and touching me, the look on his face when he realised he couldn't complete the movement. It all came flooding in and fell into place. I was stunned.

"He wouldn't have wanted you to know this," she said, still softly. "He would be mortified that I have betrayed his trust. But, you needed to know why he acted so forcefully tonight, Lucinda. He wanted to protect you, to take the decision to stake that vampire out of your hands. To give you one less thing to beat yourself up over. He had no way of knowing, you'd just go right ahead and do it any way."

Well shit. Damn.

I felt like I had to say it, I don't know why, maybe the fact that I have such a bad track record with men in my life right now. I wanted to get this out in the open, no misunderstanding, no treading the wrong path by mistake.

Again.

"I don't feel the same way about him, Amisi. He knows that, right?"

She shot me a hard look. "Yeah, Lucinda. He knows." And turned back towards the front window of the car.

So much for calming her down before meeting Michel.

I sat still for a moment longer, then thought to hell with this, it was not my problem. Nero had chosen this path, not me. And right now, I was tapped out on the problem solving front. I started the car and headed towards *Sensations*.

The club was in full swing. Being a Tuesday, that was a little unusual, but then I realised what was happening. No Norms, all vampires and their invited guests, aka dinner or entertainment. I'd inadvertently walked in on one of these functions before, it hadn't been fun. Vampires get very territorial when in a group like this, if they lay claim to a human for whatever reason, they do not like to share, or be told to take their fangs out. So, I flicked a glance at Amisi, registering her tense demeanour and said, "Stick close, all right?" I was relieved she nodded and didn't make a snarky comment, she was all professional Nosferatin, ready for action and primed for defence. She moved closer to me and kept in step at my heel.

Good girl. Despite our recent argument, if you can call it that, she knew how to switch off the emotions and play the game right. Like I've said before, she was going to make a formidable mature Nosferatin in time.

I hadn't gone straight to Michel's office when we came up from the garage, but entered the club proper, thinking he would be there. But a quick scan of my senses let me know he was out back, so I headed over to the door marked Private that led to his quarters. No one stopped us, all too busy having a good time, so I breathed a sigh of relief when the door closed behind us and turned to Amisi.

"You ready?" I asked. She may have seen Michel before, may know all about him from Nero and Nafrini and may be here staying as my guest, but meeting the master is a big thing.

She nodded, looking a little pale. I squeezed her arm lightly, she managed a half smile and we pushed on towards Michel's office.

His door was open, so I didn't knock, just walked in like I had done a million times before. He was in front of me in an instant. Amisi took a step back and lowered her face to the ground, avoiding eye contact and giving us space.

"Are you all right?" Michel looked stiff and unsure, he reached out a hand and hesitated before touching me, then obviously thought what the hell and just did it any way, stroking up my arms and cupping my face. His thumb brushing against my cheek and jaw.

I frowned at him and pulled back slightly, but he just followed me. Not breaking contact and let a low growl out between his lips.

"What's going on, Michel?" He was acting all weird, possessive to the extreme. If I didn't know any better I'd think he was wanting to mark his territory. He was acting like a threatened mate.

He looked me over, from head to foot, his *Sanguis Vitam* brushing my shields, but I held them firm. He blinked slowly and took an unsteady step back, getting

251

himself back under control. Putting some space between us again.

I was still puzzled, but now he was standing back from me I could get a decent look at him - and man he looked good tonight. He wasn't in his usual attire, but strangely jeans and a T-Shirt. The jeans hugged every curve of his legs and hips. God I couldn't stop looking at him. His T-Shirt was black and snug, showing off his broad chest and muscled arms, his dark brown, almost black, hair was loose around his shoulders and he smelled divine. Oh dear God, I had to force myself not to go to him.

He smiled slowly at me, picking up on my emotions, noticing the way my eyes lingered over his body. He reached out and stroked my face, brushing a strand of hair behind my ear. Then he simply turned away and went and sat behind his desk. I was left breathless and unhinged by the exchange, unable to get a clear thought through my head.

Oh good grief, despite everything - or in spite of it - this man could upset me.

"So, *ma douce*, are you going to introduce me to your friend?"

I shook myself out of the stupor I was in and turned to Amisi, she still had her head respectfully down, not making eye contact, pretending she hadn't been here during Michel and my little exchange. It must be something Egyptian, or maybe just Nosferatin and I had never had that training before.

"Michel, this is Amisi Minyawi. Amisi the Master of Auckland City, Michel Durand."

Amisi raised her eyes to Michel's then and bowed low,

fisted hand across her chest, just like the vampires do. A formal show of respect.

"Greetings from Nafrini Al-Suyuti, Master of Cairo City. She sends her thanks to you, Master, for your hospitality to one of her kind, as do I." She rose then and smiled at him, the most mesmerising flash of deep chocolate brown eyes. I glanced at him and caught his reaction: stunned. For a moment no one else existed in that room but them and I couldn't help the feeling of jealousy that crept into my heart. I stomped on it, I booted it out, but I still felt the echo that it had left behind.

It also dawned on me, how out of touch I was with protocol. I am a Nosferatin and for all intents and purposes, a very powerful one, but I was not raised by Nosferatin parents. I missed out on all the upbringing that Amisi has had. She knew how to act around a Master of a City. Whereas I had practically made a spectacle of myself when I met Nafrini, simply offering her my hand to shake and a simple *Hi, how are ya* kind of greeting. I cringed at the memory and once again pined for my father.

What type of Nosferatin would I have been if he had raised me as he was meant to?

Michel pulled himself together fairly quickly, returning his face to its usual blank mask.

"You are welcome in my city, Nosferatin. It brings me pleasure to greet one of Nafrini's kind."

Amisi seemed to relax at that, so perhaps the formalities were all over. Michel returned his gaze to me. I wondered then if he was disappointed in his choice of joined Nosferatin, he could have chosen one as well educated in the ways of the Nosferatu as Amisi. She has

253

been raised around them, Nafrini had a large line, who all live cooperatively with Nero's Nosferatin community. I have never heard of another like it, so compatible, so cohesive. Nothing would surprise Amisi, she'd been surrounded by vampire habits since birth. She would have made a much better match for Michel.

Just then, there was a soft knock on the door and Erika walked in.

"All sorted," she said to me, referring to the woman. I trusted that she had got the human home and nothing untoward would have happened. Erika just gave me that sense of confidence. She liked the rules, she lived by them, even if she liked to upset them from time to time.

"Excellent timing Erika," Michel said, but somehow I doubted it was a coincidence. His eyes hadn't left me the entire time he spoke. "If you wouldn't mind entertaining our visiting Nosferatin for a while, I have business with my kindred to attend."

She nodded in agreement and flashed a fanged smile at Amisi. Amisi just laughed, which only made Erika smile more.

"Come on, Hunter, let me show you my swords."

They trotted out of the room with me looking after them and then the door shut softly behind their backs.

When I turned back to face Michel, he was once again before me and this time he didn't hesitate to take me in his arms.

I felt one of his hands go around my body, pulling me against his chest, while the other ran up my back and into my hair and then his face come towards my neck and without even pausing, his fangs entered above his mark.

You are mine, was all I heard in my head as his beautiful scent filled my nose and desire shot through to my bones.

Chapter 21
You Are Mine

I felt my back hit the closed door behind us, as his lips worked the flesh at my neck, his throat swallowing convulsively as my blood poured into him. The hand in my hair kept me still, the other starting to work its way up my body, pausing at my breast. He shifted his weight slightly, so one of his thighs was between my legs and his hand could better cup my breast. And then he started rubbing against me, enough to make me gasp and then my own desire started to compete with his and I found myself wrapping a leg around him and pulling him closer.

The past few days had been Hell on Earth. So many mistakes. So much Dark. So much hurt and anger and pain. Yet no matter what, whether we had come to a fragile understanding of each other's motives or not, as soon as this man laid a hand on me, I was lost. Lost to him, lost to my utter longing to be close to him. Lost to all reasonable thought, banishing doubts, hiding away questions and just embracing the connection we shared. I wanted to cling to my anger. I wanted to keep some distance, some semblance of control over my life. But as his hands caressed me and his scent engulfed me I realised, none of it mattered. None of it mattered at all. If I continued on this path of doubting his motives, of not allowing him back in, I would die a slow death, suffocating on the loss of him. I needed Michel like I needed air to breathe.

"Michel," I whispered his name like I had only just realised who he was. He just growled and held me tighter, his lips so hot against my skin, his hand so sure under my jacket at my breast. I allowed myself to sink into the moment, no thought of right or wrong, no attempt to keep my distance, not a single Prophesy problem entering my head. Not a single thought of control or manipulation or stupid Dark-induced mistakes.

Just me and him. My kindred Nosferatu and the feel of his hard body against mine, my blood flowing to his. I felt the weight of the world leave my shoulders, I felt light and free. And complete. I melted into him and he responded, lifting my body up off the ground, forcing my skirt, which was longer than I usually wear, up around my hips, until I could get both my legs around him and feel his hard erection at my centre, straining against his jeans. The gentle rocking of his hips sending me into overdrive, making me want him so badly, making my body move in a rhythm against his.

He swung us around and headed for the desk, reaching out and wiping whatever had been on it off to the floor, then gently placing me on my back on top of it. His hand came up between my legs, removing my underwear in a simple flick. I have no idea how he manages that move, I seem to be too distracted at the time to comprehend. Then his jeans and boxers were removed, out of the way and he entered me in a rush. There was no slow building penetration, this was all about possession. He had marked me at my neck with his bite, which he was still feeding from I realised and now he was marking me inside.

His rhythm was urgent in a way I hadn't experienced from him before, but despite the fast pace and sudden invasion, I couldn't seem to stop myself from responding. I kept begging for more, for faster, for deeper and harder. And he kept giving it to me, equally as frantic as I was to be together, to be as close as we could get, to not let anything stand between us anymore.

I don't know how long it had been since he bit me, I had lost all sense of time, but as we both came together in a fantastic burst of release, he was still feeding and I hadn't even realised I had gathered my Light and sent it flooding through him. The sensation of his mouth on my neck, his fangs in my flesh and my blood being sucked out of my body, while my Light flooded through us and around and over us, was so intense, so personal, so intimate. I felt tears rolling down my cheeks as we continued to ride wave after wave of orgasms that washed past us, clinging to each other, unable to let go.

Finally, after an eternity of bliss, he retracted his fangs and licked my neck to stop the flow of blood. I could smell him all around me, his fresh clean scent, salty sea spray and newly cut grass, mixed in with the smells of sex and sweat and something else I couldn't quite place, but it was everywhere. All over me, all over him, all around us.

He pulled his face back from my neck and looked at me, his hand brushing my hair aside, stroking my chin. His eyes dancing an indigo, amethyst and magenta maelstrom of colours before me, his lips still red from my blood. He licked them slowly and I couldn't stop myself lifting my head to kiss them, his hand coming behind my neck to help raise me, his tongue stroking across my mouth when we met. I could taste the blood, slightly metallic and I heard myself groan. I don't know why, it's blood and I do *not* drink blood at all, but the erotic sensation of my blood on his lips just did it for me and I shuddered against him at the images it created in my mind. These images were wanted, invited. I welcomed them in.

He sighed as he lowered me again to the desk.

"Please forgive me, *ma douce*. I had not meant to act... so... possessively. I heard your thoughts of Nero and I couldn't stop myself, I needed to make you mine." On top of everything else that happened over the past few days, this I could understand.

I blew a breath out and suddenly became very aware of where we were. His body against mine, both of us still half dressed, but naked where we met at our core, he was still inside me, so close, so intimate. He sensed my slight stiffening, but didn't move away, just shifted slightly, making me feel him harden inside me again. Making me feel my own heat begin to rise.

"Michel." I was going to say get off me, pull out, stop, but he just bent down and kissed me with a fierceness that took my breath away, his tongue entering my mouth in a rush, his lips pressed firmly against me, his hips starting to rotate, to grind against me. Oh dear God, I couldn't say no and he knew it.

As he gently thrust against me, he hardened, lengthening and thickening inside, he whispered against my lips, "I have tried to give you space, I am trying, I really am, but I cannot bear the thought of losing you. It scares me, I have come so close to losing you already, I cannot survive it again. Oh God, Lucinda!" His hips were becoming more forceful, his breath more ragged with each word. I was mesmerised by his movements, trapped by his words, I could no further pull away than throw him across the room. My own body responding to his call and moving beneath him, meeting him midway, my back arching off the

259

desk as he entered me again and again and again. "You are mine. I will no longer share you and to hell with your need for independence. On this you cannot argue. You. Are. Mine."

Each of the the last three words were punctuated with a thrust of his hips making his hard length enter me as far as he could reach, shoving me back against the desk. Each movement a punctuation mark, an exclamation mark. The smell of him surrounding me, encasing me, caressing me.

"Say it," he breathed against me.

"No," I managed to reply, but he just moved his hips in a circle making me lose my breath and whimper beneath him.

"Say it." Still whispered, still accompanied by the most erotic swirl of his hips.

"You can't make me."

He laughed, a chuckle against me, his body moving with the rumble of his chest making me clench tight around his length and my eyes close of their own accord.

"I will have you say it." This time his voice was low, almost a growl, but I was losing ground. Not only because of what his body was doing to me - the damn man had no shame - but also because my body, my mind, my heart craved it. I couldn't deny it, even though I knew I had to. I'd made such ground in separating from him, in gaining some distance to do what it is I will have to do. To admit I was his now would be the end of me.

I knew I couldn't hold out much longer, so I did the only thing I could think of to distract him, to stall for time, I kissed him. And I kissed him with as much of me as I possibly could, letting him know what I was capable of, who I was; not showing fear, not giving an inch, but always staying on guard. He groaned against me and couldn't pull out of the kiss. I had him trapped, as he had me and I felt my inner monologue - that had remained suspiciously quiet throughout all of this - stretch and purr, like a satisfied cat, then settle again as the kiss deepened. And then his rhythm faltered and my body responded to his urgent demand and we both crested the wave again, for a second time, together. Panting against each other as he let his full weight fall on top of me, pinning me like a heavy blanket, wrapping me in all of him.

"You are impossible, *ma douce*. You know you are mine. I know this, you know this, you *will* acknowledge it one day."

I didn't disagree with him, I just didn't say a word, suddenly exhausted and replete and so very proud of myself for not giving in. But a small voice in the back of my head just whispered, *and he is yours too.*

I pushed that aside. I didn't need the complication. I had stood against him and held my own, for now that was enough. The sex aside, I could accept this as a victory.

He slowly lifted off me, but not without stroking my face, kissing my cheek, running his hand down my side. He wasn't pulling away, he was making that quite clear. I got the impression that casual touching was over for him, he was going to continue to claim me at every turn. I sent a silent prayer to Nut that I would survive the attention, even knowing I'd be unable to walk away from it, but praying I could still remain me. That I wouldn't crumble under the euphoria he created and let him all the way back in. I couldn't function like that, I couldn't let him have that kind of control.

He stood and covered himself with his clothes, tucking his T-Shirt back into his jeans. I managed to smooth my skirt back down and straighten my top and jacket, but when I went to stand, the world went black and I tilted sideways.

"*Merde,*" I heard Michel mutter as he lifted me in his arms and carried me to a couch in the corner of the room, lying me flat on my back and kneeling down next to me.

I blinked a few times to get the world to stop spinning and make the fuzzies disappear, but to no avail.

"I have someone bringing you something to drink, *ma douce*. I took more blood than I should have." He didn't sound particularly happy with himself right now, but then he shouldn't, should he?

"You've never done that before." My voice sounded a little far away, almost down the end of a tunnel. Whoa, the room seemed weird right now. I was actually seeing two of him.

"I am sorry, *ma belle*. I seem to forget how much of me is vampyre. The need to mark you, to claim you, overcame all reason."

I thought that might have been my line. I seem to forget how much a vampire he is too. Which made what he had just done and what he had been doing over the past few days, weeks even, make so much more sense. I didn't really want it to make sense, but a part of me just sighed. Maybe it was time to let it make sense. To not give in, mind you, *never give an inch*, but to accept. To move on. I think I had reached that point where I could just manage that. I think he had reached it too.

Just then he stood up quickly and went to the door,

returning a second later with a glass of what looked like *Coke*.

"Drink this, it is full of sugar." He helped me sit up slightly, with his hand behind my back as I sipped the drink. I detested the taste, I'm a *Diet Coke* kind of girl all the way. He made me drink all of it though, before letting me lie back down on the couch.

I must have closed my eyes for a while, because when I opened them, Michel was sitting on the floor next to me, legs stretched out in front, arm resting on the couch seat cushion beside my body, his eyes on my face. He looked gorgeous. I frowned at that.

"What is it, *ma douce*?"

"You have no right being so damn gorgeous." I could only put it down to my lack of blood that made me say that out loud.

He smiled, which made him seem even more edible and started stroking my neck, above his mark, with his fingers.

"Did you mark me *again*?" I asked, watching his eyes follow the movement of his index finger over his mark.

He chuckled, that delightful sound I couldn't seem to get enough of. "I did try, you wouldn't let me though."

Ha. Score for me.

"Just how many times do you want to mark me, Michel?"

"As many as it takes to get your attention, *ma douce*."

I let that statement settle between us without comment.

"You know, you could have done better for yourself than me." I couldn't help remembering the look on his face when his eyes met Amisi, or the way she had carried

263

herself in front of him. Jealous, me? Nah.

"You were made for me, as I was for you," he replied simply. "There can be no one else, you just need to accept that idea and then all these distractions you seem to entertain will disappear." He said it with a twinkle in his eye, but I knew he was serious. The distractions he spoke of were Gregor and to a certain extent, Nero. I think he'd made himself quite clear on where he stood on both those counts, tonight even pushing home the *I will not share* line with force.

When I didn't say anything else he decided to change the direction of the conversation, no doubt feeling he'd harped on about it enough for one night. I certainly felt that way.

"What happened this evening, *ma douce*? You seemed to require some more power through the Bond at one stage, yet I sensed you were still at St. Helier's."

Huh. I hadn't even realised that had happened. The Bond just stepped on in whenever it felt the need and to hell with asking permission from me.

Ignoring his question altogether, but not intentionally, I asked, "Does it compromise you when that happens? I don't even know it's happening, I don't think I have control over it." That sounded familiar.

"Not at all." His hand was still stroking me, unable to stop the movement against my skin, it didn't annoy me, it felt good. Too good in fact. "I can only sense that you have a need and the Bond takes care of the rest. Likewise, if the tables were turned, you would feel my need, but not feel drained. It... well for me, it creates a desire to protect you, to be near you. To know you are safe."

264

He looked away then and his soft stroking stilled. My head moved all on its own, betraying my feelings, as I made my neck rub against his hand and bring his attention back to me. He smiled and started stroking me again.

"Why didn't you come to me?" I think I already knew the answer and my heart had skipped a beat with the thought. A part of me didn't want it, still clinging to the need to have my space. I wanted to believe he wasn't trying, but I knew, before he opened his mouth, what he would say.

"I was giving you space. You didn't seem in immediate danger, it was not my place, so you have made clear, to interfere." When he saw the look on my face he added, "I have been trying, *ma douce*, please believe me and I won't stop trying to honour your request for space, but I will still claim you as mine. That, has already been set in motion and as a vampyre I cannot stop it now."

Somehow I knew *claim* was a euphemism for much, much more. But, the knowledge that he was trying to give me space, to give me the independence to do what I needed to do, what I had asked him for, was a surprise. And despite previous thoughts on this matter, I was pleased, relieved and a little scared.

"So, will you tell me, *ma douce*? What happened?"

I gave him a brief run down on the whole *Prohibitum Bibere* situation, plus the theory that I would also inherit or had inherited the *Lux Lucis Tribuo* too. There had been a time when I was sure Michel would use these new powers of mine, for some power hungry reason, but he had yet to prove that thought. So far he had only shown his pleasure at having that power so close, but he had not acted on it. I

265

still wasn't sure if he would, but not telling him seemed pointless. Besides, if I couldn't confide in my kindred, then I was really limiting my choices right now. Nero was *persona non grata* to me. My choice, but his confidence had been lost, hopefully only temporarily, but we'll see.

"Are you OK?" His concern made me smile. He meant it, he understood what I felt, he could no doubt feel my emotions regarding it all right now.

"No, but what else can I do? It's chosen me, or Nut has. And I have no idea why, or what to do, or if I can do it all, but it's done, so here I am." I paused and reached up a hand to touch his face. It didn't bother me that it was showing too much of how I felt, right now I needed to touch him. Probably the damn joining thing again. "Do you understand why I can't be kept under lock and key now? Do you see I don't have a choice?"

He leaned his face into my hand, turning slightly to lay a kiss on my palm and then returning his gaze to me. "I understand, but can you also see how hard it is for me to let you do this?" He saw I was about to protest, so he silenced me with a finger on my lips. "I *will* let you do this, but will you at least let me help?"

How could he help? I'm the one designed to *seek* them all, I'm the one designed to *lure* them in, I'm the one who has to figure out how to use my Light to turn them from Dark, from evil, to good. Without frying each and every one of them in the process. How could he help?

"How did you feel just now, Lucinda? When we were together, when we were lost in our love making? How did you feel?"

Well, that's a personal question isn't it? I bit my bottom

266

lip and just looked at him. He smiled and shook his head.

"Let me tell you then. You forgot about the Prophesy, you forgot about the role you have to play, you let it and everything else, go and you had a moment of peace, a moment of just you and just me, no one else, nothing else. Is that not a help, my love?"

I raised my eyebrows at him. "So, you're suggesting by having your naughty way with me, will *help* in the fight against the Dark?"

His face beamed at me, making his eyes light up and the amethyst and indigo that suddenly appeared, bounce around the room.

In a low, husky voice he said, "Do I need to show you again how good I am for you, *ma douce?*"

I couldn't help it, I just laughed.

Chapter 22
Back Seat of a BMW

It wasn't easy, but I did manage to distract him enough for the lesson not to be repeated. His hold on me was already too strong. Despite the progress I had recently made, he was working his way back into my life, my psyche, my body. Part of me knew it was futile, this resistance I was insisting on, Michel had an effect on me that my body craved, even if my mind rebelled. Sometimes my mind won the battle, but most of the time, my body did.

The fact that I was lost to him in a big way did not sit well with me. So, I fell back on that old stalwart, denial and shoved the thoughts to the back of my head.

After convincing him that I had to go - it was late and I had work tomorrow - I managed to disentangle myself enough from his arms to escape. I think he would have fought harder, but the fact that I was still a little dizzy from his blood letting and no doubt quite pale, made him behave himself a little better than he otherwise would have.

His goodbye kiss at the office door was long and deep though, a reminder of just what effect he had over me and also his determination to prove it at any turn.

When I finally managed to pull away, after several half hearted attempts, his face was flushed, lips swollen and eyes glazed. I dreaded to think what I looked like.

"Right, well, I'll be off then," I said with as much of a determined air as I could muster.

He smiled languidly.

"If you insist, *ma douce*."

I took a step away from him, losing the support of his hands on my hips and promptly losing my balance too, banging into the door jam.

He automatically reached out to steady me, his face more serious now.

"Let me drive you home."

I took a deep breath in and tried to stop the world spinning, but did manage to shake my head, not that it did any good to the spinning, or the headache that had started up on either side of my head. And now I thought about it, the nausea that rolled across my stomach. Man, he had done a number on me, hadn't he?

He swore quietly under his breath, probably having heard that last thought.

"At the very least, *ma douce*, let me walk you to your car. Erika is bringing Amisi and will drive you both home."

I nodded, swallowing several times in an effort to not give in to the nausea. Michel must have noticed, because he lifted me up in his arms and simply carried me to the garage. At the car, he placed me in the back seat, so I could lie down. I didn't bother about a seat belt, the way I was feeling, lying down was definitely the only answer.

I had closed my eyes briefly. When I opened them, Michel was still leaning over me, but I got the impression he had been there for a while. His face was full of concern and anger.

"Why are you angry?" I asked, my voice slightly slurred.

"I have hurt you this night, I have weakened you." He shook his head, a look of utter despair on his face, as though he couldn't believe what he done, how far he had taken it; feeding for so long from me and causing me to end up like this. I knew he was beating himself up, just I like I did all the time. It was a feeling I was very familiar with, I recognised it in him like an old friend.

I crooked my finger at him, to make him come closer. He leaned down towards me, his face now slightly puzzled. When he got within reaching distance I grabbed him by his T-Shirt and pulled him all the way on top of me in the back of the car. He yelped slightly, trying not to squash me, but I was having none of it. It wasn't quite as smooth as I would have liked, but I did get him where I wanted him in the end.

I kissed him softly on the lips, at first he kind of resisted, he was too busy trying not to put all of his weight on me, but I wrapped my arms around his neck and pulled him in closer, making him lose the last of his balance and sink into the back seat with me. My tongue ran along his bottom lip and when he parted his mouth slightly to sigh, I darted in, swirling his own tongue around, making sure he knew just how much I wanted him right then.

His body moulded against mine. Despite the small and slightly awkward setting, I managed to shift my legs around him, encasing him completely and getting a satisfying groan from deep inside his throat as I moved against his groin. His body responded instantly, his hands began to work their magic and the kiss took on a new level of urgency.

Perhaps it was cruel, or perhaps I just wanted to prove not only to him, but to myself, that he was just a little under my control too. Because I knew this wouldn't get finished, I knew it when I started it, because I could sense Erika and Amisi nearby. They had held back, when they saw what was happening, but I was counting on them being there to stop this, so I slowed the kiss down, stopped the movement of my hips against his now vibrant erection and pulled my face away from his. He continued to try and kiss me, when he couldn't get to my lips, he shifted his focus to my ear, to the soft sensitive skin right behind my lobe, making my breath catch and for a moment, my plan disappear entirely from my mind, but I rallied.

"It's time for me to go," I breathed against him.

"No." He was equally as breathless, but determined to get my attention.

"Michel. Erika and Amisi are here, you need to stop."

"Never."

His lips and tongue had moved to the skin on my neck above my throat, kissing, licking, nibbling. His hips had started moving rhythmically against me, making it damn near impossible to think. I thought I had been so clever to entice him into the back seat. I thought I could get him all excited and then simply walk away and say *payback's a bitch*, but I had forgotten how good he was at this, how experienced he was at this. And just how much of an effect he has over me.

For a brief moment, I thought of giving in to the sensations, to giving in to him and then I felt my heart flutter in fear. I was strong, I could do this.

"Erika. Amisi. It's time to go!" I shouted over the top of his head.

He paused, stopped moving against me, just gave me one or two more slow, small kisses on the neck. His breath was hot against my skin when he spoke and sounded very low and uneven.

"I shall not forget this, *ma douce*. Two can play at this

271

game and you know how much I like to play with you."

I smiled, I couldn't help it. Michel was back to himself again, threats and innuendo, familiar ground, but at least he wasn't beating himself up anymore, that I just couldn't stand to see in Michel. Michel was my rock; solid, strong, unflappable, well at least as far as the normal day to day stuff goes. I don't mind him being a little unbalanced when in my arms.

He lifted his head and smiled at me, eyes flashing bright amethyst and swishes of indigo.

"Very clever, *ma douce*." He'd heard my thoughts again. Man, was I projecting everything tonight, or what?

"Yes, it seems you are, but I love it." He kissed me again, long and hard, then lifted himself off me and somehow managed to get out of the back seat with grace, despite trying to adjust the front the his jeans.

"Sleep well, *ma belle*." He turned and simply vanished. He's done that before, there one minute, gone the next. I was surprised he had enough wherewithal to do it right now, but it did accomplish one thing, he hadn't had to face Amisi and Erika up close. He had probably avoided them seeing how ruffled he actually was. Self preservation can make you accomplish amazing things when under pressure.

I heard their footsteps on the concrete floor of the garage before I saw them, but finally two faces peered in the side of the car. I must have looked a sight because they both burst out laughing. I tried to straighten myself up, but didn't have the energy. Fuck it. They're girls, they can handle it.

"So, have you learnt yet, *chica*, the master always wins."

272

"Ha bloody ha, Erika. Just get in the car and drive me home would ya?" I could do without the smart-ass routine.

They both slid in the car and Erika started it.

"Oh, I don't know," Amisi said casually. "Michel did look a little flustered there, wouldn't you say, Erika?"

Erika barked out a laugh, not her usual style, it was too forceful, almost as though she didn't want to give in to it. "I have to admit, I can't say I have ever seen Michel running from a scene with such urgency before. It was almost as if he didn't want to face us, Amisi. What do you think?"

Amisi answered straight away. "Absolutely, most impressive speed. He did look uncomfortable though, as though a cold shower might have been on the agenda."

Erika was laughing outright now, it was a wonder she could see where she was driving. "I seriously doubt he's had to exit a scene like that in such a manner before. Michel likes to see things through to completion."

"I'm sure he'll rethink his strategy as far as our Lucinda goes," Amisi replied, laughing just as hard.

"Got his work cut out for him that's for sure."

"He'll think twice before tangling with the Forbidden Drink, wouldn't want to drown."

"Too late." Erika was hysterical now, I could hardly understand what she was saying. "He's addicted, there's no going back for him after this. You couldn't have played it better, *chica*, Michel will already be planning his next move."

"He'll also be able to think of little else," Amisi added. "His dreams will be completely filled with images of you in the back seat of this car."

I couldn't believe what I was hearing, but it did make

me laugh. Sometimes having girlfriends could be a real bonus.

"Oh crap," Erika suddenly said, swerving slightly with the steering wheel of the car. I thought she must have been trying to avoid something on the road, so sat up slightly. She glanced over her shoulder at me, still laughing. "You're projecting your thoughts, *chica*, he can hear everything. He just told me I was fired." She laughed even harder. "Michel, you are so lost, *chico*. So very, very lost."

We all started laughing together after that, somehow unable to stop ourselves, just getting caught up in the moment and letting it wash away everything else. It was cathartic and I felt a sudden strong connection to the two new women in my life. Yeah, as far as flatmates went, they were going to be all right.

I was exhausted when we made it home though, so even though Amisi and Erika planned on staying up and gossiping about me, while watching an old *Angel* DVD, I took the coward's way out and ran a bath. Mandarin heaven always makes me feel better, so by the time I fell between the sheets, utterly exhausted, it didn't surprise me that I fell asleep instantly.

It also didn't surprise me that he came to me in my dreams.

Usually when he visits me here it's on my parents' farm, overlooking the lambs with the waggly tails and surrounded by the sights and sounds and smells of Spring. It's beautiful and always refreshing. Going home charges my batteries, Michel always takes me there when I dream, allowing me a sense of calm and fulfilment. But, not this time.

This time I woke in the back seat of the BMW and Michel was on top of me.

"Now, where were we, *ma douce?*"

Oh shit.

"That's right, I believe I was about to show you how the game is played."

His hand went up under my blouse, stroking my nipple until it was tight and taut. His lips were all over my neck, his teeth nibbling here and there, his tongue running a hot, wet line across my skin and his hips were gently rocking against me. I was immediately back where I had been before, but not just in the back seat of the car with Michel on top of me, but also with the erotic heat that had started building inside. My own body responding instantly, moving with the roll of his hips, tightening my legs around him, my hand running up into his hair, the other down the strong line of his back, digging my fingers into his flesh through the thin T-Shirt. I moaned and arched my back up off the seat.

"That is better, *ma douce.* Feel me, want me, take me."

His mouth found mine again and I was lost in his desire as it rushed though my body engulfing me, threatening to drown me. Amisi was wrong, it wasn't Michel who would drown, it was me.

"No," he whispered against me. "We are both drowning, do not fight it, let it take us under."

It was my hands that undid his jeans, pulled his T-Shirt off over his head. It was also me who managed to untangle myself from my jacket and help him undo the buttons on my blouse. When I was fully exposed to him, he paused, just taking me in, but it went on longer than I had expected.

"Oh God, Michel, if you are going to just stop and leave me here like this as payback, I *will* hunt you down and stake you."

He laughed, a full throaty laugh. "Now, could I be as cruel as that, *ma douce*?" His lips found my breast, his hard length resting at my entrance.

There wasn't much room to manoeuvre, I think he would have liked to have spent more time discovering me. This evening had been a series of quick and urgent sessions, nothing like Michel's usual languid pace. So, he wasn't in a hurry to enter me, but still, it was a tight space, he couldn't move down on me, he couldn't turn me over and change things up a bit, but he did lavish my face and neck and chest with attention, all the while using his hand and fingers to pleasure me, to bring me to climax again and again and again.

Finally, I was begging for him to enter me, to fill me up, to take me now. I needed him inside me like it was the solution to all my problems, like it was the answer to all my prayers.

"Now, Michel, now!"

He growled against my neck, where he had been placing gentle fang marks all over the side of my skin. The pierce of his fangs, followed by the rush of his desire, only to be repeated again and again. He had me at such a high, on such a sharp edge of hunger for him, for this, that I was shaking all over, unable to breathe, unable to think, but managing to whimper all the same.

"You are mine." He said it, like he had earlier in the evening, as he entered me. Slowly this time, laboriously slowly, teasing me, tempting me, frustrating me, making me shout out in desperation and then do something I had not had any intention of doing now, or if in fact ever. I gathered my Light and I held it close, letting it build, like he was letting my body build with sharp delicious sensations and then thrusting it out towards him, surrounding his shields, climbing his walls, wrapping around his protection, until he could hold against me no more. And then I let it pour from me to him while all I could hear in my head was *mine, mine, mine, mine*. But, it wasn't Michel's voice, it was mine. It was me. And I was marking him.

He hesitated in his movements, realising what I was doing, shocked, with a little flash of sorrow there as well and then he couldn't help his shout of victory as he began to claim my body in return, in hard and fast thrusts, pumping himself as far and as hard as he could inside me.

My Light flowed through us, his hips moved against me, my legs wrapped around him and we moved as one, riding the wave of elation and rapture in a frenzy of sounds and sensations. His body pounding into me, while my Light flooded into him and eventually they both met in the middle in an orgasm like none other I had ever felt, making us both shout out in alarm and then collapse against each other in triumph.

We both lay still, unable to move because of the tight spot we were in as well as the total inability to physically command our limbs to respond. I felt like jelly, so liquid and replete, so safe in his arms and so sure that he was mine as I was his.

Shit. This wasn't meant to happen. I was meant to stay in control, not lose it like this. Damn. This had not been the plan.

I felt Michel's hand stroking my face, pushing my damp hair out of my eyes, his lips kissing the side of my neck. When he spoke, his hot breath against my sweat soaked skin sent shivers down my spine.

"This is only between you and me, *ma douce*. No one need know, this is a dream. Nothing more, it is not real. You have not given up your control, or anything else this night, only here, only now, not in reality."

I felt a little part of me sink at that statement. I know it was silly, I didn't want to lose myself in such a total and irretrievable way as I had just done now, but then, part of me obviously did and was disappointed that it wasn't over. My capitulation wasn't yet achieved. It would have been easy to just accept it, to think I had made that step, the final act had been done, that I had given him my *Sigillum*. But now, the question still remained, didn't it? Would I ever give myself to Michel completely?

When rationale returned the answer would be no. And I wanted to cry at that.

"Sleep, *ma petite lumière*. All will be back to normal in the morning."

I felt him lifting off me, but not as though he was standing up, but more that he was becoming less and less substantial, the dream disintegrating around me, the world starting to shift. I reached out for him desperately, not wanting this moment to be gone, not wanting it to return to normal at all, but to cling to this, what we had just shared and to never let it go.

His fingers brushed mine and right before he and the car and the smells and sensations of the moment were lost

278

forever, he whispered, "*Je t'aime, ma douce. Je t'aime.*"

I woke up in bed sweating, and rolled over to curl up in a little ball and cried.

Chapter 23
The Spy

I spent the next three days avoiding him. I didn't go near *Sensations*, spending my time divided between work and home. And practising with the Svante sword and Erika, or out hunting with Amisi. When not training or fighting, we watched a selection of old vampire T.V. series on DVD, spent time eating decadent and indulgent treats and worked off the calories in the gym. I was surprised at how fast the time sped by and how much fun I had with both girls.

I was getting good with the sword. Much better than I think Erika had thought I would be at this stage. We had progressed to practising in the back yard under the moon with real swords, no more *bokken* for us. The clang of steel on steel filled the still night air. Amisi was in awe of the skills Erika had taught me and even had the odd training session with her using the *bokken*. She was agile and a quick learner, but she didn't take to it like me. For me, it was as though I had used these instruments of war in a previous life. They felt so familiar, so right in my hands, that every move I made was natural, not forced, completely ingrained.

By Friday, I was wearing the Svante sword Michel had given me in its holster against my back, under my jacket when out and about. I had mastered unsheathing it, swiftly and cleanly, as well as getting it home again and switching to my stake. The holster was amazing, it fitted like a glove and felt so snug and comfortable against me. It also had the ability to shift the angle of the sword slightly, meaning I didn't have to withdraw it out vertically from behind my head. When I reached for it, the sword simply slid to my left shoulder and with my right hand I could reach across my body and pull it free. Getting it back in position was just as smooth and once re-sheathed, it fell back into its vertical hiding place automatically. Sheer brilliance. I practised that un-sheathing and re-sheathing again and again and again, until it was one fluid motion, something so natural I didn't have to think.

I couldn't imagine not wearing the sword when I hunted now, it was as much a part of me as the silver stakes and silver knife I wore in my jacket.

By Friday evening though, I knew I'd have to see Michel. So many days apart and I was starting to notice the effects. It started out with just the odd shiver, a tingling in my hands and fingers, then progressed to shakes whenever I thought of him. I felt weak and couldn't stomach any food, I hadn't eaten for twenty four hours. It took me a while to realise what it was I was experiencing and why. It was Amisi who spoke up first.

I had just walked in the door from work. She'd had the use of one of Michel's Land Rover Discoveries during the day - one Erika used in the evening if she had to do something without me - and had made it home at about the same time as me, having spent her free hours exploring Auckland and getting used to Kiwis and their habits. Erika was working out in the gym, but the shutters were all still down, the sun hadn't yet set.

I came in and stripped off my uniform jacket, chucking it unceremoniously on the sofa and landing flat on my face on top of it. Unable to think about moving again. Amisi followed me in from the garage and just stood inside the door to the lounge.

She cleared her throat softly and I managed to shift my head to the side and look at her from my prone position on the couch. She looked concerned and determined. Great. Lecture time.

"You need to go him, Lucinda." At first I didn't quite get what she was talking about, who she was talking about. She must have seen the confusion on my face, because she continued. "You need your kindred, you're drained, you haven't had contact with him for close to 72 hours, it's too long. He will be suffering too."

Shit. I hadn't thought of that. He could not afford to feel drained, he was Master of the City, he needed to stay on guard always. Hell, I couldn't afford to feel drained. I groaned and buried my head in the seat cushion of the couch. I so did not want to face him.

"Come on, let's go now. I'll drive."

I sat up slowly and shook my head. "Let's wait for nightfall, I need to get changed anyway and Erika can come with us then."

"OK." She nodded and started heading towards the kitchen. "But, I'm making a snack, so you better high tail it back down here and eat it before we go. OK?" She looked at me pointedly.

How had she got so good with English? And so bossy?

I showered quickly and when I came down, Erika was freshly dressed in the kitchen and a beef and salad sandwich was waiting on the bench. I sat down quietly at the breakfast bar and forced it down, following it up with a *Diet Coke.* We sat silently like that for another half hour until the whirring of the shutters retracting broke us from our meditations and I stood and stretched out some of the

282

aches that had taken up residence in my body.

"OK, let's get this over with."

Amisi shook her head in disbelief. She probably wasn't used to having a Nosferatin so reluctant to see their kindred Nosferatu. Where she came from, joinings were expected and carried out as part of a normal routine. Not necessarily as intimate or complicated as mine, but more as a means to an end, strategic and platonic.

Michel and I just had to be different, didn't we?

I was determined I would stay in the public area of the bar, not go to Michel if he was in his office. That would just be asking for trouble. So, when we arrived, we headed straight out into the club itself and commandeered a table once my senses told me he wasn't even there. I was momentarily unsure of what to do, I had expected Michel to be waiting for me, but he was nowhere on the premises. I could have sent the sense of our Bond out to him, to locate him, but I really didn't want him to be aware of my need to be near. I had to keep up a strong front, I couldn't lower my guard. *Never show fear. Never give an inch. Always stay on guard.*

It was hard to concentrate on my surroundings though, his absence was like a hole in my heart. Erika and Amisi, on the other hand, were having a blast and before long their antics couldn't help but draw my attention. They both looked stunning tonight. Erika was in her usual tight, tight black jeans, red knee high leather boots, red singlet and this time a black fitted leather jacket. Her Svante sword was invisible under the tumble of her blonde hair. Every eye in the bar was on her, well every human eye that is, the vampires were fixated on Amisi. Tall and elegant in tight

283

fitting black trousers and a tight fitting black shirt, her stakes hidden in a bolero style jacket, this time black with gold detailing, her long brown hair loose down her back. And those big brown eyes, pools of liquid on her perfect golden brown skin. She was lean and feminine, but also deadly. And the vampires could practically taste it.

I had to stifle a laugh, their desire was rolling off them in waves. I realised just how important my role as her chaperone was going to be. And how hard. She was playing it up like a pro. A swish of her hair here, the cock of head there, the soft laugh, the poise, the presentation. Good grief, did they train them like this in Egypt? She was a vampire disaster waiting to happen. Sooner or later a brawl was going to break out over who had rights to approach her first. So much for me being the Forbidden Drink, the vampires in the room right now were licking their lips in anticipation of tasting her, to hell with me. Jeez.

It was Dillon Malone who approached first, which kind of took me by surprise, he was usually someone who played things very close to his chest. Being Michel's spy, the one who was always travelling here and there throughout the country, coming back to give brief and quietly whispered reports now and then. I wasn't really familiar with him, like the rest of Michel's gang. He had always been courteous to me, but aloof. I don't think I had ever had one decent conversation in the entire time I had known him.

He was good looking of course, they all are, but he wore his hair short, unlike most vampires. I often wondered if that was because he spied on humans throughout the country, if he was spying on vampires, wouldn't he have needed long hair to blend in? I'd never asked Michel, somehow I just intrinsically knew Dillon was off limits, a topic not to be discussed. His hair was thick and sandy blonde, but he wasn't covered in freckles like you'd expect, just a pleasant cream complexion that seemed to complement his hair colour, not drain it. It was his eyes, however, that made you notice him, they were a stunning shade of Periwinkle. A pale blue with a dusky overture, stunning despite its lack of depth. It was as though his eyes held more power than just the colour differentiations of vampires. It was as though when he gazed at you, he could see right through to your soul.

They were trained on Amisi's now and dammit, she had been caught by his gaze.

She should have known better, even with Nosferatin anti-vampire skills, we can get caught by their glaze. Dillon wasn't trying to glaze her now, thankfully, but he might as well have been, she was already breathless and unable to pull her eyes away from the approaching predator that he was. He was, of course, in full vampire predator mode, gliding towards her, enticing her with his body, the fine lines, the broad muscles, the hunger in his look. God, even I was having trouble looking away. For some inexplicable reason I couldn't open my mouth to warn Amisi, I just sat there and watched it all unfold without lifting a finger to stop any of it.

He didn't ask to be invited to sit, he just grabbed a chair from a nearby table, turned its back towards Amisi and sat down across it, legs spread either side, his gaze never leaving hers. He rested his chin on the back of the chair and just looked at her, almost a little lost boy look, just taking

285

her all in and waiting for her to talk. I'm sure that look had worked for him in the past, it was doing a number on Amisi now, her smile very friendly back at him.

"So, do you have a name?" His Irish accent was lost some time ago, probably 100 years or more, he just had a slight Kiwi twang. He really would fit in anywhere in this country.

"Amisi."

"That's beautiful. What does it mean?"

She blushed slightly. "Flower."

Out of nowhere he produced a single red rose and handed it to her like a magician. I couldn't help laughing out loud, but neither of them heard me. I flicked a glance towards Erika, she was on guard. Which made me sit a little straighter in my own chair and take another look at Dillon. Erika would only be on guard if she felt a threat towards herself, me or Michel. I was wondering now if she had extended that blanket of protection to Amisi too.

Dillon looked harmless enough, but he did hold Amisi spellbound and now that I'd had a shot of adrenaline go through me from the look on Erika's face, I felt removed from the situation and able to actually speak.

"What do you want, Dillon?" He was surprised I had spoken, which made me think my reticence before was no doubt due to some vampire mojo he had surreptitiously been spreading.

He glanced over his shoulder at me and smiled, turning slightly to face me, as though he wanted me every bit a part of the conversation. I had no doubt that wasn't the case though.

"Lucinda. A pleasure, as always. You know, you can't

286

keep her all to yourself, she will be snaffled up by one of us."

Oh, now didn't that just make me bristle.

"Back off, Dillon, or I'll make you."

Amisi chose that moment to enter the discussion. "It's all right, Lucinda, he's just talking to me, that's all."

I gave her a really good hard stare, one I think Nero would have been proud of at that moment and turned my attention back to Dillon.

"She is my guest and as such a guest of Michel's. Do not overstep your mark Dillon Malone." The use of his full name carried the weight of Michel's command behind it. It was a natural thing for me to do and obviously something he was either channelling into me right now, or the joining/ Bond was forcing me to do in his stead. Either way, Dillon got the message, stiffening slightly and pulling away from me.

He looked back at Amisi and she blossomed under his attention. "Perhaps, little Flower, you and I can meet again without your chaperone." I growled, an actual, honest to goodness, vampire growl. Either Michel was really channelling me right now or I was way more Nosferatu than I had previously thought. Dillon stood up quickly, I think he may have been scared I was about to do something, like grow some fangs and bite his neck, who knows, but he definitely wanted space between me and him. His chair was now in front of him, between us and he was closer to Amisi than he was to me.

I didn't think he'd be stupid enough to do anything, so I just stood there and waited for him to move. But, I obviously underestimated his attraction to her and his

287

desire to test a theory, because the next thing I noticed, was his hand taking hers, their eyes meeting and *Sanguis Vitam* filling the air as he said, "Such a beautiful Nosferatin." The emphasis and power on the word Nosferatin.

I knew what was going to happen next, but not what shape it would take. All immature and unjoined Nosferatins have one massive failing: their name. Or more to the point, the name of our kind, *Nosferatin*, can be used against us. It's not designed as a weapon as such, but more a tool, to help Nosferatu and Nosferatin who are suitably matched as kindred recognise each other. When a vampire knows how to wield that power they can elicit a response from a Nosferatin. The response is usually an indication of how well matched they would be should they join. My response to Michel was to fall asleep. Anti-climactic I know, but Michel had been visiting my dreams for some time by then and in them I had already fallen for his charms. When Enrique, a master vampire with an accord with Michel, tried that line on me, he got a silver stake. So, yeah, our reactions to the power behind that word can vary, from one vampire to the next.

Just how Amisi was going to react was uncertain, but I had my stake out and against Dillon's back, hovering over his heart, before she fell into his arms with abandon. He caught her and pulled her tight and I pierced his skin, maybe only a few millimetres, but enough to get his attention and everyone else in the bar too.

The room was silent for a moment, everyone's eyes on us. Dillon had stopped breathing, but still held Amisi tight.

"Bruno," I said quietly into the room, never removing my gaze from Dillon or shifting the stake. I had no idea if

Bruno was here or not. It was Jett, however, who answered. "He's not here, Luce, but I'm happy to help." He stepped up beside me.

"Secure the room, look after the Norms."

"Yes, mistress."

I never could get used to them using that phrase with me, but as Michel's kindred Nosferatin, whenever I issued a directive in his absence, they tended to call me that. Creepy, but handy.

"Now, Dillon, you're going to let her go, slowly and carefully. And Dillon, one false move and the stake slides home, I don't give a fuck who's pet spy you are."

He swallowed slowly, but did as I asked.

I noticed Erika at my back, I sensed rather than saw her Svante out, she had her back to me, so was covering my arse, like a good little bodyguard should. I recognised the heightened amount of *Sanguis Vitam* in the room right then, the other vampires were a mixture of scared and turned on, all of them avidly watching the scene though.

I removed my stake from Dillon's back once Amisi had sat down. She looked drained and dazed, not quite with us, as though she had been under a spell too. I didn't doubt it, whatever mojo Dillon had going on, it was powerful and clever. I hadn't even felt it, even though I'd seen it operating right before my eyes.

"Here this, all Durand Nosferatu," I let my voice carry to all in the room. "Amisi is off limits. Your sole objective is her protection and nothing else. Is that clear?"

Really Michel should have issued this directive already, it would have held more weight coming from him, but as his kindred, I could only hope it made it through their thick skulls and rampant hard-ons when they looked at the girl. I could not hand her back to Nafrini and Nero harmed. It would be tantamount to starting a war with the Egyptians and as they are the strongest vampires in the world, aside from Michel, that was a path we just couldn't afford to tread.

No one had spoken, the Norms had been removed from the club, their memories wiped, so it was just me, Amisi and a bar full of vamps. Cool.

"Is that clear?" I said and followed it up with a flash of Light around the room. If they wouldn't listen to me as Michel's Nosferatin, then they would bloody well take heed of my Nosferatin powers.

Immediately they all nodded, whispered words of agreement, even bowed in the case of some of the more fragile amongst them. Dillon just looked at me with cunning. I don't know what he was thinking, but I had the distinct impression that he and I were no longer on the same side.

"She's just one girl, Dillon, no need to fall out over this."

He stared at me long and hard and then gave a short nod and turned away. In his wake I felt his power wash around me, almost stripping me bare. What the fuck? This guy was definitely more of a concern than twenty minutes ago. Did Michel know how strong he was?

It was as if thinking of Michel opened up a door I hadn't realised was closed. And it wasn't one I had closed either. It was Michel, trying to keep me out of his head. Not that I'd been going there a lot lately, but he obviously didn't want to risk an unannounced visit. Too late, I was screaming down the tunnel towards him and all I could see at the other end was his fear and pain and a whole lot of fucked off-ness.

And he wasn't alone.

There were Taniwhas around him. And lots of them.

Chapter24
We Meet Again Old Friend

I stumbled against the table and let out a gasp. Michel was hurt and chained, silver I think and he was pleading with me not to come.

Amisi was on her feet, stake out at the same time that Erika spun around to look at me, Svante still at the ready.

"What is it?" They both said in unison.

"Michel." It was a whisper, but the entire room stilled and sprang to alert.

Jett was beside me in an instant. "Where? What does he need? He hasn't called to us, is he out cold?"

I took several shattering breaths in, trying to stop my world from spinning out of control. Oh God, Michel. Oh my God.

"Where's Bruno?" As his second in command I wanted Bruno here, he'd know what to do.

"He went out with Michel earlier this evening, neither said where they were heading."

I held my hand up to Jett to stop him continuing and let myself sink into the Bond connection and go to Michel.

Is Bruno still with you?

He grimaced as I spoke in his mind, I'm not sure if it was from the pain of my voice in his head or the fact that I had come to him, even metaphysically, when he so obviously didn't want me involved.

His reply made me collapse to the floor.

No. He has met the final death. I felt his pain at the words, I felt his desolation at the loss of a close ally and friend. I felt his heart weeping.

And mine wept with him too.

I'm coming for you, stay strong.

No, Lucinda! That is what they want, they want you. They won't kill me until they have you. When you turn up they will stake me, just to watch you die.

As far as plans went, it was a pretty good one. How could I stay away from Michel when he was like this? Yet, how could I go to him knowing this would lead to his death as surely as if I thrust the stake in myself?

There was no simple answer, but the only path was the hardest. I had to stay away. I knew without a doubt that Rick and his Taniwhas would stake Michel as soon as I arrived in that clearing and because he and I were joined - and Rick knew this - I would die too. They were all on Hapū land, they knew the terrain well, they had laid the trap, but how had they caught Michel?

Call all your vampires to Sensations, Michel. I'll stay away, but let them come get you.

I could feel his relief at my words, not the vampires part, but me saying I would stay away. That's why he hadn't called them yet, he knew I would have just come running, now at least he had convinced me to stay safe.

The vampires in the room shifted suddenly and I heard Jett beside me say, "He's summoned us to you here."

Go, ma douce. I cannot concentrate on you and the Taniwhas at the same time. Je t'aime, ma belle.

I love you too.

I fell back out of the link and into chaos.

"Jett, you're temporary 2IC." The room stopped in motion, the realisation of my words sinking in immediately. We had lost Bruno. But I couldn't afford to dwell on that right now. There would be time enough to grieve later, hopefully. "How long until the bulk of Michel's line gets here?"

He coughed slightly, obviously trying to come to terms with his new, albeit, temporary promotion. I knew Jett was who Michel favoured as his next in command under Bruno. He had spoken of it to me before. Despite Jett being from another line originally, he had proven loyal and strong. He carried himself with an air of regal standing, Michel was always his *Master*, not just Michel. He believed in the sanctity of a family line, he had pledged himself wholeheartedly to Michel's. If Michel trusted him, so could I.

"Another ten, maybe fifteen minutes. The command was urgent. They will sense the repercussions. They will know our master is in peril."

I just nodded, still sitting on the floor. I seemed to have lost all ability to use my legs. It was Erika and Amisi who helped me into a chair. Jett sat down next to me at the table, as did Amisi and Erika, then out of no where, Doug slipped a *Bacardi and Coke* in front of me and simply said, "Drink."

I didn't argue, I downed half of it in one go, before realising it wasn't a double, or a triple for that matter, it was practically a *Bacardi* with a hint of *Coke*. Still, I needed the wakeup call and once I got the the sudden influx of watery tears in my eyes under control, I felt the warmth of the alcohol seep through me, warming me up and making me clear headed and ready to face the minutes ahead. Doug, a man of little words, but great virtue. He knew exactly what I had needed.

"He's being held on Hapū land at Whenuapai. You

know where that is?" I asked Jett.

He nodded. "We've had it surveyed. Michel has never felt confident with their compliance. We know the layout of the land, even if we haven't ventured on it before."

"Don't get too cocky, they live and breathe that forest surrounding their homes. They could run in it blindfolded and they are fast."

"You escaped."

I hadn't realised Michel had told anyone about that. "Well, I was lucky and I think we're going to need a bit of luck tonight."

He nodded again. A good soldier.

"He's in the clearing, by the houses in the middle of the land. They've got him strapped to a table top, silver chains across his entire body."

There was an audible gasp in the room, the vampires cringing and looking stricken.

"How much damage will the chains do?" I asked quietly.

Jett flicked a glance at Erika, I didn't see her response, too busy looking at him. She must have given an indication to go ahead and tell me. Good girl, I didn't need protection from the truth, not now.

"If he is at full strength, then he will be ale to tolerate them for a few hours, but he's been gone since sundown, so we can assume he's been there at least one hour already. And as to if he is at full strength, you would probably know that better than I."

I felt my shoulders sag in defeat and couldn't bring myself to look at Amisi. Her hand came out and clasped mine, offering a meagre amount of support.

"OK," Jett said, equally as quietly as I had. "I'll take that as not at full strength then." He paused. "In that case, he will be suffering and the longer he is under silver, the more damage it will be doing to his *Sanguis Vitam*. If he is left there too long, even a stake won't be necessary. His flesh will begin to melt where the silver touches and the contamination will quickly spread. He will be using everything right now to stop its progress."

I couldn't hear anything else for a moment, there was a thudding in my ears, a thumping that drowned out all other sound. It took a moment for me to realise it was my heart and it was racing. My Michel. In pain, suffering. I tried not to let the images of Jett's words play out in my head. It would do no good to succumb to the grief and heartache I felt knocking at my door. If we were going to get Michel out, I needed to stay strong and focused. I needed to give him strength.

I brushed at non existent tears and took another swig of my drink. Fortification, I told myself.

"There are approximately fifty fully grown shape shifters, I'm not sure how many were surrounding them, but at a guess I could see twenty, all in Taniwha form. The rest may be spread out on the land, but that's just a guess. I could only see Michel and those nearest him."

"All right, that's enough to go on. I have a plan of attack. Michel and Bruno had already thought of events such as these, however, it was always under the assumption they would be coming to rescue you, Luce, not the other way around." He stood up and turned to speak to the whole room then. "We'll be approaching from several directions in a unified attack. It'll be a snatch and grab. We're not concerned with taking them out at this point, that can come later. For now, the priority is Michel and getting him and us out of there in one piece."

He looked down at me then and in a quieter voice said, "You up to this, Luce?"

And now the truth. They wouldn't even have me.

I took a deep breath in. "I won't be going. The moment they spot me there, they intend to stake him. Their goal is to watch me die and they have chosen to use Michel as the weapon."

Jett just nodded. "Enough said. I'll leave a contingent of guards here with you."

"No. There's no need. You'll all be needed for this. Amisi will be here with me."

"And me, *chica*," Erika said laying a hand on my shoulder.

But I couldn't have that, could I? She was probably the best suited to this type of job out of all of us. Wielding those swords of hers, slashing and hacking her way through the throng to get to him. I stood up and turned to her, clasping both her hands in mine.

"No Erika. Bring him home to me." I looked her in the eyes and let mine tell her how much I was depending on her for this, because I couldn't do it, she had to do it for me. I wouldn't trust any other to the task. If I couldn't go, then she had to in my stead.

She nodded slowly. "I will bring him back."

The club was of course shut to the public, every one of Michel's vampires going on the rescue mission. Numbers would be needed, this was no stealth job, they planned on making maximum chaos in a minimal amount of time.

Erika was the one responsible for reaching Michel, Jett would be at her back. The rest were to scatter the Taniwhas and keep them all busy.

The attack would happen all at once but from several different egress points. All in all, there were some 70 of Michel's vampires who were able to respond to his call. He has more in his line and they would have felt the call too, but they either lived overseas, or too far away in NZ to make it in time. Jett warned me though, that some may still arrive and come knocking on the door, so not to be surprised.

With that, they were gone, in a caravan of sleek black Land Rover Discoveries travelling at warp speed nine towards Whenuapai. I pitied any cops who tried to pull them over, they looked formidable and scary as hell. All of them dressed in dark clothing, intent on staying camouflaged with the night.

I spent the first ten minutes after they left praying to Nut and God and anyone else who would hear and trying to send power and Light down the connection to Michel. I have no idea if it worked, or if the Bond was just doing it anyway, taking what Michel needed to stay alive until they got there. I just had to trust that it knew what it was doing and would look out for him as it had looked out for me.

Amisi poured me another drink. She had some skills behind the bar, which surprised me, I really hadn't seen that coming from a young Egyptian girl, but then, I was coming to realise there was more to Amisi than meets the eye. Egyptian or no, she was quite capable of doing whatever the hell she set her mind to. I couldn't have thought of a better person to be flatting with me right now. My life was, once again, turning into a danger zone. *Warning Will Robinson* kind of scenario. Anyone who got close to me, needed to be able to take care of themselves. At least Amisi could do just that.

We had one phone call from Jett to say they were all staged and about to strike, then it was just a waiting game. I tried to feel Michel, I tried to sense him, hear him, go to him down that line that connects us, but all I got was fuzz and white noise, as though the antenna was busted. He had to still be alive, because I was, but anything other than that was pure conjecture. I had no idea and it was eating me up inside.

Amisi had stopped talking to me, had stopped trying to fill the silence and was instead talking quietly on her cellphone. I had no doubt it was to Nero, keeping him abreast of the situation, maybe just seeking council and comfort of sorts. Who knows, maybe she was checking on a vampire back there that she was attached to and wanted to join with. I didn't know, but she kept her voice low and made sure I didn't hear.

Not that I was paying too much attention. I was too busy flipping my car keys in my hand. Michel has tried to gift me many things over the years that I have known him, from roses and jewellery, to the latest being the car. The only thing I had on me right now that he had given me was the car keys, so they were the things I was fingering, tossing up and down, smoothing my fingers over the key ring. Those and his marks.

I don't know how loved ones manage to sit outside the operating theatre and wait for news of their beloved. It is torture, it is Hell on Earth, it is not right. Nobody should

299

have to wait this long to find out the answer. At least for me, if he died I would too. I knew I'd go to Nut, I've been there before, I've met her, I've heard the children laughing. So I knew what awaited me, to some degree. What I didn't know was whether Michel would be there too. He hadn't been when I visited with my goddess mother, so where do the Nosferatu go when they meet the final death? Do they have somewhere just for them? And if so, does that mean I will live eternity without him on the other side?

I couldn't stand that thought. I couldn't bear to be parted from him? Funny, isn't it? Here I am trying to be independent, trying to have distance between us, so I can go out there and do whatever the hell it is I am meant to be doing, without him worrying like a mother hen. And yet the thought of not having him beside me for eternity when I die was excruciatingly painful.

Part of me realised I needed to make better use of the time we had together alive, before I started worrying about the afterlife. Let's just hope I got a second chance at that then.

It had been 25 minutes since Jett had phoned, so they would be at war, there would no doubt be casualties, who would we lose? But, the more time it took, the longer Amisi and I sat there, the more desperate I became. Why had Jett not phoned yet? Was Erika OK, was he OK? How about Shane Smith and Doug the barman? And even Dillon bloody Malone? Not knowing was torment. I started pacing, wringing my hands, which quite frankly is a miracle I hadn't started doing that before now, but my patience had finally worn out at the half hour mark. Shit. What now?

There was a sudden rapping on the door to the club. Amisi and I both jumped where we were standing. She was off the cellphone now and had just been staring into space, probably trying not to think of anything, just like I had, but she was closer to the door than me.

"Probably one of Michel's late comers," I offered and she went to the door.

Unfortunately, there isn't a peep hole in the front door to the bar, and no windows to look out of, they are all painted over in black. It didn't even register for a second that she should ask first, who was on the other side. Neither of us contemplated it being a problem. If it wasn't a vampire, then it was probably a Norm, wanting to know why the hottest club in town was closed up like Mt Eden Prison on a Friday night.

She went through the internal door and it swished closed behind her. A safety measure if the doors are opened during sunlight hours, one door always shuts before the other opens, so no light can spill into the room and toast a vampire. The ante chamber is big enough for a few people to mill around in, before being admitted into the bar proper.

She had been gone a minute before I started to get a bad feeling. Not really that long, but my nerves were already on a razor thin edge as it was and no noise and no reappearance straight away, just had me hiking up the adrenaline all over again. I started to head toward the door when it opened slowly towards me. I briefly felt relief, only to have it completely dashed by abject fear.

In walked Rick with his arm around Amisi's throat, holding her in a deadlock, her feet scraping across the floor, her fingers scratching at his thick forearms and having little effect on him at all.

I didn't reach for my Svante, I didn't flick out a silver knife and a stake would do fuck all. I just held my breath and waited.

"Lucinda. We meet again old friend."

Somehow the sentimentality of the words was lost by the hostage in his arms and the grimace on his face.

And then before I could even think of an adequate reply, his hand flicked out of nowhere, the flash of shiny metal caught the lights of the room and a knife sliced through the air towards me.

Chapter 25
Going Home

If I had only moved to the right, the knife would have missed me altogether, at the very least just nicked my arm, but of course, I shifted left. So the knife, which had been heading for my heart, hit me fair and square just under my right hand shoulder. The pain was blinding and suddenly it was very hard to breathe.

Miraculously, I had unsheathed my Svante sword before I had hit the ground, probably even before the knife broke the surface of my skin. I'm fast when I want to be. Shame I hadn't been fast enough to get out of the way of the three inch blade though. Man, it hurt like a bitch and why couldn't I draw air?

There was no time to think about it though, Amisi had managed to stab Rick in the thigh with her stake and he had thrown her across the room, some three metres, into a wall. I managed a quick glance in her direction, she was sitting stunned, but trying to get back on her feet, another stake in her hand already, before he came at me.

I swiped, a half-arsed swipe of the Svante sword, down in front of him, missing him by mere inches, but making him take a step back and reconsider his approach. If he had another knife on him, I was toast, there was no chance I could dodge a second. My movements were laboured and imprecise, my breathing was ragged and caused the already fierce pain in my chest into a stabbing frenzy. Sweat was coating my skin and blood was running down the front of my jacket, dripping onto the floor in front of me. I was vaguely aware of just how much shit I was actually in, but I was determined to keep Rick at bay and protect Amisi.

Rick just smiled at me, his head cocked to the side, his eyes an angry red and his teeth way sharper than a human's should ever be. The overall effect was not comforting.

"You look like shit, Luce."

"You're not a pretty picture either Taniwha-man." My voice was strained and weak. Shit, not a good sign at all. I shifted the hold on the Svante and almost dropped it, my grip tightening in response, making my knuckles go white. I gritted my teeth through the pain in my chest at the added force I was using just to hold onto the damn thing.

"This doesn't have to be hard, Luce. You know what the outcome will be in the end, just let it happen. And if you do, I promise I won't hurt your girl there." He nodded towards Amisi, who was still trying to get up off the floor, having collapsed back a couple of times now.

"Why Rick?" I had to ask. I'd been asking myself this again and again. Why was Rick doing this? Why had he killed Jerome, a man he had recently loved and respected like a father, why was he insisting on killing me? We had been friends, once upon a time, how had it come to this?

"You know why. They have to die, all of them. They are unnatural, they are dead already. They prey on the living, they consume everything around them, turning it evil, tainting this world." He laughed, a bitter bark of a laugh. "Look at what they did to you. You are just as evil as they are, because of him, because of them. Can't you see? You all have to die to keep us safe, to keep out the evil you breathe."

He had that fanatical look to him, the one hard core evangelists have. They truly believe they are preaching what is right for everyone. There is no reasoning with them, there is no argument to be had, they have already signed on the dotted line, they are committed to the end.

The fact that he was so far from the truth was irrelevant. The fact that I am the one who is meant to protect the world from Dark, from evil, would not compute. I could try to tell him about the Prophesy, about my role in it, about the consequences of having me killed now, before the war has even truly begun. But it would be to no avail, it would be futile, useless, he had already started his crusade and he would die finishing it.

My sword hand had lowered, not intentionally, just holding it up had become a mission. I was starting to feel so cold, so numb and shivery, I don't even think I could feel the pain any more, but the room had dimmed. Rick was starting to look blurry. I struggled to raise the sword when he stepped forward, noticing my strength was waning. I managed to get it back up, but my whole arm was shaking. The blade was a blurring mess of shiny metal under the artificial lights of the room, it was vibrating like a tuning fork, but I held it firm, straight out in front. I would not give an inch.

"Then let's end this," I whispered. I was done trying to convince myself that he could be reasoned with, that the path he had chosen could be changed. He was what he was now, for better or worse and certainly not because I had put him there. I would not fight the losing battle of turning him back toward the Light, but I would fight him. I could not let him kill me or the vampires. It was wrong.

Besides, he had killed Jerome, he had killed Bruno, if not by his own hands, then by his command. He had chained my kindred and caused him pain and wished him the final death. And he had trashed my house. My coffee machine, dammit. There was only so much a girl could tolerate before she lost her rag completely.

I felt myself pull on what tiny reserves I had left and I steeled myself for the final clash.

Three things happened at once. Rick changed into a Taniwha in lightning speed and with the glorious colour display that accompanies a shift to animal form. Amisi threw her remaining stake towards him, the sliver point tipping end over end, sparkling in the lights of the room and then getting engulfed in colours of his magical change. And I ran towards him with my Svante sword held high and a war cry ringing from my throat. Slashing downwards as I approached that wall of magic, slicing through the the colours, making them split like a prism catching the sun's rays and spreading them around the room.

There was a loud crack that reverberated around the club, shattering the top shelf bottles at the bar, making the glasses splinter one after the other like falling dominoes and pushing what little air that remained in my lungs out. I collapsed back on the ground, my sword lost, the knife in my chest having long fallen out and the world quickly fading. I struggled against the black that was encroaching, rolling onto my side to see where Rick was coming from next, trying to get my silver knife from its sheath at the waistband of my skirt. My fingers were numb, I couldn't even tell if they were touching the knife hilt or the skirt material, or simply just twitching in thin air. I couldn't breathe, I don't think I had taken a breath in since I had struck down with the sword and although I tried now to get some precious oxygen in my lungs, to stop the scream of pain that clenched them tight, nothing happened. Nothing moved, not my fingers, nor the knife, nor my mouth to inhale much needed air, nor my lungs. And if I was quite honest, I didn't care. Not for me. My thoughts were of Michel when the blackness finally came, engulfing me in its bitter-sweet blanket, surrounding me like a tomb.

I didn't visit Nut, nor hear the wonderful sound of children laughing. I was looking for it. I had expected it. I was prepared to welcome it. Maybe, she was angry with me. I had failed the Prophesy, I had died needlessly, fighting a shape shifter who shouldn't have even been part of the fight for Light over Dark. He was a meaningless distraction in a world subjected to war. I shouldn't have let it happen. I had failed Nut.

I wondered if the void of blackness I was now in, was what my fate for eternity would be. No sound, no sight, no sensations, just a suspended void for my conscience. Aware, but not aware. As far as punishments go, it was pretty nifty. I could think about the consequences of my actions, the fate I had left the world to. Dark would be rallying, the Light would be growing weaker without an advocate to shine bright. I could think about who I had left behind, to suffer in that increasing Darkness: Amisi, Nero, Erika, Gregor. Michel's vampires, who were now masterless, trying to find their way, trying to join other families for protection. Maybe they would band together under Jett or Erika, maybe they would continue the battle without us.

I could also think of Michel. Was he in the afterlife set aside for Nosferatu? What had Gregor called it? *Elysium.* Was he happy? Did he even remember me? The thought that I no longer existed for him brought tears to my eyes. I could feel them hot and wet rolling down my cheeks. I could feel them being brushed away by something soft and warm. I could feel.

I could feel.

I could feel.

And then not just the wet streak of tears but the stabbing pain in my chest, the throbbing ache in my head, the rasping agony of my breath. My body spasmed at the onslaught of pain, the agony that was my physical self, meeting my cerebral. Everything I had been thinking now associated with everything I was feeling.

My eyes flickered open and it took a moment for the scene in front of me to make sense. Everything was at an odd angle and then it dawned on me, that it wasn't the sight that was off kilter, but me. I was on my side on the polished concrete floor of *Sensations*. Amisi was stroking my cheek, wiping away the tears and Nero was trying to stem the blood flow at my chest, with towels from behind the bar. I could smell the faint hint of beer and wine and spirits, mixed in with laundry powder and detergent as he shifted the material into a better place. Pressing firmly against the knife wound, sending a shocking wave of stabbing pain straight down to my toes. I whimpered, but tried to move. I really wanted to sit up.

"Hush, my Kiwi. Stay still. The paramedics are on their way."

It took several efforts and he had to lean in to my mouth to hear what I was trying to say, but finally I managed a very weak, "Rick?"

It was Amisi who answered. "He vanished, just

disappeared. I don't know where he is, or what happened. The colours were everywhere and then, when your sword shattered the pattern, he just flashed out of sight."

I wanted to ask more, I wanted to ask about Michel and the others, but the blackness was returning as the front door to the club opened and two uniformed figures walked in, carrying bags and bottles and God knows what else. I didn't get a chance to see, because the pull was too strong, the black too inviting and I was just so tired. I couldn't resist it any more.

I couldn't tell how much time had elapsed, but I woke up feeling like a train had run me over. My body ached, my head thumped, I could even feel my blood moving through my veins and it hurt. There was lots of pale blue and white. Blue on the walls and the blanket that covered me, white in the lights and sheets and ceiling. Tubes and wires, flashing lights and silently blinking buttons. A heaviness to the air that felt oppressive and someone at the side of my bed.

I didn't know them, I had never seen this person before. She was pressing buttons and checking wires and tubes and writing something on a board. I tried to turn my head to watch her and found I couldn't, something was holding me in place. I realised that something was coming from my mouth, down my throat. I tried to swallow past it, but couldn't and that's when I got scared. That's when I felt really trapped.

My fear must have spiked my heartbeat, or my respirations, because the person next to the bed turned to me and frowned. Reached for something on a tray beside her and then lifting a syringe to a bag hanging at my head. I watched helplessly as she pushed the syringe plunger home and whatever had been in it mixed with whatever was in the bag and flowed down the tube to my arm.

It took mere seconds for it to have its effect on me, making the world turn black again and my heartbeat slow. And all I could do was scream in my mind while I listened to the sounds of quiet that taunted me.

When I awoke the second time, I was in the same bed, screens on two sides, open at the end, machines still surrounding me, but nothing down my throat. I could swallow, though my mouth was dry. There were still tubes in my arm and one down my nose, but that was all. The air was still heavy and silent. It took a few minutes for cognitive thought to return and then I recognised where I was. Hospital. A public hospital, maybe on a ward, but there was no one else in my room, or my opened cubicle, so maybe ICU, maybe post-op recovery rooms, I wasn't sure. But I knew I wanted out.

Where was everyone?

The nurse returned, the same one from before and this time she smiled. She had a friendly open face, but a short severe haircut. She was in pale green scrubs and had a name badge pinned to her breast pocket, *Sally*. Sally was friendly but a little intense, I was guessing, probably very good at what she did and dedicated to her job.

"Hello there, Lucinda. How are we today?"

Why is it, that caregivers always talk in the plural?

We feel like crap, thanks. "Fine." It was croaked out of a very dry throat. The nurse let me sip from a straw in a cup of water. Relief.

"What time is it?" I needed to know if it was nightfall, if I could see Michel. I needed Michel as much, if not more, than I had needed that drink of water.

She glanced at her watch. "It's almost 7.30 pm. Your husband should be back soon, visiting hours start at 7.30."

My husband? Oh. Michel? Couldn't be anyone else, could it? Please God, please let it be Michel.

"You are one very lucky lady. That stab wound punctured your lung. The doctors have patched you up, but we've had you in an induced coma for two days. It'll probably be another two or three before we release you to a ward and another week or so before you are released altogether." Like hell, I thought. "Do you remember what happened?" Her voice had softened when she asked that last.

I shook my head. No point telling a Norm that a shape shifter had thrown a dagger at my heart while trying to rid the world of vampires.

"Never mind, it may or may not come back to you, but the police will want to know. You should expect a visit from them soon. We'll try to delay them as long as we can, we don't particularly like them up here in DCC, but once you're back on the ward, they'll come calling."

DCC? Department of Critical Care. I'd seen the directory in the hospital foyer before, when I'd visited ED, or the Emergency Department, after particularly bad hunts. I wondered what my hospital file told them. Was I a repeat trauma patient, did they think I had an abusive partner perhaps? Jeez, just what I needed.

She finished up whatever it was she was doing, checking machines, fiddling with buttons, then fluffed my pillows, gave me another sip of water and left. I heard her soft rubber soled footfalls on the linoleum floor as she walked away and then her hushed words from the distant end of what was obviously a large open plan room, the cubicles were situated in.

"Ah, Mr Durand, you'll be pleased to know your wife is awake." Her voice had a sing-song timbre, she was actually flirting with him. I couldn't hear his reply, but I did get her soft laughter as she headed further away.

Was I even well enough to be jealous? Nah. Especially as she had called me his wife.

I held my breath in anticipation. I wanted Michel so badly, but I was scared of how hurt he was, of what news he would bring, of everything. I suddenly felt so small in the big hospital bed I was lying in, surrounded by bulky machines that I didn't understand and the weight of a Prophesy crushing into me.

He rounded the end of the partition and just stood there. He could have been an angel, he was awash with light. Maybe it was just the position he was standing under the fluorescents above, or the fact that my eyes had welled up with tears and everything seemed a little blurry, but he was beautiful, perfect. And apart from some faint marks at his neck and wrists, I couldn't see any other injuries, despite my eyes moving over him and devouring every inch of him that they could.

He was beside me a second later, his hand on my face, his mouth on my neck, words and sentences in French tumbling out against my skin, hot and fervent and alive.

I had my hands in his hair, pulling him closer. I wanted my lips on him too, but he seemed unable to move, unable to let me go, unable to pull his face away from his marks on my skin and unable to stop the desperate spill of French from his mouth. I couldn't understand a word he was speaking, it was all so fast and his accent so strong, but I understood what he meant. I was glad he was alive too.

Finally, he ran out of steam and the odd English word started slipping into his monologue. I hadn't interrupted, I kind of felt like he needed to get all of that out before we could actually have a conversation. But when he slowed enough for there to be pauses, I pulled his head up off my neck and dragged him to my mouth.

He managed to keep his weight off me, placing his arms on either side of my head. His mouth was perfect and soft, the touch of lips, like coming home. He sighed against me.

"You had me worried, *ma douce.*"

"Likewise, you."

He didn't pull away, just rested his forehead against mine, letting his breath wash over me, his scent fill my nostrils, his *Sanguis Vitam* flood against my shields. I lowered them automatically, but he didn't rush in, he pulled back slightly and looked over his shoulder, then said, "If I do this, they will know and there will be questions. I can glaze the staff now and remove your records, but there could be a chance that I miss something or someone. This could prove troublesome for you in the future should you require medical attention again."

Plus, he knew how I felt about glazing.

"You could do it though, couldn't you? Cover it up, I mean?" I asked biting my bottom lip.

"Yes."

"Then take me home, Michel. Get me out of here." To hell with the repercussions, to hell with glazing up a storm,

313

I needed to be back on my feet now, not in two week's time. I needed to be with Michel.

His *Sanguis Vitam* came flooding in as soon as I had finished talking. It felt like sunshine on a winter's day, like your first taste of ice cream as a toddler, like the moment you realised you were in love and that person loved you back. It was filled with light and love and happiness and was so much more powerful than I had ever felt before. It also went on longer than Michel ever had to before, when healing me. I gathered I had quite a bit to heal. No wonder the Norms would have kept me for two more weeks and even then I would have been a battered and bruised wreck.

Finally, it pulled away and I felt relief from the aches and pain, but also so tired, I could hardly open my eyes. Michel was breathing deeply beside me, leaning on the edge of the bed.

"Are you all right?" I asked sleepily.

He nodded, but looked a little pale. "I'll deal with the staff and the records. Erika and Jett are here, they'll help you out to the car."

He turned away slowly, moving at a much more deliberate pace than usual. I was suddenly a little concerned for him. That had taken a lot to do.

Erika appeared around the corner of the partition, all smiles and bright eyes.

"Hey, *chica*. You call for a taxi?"

She started to help me out of the bed, removing tubes and lines and God knows what else from God knows where else. She knew what she was doing though, as though it was all par for the course. Then Jett came into view.

"Need a hand?" he said smiling at me.

I shook my head. "We'll be fine, go help Michel. Healing me was harder than he expected, I think."

Immediately Jett was on full alert, he nodded and swung away to cover his master.

I swayed a little when I made it upright, but with Erika's arm around my waist, she steadied me and somehow we made it out of DCC and to the lifts without bumping into a soul. I was guessing there was a fair bit of *Sanguis Vitam* floating through the air, but I couldn't concentrate enough on sensing it, all my attention was on putting one foot in front of the other and not blacking out.

I was healed, physically all the holes were fixed and the connections remade, but my body was screaming for rest. Even vampire healing mojo can only do so much.

We made it to the car parked in a special temporary car park at the front entrance, no doubt hidden by a ward and Erika helped me into the back. She slid in next to me, but I didn't register anything else, falling asleep pretty much straight away. When I awoke, the car was moving and it was no longer Erika at my side, but Michel, holding me in his arms and kissing my head.

The last thing I heard before succumbing to beautiful slumber again was Michel's sweet voice in my ears and breath on my skin.

"Sleep, my love, I am taking you home."

I wondered briefly, before blackness came, where home actually was.

Chapter 26
Wake Up Call

I don't know how long I slept for, but when I awoke the shutters on my bedroom window at the house in St. Helier's were down. And Michel was wrapped around my side, one arm under my shoulders, his face nestled into my neck, his other arm across my chest, a leg over my thigh. He couldn't have got any closer if he had tried.

And we were both naked.

I pulled the covers up on the bed as they were down around our hips and snuggled down under their and Michel's weight, allowing myself to drift back off to sleep.

When I awoke again it was to the soft touch of Michel's hand on my stomach, tracing patterns with his fingers around my belly button, slowly working his way lower in swirls and circles. The warmth of his touch sending shock waves through me. He sensed I was awake, but didn't stop, just kept moving millimetre by millimetre closer to where butterflies were dancing and I had suddenly felt a rush of slick, hot heat. He shifted his body closer to me, allowing his erection to press hard against my hip. I could feel it throbbing between us, an unspoken hint of what was to come.

I knew this was the point of no return. I knew this was what I had been dreading and been craving, all at the same time. Now, was the time to decide. Push Michel away or let him back in? As I felt him hesitate, the closer he got to where he wanted to be on my body, I knew he was waiting for me to finish that thought. I had been struggling with loss of control for a long time now. It felt familiar, not exactly a friend, but an old acquaintance. I realised then, that I had let it have that effect on me. I had given it power, when it may not necessarily have had it all on its own. I asked myself the one question that only really mattered. Could I live without him? I knew the answer immediately: no. I couldn't live without Michel. I didn't want to either. I choose this.

This was my decision to make. I was making it now. I was taking control of my life back, allowing Michel to be part of it, on my terms. I was back in charge, at least of this.

Suddenly his hand had made it to its destination and he slowly spread my thighs and placed his palm against my centre, his fingers running back and forth across the sensitive folds there, making them wetter and wetter. And making my body start to arch up to meet him. He answered with a quick thrust of a finger inside. I groaned and threw my head back on the pillow, shutting my eyes and letting the sensations he was creating take over.

I could think of worse ways to be woken.

He started kissing down the centre of my body then, past my breasts, over my rib cage, around my belly button and then lower. He didn't stop, just repositioned himself between my legs, pushing them further apart to allow for his broad shoulders. His hands began running up the undersides of my thighs, to rest on either butt cheek and then he lifted me off the bed and kissed me, taking a soft, wet fold between his teeth and biting down.

I lost it then and had to fight to catch my breath, but he was determined and continued to suck one fold after the other, with the odd tongue thrust in between. And then finishing off with a bite, his fangs piercing once, twice, three times, the intensity so strong, the line between pleasure and pain so thin, I couldn't tell which side I was treading, but wanted it all. The sharp sting of his fangs, the flow of heat and lust and desire, to be repeated again and again.

Finally, he stopped biting and just sucked and licked and found that precious little spot that sent me thrashing beneath him and screaming out his name when I finally came. He moved up beside me and held me in his arms, whispering in French again, as I slowly came down off that high. I felt him rubbing his hard length against my hip, then when my breathing settled, he kissed my neck and shifted his weight, so the tip of his sex sat at my entrance.

I opened my eyes and stared up at him as he stayed poised above me, his eyes were flashing amethyst and indigo, his mouth a perfect Cupid's bow, his face flushed with hunger and need.

"Welcome home," he whispered against my lips as he kissed me.

"It's good to be home," I said shifting my hips, making my wet entrance press against his hard length. He sucked in a sharp breath and closed his eyes, but didn't enter me, just sat there teasing.

"I am hungry for you, *ma douce*." I don't think he was just talking blood, but blood was there in the question, so I lifted my chin and exposed my neck, a sure invitation to a vampire.

He growled, but said, "I had another place in mind."

He moved in lightning speed and was between my legs again, his fingers thrusting into me, not quite as welcomed as his hard length would have been at this point, but

318

managing to get me writhing again, thrusting back against his digits, meeting them with every flick and movement he made inside me. I was just about to crest another wave of a mind blowing orgasm when his head dipped to my upper thigh and his fangs pierced so close to my entrance that I couldn't really tell if he wasn't there or not. His fingers working magic, his mouth sucking blood, every sensation I had pooling right there, right at my centre and the feel of it all was so intense, I exploded in a rush of wet heat that went on for as long as he fed, washing over me again and again, not retreating but making me ride the wave longer than ever before.

My body shook, my screams went on for minutes, hours, days and the world ceased to exist. But for him and me, his mouth, my blood and his fingers.

He released me eventually and I sank back against the sheets exhausted but more alive than I had ever felt before. I felt his tongue licking his fang marks and it was still so sensitive there I whimpered.

"I would allow you a moment to recover, but I am afraid, I need to be inside you, right now." His voice was husky and low, so strained I could barely understand him, but I got with the programme as soon as I felt his bodyweight above me, his straining hard and wet sex at my entrance and then I felt him slide it home.

His face came down to nestle against my neck and he growled, "You are mine." I couldn't help feeling that that possessive statement was going to be around for a while. He hadn't stopped uttering those very same words every time his hard, long, thick sex entered me since I had returned from Wellington and the fight with Nero.

With every thrust he made inside me, I kept hearing the words in my head. I don't know if he was projecting them to me in his thoughts, or if the erotic notion of him possessing me not only with his body, but with every fibre of his self, made me think of them. Like a beat of drums as his hips rocked and his shoulders flexed and his cock entered me as far as it would go.

It didn't take long for either of us to orgasm. I was still so sensitive down there, from what he had just done and he was so desperate to mark me with his scent and seed, that within seconds we were spent and collapsed together on the bed. Our breathing ragged, our heartbeats motoring and our sweat soaked bodies moulded together in a tangled pile of intertwined limbs and intertwined hearts.

Neither of us moved for a good five minutes, still floating down off the crest of the wave, still trying to catch our breath. Finally, Michel reached for the coverlet and pulled it over us, snuggling back into the same position we had been in when I first woke.

"You are still so tired, *ma douce*. Sleep."

It was as though his words were commands - which they can't be anymore, the joining does not allow it even when I'm having trouble maintaining my shields - but I drifted off to sleep in the comfort and protection of his arms.

The shutters raising for the evening is what woke me. Michel was on his side, awake, watching me. I got the impression he had been watching me all day.

I stretched and yawned, like a Siamese cat, beside him and basked in the glow of his smile.

"You're still here?" I reached up and stroked his face.

"I could not leave you. You are my miracle. My dream come true." He bent down and kissed me long and slow. "Is it nice to be home, *ma douce*?"

So, this was my home, huh? I nodded. I could handle calling this my home for a while, as long as he was here too. Shit. Where had that come from?

His smile quirked a bit at the corners. I closed my eyes and swallowed a groan.

"I'm projecting again, aren't I?"

"Yes," he said laughing quietly.

"I bet you're just loving that."

"It would be a lie to say otherwise. You hold so much of yourself back normally, it has been a pleasure recently to see what you truly feel."

"And what is that?" Because, I'm not entirely sure even I know the answer to that question.

He paused. "Perhaps it would be better to let you discover the answer to that on your own." He kissed my nose and got up off the bed, all six foot two naked glory of him. I watched him walk into the bathroom and turn the shower head on.

The shower wasn't as big as the one at Sensations, it only had one shower head, no massaging nozzles, couldn't fit a rugby team inside, maybe just one or two forwards at a pinch.

"There is still room for you, *ma douce*." He called out above the water splashing, before stepping inside the stall and adding. "I can always have it renovated if you wish."

I bet he could, I thought. Why don't you throw a jacuzzi in while you're at it.

As you wish, ma belle. Anything for you. Now are you

joining me?

I stifled a laugh, just letting the air rush out in a semi huff. He was impossible and the sooner my thoughts were my own again the better. But, what if this was permanent? Crap. That just really would make his day, wouldn't it?

I lay there awhile, listening to the water falling in the room next door. Shifting my body weight from side to side, fidgeting a little, until I could stand it no more. I stepped into the shower stall in a flash, having covered the distance to the bathroom without even realising it.

Michel murmured, as he pulled me under the hot spray, "When you make your mind up about something, there's no holding you back is there?" I could feel his shoulders shaking from laughter.

Then he was soaping me up, gently washing away the after effects of our love making, cleansing me from the hospital smells that lingered and rediscovering my body all over again.

Twenty minutes later we were both panting and needing another soap up before we could actually make it out of the shower stall.

"I can't take you anywhere, can I?" he said as he finished washing me down, again. "Every opportunity there is, you assault me with your feminine wiles."

"I think the sentence is: you *can* take me anywhere, as you have just so aptly proven yet again. Showers, car seats, office desks..."

He raised his eyebrows at me. "Are you trying to go for a record here, *ma douce*?" He pushed his now fully erect sex against me again, I just closed my eyes and shook my head.

322

"You are way too highly strung, Michel."

"Ah," he said in reply. "I can take the hint." And pulled away.

I didn't let him get far before clasping his arm with one of my hands and pulling his head down towards me with another. I whispered against his mouth right before I kissed him, "Horizontal, that's my only request. I don't think I can stand another minute upright."

I was in his arms and on the bed in a second, the shower still running, our bodies still wet and soapy, his hard length inside me once more. Those words, his new mantra, whispered against the skin at my throat as he thrust deep again and again, "You are mine, *ma douce*, you are mine."

Suddenly he pulled out and flipped me over, repositioning himself behind me, bringing me up on my knees and pushing my head down onto the bed. He re-entered me with a groan, moving more slowly now, savouring the angle, enjoying every movement, every sensation.

"I believe you had thought of this when we were in the car in your dream, had you not? I must pay more attention to your desires, *ma douce*. From this angle, you are sublime."

I couldn't answer right then, as he had leaned forward and started playing with my wet folds with his fingers, as his hard length slipped in and out in a constant rhythm. I could feel every stroke of him. Every touch and rub of his fingers had me panting and begging and moaning within seconds and as I came his fingers soaked up my wet release and then he started moving in earnest. His hands both returned to my hips, he rocked back and forth behind me, bringing me against himself as he thrust forward, going so deep, so far. I could feel him stretching me to my limit, his strength, his size, all this side of too much, but tipping me off the edge of a cliff all over again as he pumped himself inside me and cried out in release.

This time, I couldn't move a muscle. Michel had collapsed down on top of me, pinning me to the bed. His upper body had slid to the side, so I could still breath, but his waist, hips and legs, had me trapped. I couldn't have cared less. I was replete.

"I think you've killed me. I've gone to heaven," I mumbled into the pillow.

His hand came out and started stroking down my back, sending tingles along my spine that my body was too tired to respond to. But, it still felt deliciously good. His breathing was uneven and I don't think he was able to formulate a reply straight away, so we just lay there and luxuriated in the warmth of our bodies and the total satisfaction of unbelievably great sex.

Eventually, he rolled off me and pulled me up the bed into his arms, grabbing the duvet cover to throw over us with a flick of his wrist.

"I think we should just stay here for the night, *ma douce*. To hell with responsibilities." He kissed me softly on my head.

"I bet you've already told someone to handle things for you at the club."

He chuckled. "Perhaps. I had intended to head in though, the line is still fragile at the loss of Bruno. They need reassurance."

Bruno. Shit. How could I have forgotten about Bruno? I felt like such a selfish bitch all of a sudden.

Michel pulled me closer and placed a hand under my chin, lifting my face to his.

"My sweet little one, when have you ever not put others before yourself? A moment of happiness for just you is not being selfish. Besides, my need to claim you is still too strong, I would not have allowed you to turn me away to mourn." His lips brushed my mouth.

I let my head fall against his warm chest and just listened to the beat of his heart, so calming, so much like home.

"Still, we should go in and see them, if you think it would help," I said, still wrapped up in his arms. "Did we lose any others?" A question I had been dreading asking.

"No. Just Bruno and he fought like a warrior, like only Bruno would. He.... he died for me, for the chance for me to escape. It was futile, they would have caught me anyway. At least he went to *Elysium* as a true vampyre warrior. He would have been proud."

I held on tight as Michel remembered his fallen friend. Bruno had been turned by Michel, he had been by his side for over 200 years, they were more than just master and servant, so much more than just that.

"I'm sorry," I whispered, letting a single tear flow down my check onto his chest. He picked it up on the tip of his finger and took it in his mouth.

"*Ta chagrin calme mon coeur, ma douce.*" And then he translated in a whisper as he bent to kiss my head. "Your sorrow soothes my heart."

I still needed a moment to recover, so he opted to

325

shower alone, with reluctance I might add, but a necessity. We decided the 'family' needed us more than we needed the solitude together. So, to *Sensations* to rally the line it was.

I could have easily wiled away the night with Michel in my arms, or at the very least curled up on the couch and watched T.V. with him. I realised that he and I had never done that before. Sure we've spent down time together, usually in his chamber, or occasionally at my apartment, but only for a few hours at best. A whole night doing nothing but normal around home things would be my dream. If there was one gift he could ever give me that would be priceless and I would be unable to resist, it would be his time. One night, just him and me, no pressures, no responsibilities, just us on the couch at home enjoying each other.

We could have made it happen tonight, I think he really wanted to. But the health of his line, right now when so much more was going to be asked of them in the coming days, as we faced whatever the Dark had in store for us, was more important than just me and him. I knew this, but I also pined for what he couldn't yet give me.

I lay there and listened to the water falling and let my body enjoy the last moments of blissful rest before duty called. My thoughts though, were rudely interrupted by the phone on my bedside table. I thought perhaps Erika or Amisi would answer it, but when they didn't I lifted the handset and lazily said, "*Bonsoir!*"

"*Bonsoir, ma petite chasseuse.* Have you been practising your French for me?"

Gregor. Shit.

Chapter 27
Distractions

"Hello, Gregor."

"Lucinda." I could practically hear the smile in his voice. "I hope I haven't disturbed you, little Hunter. I have missed you this past weekend. You know, you really shouldn't stand me up."

I wasn't sure if anyone had told Gregor what had happened, I assumed they had, but just in case...

"It wasn't intentional. I was kinda laid flat."

"You are better I trust? Your kindred healing you, as he should no doubt. So, when will I see you again?"

I don't think he was really too fussed about whether I was well or not, or whether Michel had healed me or not. He wanted me in Wellington and that was all that mattered. I sure as hell didn't want to go there.

I stifled a sigh. "I'm not sure, Gregor. I have some things that need sorting here." The health of Michel's line. Finding out what's happened to Rick and blasting his arse if he's still around. These were far more pressing things to me than Gregor and his wayward human assassins.

"Lucinda, we had an understanding. You were going to help me with my little human problem and fill the gap of a Nosferatin until one could be found for my city and I was going to keep the *Iunctio* from your shores. It is getting increasingly harder to hold up my end of the bargain when there have been so many more attacks since you were last here."

Bugger. More attacks?

"How many more attacks?" I could feel his grin from here, he'd hooked me and he knew it.

"Three Rogues killed and two of my line attacked, but now safe."

Damn that's not good. "Have you managed to find anything else out about the humans?"

"We have made a dent in their numbers. I believe our tactics have - how would you say? - scared them shitless, I think that is your phrase, but they are still rallying. Determined doesn't even cover their psyche, I'm afraid."

I didn't like the sound of that. Gregor making a dent in their numbers could only mean one thing, he wasn't even trying to avoid death as a solution. Killing off all the humans, who are part of this whole humans against vampires thing, would be a perfect solution in his world. I couldn't ignore this. I had to step in.

I was rubbing my face in frustration when Michel came out of the bathroom and began to get dressed. He didn't say anything to me, he could probably tell who was on the other end of the line, hear my thoughts, hear his voice. His presence was a balm though, a soothing balm, calming my jangled nerves and rising temper.

"Ah," Gregor breathed down the line. "Your kindred is near, is he not?"

Huh? "How do you...?"

"I sense your calm through our bond, *ma cherie*. I also sense you moving further away from me. I admit, my desire for you to be in my city is more than just political, my dear. Much, much more."

Michel was standing over me in an instant, growling low and long. I knew Gregor was doing it on purpose, his laughter at the other end of the phone line made that quite clear, even if I didn't know him well enough by now to

328

have figured out his ulterior motives already.

"Gregor, I'll have to get back to you on this."

"Of course, *ma cherie*. Go calm your beast. I am, if nothing, a patient man and I have already tasted the dessert, I can wait a little longer for one more mouthful."

The phone was snatched from my hand and hurled across the room in an instant, where it shattered against the far fall. The call disconnected with finality. Michel hauled me up into his arms and growled as he grabbed my hair and tipped my head back, exposing my neck.

I managed a, "Michel!" before his fangs bit into the side of my neck and his words shouted through my mind, the room, hell, even the universe: You. Are. Mine!

Possessive, much?

The bite didn't last long, just enough for him to feel he owned me again. I was getting used to it, I wasn't sure how much longer my neck was going to survive it though, but I understood it. For the first time in my association with vampires, with Michel, I understood. This wasn't about controlling, this was about not sharing. I was his, he didn't want to share me and for the first time I didn't want to be shared either.

"Oh God, *ma douce*," he said in a shaky voice as he crushed me to him. "Thank you. Thank you so much."

Maybe, this reading my every thought was going to be helpful after all.

He let me go so I could have a shower, but he didn't go back to getting dressed, he just sat on the side of the messed up bed and stared off into space. His hand running along his jawline in a soothing contemplative motion, leaning forward with his elbows on his knees. He was beautiful to watch, even in this distracted moment. He was gorgeous. I wanted him again right then and there.

His eyes shot up to me still standing in the doorway of the bathroom and his lips quirked at the corners.

"I think I should perhaps leave you to shower, *ma douce*." He slipped on some trousers while I watched with hungry eyes, he didn't bother with a shirt. "I'll be in the kitchen fixing you something to eat. I will have you eating again properly, if it the last thing I do."

He blew me a kiss from the door and headed out of the room.

Coward! I sent him.

Sweet temptation, thy name is Lucinda.

I laughed as I got under the shower, finally and had the most luxuriously warm and wonderfully imaginative few moments alone. Aware that I probably wasn't really alone, that Michel would be hearing every thought, probably seeing every image, I was painstakingly playing in full HD colour and surround sound in my head. I have a very good imagination.

I heard a loud growl from outside the room and just laughed harder. He probably hadn't even made it down the stairs yet.

He was sitting in the kitchen when I came down though, still shirtless, still gorgeous. Still looking very frustrated.

"So, how's that reading my mind going for you?" I said as I slipped into a seat at the table and picked up the delicious and extremely tempting looking sandwich he had put together for me. Ham, cheese, tomato, lettuce, mayo, oh and pickled cucumbers, my favourite. Divine.

330

He sat back, placing his tablet computer carefully on the table and looked at me. I could see the *New Zealand Herald* website on the open browser page. I hadn't realised he'd brought his tablet here. Maybe he had one in every house he owned.

"Entertaining, *ma douce*. You must demonstrate some of those more acrobatic moves you imagined some time. I would be keen to help you realise your potential."

I just looked at him over the top of my tasty sandwich and winked.

"Whenever you say the word, lover boy, I'm your girl."

He smiled broadly at that.

"You are?"

"Ah-ha," mumbled around a mouthful of sandwich.

"Promise." His voice was low, sexy, inviting.

I started chewing my mouthful more carefully, he was up to something, I couldn't tell what. Hell, who cares, I was so his it wasn't funny any more.

He burst out laughing. "That is so good to know, *ma douce*. I shall hold you to it."

Okaaaay.

He relaxed back into his seat and just watched me eat. I was used to it, this was familiar ground, he's watched me eat so many times, I can no longer count. It's almost a ritual for us, so comforting.

"Will you stay with me tomorrow?" I have no idea where that came from. I was quite prepared for Michel to stay at *Sensations* and for me to go back to work.

He looked curiously happy, but almost as though he was unsure whether to believe his good fortune or not. He reached out and took my free hand.

"I would stay with you every day if you would let me. But, if it is just tomorrow, then so be it. I am yours. Tomorrow I shall stay here with you."

I had a sudden attack of the guilts. "I suppose, I should really go back to work."

He shook his head, still holding my hand and slowly stroking the skin on the back of it with his thumb. "You are on leave for the rest of the week, *ma douce*. We were not sure how quickly you would recover, or if we could get you out of the hospital as soon as you came round. It was a safety measure, but I believe you should take full advantage of it. We must sort this Taniwha issue, before it gets too much further out of hand. We have to take a more proactive stance."

I finished my last mouthful of sandwich, aware that it was the first time in days I had eaten without feeling nauseous. I took a sip of *Diet Coke* to wash it down and sat back in my chair.

"Rick is still out there, I take it?"

"Yes. He has made sure we are aware of it, he expects us to act first I think."

"How did he capture you, Michel?" The sixty-four thousand dollar question.

Michel ran a hand through his hair, which he hadn't tied back since showering. Oh yeah, that's right, the urge to escape the bedroom was too strong. I say again, coward.

"Harsh, *ma douce*, very harsh." But he was smiling slyly at me. "I am afraid, he caught me at a weak moment. I had thought he was prepared to talk. I have been trying for a discussion for days, he seemed amenable to negotiations. I was a fool and also, I admit, not at my best, so the mistake is all mine. I had wanted to solve this for you, *ma belle*, without further bloodshed, if I could."

Wow. That was interesting, wasn't it? Here's Michel trying to do the humane thing, something he knew I would have wanted above all else and there's Gregor slicing down humans because he can and it's easier that way.

I shook my head in amazement. "Is there any wonder why I love you so much?"

I think he had stopped breathing, he just looked at me in shock. Oops. Maybe I hadn't said that aloud before, I know I'd thought it to him plenty.

He moved with vampire swiftness, one minute stock still staring at me from across the way, the next on his knees between my legs, his head resting on my stomach, his arms wrapped around my waist.

"Ma belle petite lumière, la raison de mon existence. Je t'aime, je t'adore, je t'aime."

I hesitated for a second, his words so sincere, so full of love, but I couldn't stop myself for long and found my hands running through his hair, soothing him, touching him, calming him. I reached down and cupped either side of his face, raising it up towards me. It was a bit weird looking down at him, I usually have to look straight up to reach his face, but his lips felt the same as normal, when I brushed them with mine.

When he sighed against me, I slipped my tongue inside, just a hint, running it along the inside of his bottom lip, dipping in then out, making him moan for more. I had intended to just leave it as a soft, intimate kiss, nothing more, but Michel responded with his usual hunger and need. He took command of the kiss and deepened it, his

333

tongue taking over possession of my mouth. His hand at the back of my head, in my hair, pulling me to him. His other arm staying around my waist, then using that arm to pull me onto the floor and into his lap. He was kneeling, I had my legs either side of his, straddling his lap. A handy position, I must say. He continued to kiss me with deep urgent thrusts of his tongue. I was taking much delight in the fact he didn't have a shirt on, running my hands all over his bare skin, digging my nails in to his flesh, making him growl against me.

I knew where this was heading, we just couldn't keep our hands off each other tonight, but I didn't care. We'd get to *Sensations* eventually, do the whole make happy the line thing and then come back here for more. But right now, I wanted him. Here, on the floor, or maybe the kitchen table. Either would be good.

He quickly lifted my T-Shirt off me, then made even quicker work of my bra, his lips leaving mine, which were now swollen and red no doubt, to wrap around a nipple, his hand from my hair now gently fondling the other breast, not to leave it out. I could feel his erection stirring, pushing against the fine material of his trousers. I wanted it out as much as it wanted to be out. I think we were safely on the same page.

It did occur to me that we were behaving a bit like rabbits recently. I mean Michel and I have always had a healthy sexual relationship, when I wasn't running from him that is, but lately, it's been absolutely anything that sets us off, gets the flame burning, the desire pumping. Since returning from Wellington, we'd been unable to say no once the ball started rolling. Why?

It is the claiming, I am giving off pheromones, I can not help it. I want you so badly, your body is simply responding to my scent. I am sorry, I will try to stop.

He did, he tried to pull away, to give me distance, but I didn't care if he was scenting me into a frenzy, I didn't care that it made me want to jump his bones the second he walked in a room. It had no effect on how I felt about him as my kindred, as the love of my life, it was just a sexual stimulant. I'd still want him under normal situations, but just not quite like this lack of inhibitions we were displaying right now. I mean, come on! The kitchen floor? What if Erika or Amisi walked in right now? My body didn't give a shit. And neither did I.

"Oh God, you are amazing. You know that? Simply irresistible." He was undoing his trousers, freeing his erection.

"How long does this claiming go on for?" I panted against him.

"I am unsure. It depends on how long until my vampyre-within accepts that you are truly mine."

He was lifting me off the floor and placing me down on the kitchen table, removing my panties and skirt carefully, but quickly, stepping out of his trousers, shoes and socks. We were both naked again in a fraction of a moment.

"I guess I'll just have to keep it guessing for a bit longer then, won't I?" I managed to get out in one breath, only to have it stolen completely as he growled in appreciation and thrust deeply inside me. Once again the words *you are mine* ringing through my head.

"*Mon Dieu, ma douce....* I am sorry, I can not seem to slow this down. Your desire to couple is overwhelming and my desire to claim you is insatiable right now. The combination is... unbelievably volatile. I hope I am not hurting you." His breath was hot against my skin as he managed to get the words out between frantic thrusts of his hips.

I couldn't reply to save myself. I sent the thought *don't stop* towards him, hoping that covered his question adequately. He growled again and sped his movements up until the table was moving across the tiled floor in little hiccups as he pounded into me with abandon.

I'm not sure I would have been able to come, the sex was actually quite rough and so very fast, but I suddenly had an overwhelming spicy scent invade my nostrils, filling me up, making it impossible to smell anything else. It was like mixed spice and cardamom and the sweet, sweet smell of Freesias and it was wonderful. The spice and cardamom making the sickly sweet smell of Freesias less, now just a hint, not overpowering any more. Calming it, complementing it, but combining to make something impossible to resist. I managed a deep breath in, savouring every little subtle scent and felt myself suddenly on the verge of orgasm. Michel's movements at that moment faltering, the change in rhythm setting me over the edge, the orgasm making me shout out in surprise and dig my nails into his lower back as he purred in my ear, "Yes" and came with such force inside me.

Holy. Fuck. I was never going to be able to walk again.

Chapter 28
The World of Vampyre

"Did I hurt you?" Michel whispered against my ear. He was carrying me back upstairs to my bedroom and through to the ensuite bathroom. This really felt a little like deja vu, didn't it?

"You're quite an animal when you get going, aren't you?" I was stroking his chest, my head resting on his shoulder.

He swore softly. I hadn't answered his question outright, but I guess the reply told him enough. I was sore. I really, really wasn't sure if I could walk without hobbling. It kind of made me laugh.

"You are laughing? You find this funny?" He sounded incredulous.

I couldn't help it. I'd never had so much unbelievably fantastic sex before in my life. To hell with feeling sore, I'd wear it with pride.

He let a slow breath out and stood me up next to the shower, still hugging me to him.

"Let me heal you, *ma douce*. Please?" I think he was concerned I would say no. Even if I liked the thought of being reminded of what we had just done, I did think a little less ache was a good thing, after all. I lowered my shields and his *Sanguis Vitam* poured in, washing away the aches but leaving the beautiful sense of tired satisfaction, leaving enough to remind me of what we had done.

"Is that good?" he asked kissing me on the forehead. I nodded.

He still didn't let me go, or turn the shower on next to us. I had the impression he was trying to frame a sentence in his mind, trying to organise his thoughts. I just waited until he was ready, enjoying the closeness of him, his skin against mine, his strong arms around me, the scent still lingering on him, making me shift with desire against him. He growled and held me still.

So much for it being just his claiming that made us hot for each other, I was just as keen for a repeat performance.

"It will be difficult for me to resist proving my claim for a while. I do not wish to hurt you. I will try to behave myself, but claimings are ruled by the vampyre-within, mostly, not the mind. And until my vampyre is satisfied you are mine, it *will* continue to prove the point."

"Why now, Michel? We're already joined and have a Bond, why this claiming too?"

I listened to his breathing for a while, waiting for him to answer. "It started with Gregor, I wasn't aware it had taken hold, it was just in the background, but Amisi's confession of how Nero felt towards you sealed it. It just.... kicked in. And now, I am sorry, there is no stopping it."

I'm not sorry, I thought. "What if I didn't want to be claimed?"

"Do you not?"

"That isn't answering my question. Just humour me."

"I suppose, a claiming *could* start when a vampyre wishes to claim someone who does not return the favour, but I have not heard of this before. Claimings are usually triggered when a mate is desired by someone else, it is a natural response to a threat on something that is already theirs. With time and the level of threat, the claiming becomes more intense. I think it is safe to say we have reached that point now."

Bugger. How was I going to be able to do my job if he was wanting to *claim* me at every turn?

"It does not affect my ability to reason, *ma douce*. I will be able to give you space, should you wish. Just not if you are planning to spend it with a rival."

Wellington. Shit. I didn't want to go back there, but I had to if we were going to keep the *Iunctio* at bay and solve the problem of the humans attacking vampires. No one else could do it, it had to be me.

Michel had stiffened, he'd heard every thought of course. He was rigid, his arms steel around me, unmoving. I could not have broken free of his grip if my life depended on it. It didn't and he wasn't hurting me, his body had just simply solidified, become a prison of flesh and muscles and bone around me, unbreakable, immutable, fixed.

"What about Amisi? She could go." His voice was even, under control, but very low. It always took on this tone when he was about to pounce on some poor soul. The calm before the storm.

"No. She is my responsibility. I am not sending her to Gregor without me there to protect her."

"Erika could go."

Erika was good, I knew this, but Amisi was my responsibility. Like I have said before, returning Amisi harmed to Nafrini and Nero was tantamount to declaring a war with the Egyptians. Another enemy we did not need.

Michel sighed. "You are right." Michel was, if nothing else, always a good reader of the political climate in any given situation. Survival at all costs, the old vampire stand by.

"I will need time to digest this, *ma douce*. To prepare

339

myself. It will not be easy to let you go to him."

But, perhaps necessary. I needed to face him for myself too, not just for Amisi.

His arms relaxed and he tilted my chin up, looking me in my eyes. His were dangerous swirls of magenta in amongst the amethyst, a little startling, but not unexpected.

"You are mine," he said softly, then kissed me. I expected him to be demanding, possessive in his kiss, but it was sweet and soft and so beautiful, making me crave him more than if he had simply forced a dominant invasion of my mouth.

He laughed against me. "The claiming is not stupid, *ma douce*, it knows how to entice." He kissed me once more and turned away, leaving me standing alone in the bathroom completely awash in my desire for him, my need for him to take me now.

Damn, this was going to fun wasn't it?

I showered slowly, letting my body return to me and when I came out of the stall and glanced in the bedroom, I saw my clothes neatly stacked on the edge of the bed, along with my Svante sword. I'd wondered what had happened to it when the paramedics had come. Had they cut the holster away from me? It seemed complete now, maybe Michel had replaced it. I stroked my fingers over the hilt, tracing the design, imagining the dragon dancing all over the handle.

When I came downstairs dressed and ready to face the night, Michel had also showered and changed and was in the lounge talking on his cellphone dressed in his immaculate Armani suit.

He glanced up at me and his now deep blue eyes

340

flashed amethyst, then he returned to his conversation. I didn't bother to listen in, just went into the kitchen and quickly made a coffee. I needed caffeine now.

I was just sipping my cappuccino when Michel came in slipping his cellphone in his pocket.

"The Taniwhas are on the move. A group of twenty have just left their land in a convoy of cars, heading into the city. I have some of my human servants following them, they will appear less obvious than any of my line. Despite our formidable skills, the Taniwhas are somehow able to sense us. I think it best we not delay and get to *Sensations* quickly, *ma douce*." He picked up the keys to the BMW off the kitchen bench. "Would you object to my driving?"

I smiled slowly, I kind of guessed he wasn't going to obey the speed limit and the thought of Michel behind the wheel of that car made me hot all over again. His eyes flashed in recognition of my desire and he swallowed slowly, no doubt forcing himself not to act on my signals.

"You are not making this easy, *ma belle*. Get. In. The. Car." His voice was a low growl.

I jumped, almost spilt my coffee, but managed to catch it before it slopped over the side of the cup and placed it slowly down on the bench, my eyes never leaving his. He took a step towards me, a low noise coming from the back of his throat, almost a hum, but more like a growl. I kept my eyes locked on his a second longer, then spun and ran to the garage. Of course, I knew what running would do to him. I was really suicidal right now, wasn't I?

The predator in him chased me, but I was fast, faster than he was used to. And I knew the layout of this house

341

well. Of course, so did he. By the time I made it to the garage, I thought I had him, though. I looked over my shoulder briefly as I entered the room, but he wasn't there. I realised my mistake as soon as I ran straight into his solid body. He'd moved in front of me and now stood beside the car. I'd run straight into his arms without even realising.

He lifted me off the ground and spun me around, opening the passenger side of the car at the same time. He all but threw me in the seat, fastening my seatbelt and leaning over me. He was breathing heavily, his eyes beyond magenta. "We will continue this at a later time, *ma chasse.*"

My hunted. I thrilled at the idea of being hunted by Michel. He took a shattering breath in, still leaning over me, closing his eyes and inhaling deeply.

"*Mon Dieu, ma douce. Tu appelles sur moi.*"

I smiled at the fact that more and more French was slipping into Michel's vocabulary. He was losing it big time.

"Big time," he whispered and pulled away appearing at the driver's side door in an instant.

He slid in, all sleek moves and gorgeous motion. After adjusting the seat to suit him, he pushed the button for the automatic garage door opener and started the car. He didn't look at me, but a small smile was playing on his lips. He knew I was watching him, my breath an uneven rhythm in my chest.

"Hold on tight," he said and spun the car backwards and in a slide out of the garage, somehow getting us facing the right way on the road outside the house. I tried not to smile, but failed. I had complete trust in his driving ability, but I knew he was going to push me to the limit of that trust right now. I made myself not close my eyes. He laughed, before placing the car in gear and then we were off.

It was like that scene from *The Bourne Identity*, the car chase where Matt Damon makes the mini do unbelievably stupid things, except this was no mini and we weren't tearing down steep steps and narrow Parisian streets against the flow of traffic. The BMW slid in and out of the vehicles along Tamaki Drive at close to 180km/h, barely missing obstacles, just staying within the lines on our side of the road. We would have seemed little more than a blur to pedestrians and just a flash of dark colour to those cars we passed. He had to slow as we approached the city and the traffic became more dense, but he still managed to slip through tight gaps and ignore traffic signals, bringing us to Queen Street and then *Sensations* in a matter of seconds, not minutes.

I had hardly drawn a breath the entire way, it had been thrilling, disturbing and strangely satisfying all at once. My pulse was racing as the car negotiated the garage entrance at the club, the tyres squealing on the smooth concrete of the garage floor as it tore into the underground space and slid to a stop in the usual spot reserved for me, close to the doors, right next to a security camera.

I was out and around his side of the car before he had even taken a step away, throwing my body into his arms, kissing him with fervent need. He laughed against my lips and kissed me back, then pulled away slightly to whisper, "We are being watched, *ma douce*." Nodding his head towards the security camera.

"Were we being watched when you tried to have your

way with me in the back seat of my car?"

"Yes." He kissed me again and then spun me back towards the car, pressing his body against mine, moulding himself to me.

"You naughty boy. You like an audience?" I was getting breathless, he just growled in response, moving his hips against me.

"I like my own to see that you are mine."

I laughed against his lips, but before I could reply the garage door whirred into action again, the headlights of one of Michel's Land Rover Discoveries shining through the grating of the door as it slowly rose up and out of the way.

Michel pulled back slightly. "Right," he said between clenched teeth. Then again, "Right." He shook his head, unable to take his eyes off my mouth, unable to pull all the way back from me.

"I should like to hunt you sometime, *ma douce*, to chase you." It was almost a request, as though he needed me to accept his right to hunt me down. How could I refuse? I just nodded, a little star-struck by the look of hunger on his face.

He smiled slowly, took my hand in his and turned towards the door to the club. I followed, a little stunned and way more meekly than I would usually. He was really doing a number on me, wasn't he?

The club was obviously closed to the public, being a Monday, that wasn't entirely unusual. It was just Michel's vampires, quietly drinking, talking and I had the sense, grieving. They were gathered for Bruno, to say goodbye. My heart began aching immediately. Michel just squeezed my hand and walked in as though he owned the place. Duh,

344

he did. The vampires perked up straight away, an almost tangible lift in spirits. They needed to see him all right, they needed him amongst them, reassuring them. I also gathered, by the looks his hand in mine was receiving, that they needed to see Michel with me, touching me. As though his happiness, completeness, was also theirs. I guessed it was the blood bond they all shared with him, a certain amount of his wellbeing was transmuted through the connection he had to them. They all seemed to relax and smile more as soon as their eyes landed on his hold of me.

He made sure they had all seen his hand in mine before he released me, but his arm shot around my shoulders and he drew me to him, laying his lips against my forehead and running his finger along my jaw.

"Go find your Amisi, *ma douce*. I must commune with my line." I nodded and stood on the tip of my toes to kiss his lips. There was a collective sigh through the room. It was a little creepy. Michel just smiled knowingly at me and whispered, "We are vampyre."

I pulled away and glanced around the room. All eyes were on me with a type of hunger, but not the type that scares you, it was more an ownership thing. They were looking at me as though I was also theirs. Theirs to protect, theirs to serve, theirs to worship. Like I said, a little creepy.

I spotted Amisi with Erika and Jett. The vampires a little closer than I had seen them before, practically up against each other, as they sat opposite Amisi. At least Erika had been looking after my girl.

I went and sat next to them, a *Bacardi and Coke* appearing over the top of me, Doug's hand resting on my shoulder as he placed it on the table top. He didn't say anything, but the fact he had touched me at all was a bit weird. He quickly removed his hand and walked away. It was Jett who answered the puzzled look that must have appeared on my face.

"Every vampire in the room will touch you at some point tonight. Doug was selected as the first, we felt you would not be opposed to his affection, albeit brief."

I blew a long breath out of my mouth slowly and lifted the drink to my lips. Vampires, crazy fuckers that was for sure.

"How are you feeling?" Amisi asked, taking a drink from a glass of white wine.

"Great." I was pleased we were onto more normal topics of conversation. She just smiled knowingly at me.

"When did you guys leave home today?" I asked.

"At sundown." Erika this time. "We thought you'd like some privacy." Now she had that damn knowing smile on her face. I felt my cheeks blush slightly. They both laughed.

"You make a fine couple, Lucinda," Amisi said, eyes all serious again. "That is why he did not act on how he felt, he saw it too."

I frowned at her, unable to keep up with what she was saying.

"Nero," she offered. "He recognised it the moment he saw you both together. The moment he saw your Bond glow in fact. He has accepted it, Luce, trust me on this."

I didn't know what to say to that, so I just sipped my drink and watched the crowd. My eyes of course found their way to Michel. He was surrounded by some of his line, they were sad, but happy at the same time, reliving

346

memories of Bruno, *communing* with Michel. His eyes lifted over the shoulder of one of his vampires and locked with mine.

I didn't need to hear the words he whispered in my head, I could see his desire in his eyes. *Mine.*

Maybe the claiming was feeling threatened by the number of vampires in the room right now, even if they were his, but I got the distinct impression that he would gladly take me right then and there to prove his claim. His lips curved in a smile at my thoughts.

Oh boy.

Jett stood then, I noticed his hand briefly touch Erika's and then he picked up his drink and said, "I think I'll catch up with the master." He nodded at Amisi and as he passed me, he brushed his hand along my back. It didn't feel nearly as creepy as I had thought and I was guessing the more of Michel's vampires who did it throughout the evening, the more natural it would in fact feel.

Welcome to the world of vampyre.

I guess I was finally home.

Chapter 29
Communing

"So," I said to break the silence that had descended on our table. "What's the news?"

"Erika has been letting me practise with the swords. The set-up downstairs is great. I'd like to get proficient before I have to return to Egypt. It would be nice to be able to do something Nero has not done before."

"Showing the boss up, eh?" I asked, winking at her.

"Absolutely." She smiled cheekily at me. "He's too damn confident for his own good."

I agreed with her there.

"Aaaand what about you Ms. Anders, anything new to report?" I grinned at Erika. She blushed, such a cool response in a vampire.

"He's sexy, OK? That crooked nose just does it for me."

Both Amisi and I burst out laughing. "Each to their own," I managed between guffaws.

The whole mood of the room had lifted. Not just because Michel had arrived, but in direct response to my laughing, I think. I could feel it lifting as Amisi and I were choking back tears, laughing at Erika's expense. She had also joined in, unable to stop herself. Music started up, cheerful and upbeat, voices started to rise and before we knew it a party was in full swing.

Vampires do mourn their dead, but it is more a celebration of their death, than a sadness at their passing. Bruno had gone out fighting for a noble cause, protecting his master. I don't think the vampires here could have been prouder to have known him than they were right now. That nobility of his actions made their celebrating his final death so much easier, so much more convivial.

Drinks were being handed out, some vampires had actually started dancing. Although Michel has always seemed to have more male vampires than female, all of a sudden, there seemed to be a fairly even split of the sexes. I realised there were a lot more vampires here than I had seen of his at any one time. And a hell of a lot I didn't recognise, mainly females.

"Is it just me, or are there a lot of female vampires here all of a sudden?" I asked no one in particular.

"All of Michel's vampires were called home after Bruno's death. It is always the way when one so high in the echelon is lost to us." Erika took a sip of her drink. "As to there being more females here than you have seen before, I would say that is by choice. Michel has kept the women away. He probably did not want you to dwell on the fact that he has turned so many over the years."

I looked around the room and was struck by the sheer beauty of them all. They were stunning, typical vampire sleekness, all sexy curves and feminine lines. I had to smile, albeit a little bitterly. It had actually never occurred to me that Michel would have turned so many females, it made complete sense. How could they not have been attracted to him, lured in by him? And, I reluctantly acknowledged, it did stir some jealousy deep, deep inside. To have turned a female, he would have had to have been close to them. Very close. I suddenly had an urge to find him in the room and lay my own claim then and there.

He appeared at my shoulder instantly, leaning down and whispering in my ear. "You called?" I spun in my seat and immediately felt trapped by his gaze. He smiled slowly. "I do believe I approve of your jealousy, *ma douce*. I approve very much."

Amisi and Erika had gone quiet. Just watching the scene play out in front of them. It was probably better than any soap opera on T.V. and they had front row seats.

Michel held his hand out to me. "May I have this dance, *Mademoiselle?*"

I didn't hesitate, just slipped my hand in his and let him lead me to the dance floor. The vampires making way as we approached, parting as they would for royalty. I didn't even register the movements, my heart was in my throat at the look on Michel's face. It was utterly sexy, totally captivating and entirely mine.

He took me in his arms and started to dance, moulding my body to his, making me lay my face against his chest, unable to look up at him when this close. He moved with smooth grace and confidence, owning the dance floor, making us glide over it, turning us in circles, making my head a little dizzy, or was that just the scent of him? The music went on for an eternity, no one else existed, just me and him. The feel of his hard length against me, his strong arms around me, his broad chest beneath my cheek.

As the music came to an end and another song started up he stilled us, now in the middle of the dance floor and raised my chin, allowing me to see the hunger in his eyes again. I licked my lips and he purred against me, his chest vibrating with the sound.

"May I kiss you?" He didn't need to ask, but the fact he did made the moment so much more surreal. I just nodded, unable to find my voice.

He slowly cupped a hand behind my head, continued to rub his thumb along my jaw and keeping his eyes fixed on mine, lowered his mouth to hover above my own.

"How much do you want it?" he whispered, his hot breath against my lips making me shiver in his arms. I still couldn't find my voice.

"A lot?" he asked quietly, still not bridging the gap. "Tell me?"

I shook my head slowly from side to side. I was trapped, barely breathing. For the life of me, I didn't want this moment to end and I was getting the impression he was more than happy to drag it out for me.

"I am betting, you would beg for it if you could find your voice. Will you beg for me, *ma douce?*" He held me firmly, not allowing me to pull away, his eyes devouring mine, his mouth still so close. I tried to move against him, to finish the moment, to lay my lips on his, but he held firm and just growled softly and whispered, "Beg me and I am yours."

I would usually be fighting this, my internal monologue was humming, not scared, not in warning, just letting me know I could do better than just acquiesce to his demands. I was thankful for its reminder. He was playing a game, of course, having some fun, but it was in front of his entire line, who were all avidly watching their master seduce his kindred, right in plain sight, in the centre of the dance floor. For the good of all Nosferatin, I couldn't let him win.

"What if I say no?"

He seemed surprised, momentarily taken aback. I had not only found my voice, but denied him the answer he wanted. I saw a flash of amethyst in the blue of his eyes and his smile became a definite one of appreciation. I was making him work for it, all the better.

"I am sure I can convince you otherwise," he whispered, shifting his hips against me, making me go weak in the knees. He would have been able to tell, my weight suddenly heavier in his arms. "That is better, my sweet little one. How much do you want me?"

I flashed him a smile. "How much do *you* want me? Make it worth my while to capitulate. Make it impossible for me to say no."

His mouth opened in further surprise. I don't think he expected me to challenge him so. He swallowed, blinked slowly and growled very low. It would have been impossible for anyone in the room to miss it.

I just laughed, but my heart was now racing. I was pushing Michel to the limit and that was never a safe thing to do with a vampire. Especially, it would seem, one in the process of laying a claim on me.

He was stunned, unable to reply, unable to move away, unable to close the distance. I gently pushed back on his hold, keeping eye contact, moving very slowly. He only let me, because, I was sure, he just wanted to see how far I would take it, how far I would actually go. He was mesmerised by my resistance, by my strength.

I took one step backwards, then another, then another, as he stood stock still in the middle of the dance floor, the music still playing but not a vampire in the room moving.

"You wanted a chase?" I said a little breathlessly. He cocked his head and smiled. "Come and get me."

I spun away before he could reach me, dancing through

the air in my Nosferatin spin. The room was suddenly alive with *Sanguis Vitam*, the tension not frightening, but exciting. The vampires approved. It only made me more determined to show them what Michel had got himself into.

He was a flash as he followed my every spin, but he was good. He let me have a few seconds, maybe a full minute, of a lead, he let me show my talent, the beauty of my moves to the room. He let them all see just what a prize I was and then he simply appeared in front of me when I landed, after a long spin and held out his hand, palm up, ready for me to take. I stood swaying for a moment, catching my breath, finding my balance. My face was flushed with excitement, my smile broad on my face, I bit my bottom lip and looked right at his outstretched hand, then let my eyes slowly shift up to his. The magenta was bright and clear, dancing in depths of the blue.

"Kiss me," I breathed. "Please."

He smiled and took me in his arms, tipping me over backwards in an old style romantic movie scene move, claiming my mouth with his. The room erupted in applause, the vampires now all on a high. They began to move and return to their conversations, allowing us a moment of privacy as he devoured my lips and tongue. And me.

"You are a challenge," he breathed against my cheek as he righted me again, still holding me tight against him. "A worthy challenge."

"I'm glad you approve." I was still breathless, still quite flushed and excited. He purred again, that beautiful sound from so deep inside him that made his whole chest vibrate.

"I would have you, right here, right now, but we must play our part. The night is still young and I believe some of my line have yet to lay hands on you. It would be selfish of me to deny them that right."

"Deny them for a few minutes, I'm sure they would understand."

He growled and lifted me off the floor, not cradled in his arms, just up against his body. I could have wrapped my legs around his waist, but even I have my sense of pride, despite recent evidence to the contrary.

"Temptress. You shall be my downfall. I welcome it." He kissed me this time fiercely, letting me feel his fervent desire, letting me see how much he did want to take me to his chamber and spend the next hour proving how much he really wanted me. But, he was right and also damn stronger than I had been giving him credit for. He gently lowered me to the floor and in a slightly cracked voice said quietly against my lips, "Go. Before I start stripping you of your clothes right here. I have instructed my line to hurry up and get communing with my kindred, my patience is running thin." He was laughing as he said it. "You have no idea how much of myself you have made them see tonight. You are both my strength and my weakness. And now they know."

Somehow I got the impression that that was a pretty big deal. He held my gaze for a moment longer, making sure I understood what he had just said and then he let me go and took a slow step back, adjusting his suit and keeping eye contact with me.

Later, he whispered in my mind and smiled. In an instant he had disappeared to a spot across the room, picking up a glass of what looked like Bourbon or Whiskey - straight, on ice - and downing it in one. He was shaken

354

and he was desperately trying to get himself under control. Doug presented him with another shot and he simply downed that too.

I turned away, allowing him time to recover. Erika was at my side immediately and led me back to the table, her hand on my wrist; a reassuring touch. A small smile playing on her lips. Vampires brushed against me as we walked, not too much, just a brief touch here, soft brush there. Comforting, not claustrophobic. I relaxed into my seat and took a deep drink from my glass.

"*Chica*, you are amazing. I have never seen Michel so rattled before. He *lurves* you. He really, really *lurves* you." She said the lurves part in a sing song voice, which Amisi found hard not to laugh at. I just smiled and shook my head. I could blame it on the claiming, but somehow I didn't think it was that. Michel was mine and now everyone knew it.

The next ten minutes were relatively relaxing, all the vampires making their way past our table, gently touching me, stroking my shoulders. None of it seemed weird. I flicked a glance at Amisi to see if she felt uncomfortable, but she had that slightly bored, been-there-done-that kind of look on her face. I guess this was well known in normal Nosferatin circles. I've just never been in normal Nosferatin circles before.

I had the sense, as time passed, that the vampires were feeling whole again, despite the loss of Bruno. Whatever this communing did for them, it was important and it strengthened Michel's line. I also couldn't deny the sense of peace I felt too. I had never considered I needed Michel's vampires for anything, other than the occasional protection squad and just an extension of who he was. But, now I realised it was more than that. I was joined to Michel, so I always knew I had kind of come under his line, but there was more to it than that. It felt as though, all of a sudden, I was part of them too. Or they were part of me, it was hard to define.

I'd always felt at home on my parents' farm. They raised me from when I was only a few months old, they nurtured me, provided for me, protected me and made me strong enough to venture off into the world without them. I will always be grateful for that love and care. But, since finding out I was a Nosferatin and they were not part of that side of me, I have felt alone. Nero had filled a gap, even meeting Tim had filled a gap. But sitting here, right now, in amongst vampires of my kindred's line, I felt more at home than I had ever felt anywhere else before.

I was a lost Nosferatin, but now I belonged. And it was not anywhere that I had ever suspected I would feel that kinship. Vampires are what I hunt, evil vampires are what I kill, yet here I was surrounded by vampires, save one Nosferatin and it was home.

You are home, ma douce. We are your home.

I couldn't see where he was in the room, but I felt him. In me, around me, with me. Is this what claiming someone as your own felt like? This utter calmness, this acceptance? Or was I just happy to share a part of me only with these vampires, with Michel? How would I know when I had given all of me? If I ever did.

You will know.

I felt his slight sorrow, when those words were whispered in my mind. It was familiar. I had felt it before. I couldn't place where or when, but I had a suspicion that when I did, I'd know I had made that final move and given myself completely to Michel.

I prayed I could. I wanted to, but I also knew part of me was still holding back. I just didn't know why yet.

I was just reaching for another sip of my drink when I felt it. It seems that any significant sense of mine creeps up on me, taking me by surprise. I had forgotten all about my new found power. The *Prohibitum Bibere*. But here it was, flaring its ugly head and roaring through my mind. Not just one vampire, but several and they were close. So close. They had crept up on me as the last one had, surprising me, ambushing me almost. Trapping me.

I felt my heart rate quicken, my throat go dry and the awful sense that this was not going to be good at all flood through me.

Michel was beside me in the next instant, his hand on my shoulder. "I shall come with you. You will not be alone."

Simple words, but tonight they seemed to mean so much more. I relaxed slightly against his body, as he stood next to my chair. Only to have a jolt of adrenaline rush through me as his cellphone went off and I knew, without a doubt, what it would be about.

He answered it crisply. I heard his sharp intake of breath and stiffened for the hammer blow.

He rang off with a few curt words and slipped his phone away. I had already stood to face him and knew what he would say before he opened his mouth, just not how bad it would actually be.

"The Taniwhas are at Albert Park and they have

357

hostages. Humans. Your neighbours, your work colleagues, everyone you know in the city, save from mine."

Rick had finally crossed the line and I wanted so badly to face him, but they called with a sense of knowledge for my predicament, although how they could know I was at a crossroads is beyond me. But, the six vampires waiting for my Drink were laughing and rubbing their hands together with glee.

Chapter 30
Fight Night

I turned to Amisi and said, "Phone Nero." She was on it immediately. I needed back up and it couldn't be Michel.

He spun me back towards him, a look of pain on his face. "I will stay with you."

I was already shaking my head at him. "No. You must avenge Bruno's death, you must lead your line against Rick. You know this." I saw the acknowledgement in his eyes, mixed with fierce denial. He wanted to protect me. He needed to protect me. But, his line needed him to lead.

"Let me do my job, Michel. This is what I am." If I couldn't face those vampires that came calling, then what was the point of me being the Prophesied.

He nodded, slowly, painfully, gripping my shoulders tightly. He pulled me into a close embrace and whispered, "You are my Light, Lucinda. You call to me. I will always hold you dear."

I let a breath of air out in a rush, he could not have chosen anything more perfect to say. No doubt he had heard me think those words in my thoughts. *I am the Light to your Dark. I call to you, as you call to me. I will always hold you dear.* It's the Prophesy. Or part of it. I guess, you could say, it's the part that is me.

Michel kissed me on the lips lightly and then vanished out the door with most of his vampires in tow. A dozen of so were left behind and they all looked at me. Great. He'd left a contingent of guards at my disposal, one of which was Erika. The moment my eyes met hers, she shook her head.

"He has commanded me to stay at your side. I cannot

359

disobey. And he asked, respectfully, if you would not counter his command with your glaze." She held my gaze for a moment and then added, "For him."

I have been able to overcome commands given by Michel to his line before, with my own glazing power. In particular, Bruno. The thought of Bruno made an ache creep into my heart, but also made me wish to honour this request from Michel. He had enough of his line with him to face the challenge the Taniwhas laid down, but I didn't want to scare the vampires I was going to meet with a huge entourage of people, so I nodded agreement to Erika and turned to Michel's vamps.

"Erika can come with me, but the rest of you stay here. If we need you, we'll call, but I have to see if we can meet these vampires half way and not scare the shit out of them with you lot first." They all nodded, they were quite used to my turn of phrase by now, these were Michel's regulars. All vampires I knew fairly well.

Just then Nero flickered in to sight.

"I trust I am not too late, Kiwi."

I turned and gave him a smile. The last time I had seen him I was barely conscious and the time before that, I had told him to rack off back to Egypt. I suddenly felt like an utter twit.

"Perfect timing as usual, Nero. We're just heading out."

He smiled back and bowed slightly. It had been a while since I had seen him do that old slow bow of acknowledgement. I hoped it didn't signify a return to stiff formality between us, but if that was what he needed to be to remain around me, I'd let him have it. It was the least I could do.

The six Dark-filled vampires were waiting in Myers Park, which was closer to *Sensations* than Albert Park and smaller. As we headed out I sent my senses down the line to Michel, he had clamped himself shut. I couldn't gain an idea of what was happening, but just that he was OK, focused and on high alert. Perhaps, they had already confronted Rick and were negotiating, or perhaps they were surveying the scene before rushing in. I couldn't tell and he didn't want me to be distracted by it. His shields were held tight.

I decided to do the same with mine and fortified my walls accordingly. I turned to Amisi and Nero, determined not to have a repeat of last time.

"We go in as one group and no one moves unless I say so, OK?"

They both nodded immediately. I don't think they wanted a repeat of last time either. I let my senses seep out as we neared the entrance to the park. All the vampires were in the middle, in the open, no humans, just them. They hadn't needed to go to that extreme, they knew I was close and they knew I was coming. They were just waiting. I still hadn't got used to this.

"They smell of evil," Amisi whispered, fingering her stake.

I always think it's a smell too, usually that they reek of it, but maybe Amisi just doesn't know that English word yet. Her nose was scrunched up in disgust though, so I'm guessing it was more a reek than just a smell. These guys were bad boys, through and through. Just what the hell was I supposed to do with all that Darkness? How was I to help them toward the Light and not kill them? I crossed my fingers and took a deep breath in as we walked up to confront them.

They had fanned out in a straight line. All of them dressed similarly. Dark clothes in good order. Their hair was a little wind swept, differing colours and lengths, but they all looked like they had travelled a distance to get here and not paused for a rest. They had been determined to see me without delay.

Six vampires together, unless they are of the same line, is unusual. Especially if hunting. Vampires are solitary hunters and if this lot wasn't here to hunt, then what? They didn't look hungry, not for blood anyway, well not for blood of humans, maybe just a little hungry for mine, I'm not sure. They kept steady eyes on me, aware no doubt of the group surrounding me, but only interested in its leader.

OK.

"What do you want?"

I couldn't deny the sense that they wanted something, I just couldn't quite fathom yet what.

The one in the middle, standing forward slightly, was obviously the spokesperson for the group. He had beady little eyes, all black with a hint of red and long brown wavy hair. His accent was European, perhaps Turkish, hard to say.

"So, you are the *Prohibitum Bibere*." He looked me up and down.

"I know, I'm shorter than you thought I'd be, right?"

He laughed, a little darkly, but his words were darker still. "I am sure you will still taste as good as we believe."

Okey dokey.

"Just what do you hope to gain by tasting me?" I was

curious, why the attraction?

He rocked back and forth on his heels, his hands held loosely in front of him, he looked quite relaxed actually.

"Eternal happiness."

Riiight. I just wasn't buying that one.

I glanced at Nero for inspiration. I may have been pissed off with him recently, but he is my only connection to the Prophesy and what it means. Of course, the vampires couldn't see him, he was Dream Walking. For all they knew it was just me, one other Nosferatin and a short blonde female vampire with a sword. Nero didn't exist.

"I do not know what to suggest, Kiwi." He shook his head. "There is no guidance on this, save that the *Lux Lucis Tribuo* is meant to complete the exchange of Light. Somehow easing their burden."

"And how does the *Lux Lucis Tribuo* achieve that?"

By now the vampires had started shifting uneasily. They knew Nero was here now, they could hear him, but still not see him. That's enough to put anyone on edge.

"I do not know," Nero said softly. "I am sorry. The Prophesy only says that *the Light will capture the Dark and hold it dear.*"

Yeah, yeah, I knew the Prophesy word for word, but still, how the fuck was I supposed to do that? Anyone?

Well, there was no way I was going to let them taste me, I had a sneaky feeling that once their fangs got in my flesh, they weren't going to let go until they had consumed all of me and a fat lot of good it would do them. It's not like Michel gets extra Light from drinking my blood. No, Light comes from in me and is directed by me. Well, most of the time.

So, here goes. I tried to gather my Light up inside me, I tried to bring it all together, build it up, ready for release. I was going for a burst of Light to cover all six of them hoping it would do the job and we'd be done. But, they could tell I was doing something, maybe I start to shine or something, or maybe I just give off lots of Nosferatin mojo, but they became restless and started to fan out more around us.

"Hold still boys. I've got a little something for you to taste."

Perhaps warning them wasn't the best idea, because by the time I released the Light towards them, three flew straight up in the air, two more flashed behind us, so that only one got the full benefit of my Light. I needed more practice at this. But even then, the one that got the full frontal of Light, didn't seem that much Lighter, if anything he seemed Darker, just a little unsteady on his feet with a look of someone who had just had awesome sex. Yuck. I'd not tried to make my Light anything other than its normal manifestation, which embarrassingly, is my desire and lust and a metaphysical orgasm to boot. Damn. I really was going to get a name for myself at this rate.

"Hot damn, *chica*, that's some awesome magic you got going on there." Erika was already holding a couple of vampires off with her Svante, but looked equally awash with post sex glow. The two vampires she was holding at bay, also seemed to have received a throwback from the Light blast. Not quite as potent as the one in front of us had, but a fair indication of what I could do.

Of course Nero and Amisi hadn't felt anything other than a warmth from the Light, a recognition of what they

364

already are. They were also battling vampires themselves, one apiece. That left two for me. The one still recovering from the main blast and another who landed back on the ground about three feet away from me. I still wanted to figure out some way of getting through to these guys, rather than just staking them. It seemed cruel that they had just come here like love-sick puppies, unable to resist the call, simply to fight for their lives. Despite being full of evil, there had to be a way to save them. There just had to be. They hadn't been chewing on humans, they hadn't been breaking the rules, they simply were threatening us.

Enough to fight back in self defence you might say, but still. I felt uneasy about the situation, there had to be an answer. There just had to be. I couldn't think of one though, so I circled my main threat, keeping a wary eye on the other one and settled my stake firmly in my hand.

"How do you think this will end, vampire?" I asked, studying him.

"With my fangs in your neck."

"And if I get my stake to your chest first? Is that odds you're prepared to accept for a chance to taste me?"

"Absolutely. I will have my drink."

I saw it then, in his eyes. A complete conviction that this was what he had to have. I was fairly sure in that second, that he had been denying himself blood in the days leading up to finding me. To answering the call. Nothing else would have done, nothing else would have satisfied the crave. He wanted my blood and no one else's would do. Shit. Even if I could think of an answer to this problem, a way to use my Light to help them, it wouldn't be tonight, not now, not facing off against this lot. I was at a loss and the best I could hope for was to come out of this alive.

And to make it quick for them. No more banter, no more delays resulting in torment. Time to end this.

I noticed the others; Amisi, Nero and Erika, had been holding the vampires off, but not striking. They had taken my request to heart, they were waiting for my signal. Good little soldiers. Bless them. But, my decision had reluctantly been made. I would live to fight this battle another day and so would they. I would work on a solution and the next time we faced off with the disciples of the *Prohibitum Bibere*, we would be prepared.

But not today.

"OK guys, enough is enough. Let's just end this."

The second the words had left my mouth they moved. Svante slashing, now on attack, Nero spinning staking a vampire with ease and Amisi moving in for a strike, but being thrown backwards. I couldn't see what happened next, because the vampire in front of me smiled slyly and jumped. And the one who had been enjoying post coital bliss, sprang at the same time too. Two for the price of one. Yippee.

I rolled out of the way of number one and managed a slice on the arm of number two, then sprang up from the crouch I had ended in and braced for the comeback. Number one got to me first, a swipe of his hand, a simple flick, which I dodged, but he followed through with a swift roundhouse kick to my head. I'd dodged the swipe of the hand, but set myself up completely for the kick, so couldn't avoid the impact. I went with it, letting the momentum roll me backwards and flicking my feet out as I went head over arse, landing in a half crouch.

366

By this time number two came back, like some evil tag team twin at Fight Night - WWE style. These guys knew what they were doing. And then he landed a brilliant side kick to my chin, spinning my head around and making my brain go to mush. Those sideways movements are the worst, it's a twist the brain just doesn't appreciate. Mine was complaining loudly.

Nero must have helped Amisi dispatch her vampire, because he quickly made short work of number two, or at least took his attention away from me and that was enough to get me back on my feet and facing number one again. He came at me low, one of my favourite attacking positions. I love it when they assume there is nothing that can be done to them if they take out your legs, but I jumped, not quite getting enough of a forward motion to flying head over heels above him, but splitting my legs wide - who knew I was so nimble, Michel will be pleased - avoiding the vamp's outstretched arms, but allowing a fantastic open spaced opportunity to gain access to his back.

He knew immediately he was in trouble, so twisted slightly, to try to meet me face to face. So, when my stake entered, it missed his heart and jammed against his shoulder blade. Painful, but useless. He kept moving forward, taking my stake with him, but by the time I had landed on my feet again, I had my spare out and ready to go.

Nero had taken out number two, flicked a glance at me and saw I was armed, so returned to help Amisi and Erika. Being invisible he had a hand up on the game. Erika had sliced one vampire really beautifully, but not fully decapitated him. Both she and Amisi were still head to

367

head, a vampire apiece, so Nero went in to finish off old Slice and Dice, and I went back to work on number one.

He had recovered from his close encounter of the silver staked kind and now decided coming in low wasn't a good idea, so chose to fly high. I was getting a bit sick of all of this by now, usually it didn't take quite so long to take a vampire out, but these guys were like the elite fighting force for some battle ridden country, or some such thing. A cut above the normal Rogue I dealt with. Still, I really wanted to finish this. So, although he was coming in at me all large and at full height, I started running full speed to meet him head on. I suppose, I could have spun, that would have worked too, but I felt like getting a little dirty, so just as we were about to meet, I skidded to the ground and slipped past his feet, coming to stand up behind him and landing the stake with ease. This time I didn't miss and dust exploded in my face, gently wafting to the ground around me.

I took a moment to catch my breath as I checked on the others. Within a minute, Nero helped finish them off and the sounds of fighting left the air. Erika glanced around and sniffed the air, checking for Norms, no doubt. She must have smelt some because she took off at a run no doubt to glaze away any memories. Myers Park is a popular place after dark, for various human activities, if you know what I mean. The chance of someone having seen us and called the police was high. Sometimes having a vampire with you can be handy. I may be able to glaze vampires, but not humans. I usually don't fight in such public places. I prefer dark alleys and shadowy spots out of sight and tucked well away.

She was back a few seconds later, sliding her Svante back in its sheath and dusting off her hands.

I turned back towards Nero and Amisi.

"You guys OK?" Amisi looked all fired up and full of beans, excitement shining in her eyes. Nero looked unflustered, calm and nothing like a hunter having just dispatched almost half a dozen very well trained vampires.

They both nodded, but it was Nero who spoke.

"They were experienced fighters."

"Yeah. Their moves were familiar," Erika added. I swung back to look at her and raised my eyebrows. "The *Iunctio* guards fight like that. Close quarters, some dual action fighting, cohesive, tight. They were *Iunctio*, no two ways about it."

Iunctio. Shit.

"What were they doing here?" I asked, stunned at the repercussions. If we had just taken out some *Iunctio* guards, surely they would be missed. Double shit.

"That.... is a very good question, Kiwi. Very good indeed."

We all stood staring at each other for a moment, letting that little bit of news sink in.

It seems every which way I turned I threatened to bring the *Iunctio* down around my ears. I wondered if Gregor knew some of their guards were here in NZ. I'd have to ask him, but it could wait.

Now... now we go help my kindred and kill an old friend.

Chapter 31
Now You Die... Old Friend

Albert Park was downhill from where we were, but still a fair distance. There was no point going back up hill to *Sensations* and the car, so we just ran as fast as our legs could carry us. Which was pretty fast, all things considered.

My head was still a little trippy from the whacks I had sustained and pounding the pavement was not making it any better, but I didn't have the luxury of grabbing some asprin, so sucked it up and kept at it. The thumping of my head and the jarring of my feet on solid concrete pavements was not making me a happy chappy though.

Not to mention what would wait for me at the bottom of the hill in Albert Park. I tried to reach Michel to let him know we were coming, but he was still bound up tight, there was no getting through those shields of his, so what awaited us was very much a mystery still. And then there was the train of my thoughts. Rick. I was heading towards a confrontation with Rick which could only end one way.

I had been trying not to think of the possible outcomes, I had been in denial to a certain extent. Part of me knew I had to end this. People I cared about were dying or being hurt and it wouldn't stop until he killed me and hunted down all the vampires in Auckland. I didn't want to have to do what I had to do. I really didn't. So, I had been ignoring the issue altogether. But as my feet hit the ground and my head responded with a sharp explosion on every downward strike, I forced myself to face what was ahead of me tonight.

I was running head on into a fight for my life, but not only that. A fight to stop Rick and there was now only way to achieve that. I was going to have to kill him. Even as I ran, my breath getting quicker, my heart rate rising and my head about to explode, I still managed to feel despair at what was about to happen. My friend, my once best-friend. The person I had told all my deepest darkest secrets to, who had been there when I killed one of my first vampires and let me cry on his shoulders when I realised what I had done. Who had shown me the beauty of shape shifting Taniwhas, who had welcomed me into his home and life. Rick. He wasn't that Rick anymore and it wasn't my job to save him. I wanted it to be, even now, after he had killed Bruno, tortured Michel and trashed my house. Even now, I wanted to save him. But it's not my job.

My job is to protect the innocent and if the Prophesy is correct, to bring Light to the Dark. Rick is not the Dark that the Prophesy refers to, he has his own demons, but he doesn't answer to me. I am not born to save him, like I am others in this world. So, this was it, this was the moment I turned from being one of the good guys and did something quite horribly wrong, to keep the Light going and be able to battle the Dark.

They say there are always casualties, collateral damage, in war. Is Rick collateral damage? Or is he just one more creature in this world who has given in to their dark side and just happened to cross my path? I wish I could honestly say there is no choice here. I wish I could tell myself, this is out of my hands, I have to do this no matter what. But, all I can hear in my head is: this is wrong. This is not me. This is not what I have been made for.

But, and I am clinging to this *but* right now, if I am to commit to the Light, the Prophesy and to Nut, this is what I must do. To fail in this, would be to either get myself killed, or allow something unrelated to the Prophesy to stuff it all up for the rest of us. Prophesy or Rick?

I choose Prophesy.

That doesn't mean I have to like it.

We could hear the sounds from a block away. This was going to have ramifications far beyond the supernatural world. For some reason, there weren't any wards to keep the noise from the Norms, I could even see people approaching, cautiously, inquisitively, towards the main entrance of the park. Either the vampires didn't have time to set up perimeter wards, or they had failed. Either option was not very reassuring.

I knew Erika would be essential in the coming battle, but Nero and Amisi did not have to get their hands bloodied like this. I could keep them from the Dark a little longer, I could at least protect their Light.

I made everyone stop before we got too close and turned to Nero and Amisi.

"We need wards and we need to keep the humans back. Can you both do that?"

Amisi looked unsure, but Nero looked furious.

"I will not leave you to this alone, Kiwi. It will not be pleasant in there, you need us."

I hated this, but... "No. I don't. This is Auckland's battle, not yours. You're here, so I ask for your help in placing the wards and protecting the innocent. That is your job, Nero, not interfering with a local issue."

I swear the air got colder around us. My heart ached at the look of disbelief on Nero's face, accompanied by the look of shock and maybe a little hatred, on Amisi's.

372

Sometimes you have to harm those you love to save them.

I held Nero's gaze firmly, I didn't blink. He was the first to back down and he didn't nod, he didn't agree, he just turned away and Amisi followed. He'd do it, I knew he would. Not necessarily because I asked, but because there were too many Norms here and they needed to be protected. That's Nero. The protector. Protects me. Protects Norms, would protect everyone if he could.

I took a deep breath in as they walked away. It felt like they were walking away for the very last time. It felt so final. I didn't allow myself to second guess my decision, I didn't have time to be weak. *Never show fear. Never give an inch. Always stay on guard.*

Nero had taught me that.

I nodded to Erika, who had remained very quiet throughout and we both turned to face the roar from behind the gates.

It was chaos, just as I had suspected. Dust did hang in the air. I pushed that thought aside and scanned for Michel. For Rick. Erika patted me on the back and jumped right in, heading towards Jett, slashing out with her Svante sword, culling shape shifters like they were wrapping paper, shredding them here, slicing them there, ripping them apart over here. I pulled my own Svante out slowly and prepared for the inevitable.

I hadn't been able to spot Michel or Rick, so I just dived in where I was. Flashes of grey, streaks of white, glints of scales and sparkles of light off serrated teeth. Snapping, snarling, growling, yapping. The noise was so loud, I couldn't hear the thumping in my head any more, I could still feel it, but it was now just a drumbeat, a war cry, to my heart rate, to my arm swings and stabs and jabs and slices. Blood flowed freely, animal cries of pain filled the air and I didn't allow myself to think, for a moment, that I knew these shape shifters. That they weren't just a beast attacking my kin. That I hadn't sat in their backyards and drunk beer with them and broken bread at their tables. That they didn't make the best *Hangi* and sang the best songs. I didn't allow myself any of that, because I was killing them.

Perhaps not intentionally. Initially, it was to just ward them off, so I could get further into the park and find Michel, but they kept coming back. A small slash, a soft jab, just didn't do it. Once they saw me, they went for my throat and nothing was going to stop them unless they could no longer move. So, my small slashes and soft jabs became desperate strikes and fervent stabs, all of which were aimed at the heart, or the head. All of which were aimed to incapacitate, permanently.

All of which were killing blows. I hadn't thought before that I was a bona fide killing machine. I mean, I know I hunt and kill vampires, but it had never occurred to me that this skill, this lethal weapon of mine, could be turned on others. That I could pick up a sword and do with it, what I so naturally do with a stake. I always thought I was born a vampire hunter and that was that. Stakes, vampire, dust. But, here I was using an ancient Swedish weapon of war and achieving much the same thing with much the same ease. Shit. I *was* a killing machine.

But that, unfortunately, wasn't the last of it. I had made it into the centre of the melee. I had also left a devastating track behind me which when I spun in a circle to get my bearings, almost made me hurl. I swallowed back bile and told myself this was life or death and just to get the hell on with it. And then I spotted Michel. And Rick. Of course, Rick would be with Michel. Sticking to Michel, he knew I would eventually come.

He must have sensed I was near, maybe he recognised my scent in amongst all of the vampires. He was in Taniwha form, something I had seen up close and personal on several occasions, the last of which he had tried to kill me. His huge shark-like muzzle turned towards where I was standing, warding off a few Taniwhas and those eyes, Rick's eyes, just bore into me as his lips pulled up and back and a multitude of sharp Taniwha fangs were bared at me in a growl.

I thought he'd abandon Michel and come for me, the hunger in his eyes when he spotted me was incredible, I could taste it on the air. But he didn't come for me, he turned back to Michel, he raised up on his hind legs and struck. I'm not sure if Michel had been distracted by my presence, or if Rick was just too fast and maybe Michel was tired, or hurt, I don't know. But, he didn't move fast enough to avoid Rick's claws and he didn't move fast enough once he had been thrown back on the ground - a large slash across his chest, already welling up with blood - to avoid Rick's jaws. Rick's sharp teeth sunk deep into Michel's side, just by his stomach. He shook his head back and forth, like a dog with a bone, and didn't let go.

I saw Michel going whiter and whiter, I saw the blood gushing out of his chest and stomach and side. And I saw red. Not blood red. But the red of Darkness. My vision shaded, everything turned crimson and two dimensional. The noise of the battle ensuing around me faded and all I heard was a beat inside my head. Not the thumping of a headache, but the gradual increase of a war drum, beating as surely and as steadily as my goal, my need, to avenge.

I had always thought that spin fighting was just a Nosferatin tool when battling vampires, but it works pretty damn effectively on Taniwhas even when carrying a Svante sword. I let out a cry and spun in the air, over the top of Taniwhas, bypassing several, then when I had to land, taking out three at once with just one strike. The force behind my action so powerful it toppled all three. And then I went spinning on through the air before any of their mates could retaliate. This happened three times before I reached them. Three times too many, I was sure. Three times too long. Michel would not survive this and I didn't think about the fact that I would die too if he did, I only thought *no fucking way*. Michel was *not* going to die. Not today. Not by this ex-friend turned homicidal maniac. Not on my watch.

I struck before I even landed, slicing through Rick's back, but he had released Michel and jumped at the same time - managing to get nicely cut, but not lethally - and rolled away. I didn't hesitate, I didn't stop to assess Michel, I didn't stop to help stem the blood flow. I wanted Rick dead. Deader than dead. Nothing could have stopped me from that objective.

I felt the Darkness take over. I knew exactly when it breached my shields and surpassed the level of Light I had within. I felt it curl around the inside of my body like it owned me, like it was coming home after a long day at work. It was familiar and comfortable and full of anger like me. I let it in, I embraced it, I encouraged it. I gave myself over willingly to the enemy and I did not regret it. I prayed it could do what I thought I could not.

Rick came at me with a roar. There would be no last words of unfriendly banter. No memories shared or thoughts given. He was a Taniwha and I was Darkness, neither of us could talk. He managed to land a claw on my arm, the pain excruciating, yet invigorating. The Dark within yelled in delight at the pain it received and used the adrenaline to fight back. Nothing was wasted. Pain, agony, despair, it was all used to fuel its flame and make it fight harder. I thought briefly, how economical, how concise. A perfect engine, recycling what comes in and using all of it to push out the anger and hatred and evil that now was me.

Ironic, isn't it? I am the the *Sanguis Vitam Cupitor,* the *Prohibitum Bibere,* the *Lux Lucis Tribuo.* I am the Light to the Dark and here I was evil personified. I was aware that this might be a one way path, that there could be no coming back from this. And I did not care.

Blood dripped down my arm, sweat ran into my eyes, stinging me, making me blink to free up my vision, but Rick didn't stop to allow us both to catch our breath, his evil was driving him too. He launched again, this time managed to pin me, my sword useless at my side. He was too close for me to get the angle right with the long blade and I was too frantically trying to keep him out of my face. Drool was dripping down his fangs onto my cheek, his hot Taniwha breath was searing me, almost burning me. And he was strong. Way stronger than me, but despite evil running through my blood, despite that I had given up my Light so easily, I was not prepared to give up my life.

In a flash I had my silver knife out of the sheath at my

waist and stabbed him up through the jaw. Blood gushed from the wound into my eyes, all over my face, into my mouth. I couldn't see, I could hardly breathe, but his weight lifted off me, as he howled in pain and fury. And when I rolled to the side to try to stand, my hand landed on the dancing dragon hilt of my sword, I thought of Michel and the Light came streaming back in. The Dark banished in an instant, but my will to finish this still sound, still certain. I clambered to my feet and turned to face my old friend.

Rick had managed to shake the knife free. Being silver it had caused a lot of damage since he is a shape shifter, if left now he would eventually recover, but I wouldn't let him. He hadn't let Bruno recover, he most certainly had every intention of finishing Michel off if he got the chance and he wouldn't offer me that consideration if I was the last person left alive on Earth.

I raised my sword in shaky but strong hands, I looked directly in his eyes and I took a deep breath in and ran towards him. He bayed to the moon, then braced his feet wide apart. When I leapt in the air, he rose on his back legs, lifting his claws up and not swiping at me as I had expected, but flinging his front legs wide and exposing his chest. I hesitated, I had my sword out, pointed towards him, I was ready to drive it home, but he was capitulating. I lowered it at the last second and he struck.

I felt his claws rip through my jacket, down my arm, over my chest, across my stomach and then free. The force of the strike spun me away. I felt my body twisting, my skin tearing apart at the gashes and blood soaking my clothes, even before I hit the ground. The air was pushed from my lungs, dirt ground into the wounds across my front and my head smashed down on hard packed earth. Stars began to burst in my vision, my head felt like it had been jammed in between the door of a car and the frame of the vehicle and then been slammed a few hundred times in its metal grip. I felt nausea roll up inside me and knew this was not good. It was not good at all.

I sensed, rather than saw, a form above me. His breath on my neck, his low growl at my ear. I didn't need to speak Taniwha to understand what he was saying. *Now you die.* Maybe he tagged an *old friend* on the end there, I can only think there was some of Rick left, some of the old Rick, my old best-friend, but I wasn't sure. I clenched my fists in preparation for the killing blow and found I was still grasping my dragon hilt. I let the feel of the raised pattern on my palm calm me, I managed to get a steadying breath in and just as I was sure he was ready to do the deed, that he was pulling back to strike, I used the last of my energy, the last of my consciousness, to roll over. Gritting my teeth through the pain and using the adrenaline like a weapon - just like the Dark had, but now there was only Light within - I sunk the sword hilt deep in his chest.

I don't remember anything else. My Light washed through me, it felt like it was bathing me and filling me up and then bursting from me. I wasn't sure, but it was too big to contain, too big for all of me. I'm only small and it felt enormous, bigger than the world, bigger than the universe. It felt like an explosion from deep within. I tried to hold on to it, I didn't want it to harm the vampires in the park, I tried, I really did, but it was strong and it was determined and it kept telling me softly: *it's OK, it's OK, it's OK.*

Still, I fought it as best I could, even though it was

379

comforting me, even though it was soothing me, I fought it.

And the last thing I heard was my voice in my head saying over and over again, *please don't hurt my vampires, please don't hurt my vampires, please don't hurt my vampires.*

And then nothing.

Just white light and soft laughter, that after a while I thought might just belong to children.

Chapter 32
Butterfly Kisses and Fairy Wishes

I dreamt of happy things: children laughing, children playing, hopscotch, tag, jump rope. Butterfly kisses and fairy wishes. Candy floss and bouncy castles, cuddly toys and mud pies. Colourful dresses and Cowboys and Indians. Laughter. There was so much laughter. It left me smiling in my dreams. It left me happy, even though I knew deep down inside, there was a reason I shouldn't have felt happy at all.

When I woke it was day time, I knew this because the shutters were down. I couldn't remember going to bed, I couldn't remember much after dancing with Michel at *Sensations*. I reached out a hand and he was there, like he said he would be. Spending the day with me, in my bed.

I decided I'd wake him up, so I rolled over to throw my leg across him, to snuggle in against his hard thigh, to run my hand down his stomach, lower and lower, but instead of rolling over I screamed out in pain. I ached all over and with the pain came the memories and the scream turned to a whimper. *No. Please no, it didn't happen.*

"*Ma douce, ma douce*, it is all right. I am here." His voice so soothing, his fingers on my cheek, my neck, so soft, his breath against my face so warm. My eyes flickered open and his deep, deep blue eyes shone back. Reassuring, loving, here.

"Are you OK?" I whispered.

He smiled and laughed softly. "Only you would think of someone else when you are injured so."

I did feel like shit, now that he mentioned it. I winced as I tried to shift my body slightly. Not a good idea.

381

"Do not move, you have stitches. Let me heal you. Lower your shields."

I shook my head, relieved to notice it no longer hurt, the thumping headache subsided. "You're hurt too, don't waste your energy, I'll be fine."

He smiled more broadly. "I have almost completely healed, *ma douce*. It has been over 48 hours since the battle."

I just stared at him. Shit. Another couple of days vanished, lost to me forever. God dammit, this just had to stop.

Michel had started laughing next to me, making the bed shake slightly, not something I appreciated right now.

"OK. OK. Heal me before you really start going there." I lowered my shields and the familiar feel of Michel's *Sanguis Vitam* came pouring in, filling my body with warmth and washing away the pain and aching. I could almost feel the skin knitting together, the bruises fading, the scraps and cuts disappearing. He didn't stop, but let his *Sanguis Vitam* continue to pour through me, wrapping around me, stroking my skin and heading lower and lower, until I started squirming beneath its touch. No longer able to keep eye contact with him, having to shut my eyes, breathe more deeply and ride the wave he had started.

I thought he'd just leave it at that, but with my shields down and his power flowing through me so deliciously, so beautifully, I had no way to ask, instead his lips found mine, his hand swept over my body and started joining in on the fun. I was being assailed by his power, by his lips and tongue, by his hand and fingers. It was amazing. I have had orgasms before from Michel's power. Before we joined he'd sometimes play havoc with my willpower, causing me to respond to him even when he hadn't laid a finger on my body. But this time, he was using both, his vampire mind and his vampire body.

I couldn't stop him, even if I wanted to, so I just chose to enjoy it, chalk it up to an early morning wake up call and let him do his thing. It was intense, it was out of this world and it didn't last nearly as long as I wanted it to. I came with a rush, it curled me up, made me cling to him and shout out in ecstasy as he made me ride it over and over again.

Finally he released me and let me lay back into his arms, wrapping himself around me and pulling the blankets up over us to make a cocoon.

"*That*, was for scaring me half to death, *ma douce*. Don't *ever* do that to me again. I could not bear it."

"Then don't make the punishment so good," I breathed against him. I felt his shoulders shake with laughter.

"Should I lay you across my lap and spank you then, would that be better?"

I laughed too. "You could try."

He growled against me and shifted his hips. I felt his hard length press into my side.

"Do you have any idea the effect you have on my body, *ma douce*? I want you now, right this second, I am having to use all of my power to restrain myself. You need time to recover. Please do not push me."

Oh, now that was an invitation to party.

He growled deeper even before I rolled on top of him. Obviously, still able to read my mind then.

"Yes." The 's' was said long, lengthening the word,

giving it a whole new meaning.

He tried to shift against me, but I had him pinned. My legs down on either side of his body, my hands holding his arms back against the pillows. I realised then we were both naked. He certainly liked putting my unconscious body to bed in the nude, didn't he? Handy though. I started shifting myself against his erection, he closed his eyes and stopped fighting me altogether.

"Giving up so soon, vampire?"

His eyes shot open and I was rewarded with magenta and indigo, with only a few splashes of amethyst left. Jumping right to the big boys there. Goody.

He held my gaze but raised his head towards me, his teeth taking one of my bandages and slowly tearing it away. The tape causing a slight stinging sensation, sharp and painful, but making me writhe against him all the same.

"I don't think we need these any more, do you?" His voice was husky and suddenly it wasn't me holding his arms, but him holding my wrists and he was making me come closer to his mouth. He moved me around until he was able to get at each bandage, slowly, painfully removing each one with his teeth, keeping eye contact, but making me squirm and moan and whimper and generally make a right bloody fool of myself. By the time he had finished I was aware he had doubled in size beneath me, pressing so hard against me and I was wet.

He didn't let me go, just started licking all the sensitive spots where the tape had been, one slow long lick after another. The saliva from his licks helping to heal the marks, soothing the searing sensation and flooding me with

384

warmth.

"Never say I don't look after my kindred," he whispered against one wet lick making me shiver uncontrollably above him.

He lifted me up off him by simply raising my arms and then somehow managed to get me to come back down at exactly the right spot and angle for his hard round tip to be at my entrance. His eyes still on me, he pushed up slowly as I came down onto him just as slowly and his mouth opened and a shot of air left his lungs and he moaned. "God! You are mine." With those words he thrust the last few inches inside me, filling me up and claiming me again.

His hand shifted from my wrists to my breasts and we started a beautiful slow dance together, not rushed, not frantic, but still desperate to be close, just savouring each thrusting motion in and long draw out. His hips working hard, the hard length of him so big, filling me up and making me pant for more.

It was me that tried to speed things up and when I did his hands moved to my hips to slow me, as his head came up off the bed and before his mouth wrapped round one of my nipples he purred, "Not yet."

I arched my back and let him have better access at my breast. He sucked hard, leaving teeth marks as he bit, making me cry out.

"Do you want more, *ma douce?*"

"Yes." Now it was me with the lengthened 's'.

He shifted to the other breast and lavished his attention and tongue and teeth there. All the while making me ride him so slowly, when all I wanted was hard and fast.

Finally, I'd had enough, enough to make me beg, which

385

I knew was what he was after. The damn man was still trying to prove a point.

"Michel, please. Faster."

He smiled sinfully. "I am sorry, *ma douce*. What was that?"

"Arghh! Now dammit, now!"

He had me flipped over in an instant, still inside me, never leaving his hold of my body. He started moving more forcefully against me, kissing my cheek, my jaw and then my neck, just above his mark. I knew what he was thinking and his hesitation said it all, he wanted my blood, but he was trying not to get too carried away. I had the feeling that the claiming was still very much going along nicely and drinking blood while he was inside me sent that little claiming genie on a frenzied high. He was trying to resist, but I wasn't having any of that.

I ran my hand up his back, into his thick head of hair and slowly brought his head down to my throat.

"You are pushing me, *ma douce*." He was so breathless, it made me ache for him, which only made him growl.

"Drink me. I am yours."

Oh and if that didn't just do it for him. With an almost anguished cry his fangs slid in, his lips moulded to my flesh and my blood started draining, sucked into him. With each draw of blood he thrust deep into me, the two actions unified, synchronised. Suck of blood, thrust of hips, plunge of his hard length deep within me. In my mind as clear as day, his words *mine, mine, mine* with each thrust and suck.

We both came together suddenly, even before he had finished drinking, too close to the edge not to be tipped over and we continued to come as he continued to drink and thrust and suck. Finally his fangs slid out, followed by a lick of his tongue and a final thrust so hard and deep and then he collapsed beside me, sweaty and breathless, just like me.

"Oh dear God, *ma douce*. What do you do to me?"

It was kind of mutual, so I didn't bother to reply.

We lay tangled together for a good ten minutes, listening to each other's heartbeats and the sound of heavy rain against the windows outside the shutters. It was so peaceful and warm and perfect. I never wanted it to end. After everything we had been through, I never wanted us to be apart again.

"The choice is yours, Lucinda. I am here for eternity and I want no one but you by my side."

The unspoken part to that statement was still clear; *just give yourself over to me and it is so.* I wanted it, so why couldn't I just do it?

He kissed my cheek and stroked my hair, pulling me closer. Reassuring me, comforting me.

"I will wait for however long it takes, but I may just have to claim you every day to prove my commitment to you, *ma douce*. Would you mind?" The last was said with a smile. He was trying to make light of the situation. I knew how much he wanted me to give all of myself to him and I also knew how much it hurt him that I couldn't seem to bridge that final gap. Yet here he was, trying to make it easy for me, trying not to push.

I loved him more now than I had ever loved him before, but I still couldn't do it.

He sighed softly against me and held me tight, as

387

though he was scared I'd pull away. I had no intention of going anywhere right now, but I understood his need to do it, so I settled in against him and just listened to the rain.

Of course, that left room in my head for thinking, for remembering. And my mind wandered to the events two nights before at Albert Park. Rick. I presumed I'd killed him. That sword blade had gone right through his heart, right up to the beautiful dancing dragon hilt.

He is dead, ma douce. You did well.

I'm not sure Michel wanted to say that aloud, hearing his voice in my head was enough to make me cringe. I did well. I killed an old friend, that's what I did. And I know, I didn't have much of a choice. He was going to kill me, he almost killed Michel. He trashed my house, kidnapped my kindred and killed Bruno.

"Who else did we lose?" My voice was flat, but it was still controlled, I hadn't lost it. Yet.

Michel started stroking my back, my head on his chest, an arm wrapped around him, one of his hands holding one of mine.

"We lost six. Terry. Alphonse. Bridget. Marguerite. Simon. And Dillon."

I knew Terry and Alphonse, a couple of rowdy vampires who resided in Auckland, but I wasn't familiar with Bridget or Marguerite, probably recent arrivals for Bruno's wake. Simon was also local.

"Dillon? Dillon Malone?"

"Yes." Michel sighed and it was sad enough to make me shift from the comfort of his arms to look at his face. He looked tired and worn and fed up and so sad. "He died trying protect me."

388

Well, didn't that just suck? And how wrong had I been about Dillon?

"You did not trust him, *ma douce*?"

Man, I was so going to have to start vetting my thoughts.

His hand came down to my chin and lifted it back up so he could look me in the face, his head was shaking.

"Dear God no, do not do that. I have never felt as close to you as I do right now because I can hear what you really feel. I am not looking forward to going back to not knowing, to waiting for you say it, for fearing I will never hear it out of your lips." He leaned forward and kissed me lightly on the mouth. "Think whatever you want my love, but let me hear it all. Please."

I'm not really sure I can hide my thoughts, or temper them in fact. It's a wonder I have a filter between my brain and my mouth at all. My thoughts tumble and are chaotic and uncontrolled. If Michel is prepared to wade through that mess, then he can have at it, for all I care. I have nothing to hide. I just have trouble saying it, that's all.

He was laughing next me, pulling me close in his arms.

"I love your mind. It *is* messy. But beautiful. I could listen to your thoughts all day and never tire. Your dreams are somewhat interesting too."

"My dreams?"

"You dream of children, *ma douce*. I did not know you felt so strongly for children."

As a Nosferatin I cannot have children, it was another blow in amongst the multitude of hits my body took when I found out what I was. The fact that I can't have children has nothing to do with Michel being a vampire, although that of course would be a problem, vampires can't father babies. But, the real reason is it's all in my genes. Had my parents have had a younger child, that child would have been able to procreate, to conceive a Nosferatin and further children, one to pass on the gene. But never me. I would never have children. I wondered if that was why Michel was so close to his vampires, the ones he had created.

"Of course, they are all my children. They are your family now too."

But they weren't mine, were they? I would never create like he has.

I suddenly didn't feel like being held. He let me get up out of the bed and head to the shower. He didn't follow me immediately, maybe picking up on the feel of how much I just needed some space right now. Time to think. It wasn't until I was in the shower, hot water spraying over me, mixing with the the tears running down my cheeks, that he came to me. Stepping silently into the shower stall and wrapping me in his arms.

He didn't say a word, he just let me cry. I cried for Dillon, whom I had so wrongly misjudged, for the other vampires I knew not so well and not at all. For Bruno. For Rick. And last of all, always last of all, for me. For my fucked up, screwed up, messed up life. I allowed myself to wallow in it for a good few minutes in his arms and then I tucked it all up inside me and threw away the key.

Life sucked, but sometimes you just had to let it be.

Chapter 33
What Movie?

I was glad Michel was there, he couldn't leave to attend business. Despite the rain earlier, the clouds had shifted and the sun had come out by the time we dressed and went downstairs. I was starved, hungrier than I had been for days, so I high tailed it to the kitchen. He followed me, picking up his tablet computer from the lounge on the way and opening up his cellphone to no doubt check in with his day time staff at *Sensations*. I had the feeling he was going to conduct business from the dining room table, but I didn't care, it felt normal, something so very normal. Human even.

Amisi had beaten us to the kitchen and had been playing the housewife, domesticated to the nth degree. Muffins and cookies freshly baked, the latter just coming out of the oven right now.

"You have got to be kidding me. Amisi, you cook?"

"Don't sound so surprised, Luce. It's relaxing, I always bake to soothe my nerves."

I looked at her then, really looked at her. She seemed a little tired, worried even. Shit. I'd been a bad host and an even worse friend. I went straight over to her and threw my arms about her shoulders.

"I'm sorry," I said against her ear. "I suck at being a friend." And then started bloody crying again.

I could tell she was looking at Michel for guidance, she hadn't ever seen me break down before. I think she thought I was some super tough warrior princess or something. Truth is, I was a mess and getting more and more messier every day. I had really been tough on her and Nero. Nero especially, lashing out because I felt he was complicating my already extremely complicated life. But, it didn't need to be that way. I could let them in. Just like I could let Michel in.

Sounds easy, doesn't it? Shame my mind doesn't agree.

I pulled away stiffly and swiped at my eyes. She smiled and turned me around to the table, taking me over to sit down next to Michel, who was watching me closely, making me feel even more like a pathetic wuss than I already did. God, I was just breaking down all over the place, wasn't I? He gave my hand a quick squeeze then started talking into his phone. Man, I hoped he hadn't gone silent on his caller while he watched me blubber all over the cook.

Amisi came back with a couple of blueberry muffins, still warm, oozing butter and plonked them down in front of me.

"I've been practising with the coffee machine, I think I've got it sorted now. You can be my first official guinea pig." She danced back to the kitchen and started getting the bean hopper grinding.

I could get used to this. The muffins tasted as good as they smelt and I groaned softly as I swallowed my first mouthful. Michel's lips twitched at the corners as he tried to answer an unheard question down the other end of his line.

Am I distracting you? I threw the thought at him, unnecessary probably, but I was making a point.

Always, he answered, his hand running up my thigh under the table. I just smiled in response. I could literally see the relief seep into his eyes. It made me pause. He was worried about me too. He rang off his call quickly and closed his phone, looking me in the eyes. He didn't say anything, just held my gaze.

"I'm fine," I said to the unasked question.

He just looked at me. What did he want me to say? To do? I looked away first and tried to concentrate on my muffin, just wanting to cry all over again. Shit! What was wrong with me?

Amisi brought my coffee over and I could only hope that my regular fix of caffeine would jolt me out of the blues. It was good, she'd done well. I still felt like crap.

"This is great, Amisi." I'm sure my voice sounded believable, it was the way Michel just watched me that probably gave me away.

"What's wrong, Luce?" she asked softly.

Oh, I so could not do this right now. You know how it is, when all you want to do is cry and someone shows you care and concern, it just makes it even harder not to let the plumbing loose. I swallowed past a huge lump in my throat and tried to chase it with scalding coffee. Not a good combination, but who cares, it gave me something to do.

Amisi turned to Michel and said, surprisingly, "Would you give us a moment please?"

He didn't say a word, just stood up from the table, taking his tablet and touching my shoulder, then walked into the lounge.

"He'll be able to hear everything, Amisi. It's useless sending him into the next room, he's a bloody vampire."

"But he won't see you. He watches you with such attention, such care, it suffocates you."

I let a huff of air out. Sometimes it did suffocate me,

sometimes I clung to it. Right now? Yeah, I could probably do with the space.

She was silent for a while, just sipping her own coffee. Finally, she broached whatever topic had been bugging her mind.

"Luce, it's OK to be upset. I know that sounds... clichéd, contrived even, but you know what, I have no fucking idea how you do what you do." I just gawked at her. Amisi is a lady, she never swears. Hell, Nero was gonna love me when I sent her home with a potty mouth. "You have so much pressure on you, to do so much... stuff, we don't even know yet what stuff, but you're expected to do it. And on top of that, well, then there's... Rick." She sighed. "Look, I don't want to make you feel worse by talking about it, but I want you to know, you are entitled to lose it, every now and then. Why don't you just let today be that day? We're all here. Erika's downstairs gyming it - you know how committed she is to that room - and I'm here and Michel's here, we'll all look after you. We'll help you pick up the pieces afterwards. Just... just don't be so hard on yourself. Crying is not a weakness. Letting us see *you* is not a weakness. You're tough, Lucinda, one of the toughest and most extraordinary Nosferatins I have ever met. And, I have met a few." She smiled then, knowing that her little Nosferatin community in Egypt was unusual. Normally we don't get to meet that many of our kind. There's just so few of us left now. "So, what's it gonna be? Eat your muffin, cry into your coffee, do what ever you need to do, but don't hide it. Let it out. It'll be OK."

I rubbed my face in my hands. Let it out? I felt like crying before, but now, for some inexplicable reason, I felt all dried up, not a tear to spare. Call my bluff and look what happens.

She got up and went to rinse out her cup at the sink and put the muffins and cookies into containers. I couldn't help thinking she was trying to fatten me up, who else was going to eat those things, the vampires? Hell no, just her and me. We might as well throw in a tub of *Kapiti Ice Cream* as well, for good measure. Erika will have to make some space for me down in her favourite room because I was gonna have to work this lot off if Amisi kept at it.

Arghh! OK. So I was feeling bad about all the death and destruction around me, it was natural, I suppose. Amisi was right, I've got a shit-load of responsibilities and a compass that only seldom works, I'm flying pretty much blind here. Nero does his best and don't get me wrong, without him I would be well and truly lost, but on the whole, it's all down to me.

Sanguis Vitam Cupitor.

Prohibitum Bibere.

Lux Lucis Tribuo.

Me.

I scratched my head and had another bite of muffin. God damn they were good, the girl could cook, shame she has to join with a vampire, those skills aren't top of their mating list. Not that they all had to fall head over heels for their kindred like me. I guess she could have a loved one on the side, a human who enjoyed blueberry muffins.

Ah shit. Of course she couldn't. She'll be immortal, they won't. Fuck this life sucks!

I had my head in both my hands, my elbows on the table top, when Michel came back in.

He took hold of one of my hands and gently pulled me up from the chair, his other hand brushing my hair out of my eyes.

"Thriller or Action Adventure?" He cocked his head to the side. "Maybe a Romantic Comedy?" *Please say no, please say no.*

I smiled, despite myself. "Action Adventure."

"I have just the thing, *ma douce.*"

He led me by the hand into the lounge, which had been transformed into a movie theatre. I stared at him in wonder. When had he done this? The sofas and seats had been arranged like a cinema, in rows and behind each other. The ones behind on plinths, so they were higher and in between each seat a large container of popcorn and a giant *Coca Cola* Cup with straw. A huge - and I mean huge - screen had been lowered ready for viewing, the lights were dim, it was just a matter of getting settled and starting the film. It was awesome.

He took me over to the two seater sofa, slap bang in the middle of the front row and let me sit down. He leaned over and whispered in my ear, "I don't care if the crowd in the back sees me smooching with my gal." I just shook my head at him and watched him go to the *Blu-Ray* player and slip a disc into the mechanism.

He returned with the remote and wrapped an arm around my shoulders, grabbing a blanket and throwing it over our legs. He handed me my *Coke* and Popcorn and smiled.

"Ready?"

"What about the others?"

"You want them to share our movie night?"

396

I shrugged. It seemed a bit mean to turf them out of the lounge and besides, I'd seen he'd put out popcorn and *Coke* for Amisi.

He winked and called, "Amisi, film's about to start."

Just as she came in, so did Erika. No doubt receiving her summons via telepathy. They both plonked down behind us and someone, I'm betting Erika, threw popcorn at our heads. The lights dimmed and Michel hit play on the remote.

What's the movie? I threw the thought at him.

I thought it rather fitting. Plus it has Mickey Rourke in it, I've always liked Mickey Rourke.

Okaay. I watched patiently as the start up credits and ads went by and finally was rewarded with the title.

Immortals.

Ha ha!

I could feel him silently laughing next to me, he thought it was a great joke.

As soon as the credits had finished and the opening scene started he was nibbling my ear.

You're not watching, I chastised in my mind.

Yes I am.

Not the movie, Michel.

What movie?

I brushed him off me as the the first god appeared on screen, all bronzed body and absolutely over the top but delicious muscles, curly black hair. I have a thing for dark hair. They build those gods well in Hollywood.

Should I be jealous? He was now licking my neck, nibbling my throat.

Michel! Erika and Amisi are behind us, they can see

everything you are doing.

Amisi is too intrigued with Zeus to notice us and Erika knows better than to be voyeuristic. Your virtue is safe.

His hand had slipped under my T-Shirt and was now rubbing my nipples hard.

What if I want to watch the movie?

Watch it, my dear, never mind me.

Never mind him. I couldn't help it I started laughing.

Oh do not stop, ma douce. Your laughter does wonders for your breasts. His head dipped down my chest and started nuzzling in between my breasts which had now definitely stopped heaving with silent laughter.

I battered him away and made him sit upright.

You're no fun! he threw at me, but let me watch the movie unhindered, for about five minutes or so. Then started nibbling my ear again. His tongue slipped in my ear making me curl up and cringe, but I couldn't stop laughing.

He was laughing too, trying not to make a sound and had returned to watching the movie. I had absolutely no idea what Zeus was talking about or who the hell Theseus was. Damn, I might have liked this movie.

We could retire. Let the girls enjoy the movie without the side show, Michel said in my mind without looking at me.

I thought you said they weren't paying any attention to us.

It's hard not to notice you, ma douce. You are delicious.

And there goes the nibbling again. Oh, and the hand, but this time much, much lower.

Michel!

Yes?

Oh for the love of... *Stop, you're embarrassing me.*

But you want it, ma douce, I can smell your desire.

I cringed. *That means Erika can too.*

Hmm mm. Your point? The hand had now managed to find its way under my panties and a solitary finger was working some naughty magic making me forget my point, hell forget the entire room for a moment. What film. Oh dear God, he was going to make me come.

No. No. No, Michel.

Yes. Yes. Yes, ma douce. Come for me, right here, in this room, you can do it, they won't know.

Yes they would. I was sure they would, but he was sitting with his arm around my shoulder, his head resting against mine, watching the movie, that's all Amisi would have been able to see. His arms weren't moving, he was making no sound. Erika could probably tell what was up, but she's a vampire, this would have seemed quite acceptable behaviour to her, nothing unusual and certainly wouldn't have distracted from the film.

The movie was action packed, loud and I could tell both girls were into it. Squealing here, ahhing there, they were wrapped up in the film, not us. And for all intents and purposes, we looked like we were too.

Come for me, ma douce. I want to feel your slick perfume on my fingers, I want to lick them dry when you come.

His fingers were working harder, but he was holding me still, so I wouldn't writhe and squirm. I wanted to throw my head back, but I settled on closing my eyes and breathing as quietly as I could through my mouth. It wasn't necessary, there was a fight scene on the screen and the movie was shockingly loud, no dialogue, no quiet moment of conversation, all action. Good choice.

Yes, my love, yes. Come for me.

And I did. Blindingly, unbelievably, beautifully. He held me still, breathing in my ear, stroking me down from the high. He whispered in my mind, *You are amazing. You are beautiful. You are fearless. You own my heart and soul, completely. I am nothing without you.*

I turned my head towards him, I knew I was flushed and carried that post orgasm glow, his eyes flashed at the look of me, his lips brushing my mouth. He brought his hand out from under the rug, lay his wet fingers against his lips and then sucked them into his mouth, all the while keeping eye contact with me. Once he tasted me though, his eyes closed in bliss.

You taste divine. I want to bury my face in you. I want to feel you come against my lips. I want to drink from you as you orgasm, again and again and again.

I just nodded. I was so into that. He picked me up, still wrapped in the rug and carried me out of the room without a word to Amisi and Erika. And all I heard as we started climbing the stairs was Erika's voice.

"Thank fuck for that! I thought they'd never leave."

And then, much to my horror and Michel's amusement, Amisi added, "Yeah, I know. Get a room why don't ya."

Chapter 34
I Just Called to Say....

So, I'm beginning to think that Michel is an exhibitionist. He gets off on getting me off in front of people. Maybe it's a little of that control thing. Right now, I'm picking, he's feeling a little out of control. The claiming was really doing a number on him too. Michel doesn't like losing control, hell who does? But, a vampire and one who is Master of the City? Not a good combo. Letting his vampires see what kind of an effect he has on me was his way of taking back some of that control. I understood it, in theory, I'm just a little uncomfortable with the method used.

Not that I don't seem to respond to the situation. In fact, I'm beginning to wonder if a secret part of me kind of likes the danger element, the taboo. It is a little naughty.

But still, I had strong words with him when we got upstairs to my room. And of course, he simply ignored them, thinking it was righteously, uproariously, funny.

He also proceeded to show me just how much it had made him happy. I could hardly argue the point when I was unable to refuse his advances. It kind of sealed the deal for him. God help me, but I was going to have to watch myself around this man when in public from now on. He had found a new game.

I did convince him to stay in the bedroom for the rest of the day, not that that was really too difficult a task. He'd achieved his shock and awe moment, the rest was just the icing on the cake and he was quite prepared to devour that in private. So, by the time the shutters rose up for the night I was again exhausted, but in a good way and he was practically purring like a cat. Grinning like a Cheshire one too.

The distraction and his careful attention seemed to keep any more episodes of tears away. I knew I wasn't completely over what had happened, I knew I was changed in some small way, because of all the Darkness that I'd had to go through. But, I also felt like I could move on now. Maybe accept the events and not dwell on them. It was a tall ask, but I did feel stronger and it was because of Michel. Michel and Amisi and Erika. Friends who cared and didn't judge me by my occasional shows of weakness.

Reality returned with the rising of the moon, however. Rick may have been dead, plus several of the larger players in the pack, but the Taniwhas still existed and as Michel was the head of all supernatural activities in Auckland, he was also considered the boss of all the supernatural groups. Even if it was just on paper, he still needed to take control of the situation and unfortunately, that meant taking control of what was left of the Hapū.

He and Jett, plus a few others, were planning on heading out to Hapū lands to lay down the law. And I had a sneaky suspicion, to also mete out punishment. That's why he refused to allow me to attend. He said it was because he didn't want me to have to face the remainder of the Hapū, he wanted to protect me from what would undoubtedly be an uncomfortable experience. I did kind of understand, but I did not like being shut out of it either. Even after everything that had happened, I didn't want what was left of the Hapū to be tortured. To be held accountable for what their fucked-in-the-head Alpha had done. There were good people out there, they just needed proper guidance. Maybe if Jerome had been tougher, this wouldn't have happened,

402

but it did and now they needed to pick up the pieces and I hoped Michel's heavy handedness wasn't going to push them over the edge.

It's easier to catch bees with honey than with vinegar. That's what my mum says anyway.

I was still quite weary, not just from a demanding day with my lover, but from everything that had happened. So when I realised I couldn't move Michel on the Hapū visit no-go, I relented and decided a night in was what I needed. Erika and Amisi on the other hand, had spent the past few nights doing nothing, waiting for me to recover, so were unbelievably stir crazy once Michel had left.

I'd about had enough of the sexual innuendos too. Michel really owed me for the movie mayhem he had caused, but I couldn't face a whole night of the girls' constant jokes at my expense, so I sent them packing. Erika was reluctant to leave me, but I promised I'd call if I felt the pull, either the evil-lurks-in-my-city pull or the *seeking a drink* kind of pull. She would be able to meet me in the CBD, so nothing would be lost.

Peace at last, the house to myself, I enjoyed a mandarin soak in the bath tub, did typical girl's night in things and curled up on the couch to watch *Immortals* properly by about 11pm. The movie was about half way through when I received a visitor. And not through a knock on the door.

The Champion appeared in my lounge out of thin air. I just about choked on the popcorn I had just shoved in my mouth and had to try to cough it up and chase it with a swig of *Diet Coke* before I could stand to greet her. She was patient, just stood there in a kind of haze. Not quite solid, not quite transparent, almost like the first time I had seen her, here but not here. This time I was picking it was because she was projecting her image and not because I couldn't figure her out.

The first time I met her at the *Iunctio's Palais* in Paris, she had appeared just as she did now. When I shifted my head to the side she was solid, when I turned it away she was transparent. Apparently that was to do with how I perceived her, I hadn't quite figured her out at that stage, so she hadn't quite solidified to me. By the time I left the *Iunctio's* tender care, she was as solid as a rock. I got her number all right.

The Champion is the head of the *Iunctio's* council and one scary vampire as well. She is, of course, powerful. You don't get to head up the vampire's rule making team, without accumulating some power. Plus, let's face it, she's a female and even in the world of vampyre, equal rights aren't mainstream.

For their all seeing, all knowing leader, she's pretty short, but don't let that fool you, her height is not an indication of her prowess. She looked even more like a china doll today, dressed in an immaculate pale blue dress with white pinafore. She actually reminded me of Alice, from *Alice in Wonderland*, except her hair is almost black, not blonde, but it is full of curls and always perfectly coiffed. Today it was waist length and loose. Her pale and perfect porcelain skin glowed in the reflection of the movie screen, as though she sported her own 200 watt bulb under the surface.

Despite the power that rolled off her and the fact that I knew she was about 1000 years old, give or take a century, she always appeared little more than a child. Petite, perfect,

404

precious. I bet she fooled a few people with that disguise. Not me. I knew better.

But, this was the first personal visit I had ever received, I didn't even know she could do that.

"I can do a lot of things, Nosferatin." Her musical voice sounded very much here, in the room, even if her actual body wasn't.

Oh, and did I mention? She can read minds. There is absolutely no point lying to the woman, she'd just pluck the truth right out of your skull and then feed it back to you with a mallet.

I muted the movie. "Champion." Then fisted my hand over my heart and bowed low. It wouldn't be good not to show respect, even if it grated to do so.

"Mm." She had me pretty much sussed too. It's not like I'm rude to the woman, but she does rub me up the wrong way. Well, it's kind of like an itch under your skin, the type you want to scratch and scratch and scratch at until blood wells up under your finger nails. Yeah, a nice kind of itch, not. I would, however, die for her. I can't quite explain it, it's something to do with the connection Nut placed between us. I would gladly lay down my life for this woman, but I have no idea why.

"It is a puzzle, but there you go. One must make do with what one has and it seems I have you." She looked around the house absently, taking in the artwork, the fine furniture, the plush surroundings. I was betting she had figured out it wasn't my standard habitat. Bank Teller/ Nosferatin doesn't spell chic and sophisticated expensive digs.

"So, to what do I owe the pleasure of your company?"

405

I've never been afraid to jump right in there with her and I really would have liked to get on with things. Her presence was not doing my blood pressure any good. Plus resisting that urge to scratch was distracting.

She pierced me with her vivid and striking blue eyes. They're like the azure of the Mediterranean Sea, unusual but compelling. Sometimes, just sometimes, Michel's eyes turn that blue. It's lovely on him.

She blinked slowly, probably making sure I saw how lovely that blue was on her. OK. It's nice, can we get on with this?

"Patience has never been your forte."

"No, that would be staking vampires."

She hissed at me and bared her fangs, it was all very showy and a waste of time. Fangs don't impress me, unless they're a millimetre from my skin, not that I wouldn't put that past the Queen of the council to take a sip just to prove a point, but I know she can't kill me. Nut has seen to that. It kind of takes the punch out of her toothy act.

"Very well. I am here to warn you." She said it like she really couldn't believe she had lowered herself to this point, to actually do something to help me, to prevent me from harm. I was a little surprised myself. "It seems, I have an undeniable urge to ensure your wellbeing and as such, here I am." Her hand swept out at our surroundings and then back to herself.

She didn't elaborate further. Great. I'm warned, but of what?

"OK. Thanks." I guess. "Anything else you want to add to that?"

She sighed and actually shuffled her feet. "Yes. You

need to sort out your mess in Wellington. It is a distraction, much like your Taniwhas, that you do not need."

Huh. Well, it wasn't really surprising that she knew about the Taniwhas, she is the head vampire and all that. And as for the Wellington issue, of course, she knows about that, that's why Gregor is there, at her request. So, why not warn Gregor, not me?

"Wellington is not your warning." Nothing else. Just that.

"What is my warning then?" She actually paled and looked decidedly uncomfortable, her gaze moving about the room, not able to rest on me. She was swallowing convulsively as well. Man, this was so not like her, where was all the calm composure? Where was all the regal haughtiness? It was as though she really didn't want to answer my questions, but had to. And she was fighting the compulsion to do so.

Oh.

"Yessss. I must answer your direct questions. Your warning is; the Dark is on the rise and she seeks you."

Holy heck. She has to answer my questions. Well done Nut.

The Champion just glared at me. I was just frantically trying to think of a decent question. All I managed to come up with was, "So, you have to answer any question I ask? About anything?"

"Yes. And yes."

I started laughing, this was too good to be true. I felt her *Sanguis Vitam* only a split second before it struck. Stabbing me all over with little pin pricks and then sand blasting me like a concrete wall being cleaned for painting.

I ended up back on the couch curled up in a little ball. Shit. So, no killing but hurt like fuck, yeah?

She backed off, her point made.

Once I found my voice I managed an indignant but barely audible, "Fuck you! You're not supposed to harm me, as I'm Gregor's mate."

Gregor had claimed me, so he said, as his mate, while we were at the *Palais*. At the time, I was sure it was just to get us out of a tight situation, but Gregor indicated it was more. Having now experienced what a true claiming is all about, I'm guessing Gregor's was all an act.

"Exactly, Nosferatin. You are no more his mate, than I. But," - she cocked her head to the side and stared hard at me - "you are definitely Michel's, or will be soon. And as he is not on the *Iunctio* any longer, your rights to no foul play from the members of the council, have been forfeited." She smiled sweetly at me then.

I stood up slowly, stretching my limbs out and wishing like hell I had my jacket on and a couple of sterling silver stakes hidden in the pockets. Not that I'd stake her, I can't, not with Nut's little connection running interference, but they'd be bloody reassuring at this point. So, best behaviour time. Bugger. I've never responded well to authority figures.

"OK. So, Dark is after me, this isn't anything new. You called her a she, who is she?"

"This I cannot say, I do not know, only that the Dark I sense is female, this I am certain."

Kinda like Nut, I suppose. Another goddess maybe.

"Do you know what she will do when she seeks me?"

"No. That I do not, but I can only assume it has a

potential to be fatal, otherwise I would not be here."

I had a sudden thought. "Some *Iunctio* guards turned up here the other day, six of them, did you send them?"

She frowned. "No. Why would I? I cannot kill you."

OK. Forgot about that little bit of info. "Could someone else on the council have ordered it without your knowledge?"

"Yes."

Great.

"Do you have any idea who that might have been?"

"No."

She was definitely shutting down, not giving more than the question required. Back to Wellington then.

"Are you going to bite Gregor's arse off about the situation in Wellington?"

"No." And there goes the one syllable answer. I was going to have to try harder.

I rubbed my eyes. So, I've got to clean up Wellington, simply because it's a distraction, but Gregor won't get the blame if it's not done soon.

"Why won't you confront Gregor over this?" Yippee, an open ended question.

"He is not the cause of the problem."

What...? "And I am?"

"Yes. You are most certainly closely related to the problems in Wellington."

"How?"

She ground her teeth together in a most unattractive manner. Oh, I did love it when I got under her skin.

"I would suggest you look to your blood, therein lies the connection. Now, I believe I have more than done my

409

part in helping to save you from harm. I shall take my leave." The last was said up into the air, as though she was speaking to Nut herself, who I've always thought was up in the sky too, kind of like heaven. I guess vampires feel the same way.

Before I could think of another question or offer the correct farewell bow, she simply vanished. My bet, she really didn't want me to ask any more questions that she would have been compelled to answer and only live to regret afterwards. Fine by me, the shorter the conversation, the healthier.

I rubbed my arms, the memory of the sandblasting still quite fresh. I suddenly felt like a shower to wash off the contamination of the Champion, like she was a disease or a nasty illness I could catch.

I started towards the stairs when my cellphone went off. It was back on the side table next to the *Blu-Ray* remote, so I dashed back in before it went to voicemail.

I flipped it open and before I'd uttered a word Michel's slightly panicked voice came down the line.

"*Ma douce*? Are you all right?"

"Yeah, I'm OK." If you can call a close encounter with a viper fine.

"For a while there I could not feel you through the Bond. I could not hear your thoughts. What has happened?"

Hell, that was weird. "Can you hear them now? Can you feel the Bond?"

"They are starting to come back, but are still chaotic, as though the connection had been disrupted and it's trying to get re-established, but I can feel you through the Bond again. What has happened?"

I sighed, I really didn't want to worry him, he had enough on his plate, but....

"I had a visit from the Champion."

There was silence on the other end of the phone, then the sound of a door slamming shut and an engine starting, followed quickly by the squeal of tires on smooth concrete.

"Michel?"

"I will be there in five minutes." His voice was a low growl.

The line went dead. Five minutes. I'm guessing that's how long it would take Michel to defy the laws of physics and New Zealand road rules to get from *Sensations* to St. Helier's Bay.

So, not happy that the Champion made a little house call then?

Well, I guess I'd find out how unhappy in T minus four minutes and forty-three, forty-two, forty-one... seconds.

Chapter 35
Leaving

I switched the movie off, it seems I wasn't going to get to see *Immortals* any time soon and sat with my feet under me, curled up on the couch. The shower would have to wait. I really felt like it might have been a half hour kind of thing and Michel would not have had the patience, by the sound of his voice.

It seemed like time flew by, because before I knew it Michel was storming through the front door. I cast a glance out the window to see if he had left the Land Rover still running, headlights on, door open, in the middle of the drive, but it was out of sight. By the time I looked back at him, he was on me.

He pushed me back on the couch so I was lying half on half off and crawled up my body, his fangs were already down and out, his knee pushed my legs apart, his hands running up and over my body as though he was reassuring himself I was all still there. The look on his face was a little frightening, but handsome at the same time. Captivating. But it was a look of utter hunger and all fierce possession.

"Michel?"

He growled and stroked a hand through my hair, then started nuzzling my neck and his mark, inhaling. I suddenly smelt that scent he has when he's about to claim me, that beautiful mixed spice and cardamom, with a splash of Freesias. My body responded immediately and he reared his head back with a groan and sunk his fangs in. As he started sucking down my blood his hips began to rock against me and all I could do was moan and arch my back and move against him in return.

Before I knew what was happening, he had removed my underwear, pushed my skirt up and had entered me in a rush, his thoughts in my head a shout: *YOU. ARE. MINE.* There was no slow movement, it was just an urgent pumping, a desire to get as close as possible, to have himself inside me, to be drinking me, to be claiming me and I loved it. I so damn well loved it. I loved that he couldn't help himself, that he had so little control, that I did this to him. I don't think it would have mattered where we were or who was there, this urge was so primal, driven from some base instinct, some ancient call in his body, we were both just along for the ride.

His hands were all over me, his body weighing me down and filling me up, my blood in him, his thoughts in me, his scent everywhere, clinging to me, cleansing me, washing away the feel of the Champion and anyone else for that matter. All that existed was him and me and the heat that we created together.

I came first, unable to stop that beautiful build to ecstasy and when he heard me shout out and writhe against him, he quickly followed suit, still drinking me, so making both our orgasms last that much longer, drawing them out in exquisite bliss.

Finally, his fangs retracted and he licked his mark and collapsed beside me on the couch, pulling me close and kissing my neck.

"Hi," he said a little huskily. "I forgot to say hi."

I laughed. "If that's to be your new greeting, then you have my permission to forget to say hi any time."

He laughed against me, nuzzling my neck again and kissing his mark.

"I think it is safe to say that the claiming felt threatened by news of your visitor, *ma douce*. The moment you mentioned she had been here, I could do nothing else but get to you and claim you again. He started kissing my skin again, softly, so softly. And with such care.

Man, if that's how he reacts to a projected image of a vampire who can't stand my guts, how the hell was he going to handle me going to Wellington and seeing Gregor, which looked like I was going to have to do, or else suffer the consequences of the Champion.

Michel's arms tightened around me, pulling me close, I also felt his fangs come out again and scrape over his mark.

Shit. You can hear my thoughts again, can't you? I didn't even project them, I knew I didn't need to. He just nodded against my neck in an affirmation.

This was going to be hard. And if I had thought it was just going to be hard for me to face my demons and stand up against Gregor, then now it was ten times harder, because I so did not want to put Michel through this. I wanted to protect him too.

I felt his breath come out in a sigh and his head rest down on my shoulders. If I could have seen his face, I was sure his eyes would have been closed.

"I trust you, *ma douce*. I really do. I can see your thoughts, I can see how you feel about me. For the first time since I have known you, I haven't had to guess at where I stood in your affections. But, the vampyre in me is not quite so... understanding. It wants to tie you down to the bed and never let you see another rival ever again."

I kinda fancied the tying down to the bed bit, truth be known. Michel growled and shifted against me. Oops.

Better keep those thoughts under a lock and key for now.

"I'd still be able to reach them." His hand had started stroking my cheek, his finger now tracing my lips.

We were both silent for a while. It was me who said what we both were so desperate not to say.

"I have to go, Michel. She said it was because of me. The humans attacking the vampires down there. You know I can't ignore that if it is the truth, despite the fact that she was right about it being a distraction too. The more problems the humans cause, the less likely I am able to be ready for when the Dark strikes and from her warning, I'm guessing that will be soon. Why else would she have come to see me? This needs to be sorted. Now."

He was quiet for a while, just stroking, breathing against me, holding me tight.

"Why do you think she believes it is because of you, *ma douce*?"

"She mentioned my blood, I can only assume they know about my Forbidden Drink powers or something. They know the vampires are drawn to my blood. Maybe they want to use that to capture them."

"It is not your blood they are drawn to, *ma douce*. It is your Light."

Huh. I hadn't thought of it like that. Then if not my actual blood, what the hell did the Champion mean?

"Have you considered she meant it figuratively, as in blood relative? Perhaps you should start with your cousin."

Tim? What on earth would he have to do with vigilante vampire killing humans? Well, other than the fact that he approached Gregor to become the local Nosferatin, even when he isn't one.

"A good place to start then," Michel said softly, still stroking me, still holding me tight. I knew he was trying to be reasonable, to help work it all out, but I could feel his tension, he was thrumming with it. He was so close to the edge because discussing this meant I was closer to going to Wellington. To Gregor.

I felt like I needed to deflect the inevitable, at least for a moment.

"Maybe I should pay a visit to my folks, see what they know about my father's side of the family."

"Hmm mm. And perhaps you should introduce your husband to them while you are at it?"

I pulled back and looked at him. "You're not my husband." I said it with a smile.

"In vampyre terms I am. And do you not wish for me to be your husband, *ma douce*?" His smile said it all, he knew exactly how I felt about him. He could read my mind now, how convenient. And my mind was shouting that he was mine.

"It surprises me that the claiming is still in effect." He sounded puzzled, mildly intrigued. "I did not expect to hear from your thoughts that you were so certain, but you are." I knew though, that he was trying to stimulate thoughts in me, trying to fish for an answer.

I couldn't give him one, because I simply did not know. I was obviously still holding something back, but what? I started to shift uneasily next to him, it was a topic of conversation I didn't feel comfortable with at all.

He just kept stroking me and held me firmer, he wasn't going to let me run from this.

"It is all right, *ma douce*, all shall be revealed in good

time. I have complete faith in this."

We sat quietly for a moment, each with our own thoughts. Well, me with mine and Michel with both his and mine, but you know what I mean.

To steer away from the awkwardness that I felt, I put us back on to business.

"So, I think I should go to Wellington tomorrow, not wait until Saturday. I think if the Dark is about to strike I need to get on with this. Sort it out.

"I will come with you."

I ached at the tenor of his voice. The fear I could clearly hear. He may be certain of how I feel right now, but he was terrified of what would happen when I got off that plane in Wellington and was faced with Gregor again. I couldn't blame him. And I also couldn't put his fear to rest, my track record was not so great that it would be believable. But, I also knew he couldn't come with me. Gregor was still establishing his hold on the city and a visit from a Master of a nearby City, would be construed as an attack for possession. It was politically suicidal.

Michel abruptly stood and started pacing. He was so wound up, I could see the veins on the side of his neck standing out at attention. I sat up slowly and got myself straightened and just watched him pace. Like a caged tiger, he was all energy contained, the potential at any moment to explode. I wanted so much to ease his pain, to stop this slide into what I could only assume was going to be destructive to our relationship. I wanted to offer a solution, to fix it, to stop this thing that he feared from happening, but I couldn't. All I could do was watch.

After ten minutes of watching him pace and neither of

us uttering a word, he finally stopped and turned to look at me. I had to close my eyes at what I saw. Such pain, but such determination. He'd made a decision and it had cost him greatly. He was tearing himself apart from the inside out.

"Erika and Jett will go with you. And Amisi, of course. Accommodation will be found in neutral premises and neither vampyre will leave your side. This is the best I can offer."

I stood up slowly and walked toward him, taking both his hands in mine. I could almost see the knife slicing through his skin and piercing his heart, this was causing him such physical pain. Despite a claiming which he could barely refuse, he was allowing me to do my job. The vampires attending didn't faze me, I would have wanted them there myself, not only because of moral support - Erika is my rock - but because facing off against the humans in large numbers was going to require a show of force. I didn't for a moment think we could negotiate any longer, Gregor had seen to that with his high body counts. I needed a couple of warriors at my side to send the message home, if it was going to work at all.

But, what I could do for Michel was to show him how much I appreciated what he was doing and how much he meant to me. Even if *he* couldn't see past this weekend, I knew I could. I knew without a doubt that I would come back to him, so I did the only thing I could think of that would show him how I felt. I led him up the stairs to our bedroom and gave him every inch of my soul that I could spare.

I lavished him with love and attention and care and I

never took anything in return. It was all for him. It was the least, the only, thing I could do. I pleasured him until he could stand it no more and I could fight him no more. And then I let him claim me one more time before the sun rose and he whispered in my ear as I drifted off to sleep, "I will leave now, *ma douce*, because I cannot bear to watch you walk away. *Je t'aime, ma belle. Je t'aime.*"

I didn't answer, he heard my thoughts and besides, it's just words anyway.

Chapter 36
Dancing Dragons

Amisi and Erika had come home late and as I had been up all night with Michel, we all managed to sleep most the day away. It was close to 5pm when I ventured into the kitchen, after packing an overnight bag and getting myself showered and ready to face what was perhaps going to be the most awkward, or hard, or impossibly difficult 24 hours of my life. At least I would have my peeps with me.

Amisi was up, but Erika was nowhere in sight. Breakfast today, well it could be called dinner but we were only just getting started, was pancakes, bacon and maple syrup. I know for a fact that the vampire in the household would have found it painful to be around the delicious looking stack of sugar loaded goodness that sat in front of me. Just because you don't eat solid food any more, doesn't mean you can't pine after it.

"I bet Erika can smell this up in her room, she'll be getting jealous." I stabbed a thick pile of dripping pancakes and shoved it in my mouth. Bliss.

"She'll be too busy. She brought Jett home with her last night.

My eyes bugged out, I was unable to speak because my mouth was so damn full, but Amisi got my meaning by my expression and just laughed.

"It was kind like watching you and Michel all night, but very much more public. Vampires have no shame." I wasn't quite sure how much more public you could get than Michel and me, but I took her word for it. I also noticed that she didn't seem surprised. Amisi has grown up around vampires, she knows exactly what they are like and nothing surprises her.

"So, we're off to Wellington today. I can't wait to see what it's like." She looked excited, like a kid about to open its Christmas present and see what Santa brought. I couldn't blame her, this could well be her new stomping ground. Amisi had already left her life behind in Cairo, I think, she was one of the most practical people I had ever met. There was already too many Nosferatins in Cairo, she knew she had to make her way elsewhere, why not Wellington?

"You think you could live surrounded by Kiwis, Amisi?"

She shot me a look that said it all, *purlease, what do you think?*

I nodded and smiled, for some reason Amisi was more Kiwi than some of the kids I grew up with back home in Cambridge. More down to earth and approachable than the horse breeding snobs of rural Waikato. She fitted in like a well worn glove. As I watched her fluff about in the kitchen I couldn't help feeling that she was like a sister to me. Connected in more ways than just blood, although the fact that she is a Nosferatin does mean she has some of the same blood in her veins as I do. But she understood me, she understood the country I grew up in. Amisi would make a fine addition to New Zealand Nosferatin ranks. I only hoped that Gregor would accept her as his local vampire hunter and allow her to stay.

He didn't really have much choice. Wellington needed a Nosferatin and Nosferatins are thin on the ground. To have found such a well educated and accomplished Nosferatin at all, was simply a miracle of biblical proportions. If this worked, my life could become so much more simplified and finally, maybe something right could happen, instead of all the doom and gloom that seems to follow me around.

"You know, I would really like you to live here in NZ. You might be in a different city, but we would be able to meet up often, exchange ideas, work together. I really hope this works out, Amisi. I really don't want you to go back to Cairo."

She looked at me a little strangely then, her eyes were shining bright, glistening in the downlights of the kitchen.

"Thank you, Lucinda. Thank you." She bowed to me then, the formal fisted hand across chest bow. It took me by surprise. Amisi and I had well passed the formal stage, but then, she was a Nosferatin of regal standing. Sometimes I felt like the poor cousin, the country bumpkin around her. She could be so elegant, so refined and so perfectly part of this other world. Once again I was reminded of what I might have been like, had I been raised by my Nosferatin father. How much did I miss out on? Where would I be now if he was still alive?

I let my mind wander as Amisi turned back to her chores and I thought about what the world would be like with my father in it. I do think about my mother, but it's my father I wish for most. I got all the love and care I could ever have wanted from my mother's sister, my aunt, but what my biological father could have offered, none other can replace. Nero has filled a gap, for sure, but not like a father, more that of a friend and acquaintance. Imagine what I could have shared with my Dad. Michel, for starters. Michel had asked if I would introduce him to my Aunt and Uncle, I think he was just joking, they couldn't meet him, not really. To travel to their farm we would have to drive at night, they would have to meet him in the glow of the moon, we couldn't stay during the day, the farm house is not light tight. So, logistically speaking, I couldn't take him to meet my parents. Perhaps if they visited here, but they don't. They can't stand the city, they are farmers through and through.

But, my biological father, my Dad, he could have met Michel, he could have known what he was, there would have been no secrets. How nice that would be, not to have to hide who I am or what I am with my parent. How different my life would have been. I have managed to surround myself with people who I could confide in, people who are part of this world too. I have support and love and understanding, I just don't have that bond you would have with a parental figure who is also part of your vocational world. Imagine the tips and tricks he could have handed on. Imagine what I could have been with his tutelage and care.

I brushed an unwanted tear away and refused to let any others appear. It was all a dream, a wishful waste of time. He is dead, I am alone, save for those people I have picked up along the way to fill the gap, but it is never completely filled. It never will be, I think.

Erika and Jett walked into the kitchen then and saved me from my wasted dreams. I don't think I could have been happier to have seen them, they broke the hold of what-could-have-been, they snapped me free of my own empty yearnings and plunged me back into reality like a cold dip in an icy river. I needed it. Their timing couldn't have been better.

"So, you all packed, *chica*? Time to face the devil."

Erika did not like Gregor. I could hardly blame her, he had used his superior *Sanguis Vitam* on her to make her abandon me in his apartment. Her job had been to protect me from him, she had let me down, herself down and more importantly, Michel down. She despised Gregor now and I somehow thought he'd never be able to get the better of her again. Erika may not be as strong as Gregor, or as powerful, but she sure as hell could be as cunning. Gregor Morel was in for a load of crap from Erika Anders. She would not make his life easy.

I smiled back at her. "Bring it on!" I was aware they all knew it was just words. Inside I was a complete and utter mess, but I could act when needed and the next 24 hours may have to be the command performance of my life. I would draw on every lesson I had learnt in the face of vampires, pull every trick I had out of my sleeve and *never show fear. Never give an inch. Always stay on guard.*

I am Nosferatin, hear me roar. Ha. I wish.

Nightfall came, with the help of the odd jab at Erika about her house guest's appearance to speed the last couple of hours of daylight along. Jett just plain ignored the girl talk, reading from Michel's tablet computer as though he owned the thing and as though we weren't commenting on Erika's choice of bed partner or her downright lustful look when she spied her man across any room. I'm sure he found it amusing, but he sat straight faced in the corner of the kitchen and pretended we didn't even exist.

I think Erika was relieved when the shutters whirred away, as she was the first out to the garage and started loading our gear into the back of the Land Rover. All four of us in my car was just not going to cut it. Jett was a big boy, I don't think he would have fitted.

The plane was out of the hangar, fuelled and ready to go. We boarded without delay and I was surprised to see Michel's manservant on board. He usually only attended when we had a long haul flight, Auckland to Wellington was hardly long haul. I was the last to board, and Michel's guy just about tripped over himself to greet me, quietly handing me a little box.

"From the master," he whispered and went about his business of securing the door and making sure the rest of the passengers were seated and belted in for take off. I took a seat in an armchair at the back of the plane, out of sight of the others, providing an element of privacy.

I fingered the box. It was the size of a jewellery box I guess, white with a deep blue ribbon wrapped around it, slightly padded, so when you pressed it, a perfect dent was left which slowly filled in as the padding returned to its previous puffed up shape. I did that several times, watching as it slowly refilled, trying to build up confidence to open the damn thing. It's not like Michel hasn't tried to gift me things in the past. I've got a perfectly beautiful *Longines Dolce Vita* watch and a beautiful diamond encrusted bracelet hidden away in my lingerie drawer. I've never worn either. But, there was just something about the timing of this gift that made me believe it would be difficult to deny it, to pack it away between my lacy knickers and bras.

Was it so hard to accept a gift from the man I loved, I asked myself. I stared out the window for a while, watching the lights of Auckland drop away and grow smaller as the plane defied gravity and rose into the night air. Damn it, it probably wasn't even jewellery. The key to his chamber? A new fighting tool of microscopic proportions? Shit. Just open the damn thing and get it over with.

I ripped the ribbon off and snapped the lid open before I could think further about it. What stared out at me stole my breath away. His dancing dragon. A beautiful platinum dancing dragon, with bright blue gemstones for eyes. I was guessing blue diamonds, they didn't look right for a sapphire, the sparkle just too intense. The dragon also had a bolt of lightning through its heart, made up of smaller white diamonds, making the lightning bolt shimmer as though alive. I lifted it up out of the box with shaking fingers. It was suspended on a long fine platinum chain, it felt heavy in my hands and the thought of the delicate links in the chain being able to hold its weight briefly surprised me. It was a solid piece of artwork, beautiful and undeniably stunning. I loved it. But, could I wear it?

I ran my fingers over and over the dragon, the metal becoming warm under my touch. I quickly tipped the box upside down to see if there was a note, but nothing else came tumbling out. Just the necklace. I don't really think it needed an explanation. Its beauty spoke for itself.

I stared at it for a few more minutes and then thought, to hell with this. It was beautiful. It was him. And me. It was perfect. I slipped the long chain over my neck and watched as the dragon slid down my chest to rest between my breasts. I had to smile, he had even worked out the exact length for it nestle where he himself would no doubt love to be.

Thank you, I heard in my mind, his voice so soft, so beautiful.

I smiled and held the dragon tight, closing my eyes and

426

letting him see just how much I loved him, from the images I played in my head.

After a while I heard a soft clearing of someone's throat at my side, I opened my eyes and Michel's servant was standing with a small tray, the gorgeous smell of coffee wafted up to meet me with a plate of delicious looking biscuits on the side. James, the thought popped in my head. Whether that was Michel reminding me, or it just came flooding back from previous journeys on the plane with him taking care of us, I'm not sure, but the guy's name was James.

"Thank you, James," I said as he placed the tray on a side table for me. His eyes flashed when he smiled.

"My pleasure, madam." He slipped away as quietly as he had appeared and left me to my thoughts and the blissful taste of freshly ground and brewed coffee accompanied by chocolate biscuits to die for. I felt loved and cared for and precious to someone and it eased my soul, relaxed my body and let me calm before the storm hit and all hell would no doubt break loose.

We started our descent into Wellington not long after and before we had to belt ourselves in for landing, I moved out to the main area and joined the others. Enough of hiding, time to get together and face this as one. Erika's eyes flicked over the dragon and she smiled, Amisi squealed as she reached for a closer look and Jett just read the *Herald*, this time in paper form.

"That is truly beautiful, Luce. What does the dragon mean?" Amisi asked fingering the pendant.

"You know, I'm not sure, it's just Michel. It's here on his plane, at his chamber in *Sensations*, he wears it on his clothes sometimes. I just associate it with him."

"It's his crest," Erika offered. "His family crest."

I didn't know he had one, he wasn't of noble blood, just a peasant from a village in France. Did they all have family crests over there?

Erika must have picked up on the confusion on my face because she added, "It was the crest of his village, where he originally came from in France. When he was turned and had to leave his home forever, he chose the crest as his own, as a reminder of what he had lost and what he had to honour. It is now the Durand line's crest. For him to gift it to you, such as this, he is offering you everything he stands for. His past, his present, his future. It is a meaningful gift, not just a token of love."

So, not just a piece of jewellery then. Are you trying to tell me something Michel?

All that I stand for is yours, ma douce. All that I am, all that I have been and all that I will be, is yours. Will you accept?

You know I will, I whispered in his mind.

The plane touched down then and I lost the connection, not intentionally, the jarring just brought me back to myself and my current surroundings. It didn't surprise me that there was no limo on the tarmac waiting for us, I hadn't told Gregor we were arriving a day early. Bad, I know, but the element of surprise was important to me. He always seemed to be one step ahead of me and I needed a little head start tonight. I glanced at Jett, his eyes came up to meet mine and he cocked his head.

"I will take care of it," his gravelly voice announced.

Shit, could he read my mind too? I wanted him to glaze

Gregor's humans in the hangar, so they wouldn't tell their boss an unannounced plane had arrived and parked itself in his hangar. Jett just smiled.

"The master is conveying your thoughts."

Cut it out, Michel. If he stayed in my head this was going to kill him. I couldn't be worrying about his reaction to Gregor while having to deal with it myself. If I could, I'd lock him out altogether, but for the life of me, I seemed unable to right now.

I shall leave, ma douce. You are correct. I felt his touch in my mind like it was a physical caress and then he was gone. I sent my senses out tentatively and found he had walled himself in. His shields thick and impenetrable. At least one of us had the ability still to block.

We exited the plane and Jett dealt with the humans who had come out puzzled at our arrival. Erika was on the phone and within ten minutes a rental car had been delivered. A Mitsubishi Pajero, not our usual standard, but it would do. We piled in and headed towards the city centre, stopping briefly at our hotel on Lambton Quay to off load our bags and park up the car. Then, fortifying myself, we headed off to *Desire de Sang.* I may have wanted Gregor to be unaware of our arrival, but walking in his city without announcing ourselves first was just stupid. Best to get this over with.

Friday night in the capital was pumping. Crowds of pub crawlers and party goers were walking the streets. It was bustling and alive and vibrant and kicking. And I noticed how Amisi took it all in. Her eyes were darting from one landmark to another, skimming the people, the faces, the scene. She was awash with excitement, but underneath it all I saw her assessing each alley, each side road, each building, like the well trained Nosferatin she is. By the time we reached our destination, she had already committed to memory the last few blocks, the most likely places for vampire attacks, the most desirable spot to confront the enemy. I was impressed, to say the least, but not surprised.

We queued to enter, we didn't want to make a fuss and although the vampire on the door recognised me and Erika and was unimpressed with Jett, I quickly held his gaze and glazed his memory of us from him. Did I feel bad? Not a bit. I needed every bit of an advantage I could get tonight and I was prepared to cheat to get it.

We entered with a group of humans, into the sordid world that was Blood Lust. It made my lips quirk just to be here again. It was so rank fantasy vampire, that it had to make you laugh. The look on Amisi's face was priceless.

"I didn't know places like this existed," she said, barely audible above the thumping of the music. I could tell she didn't approve. It just made me smile wider.

We took a seat in the corner at a table against the wall, while we assessed the situation. Several vampires were dotted through the room, not all of them in the required uniform of leather and vinyl. Some obviously there for their own pleasure, some no doubt unobtrusive security, none of which looked our way.

"Why haven't they noticed us?" I asked no one in particular.

Erika smiled, it was the kind of smile you'd see on someone filled with pride. "One of Jett's skills is masking. He's masking us from them, all they sense is a group of humans."

I quickly shifted my gaze to him, he seemed relaxed, not working too hard at all.

"So, I didn't need to glaze the guy at the door then?"

He shrugged. "It's a team effort, isn't it?" His gruff voice murmured.

I shook my head. "Don't do me any favours, eh?" I could so do without glazing, I hated it. He nodded in understanding.

Just then Gregor entered the room from the private door at the back and stood talking to some vampires. I felt, rather than saw Amisi sit up straighter. I quickly shot her a glance, she looked slightly flushed and totally in awe. Shit. I never thought she'd find him attractive, but that's just stupid. Who wouldn't? Then suddenly she frowned.

"What's wrong?" I asked.

"He wears a Nosferatin *Sigillum*." She glanced around the room as though she would see the Nosferatin who had given it to him. Huh. Had Nero never told her?

"Yeah. It's mine."

She turned slowly to look at me and I had to hold my ground in the face of all that incredulity.

"Why would you give him your *Sigillum* and not Michel?" She sounded appalled.

I couldn't blame her, I was too. "He tricked me, all right. I had no idea I could even mark someone and he tricked me into doing it."

Now the incredulity was replaced with anger, so strong, so intense, I could smell it. Erika and Jett shifted uncomfortably in their seats.

"No one..." - she paused to suck in a breath through

431

clenched teeth - "no one should ever be forced to give their *Sigillum* without consent. That is despicable."

Whoa. Tell us how you really feel. She was ropeable. It kind of made me feel better. I pretty much felt the same way. I had never forgiven Gregor for cheating me out of that precious part of my soul. It was why I had promised myself I would never give my *Sigillum* away again. It was all I had left of me.

Just then Gregor's eyes shifted across the room to me and locked on with a shadow of surprise. I could see my *Sigillum* glow with recognition, making the silver and platinum that swirled in his eyes dance with the colours of the rainbow.

I felt my heart skip a beat and the undeniable pull towards him that I had felt in the past. And I cursed.

Couldn't I, just once, catch a friggin' break?

Chapter 37
The Offer

He glided over the dance floor towards us, taking his time, while people just stepped out of his way. The vampires out of respect, the humans out of intuition. They could no doubt feel the power rolling off him, even if they didn't know what it was they were feeling. His eyes never left me, the surprise now replaced with hunger. I shifted in my seat and Erika's hand came to rest on my own under the table.

"Easy, *chica*. You can do this," she whispered, loud enough for me to hear over the music in the bar.

Jett stood slowly, to stand behind me, a sentry making a show of why he was there. Gregor didn't even glance at him. It was hard not to notice his body, under that beautifully cut suit, he was tall and lean and moved like a panther, all sleek lines and beautiful grace. He knew the effect he had on me and he was playing it up. I allowed my eyes to travel the length of him and then I shook myself awake, breaking whatever fucked up spell I was under. He was just a man, just a vampire, he might wear my mark, but he did not hold my heart.

As soon as I thought that I realised how true it was. I felt it down to my core. I would always be attracted to Gregor, I didn't doubt it, but I also knew I could refuse his advances, I could choose not to play the game. I felt suddenly liberated. I wondered if I could have chosen this path before we crossed that forbidden line, but I didn't let myself dwell on it. The challenge had complicated things, I was angry with where my life had taken me and trying to banish Michel from my mind. And the Dark had taken

433

hold. All pretty pathetic excuses on the whole, but I would cling to them. What had happened had happened, now it was time to move on.

The detachment I felt allowed me to become more aware of my surroundings and I flicked a glance over to Amisi. She was having a pretty hard time taking her eyes off him too, but she had the determined look of someone who was not going to entertain any thoughts of the evil god who approached, despite the fact that he mesmerised her. I felt a momentary pang of sympathy for her. It was tough to covet something you despised. Trust me, I know. She'd learn to live with it, or get eaten up by it, but it was her choice and hers alone.

Finally Gregor made it to our table and he simply bent down and took my hand from my lap, raising it to his lips, his eyes never leaving mine.

"*Ma cherie*, you have entered my city unannounced. I should punish you, should I not?"

I smiled sweetly at him and pulled my hand free, catching a look of surprise on his face, which he quickly hid with his usual sex-on-a-stick demeanour.

"You were expecting me, Gregor. I am merely a day early and considering your last phone call, I would have thought you'd take my early arrival as a sign of my commitment to the task."

He cocked his head at me and smiled. "Not, it would seem, as a sign of your desire to see me again." His eyes travelled down to the dragon on its long chain, delicately resting between my breasts. I couldn't tell if his attention was captured by Michel's crest or by my boobs, either way his gaze lingered longer than it should have.

434

He stood up straight and glanced around the table for the first time. He nodded to Erika and just glared at Jett and then he finally found Amisi and the world stopped spinning. He blinked slowly, as though trying to rid himself of the vision before him, but he didn't look away. She glared back at him, unsmiling.

Shit. I better intervene.

I stood up and said, "Gregor Morel this is Amisi Minyawi from Cairo."

She stood, all smooth graceful Nosferatin lines, fisted her hand across her chest and bowed low, offering him the Nosferatu greeting of respect. Despite how she felt about him, she could play the dutiful Nosferatin well. While still bent over she uttered the greeting she had given Michel on meeting him the first time.

" Greetings from Nafrini Al-Suyuti, Master of Cairo City. She sends her thanks to you, Master, for your hospitality to one of her kind, as do I."

She rose then, but not before Gregor's hand had come out to help her up. I don't think he realised what he had done. She just looked down at it suspended between them and then back up to his eyes, returning a blank mask.

He paused and assessed her, then smiled slowly, a little wickedly. I think he may have found a new challenge. His gaze returned to me and his smile broadened.

"Two for the price one, how fortuitous."

He pulled a seat out and sat down, which I so had not expected. I hesitated and then sat myself down as well, I guess he was here to stay. Amisi slowly lowered herself into her chair, so delicately, so perfectly. Gregor's eyes watched her every move. Oh, how fickle the heart can be, I thought and hid a bubble of laughter.

It's not that I wished Gregor's attention on Amisi, although I think she can take care of herself, she has been practically raised by vampires, she knows their number. But it did make it easier on me. I admit, I liked his attention elsewhere and was I jealous? Nah. Not in the slightest. I had already moved on.

I did know that a part of me still wanted him to be saved, saved from himself, saved from the Dark. But maybe, just maybe, I could hand those reins over to Amisi. She was a Nosferatin after all, her desire would be the same as mine. To save as many vampires from the Dark and bring them toward the Light.

I was a little concerned on how he would play her though. She was my sister in all but name, I did not want her hurt. So, I pierced him with a glare and raised my eyebrows when his eyes met mine. Of course, he took it the wrong way and smiled cheekily in return.

"Jealous, *ma petite chasseuse?*"

I held his gaze and tried to stop the blush that threatened to engulf me. I was not jealous. I was not jealous. I was just unable to stop my body from responding to his look. I was the first to glance away, he just laughed.

A waiter brought over a champagne bottle and glasses, pouring a drink for each of us, including the vampires at my back.

"I think perhaps a celebration is in order," Gregor announced as he raised his full glass. "To my... *Sigillum* shared Nosferatin." He nodded to me and then he turned to Amisi. "And to the Nosferatin I intend to never share."

Oh God. This was not good.

436

He drank from his glass, but the rest of us were frozen, unable to share his toast. He didn't pull us up on it, just smiled knowingly. I think we may have made his night.

Back to business. Always a good thing to remember in the face of the wickedest of wicked vampires.

"How's your little human problem going, Gregor? Any new updates?"

He sipped his drink and then ran a finger around the edge of the rim on the glass.

"They have had a few casualties. I think they have underestimated my resolve to remain in the city."

Great, more deaths of humans. More crap for me to climb over.

"Has it stopped them attacking vampires?"

"No, unfortunately."

"Then a good plan, huh?" I offered, taking the first sip of my drink out of habit more than desire.

His silver eyes bore into mine. "I will defend my territory, *ma cherie*. From anyone who threatens it." I got the innuendo.

"I'm not threatening your hold on your territory, Gregor. I'm here to help. But, I gotta say, you're not making it easy for me. How do you think the humans will respond to all the killing? How do you think I can get them to toe the line now?"

"I have no intention of having them toe the line, as you say, but to get the fuck out of my way. This is my city."

Okaay.

We sat silently for a while, just letting the sounds of the club wash over us. He may have given up on trying to avoid conflict, but I couldn't. I knew negotiating was out,

437

but maybe reasoning with their survival instincts was still a viable option. Maybe I could convince them that if they didn't leave he would kill each and every one of them and probably their families as well. The desire to survive can be a powerful one, I prayed I could use that power.

"Will you give me the next 24 hours to try something?" I asked.

His eyes roamed over my body and then came back to rest on my neck, above his mark. "I gather you're not offering something that would entertain me?" His voice was low and husky, he didn't give a damn who heard him, or that they saw the way he looked at me. So, maybe not passed over yet. Damn.

I didn't let my body respond, just sat firm and still. Go me.

"Be serious, Gregor. I am."

"Yes. You seem to be a tad more serious than you used to be, Lucinda. Where has your spontaneity gone? Did you leave it in Paris?"

I took a slow breath in, I did not need to be reminded of what happened between us in Paris.

"Throw me a bone here, Gregor. Can you hold off annihilating the humans until after I leave?"

He laughed, a full throaty laugh, that made every female in the room look at him and not be able to pull their gazes away.

"Oh, I have missed you, *ma cherie*. Very well, you may have 24 hours in my city to attempt whatever useless thing you wish to do and then I shall finish what they have started once and for all."

I had no doubt he meant business. This was it, the

deadline had been reached. If I couldn't round up the humans tonight or tomorrow, Gregor would simply make them cease to exist. Last chance time and I intended to make it work.

"Thank you," I said rather stiffly and stood to leave. The others following suit, Jett already on his feet beginning to make a path for me toward the door. Amisi fell in behind him and Erika kept at my back. We were an obviously tight group, flanked by bodyguards the impression couldn't have been stronger.

Gregor raised his eyebrows at the scene.

"They protect you well, *ma petite chasseuse*. What are they afraid of? Me or you?"

I didn't care to answer that question. I wasn't quite sure what the correct reply would actually be.

I shook my head and started following behind Amisi, but Gregor leapt to his feet and held onto to my arm, spinning me back towards him.

"Lucinda."

Erika was up in his face in an instant. Jett having stopped and turned to assess the scene. He didn't make a move, just trusted his girl to do the job needed.

Gregor ignored her completely, but removed his hold on my arm and slowly took Michel's dragon in his hand.

"Can we talk for a moment, privately?"

I shook my head. "She goes where I go."

He smiled a little bitterly. "Michel's orders?"

"My desire."

He nodded slowly. "Very well, I will say what I have to say right here." His hand left the dragon and brushed up my chest to his mark on my neck, his thumb tracing it with a

439

soft caress. I felt it, deep down inside, the effect he still had on me. It was warm and lovely and so, so nice. It was everything good about Gregor and nothing of the bad. It was the part of him I had fallen for, the part he hid from most of the world. I felt privileged to have been introduced to it, but it was not mine to keep. Nor did I want to.

My hand came up to hold his and still the motion, my eyes told him everything he needed to know.

He smiled sadly.

"So, you have made up your mind, *ma cherie*?"

"Yes. There was never any chance of it being any other way." Not really, not now that I think about it.

"There is nothing I can do to change your mind?"

I shook my head. "I am sorry."

He smiled, but this time it was his wicked one, his slightly sinful one. The one that told you he wasn't yet down and out for the count, he was rallying and would strike back with a vengeance at any moment. I stiffened slightly and his thumb began tracing his mark again.

"I told you once, Lucinda, that I do not give up a fight easily. I could continue to pursue you and I would make it my life's goal to win you back. I have never lost a battle yet."

I didn't like the sound of this.

"But, you could offer me something in return, to let you go, without further... seduction on my part."

Oh boy. I really didn't like the sound of this.

When I didn't say anything his eyebrows raised. "Will you not ask what would release you from my sights? Are you not in the slightest bit curious? Or do you think you could stand against my fervent desires?" He leaned in towards me and whispered against me ear, "Are you really that strong?" His fingers still stroking his mark on my neck.

Shit. "What could I offer you, Gregor?"

Oh he liked that. His smile returning with much delight.

"Amisi." His voice was quiet, not raised. But somehow it managed to block out all other sound, as though the DJ had stopped the music and the dancers had stopped their motions and the people in the room had all held their breaths in fear.

"No," came my reply and I pulled away and strode out the door past a shocked Jett and an even more shocked Amisi and the sneering eyes of Gregor's doormen.

I guess I wasn't the only one to have heard his words.

Chapter 38
Family Ties

I fumed out on the pavement. That no-good-son-of-bitch-vampire! What the hell did he think he was playing at? Amisi was not mine to trade and even if she was, stuff him! He's never getting his claws on her. Never!

Jett had taken up a position with his back to us, watching the shadows, keeping an alert eye on the surroundings. Erika was in front of me, trying to get my attention, Amisi was off to the side, a far away look in her eyes. I was still fuming. I could not believe the audacity of the man. He knew he didn't have a hold on me anymore, so he shifted his sights to Amisi.

It seemed that any Nosferatin would do, it didn't matter who. I always knew Gregor had a thing for Nosferatins. He'd told me once that their blood called to him. The way he had looked at Amisi I truly believed that. There was hunger there, but more, a kind of reverent desire, an almost worshipful look to his eyes. Sure, he no doubt saw how beautiful she was, how much the epitome of Nosferatin upbringing she represented, but he was also just as attracted to her neck, specifically the vein on the side of it pulsing with her Nosferatin blood.

I would never let him drink from her. I would never let him near her again. We would do what we came here to do, then we would return to Auckland and I would send her home. The further she was away from Wellington, the better. Cairo was only just barely far enough away for my liking, but it would do. Surrounded by Nero's Nosferatins and Nafrini's vampires, Gregor would never be able to touch her. Never.

I would just have to battle his *fervent desires* for eternity and I would not cave, no matter how much he thinks he can tempt me. I would stand strong for all Nosferatin. I would keep him busy, so he never had the chance to find another again and if I had to, I would sacrifice myself to protect them all. He was a monster hidden behind the mask of a lamb. Beautiful and cruel and clever and determined, but I alone would be able to hold him off. If not from me, then from the rest of my kind.

I would not let him get her.

"Lucinda. It is not your decision to make."

My head shot up and looked at Amisi. No fucking way! I had started shaking my head at her, but she broke in before I could open my mouth.

"You think you are the only Nosferatin in this world who has to battle a vampire like Gregor? There are hundreds of Gregors, Luce, just like him. And many of them run a city. Every city needs a Nosferatin, so you can imagine how many Nosferatins have to battle the likes of Gregor. I have known his type before. Even Nafrini has Gregors. I am well versed in how to act around them, I can hold my own. If I choose to come to this city it will not be because of him, or in spite of him, but it will be because I choose to. And if I choose to help free you from him, then that is my choice. My choice, no one else's."

She held my gaze with a sense of conviction I don't think I could have argued with. She was so sure of herself, of her position in this world, of what she would face. There was no nineteen year old's naivety, she knew full well what would face her here in Wellington and it didn't scare her. And she didn't think she was immune to it, only that she

443

would have to face it somewhere, either here or somewhere else, location was all the difference. It was the only difference. The situation could appear again anywhere throughout the world.

I ran a hand through my hair in frustration.

"I don't want you to have to deal with the likes of him. It's not fair, he doesn't play fair."

"He is vampyre. He is no different from any other and he deserves to be offered the Light. The question I ask you, my sister, is can you give him up to me?"

Why is it that she suddenly sounded decades older than me? She still looked the same. Young and sweet and barely touched, but she held the knowledge of the ancients in her eyes, their strength and wisdom far beyond her years. In that moment she seemed more goddess than Nosferatin. In that moment she seemed more.

"Is this what you want, Amisi? Really what you want?"

"Yes. I do believe it is."

I stood there in the centre of a busy pavement in downtown Wellington, a couple of vampires watching my back. Humans milling around waiting to enter the confines of a vampire cesspit, be trapped in the web they weaved and I looked at this strong and capable Nosferatin. I no longer saw the young and innocent girl, but the woman she wanted me to see.

I sighed.

"I have no idea how in hell you are going to convince Nero of this, but you have my blessing." She smiled at me. "I don't have to warn you though, Amisi, but I will. Watch your back with him, he plays for keeps."

Then she said something I hadn't expected to hear her

say.

"That's what I'm counting on." She turned away with a little wicked smile playing on her lips and I found myself looking at Erika in surprise. Erika shrugged her shoulders and said, "Each to their own, *chica*. Each to their own."

I shook the last remnants of fear and uncertainty aside and fished out my cellphone, dialling up my cousin's number. Let's see if we could get that break we were so desperately in need of. Time to stop playing nice Nosferatin and get my hands a little dirty.

He answered on the first ring and was keen as punch to meet for a drink. We arranged to meet up at the *Dockside Restaurant & Bar* - the same one we had met at before - in half an hour. Enough time for us to wander down there and for him to drive there from wherever it was that he lived. It dawned on me then, that I didn't know a lot about him. His home address. His work address. Just his cellphone number. That was all.

As we approached the bar I decided it might be best to start out easy, not frighten him. I still wasn't sure if he would have the information I was after, but if he was involved I didn't want to scare him. I needed to work into this slowly and the sight of two vampires at my side might just be the totally wrong impression I needed to avoid. So, Erika and Jett agreed to watch from a distance, blending into the surroundings and using a little of Jett's masking abilities to hide them from any potential human-against-vampire-vigilante in the area. I don't know what it was, but I kept having a bad feeling about this evening, as though someone had walked over my grave, the shivers down my spine just wouldn't stop. I rolled my shoulders as we

445

entered the bar in a vain attempt to dislodge that foreboding feeling, but to no avail. I felt really jumpy all of a sudden and nothing was going to shift it.

Amisi and I sat down at a table, well in view of the front doors after picking up a drink each from the bar. The more at home and relaxed in the environment the better it would seem to anyone taking an interest in a couple of Nosferatins in their city.

Tim was late, by about ten minutes, so both Amisi and I had finished our drinks when he sauntered in and were just playing with the melted ice at the bottom of our glasses. He was dressed to impress. I hadn't mentioned having anyone with me, so I only assumed he was trying to impress me or this was his usual Friday night club scene wear. Tight black jeans and a shiny black dress shirt, short sleeved, so it showed of his well toned and deeply tanned arms. His dark brown hair was spiked up, as though he had taken a lot of time and effort to get it looking just right. He looked cute, but kind of tough, he was definitely going for the bad boy image, but he'd thrown in the boy next door for good measure. It didn't surprise me that a few of the heads of women in the bar turned as he crossed the floor to our table.

His smile seemed genuine, his brown eyes sparkling in the lights and for a moment, again, I wondered if I had misjudged Tim. If in fact my friend Pete, who had warned me to be wary of him, had misjudged him too. He seemed so normal, so nice. I couldn't help the smile I returned, he just made you want to please him. His eyes flicked to Amisi and stalled. She seemed to have that effect on men, whether they were vampires or humans, they couldn't help but look twice. I don't think she realised the power over males that she possessed. She was disarming, natural, out of this world.

He recovered and came over to give me a hug, glancing at Amisi afterwards, probably no doubt wishing he could hug her too.

"Tim, this is my friend Amisi. Amisi, my cousin Tim."

She nodded slowly, her beautiful long neck stretching as her head inclined and then she offered him her hand to shake. He hesitated - star struck I think - and then shook it keenly. Holding on a little too long. She delicately removed her hand from his grip and smiled up at him. I think he was well and truly lost.

He cleared his throat and said, "Hi." Then blushed, I guess words were failing him right now, I'd better take pity on him.

"I was just going to get another drink for us, do you want one, Tim?"

He shook himself free of the Amisi spell and said, "No, I'll get them, you stay there. You're visitors in my city, it's the least I can do. Um, *Bacardi and Coke* right?" he asked me and when I nodded, he turned to Amisi. "And you Amisi, what can I get you?"

"I'll have the same thanks."

He smiled broadly and hopped off to the bar, a nice little spring in his step. I started to laugh. Amisi just held my gaze steadily and cocked an eyebrow.

"You have no idea, girlfriend, the effect you have over members of the opposite sex."

She humphed in reply, clearly not convinced. I just laughed harder.

Tim returned a moment later, laden down with drinks and settled into a seat at the table next to us, every now and then casting a glance at Amisi. I didn't want to jump right into the nitty gritty of my visit, so I opted for a more circuitous route instead.

"How's the apprenticeship going, Tim?"

"Oh, ah, yeah, it's great, thanks. Nearly completed it and I'll finally get paid full wages, can't wait."

"What are you training to be?" Amisi asked politely.

She could have been declaring her undying love, from the look Tim flashed at her.

"Carpentry. I'm training to be a builder."

"Great." She smiled at him and I got the distinct impression she was actually well aware of the effect she had over him and was planning to use it to disarm him as much as possible. Maybe they teach more than Nosferatin fighting skills in that community of hers. Interrogation skills must come in handy from time to time in the course of our job, maybe she had been trained to use her best assets whenever needed.

From the looks of how she held him trapped in her gaze, I think she would given 007 a run for his money. Impressive.

I thought I'd drop the big bomb and see how he took it.

"Amisi is a Nosferatin from Egypt, Tim. She's here to decide if she would like to take on the role in this city."

That got a response other than the blank look of adoration he had been flashing.

"Here? In Wellington?" He looked momentarily frightened and then sad and then completely nothing. He could have been a vampire with the speed in which he rescchooled his features. But, not fast enough for me to have not seen. I have been around a lot of vampires and honed my skills appropriately. When you only get a split second to assess a weakness in your enemy, you learn to use that split second well. He didn't like the idea of Amisi being here. Why?

Time to up the ante.

"You seem unhappy that your city will have a dedicated Nosferatin to hold the vampires accountable. I thought that was what you wanted, Tim. Or have things changed?"

"No. Nothing's changed. It's all good. It'll be great that she's here. I can sleep easy now." He took a swig of his beer, straight from the bottle and leaned back, all relaxed ease. I didn't buy it for one minute.

I sighed, but kept it well hidden. "Is there something you want to tell, cousin?"

His eyes drifted over to mine and they were empty. Empty of him, empty of feeling, empty of life. Shit. Pete had been right. Ghouls never get it wrong.

"We've got a situation, Tim," I said leaning forward and placing my drink on a paper coaster with care. I rested my elbows on the table in front of me, holding my hands out together where he could see them. "There's a group of humans who think they can run the vampires out of town." I watched him closely for a response, he didn't give me one, which considering what I had just said, only made me believe even more that he was in this right up to his neck. Even a Norm would have baulked at that statement.

"They have killed quite a few of their number. Many of which were good vampires, Tim. They weren't filled with

449

the Dark. And now, the humans have got a problem. Can you guess what that might be?"

He took a slow swig of beer and levelled his gaze at me.

"Are you telling me, that you no longer care that vampires hunt humans?" His whole persona had changed. His voice was lower than he normally spoke, his stature more menacing, his eyes not friendly. This was the real Tim. Bugger.

"I care, Tim. Moreover, I care that the humans are risking their necks and their families necks, for something that they are not well equipped to handle. This is not a game and vampires don't play nicely."

He barked out a laugh. "You think you know everything there is to know about being a Nosferatin, Lucinda? You're an orphan, you weren't even raised by one. I was raised by a family who has lived the life, has fought the fight, who has sacrificed everything because of those blood suckers. We are the Nosferatin, the true Nosferatin, not you. Not an orphaned whore."

Holy hell, what had I uncovered here?

"OK. Putting the slight on my virtue aside, what the fuck?"

He laughed again, bitterly. "You weren't even meant to live past your 25th birthday, yet here you are."

It suddenly dawned on me, that we had passed the one month moon's cycle since my 25th birthday. If I hadn't have joined, I would now be dead. And he knew it.

"So, who's the lucky vampire, Lucinda? Who did you sell your soul and the Nosferatin honour out to? Was it the vampire here, you keep coming to see? Or maybe one back in your city? I bet that's it, you'd want to stay close, wouldn't you? The Master of Auckland City perhaps? I know a lot about him, he's on our list. Once we get this town sorted, we'll be coming your way."

Like fucking hell you would. Just how many arseholes think they can threaten my vampire and get away with it? I'd had enough of playing Ms. Nice.

I gave him my best *fuck you* smile and took a long sip of my drink. "I'd like to see you try, cousin."

Amisi shifted next to me, she could see I was about to lose it big time. She glanced around the room, no doubt for Jett and Erika, but they were well hidden. I knew though, they would be listening to everything that was going on here. They would be ready to act if needed.

"You know," he said, not fazed by my retort, "your father would be most upset to see you now, if he were still alive. You would have disgusted him, as you do us. His whole life was dedicated to denying the Nosferatu our powers. When he and your mother accidentally got pregnant with you, he tried everything in his power to kill you both. In the end, the only thing he could think of doing was to die alongside you in that car. But, you survived. God knows how. Over a fifty metre cliff and nothing was left of that car, nothing at all. And yet there you were, in your car seat, somehow sprung free from the wreck, but unscathed. Their bodies crushed like watermelons dropping from a tall building onto concrete."

My hand was on my silver knife and I hadn't even realised it, the tip just under his chin. "You lie." My voice didn't even sound like mine any more, but some crazed and demented lunatic, ready to slice a pub patron in a bar.

451

Somehow no one around us noticed a damn thing and then I realised Jett must have covered us with his masking power, making us all but invisible to the crowd.

Unfortunately, Tim noticed too.

"Well, well, well, cousin. You brought back up." He stood up slowly. I went with him, the knife not moving, Amisi at my side with her hand also in her jacket. "So did I. You want to take this outside?"

"I want to gut you where you stand, you lying bastard."

He just smiled and it was creepy, even more creepy than a vampire's because it was wrong on his face. A face I had come to know with a different emotion playing across it, a trusting, friendly, kind of emotion. Not this hatred, this outright disgust.

"Come, Lucinda. Think of the Norms. We can continue this in private. I'm sure you have questions about daddy dearest."

He simply turned away from the knife and me. And walked out the door.

What choice did I have? I knew I'd be walking into a trap, that there would be his vigilante cohorts waiting in the wings. But, isn't that what I wanted? An audience with the creeps.

I took a deep breath, re-sheathed my knife, but shifted my shoulders, feeling the familiar weight of my Svante sword on my back and followed after him.

Images of my parents bodies crushed in a car wreck and questions rolling around my head as I walked out into the night.

Chapter 39
Whispering Sweet Nothings

He walked across the paved expanse of the pedestrian mall beside *Dockside*. Past the bench seats he had found me sitting on last time and around a corner away from the normal crowds. I couldn't see anyone else, but it was shadowy in the corners. Plenty of places to hide out, plenty of places to spring out from. Plenty of places to remain hidden and simply fire a gun.

Guns aren't big here in New Zealand, we're a little blessed when it comes to firearms. We have them, but not every Tom, Dick and Harry owns one. Still, there was a high chance that these fanatics didn't follow the law. Hell, of course they didn't, they killed vampires - who for all intents and purposes, look like average Joes to the general public - and they didn't bat an eye.

Tim stopped in the centre of the small clearing and turned slowly to see me, arms loosely held at his sides, but outstretched, so I could see he wasn't armed. It didn't put me at ease, he may not be armed, but his back up no doubt was.

"So, fire away. What do you want to know, Lucinda?"

Great choice of words, I thought.

"There is nothing you can tell me that I would believe, Tim. You've only ever lied, so why trust you now?" It's not that I didn't believe him, I had questions screaming in my mind about my father and what he may have done to my mother and been trying to do to me, when he drove that car over that cliff. But, asking Tim was not going to give me the truth. And if it did, I'd always doubt it. I'd have to find another way to get the answers I needed, but not here, not from him. I ached inside at the thought that my father had killed my mother though, I wasn't immune from that pain. The fact that I may have been a mistake that he felt compelled to rectify with my death, made me sick to the stomach. That I may have been the reason why my mother had died. I had always believed my father would be on my side, but I wasn't so sure now.

I wasn't so sure.

I rolled my shoulders again to centre myself with the weight of my Svante. I needed grounding, I was floating away.

"I have come to warn your people that Gregor means business." I could only try to reach Tim one more time. I am, if nothing else, persistent. I needed to at least try my best before the shit really hit the fan. "He will come after each and every one of you. And he will come after your families and friends. You need to get away, to stop this, to take cover. Anything that will stop the bloodshed."

Tim looked at me as though I was filth on the bottom of his shoes. "And you defend them? They are killers, Lucinda, how can you not see this? How can you not want to kill every last one of them like your blood family does? How can you not be one of us?"

"You are killers too, Tim."

"They are dead."

Man, was I so sick of hearing that old adage. Give it a rest already.

"If they were dead, Tim, they would be six feet under, not walking around, interacting with society, contributing to the world and loving." I saw the look of disgust on his face at that last word. "Yeah, Tim. They love, they care, they can be hurt. Just like you, just like me. And before you say it, I am not naïve. I know full well what lurks beneath the surface. I've had an upfront audience with the Dark and I'm at the top of its hit list right now. But, you know what? That Dark that resides in all of the vampires, it's got a close relative. It's the darkness I see in you. You're no different, you think you are, but you're not. Not really. The only real difference is, you don't have a me. Someone who is made to bring you back towards the Light. You don't have an angel willing to die for your soul. It's all on you. And I don't think you've got what it takes to fight it alone."

He spat on the paved ground at his feet.

"Enough of this shit. You're screwed in the head. You're better off dead. We should have completed what my uncle failed to do all those years ago and taken you out on the farm when we had the chance. A sitting fucking duck and they couldn't follow through with it. But, I can. I will." He looked straight at me and said to no one in particular. "Do it!"

I don't know what made me pull out my Svante, but I just knew I'd be better off with it in my hand. Amisi drew her dagger, a long thin blade, she hid down her thigh and Erika and Jett materialised beside us. It wasn't enough to stop what would happen, but I felt thankful to have them with me right now.

Just as the gun shots rang out in the courtyard I felt the familiar pull of vampires nearby. Not the evil-lurks-in-my-city pull, but that newer one, that stronger one. The one that told me, it was time for Drinkies. They were after whatever it is they thought they would get when they drained me. The Forbidden Drink waiting to be consumed. But, I was

455

kind of busy right now, throwing myself to the ground and covering my head. I felt someone lift me off the paving and run with me to cover. I realised it was Jett and that Erika had taken Amisi to cover across the way too. I could see them and they looked OK, but Jett had taken a bullet to the shoulder. When I reached up to check him, he just grunted. "I'll be fine, but we're in the shit here. What do you want to do? Call Gregor for help?"

We were in the shit all right, but not just from the crazy humans. I could feel about thirty vampires nearby and they weren't part of Gregor's line. They were filled with evil, but there was one amongst them that left me breathless. When I tried to concentrate on their signature I got shut down. I had never been shut out of a vampire when *seeking* before, this one just slammed the door in my face and sent the deadbolt home. Before it had evicted me, I felt it, a Darkness so pure it was complete. I'd bet every vampire I held dear that this was the big bad nasty, evil personified, the *she*, the Champion had referred to. Fuck me, we were in trouble.

I quickly gave Jett a run down of the situation and watched as the blood drained from his face. Like I've said before, that's a pretty nifty trick for a vampire, right there.

"We better let Erika know."

"She already does."

"How?"

He looked at me steadily. "The master has told her."

"How the fuck does Michel know?" He was not meant to be watching this at all.

"Don't get mad, Luce, you can't afford to lose it right now OK? But, we've been keeping him pretty much abreast of the situation since we got here. He's not in your brain, but he sure as fuck is in both of ours."

That cheeky fucking vampire lied to me. He said he'd stay out of this. God dammit. Did he have a suicide wish? He'd be pretty friggin' irate by now. He's probably got a core of his line holding him down. Or did he?

"Please tell me he is not coming here right now." I said it very slowly and through gritted teeth.

"He is not coming here right now."

I looked at him, his face was straight, no emotion whatsoever. That vampire preternatural calm. Fuck.

"You're lying, aren't you?"

"What do you think, Luce? You've just told me - and in turn him - that the Queen of Darkness is around the corner with thirty vamps and you think he's just gonna sit down with a beer and chill?"

Oh sweet Jesus. We did not need this.

"Tell him to back off. We'll get Nero here and some of Gregor's vampires, but if Michel steps foot in this city it will mean war with Gregor and probably the *Iunctio* as well. We can't afford that."

I was too angry to send a thought towards him myself and besides he may still be shutting me out, but he wasn't Jett. I waited for Jett to answer me, while bullets still ricocheted around my head every few seconds or so, just checking to see if we had moved. At the moment we were all in a kind of stand off, none of us able to move from our hidey holes without getting our own little holes from a stray bullet. In the meantime, evil came closer, drawn not only by the promise of me, but by the blood and sweat and discord in the air around us.

"He's agreed to wait at the city limits. But he will enter if he fears for your life."

Great. Just great. I grabbed my cellphone and sent a text to Amisi telling her to call Nero and get his arse over here, then I started a call through to Gregor. It rang once and then he answered, his voice purring down the line.

"*Ma petite chasseuse*, you have changed your mind? You wish to spend the evening in my arms."

A bullet whizzed by my head.

"What was that?" He wasn't purring any more.

"It's a bullet. I kind of started a gun fight down by the docks with the human arseholes who happen to be my extended family and fucked in the head. And I can sense about thirty vampires nearby who don't belong to you and want to take a drink from me. And right now I'm up shit creek without a paddle, because the fucking Queen of Darkness has decided to pay me a visit as well. Wanna come play?"

"Oh, you do say the sweetest things to me, my dear. I shall be there with mine in two minutes." He rang off without saying goodbye.

"Now we just have to wait, either Gregor will get here before the bad vamps or he won't." I took a deep breath in then added quietly, almost to myself. "Either way, we're pretty much fucked."

Jett just patted me on the shoulder and settled in to a more comfortable position, making sure none of his vast bulk stuck out the side of the hidey hole we were sitting in. He shut his eyes and looked like he was taking a wee nap. Fucking vampires.

"They're close," I said shifting my weight to stretch out

an ache.

"How close?" Jett asked, not opening his eyes.

"Like the other side of the humans, close. Do you think I should warn them? The humans?"

He opened an eye at me to that. "Are you fucking kidding me? They're shooting at us, let the fuckers get what's coming to them."

I kind of agreed, but they were family. I flipped my cellphone open and rang Tim. Jett just sighed and gave me a good hard stare. I mouthed back, what? And shrugged my shoulders. I'm a good girl, I can't help it.

"What is it, Lucinda? I'm kind of busy trying to shoot you right now."

Ah, Tim, we could have had so many laughs together, but you had to turn into an evil fuckwit, didn't you?

"Listen, there's a bunch of very evil vampires about to pounce on you. They aren't mine and they don't belong to the Master of this City. They are bad news, Tim, they will kill you. Be prepared."

I rang off. I'd done my bit. He probably thought I was pissing in the dirt on this one, but hey, I tried. I had warned him.

"Gee, he's gonna believe you on that one," Jett added sarcastically.

"If you don't have anything nice to say, then shut the fuck up," I muttered.

"Such beautiful language, *ma cherie*. I shall miss it when you no longer visit. Does Amisi have your penchant for swearing?"

I spun around and just about face planted into Gregor. I threw a look at Jett. He shrugged. "He snuck up on me and

459

besides, he's on our side isn't he?"

I'm quite sure he didn't sneak up on Jett, he just had chosen not to tell me. The bastard likes to catch me off guard.

"So, where are we at, *ma cherie?*" Gregor was crouched down behind us, his hand came out to rest on my shoulder. I didn't shrug it off, that kind of seemed petty.

"Where are your vamps?" I asked instead.

"Fifteen are approaching from the rear, another five either side of us and three behind where we sit.

Almost enough, almost. If we didn't have the humans to contend with and the evil Queen of Darkness orchestrating the whole event.

I let my senses flow out and felt a sharp stabbing pain in my temple when I reached the Dark void. It lashed out a feeler, or at least that's what it felt like and tried to wrap around my shields, fingering here and there, trying to get inside, looking for a weakness. I felt Michel's presence frantically building further shields around my mind, his own on top of mine, eventually she stopped trying and I collapsed back against Gregor.

"*Ma cherie,*" he murmured against my head. "What happened?"

"I don't think I should *seek* any time soon, she wasn't playing nice."

"Are you hurt?"

I shook my head. There was an ache, but Michel was trying to calm me.

"No, I'm fine. But, they're about to strike the humans, they've been watching and have grown impatient. They see them as an obstacle to me. Any second now."

460

"Then we wait. One less problem," he muttered, but his hands were running up and down my arms. I pulled my myself forward and out of his grasp. Jett just smiled at me and winked. I could just imagine what he was thinking: atta girl, don't give him an inch.

Gregor didn't seem fazed, he was too busy communicating with his vamps I think.

The shit hit the fan about 30 seconds later, right when I noticed Nero flickering into sight next to Amisi. His eyes immediately found mine and I let a breath of air out I had been holding. Of all the cavalry that had arrived I trusted Nero the most.

The gunshots stopped firing at us and started sounding off in the other direction with a frantic boom, boom-boom-boom, boom. The staccato rhythm sending shockwaves through the air, the sound reverberating off the walls around us, even louder than those they had been firing at us before.

After what felt like an eternity, one in which we could have simply run the fuck away had we thought of it, the gunshots ended and all we heard was the sickening sound of flesh being torn. No doubt jugulars severed and blood spilled by the bucket load. Poor Tim. He thought he knew what evil vampires were all about. He knew jack shit, nothing.

Silence sounded out with a sudden finality, making my heart leap into my throat and my palms begin to sweat. I could feel her. I could feel her like she was standing right before me and she was calling my name. I went to stand up and Jett grabbed a hold of me.

"No you don't, mistress. The master can hear her too, in

461

your head. You're not going anywhere."

I struggled against him, getting more and more frantic to break free and run to that beautiful voice that promised so much. That told me I would be happy in her arms, that she could give me what I wanted; my family, my father, my mother, a sister or brother to carry on the gene, to have children for me to love and hold as though they were my own. She promised she'd make it happen, I would never be alone again. All I needed was to step out into the centre of the courtyard and she would come to me. She would save me from the bleak world I lived in alone.

I started crying when I knew I couldn't break free. When I knew I couldn't get to her. When I knew I wouldn't see my father again and I would be alone forever. Jett held me close and stroked my hair and kept repeating words in my ear I couldn't understand. And then finally, they broke through.

And all hell broke loose in their wake.

Chapter 40
Just Shut Up and Go!

Gregor leapt up and joined in with the fighting, his vampires swarming into the scarcely light area with fierce and determined looks on their faces. Some carried weapons, knives, swords, machetes, you name it, they had it. And so did the others. I couldn't see her or feel her anymore, it was as though she had vanished as soon as Gregor's vamps jumped out of the shadows, as though they had scared her away.

Jett held me firm though, I knew he wanted to be out there too, helping Erika as she swung her Svante sword with such skill and grace. I watched as Amisi staked a vampire, Gregor shouting out in approval at her side. I saw Nero spinning, none of the vampires seeing the beauty that I could. So powerful, so perfect, so sure. He staked two vampires before they even realised he was there.

"She's gone, Jett. Let me go help."

"No. The master has instructed me to hold you here. To keep you safe."

God dammit, if we were back to this crap bloody control issue, I would throttle him. This was my job. This is what I am. The *Sanguis Vitam Cupitor*, the *Prohibitum Bibere*, the *Lux Lucis Tribuo*. This is what I am meant to do. To hell with the fact that I am outnumbered. I am an emissary of Nut, Michel cannot stand in my way. I gathered my Light and moulded it very carefully, then I let it out straight for Jett.

He took a deep breath in when it hit fair and square in the centre of that broad chest of his and then he toppled over backwards out cold.

"Sorry mate," I muttered as I pulled him back behind the shield of the low wall we had been hiding behind. "I'm sure you'll thank me in the morning."

He'd wake in about five to ten minute's time, thinking he'd had the best sex in his entire life.

Lucinda!

Oh, you're back. Great. *Welcome to the party.*

She may not have left and now you are unprotected. Man, was he fuming. I could feel the fury down the line of our connection, it prickled against my skin like a bad rash.

Michel, stay right where you are. Promise me you won't come into the city. I can't feel her anymore, it's just vampires. You know the normal evil ones. Let me do my job.

I didn't wait for an answer, just lifted my Svante off the ground and headed towards the battle. I could have used stakes, but with this many, a sword allowed a certain distance. Distance was good when being attacked by multiple vampires. One on one, give me a stake any day. Multiples, I'm going all Highlander on their arses.

Besides, these bastards had swords of their own.

As soon as I entered the middle of the courtyard I knew Michel had been right. She was still here, she had just been waiting for me to play the hero.

I couldn't stop to think about that now, I was in full battle mode and those vampires closest to me were hungry. Their red rimmed eyes shone brightly in the night, when they spotted me, they saucered bigger and their lips peeled back to reveal long fangs ready to go.

Gregor's vampires tried to get around me, to hold them off, no doubt instructed to by Gregor, but I held my own.

464

Slashing one then the next, unable to land killing blows but managing to keep their weapons off me, holding them at bay. We'd been at it maybe ten minutes, neither side making much headway. I could still feel old evil chick somewhere in the periphery, but she didn't seem keen to get involved, so I blocked her from my mind. Just kept a subtle check on her location and poured my efforts into what was in front of me.

Finally, I managed to land a jab in the right place and the vampire I'd struck burst into dust in the air. I felt like letting out a cry of celebration, but he was soon replaced by another and it started all over again. I wasn't tiring yet, I'm built for more than this, but I was beginning to wonder just how long this was going to go on for. If we were lucky, the sun would rise and the vamps would all burn. Of course, that would mean Gregor and his lot, as well as Erika and Jett, would have to seek cover, but you know, it was a tempting thought.

I didn't exactly feel cumbersome with the Svante, but I did feel disconnected. I liked my sword, I really did and I could do fantastic things with it, but I couldn't help seeing out of the corner of my eye, the simple and effective moves of Nero with just a stake. Sure he had to get closer to the vampires than I was, but by getting closer he was landing more blows. I was simply using the sword to fend off their advances, unable to land a strike because I was still too far away. I missed the feel of my stake. I missed the close confines of the fight.

To hell with this, I shouted at a nearby vamp to cover me, he jumped in front of my body and I re-sheathed my sword, managing the motion in a heartbeat. Practice,

practice, practice. I slipped a stake out of my jacket and felt immediately calmer.

I let Gregor's vamp know I was back on the team and started getting busy for real. I've learned so much over the past two years, not just from Nero more recently, although his tutelage has been amazing, but also from the shape shifters, from Rick. I know every kick boxing move there is, every kick, every punch, but even more, I can fight dirty. Like a street fighter, the Taniwhas taught me that. I can roll and duck and flip and scamper like the best of them. Without my sword in tow, I became a breeze, a leaf in the air, fluttering from one point to the next. My speed has increased since I joined with Michel and came into my powers, I'm faster than even Nero sometimes, especially when I am in the zone.

I noticed Nero watching me with a look of pride on his face, even as he battled two vampires at once. I liked that he appreciated my skills. If there has been one goal in my life over the past couple of months, it would have been to have made Nero proud. He has always appeared the most accomplished, the most beautiful fighter I have ever witnessed. I don't believe I come even close to his natural style, his natural ability. Hell, he's had five hundred years to master it, maybe I could be as good as him, given time. But, he is stunning and to have him look at me right now with that wonderful look of pride on his face filled my heart to over flowing.

I was distracted from my thoughts by the vampire in front of me though, who had decided it was time to stop playing by the rules and simply tossed his mate right at my head. The vampire that flew through the air screamed like a girl and I ducked and rolled out of the way, only to have the shooter land on top of me and flatten me to the ground. Everyone was busy, no one could help, but I was used to one on one and just because he had me down, didn't mean I was out. I threw my head back against his face as he came in for a taster, smashing his nose a beauty and making him rear back in pain. It was enough to wriggle out from under him, twist over on my back and land a kick with both boots to his face as he crouched above where I had been held only moments before.

He swore and fell backwards, I didn't waste any time, but jumped on top of him to land my stake. He tried to swipe me away and managed to swat at my head, making stars appear briefly but my stake had already found its mark and simply required me to push it home. I did and landed in dust. I was up on my feet in an instant, ready to round on the flyer who had gathered himself together, crushed his inner girl and come back with fangs down and out. We danced, the usual dance, but I was getting my groove on now and had him staked within sixty seconds flat.

These guys were numerous, but not good. I picked they weren't *Iunctio* guards this time round, but effective only due to numbers. There had been a lot of them, now there were only a handful. I hadn't been the only one to get busy. Amisi was covered in dust and sweating, but still managing to look beautiful. Gregor and his vampires were like elite soldiers, all swift, economical moves, minimal effort, maximum gain. Erika and the now recovered Jett, were fighting side by side and they worked well together. Complementing each other, setting one guy up to be ended by their partner. Jett would lure them in, land a few blows, get them into position and Erika would pierce the heart. It was also beautiful, in a cat and mouse tag team kind of way. Nero was just Nero. A flash of Light so bright he dazzled. I smiled as I battled with a loner vamp. I owed Nero a big fat apology. I'd been a real arse lately and he deserved so much better. He was an amazing trainer and an even more amazing friend. I vowed I'd make it up to him, as soon I finished this piece of shit right in front of me and we wound up for the night for real.

I knew we could do it, we were almost there. It was just a matter of cleaning up the dregs, glazing any nearby humans and hiding any evidence that any of this had gone down at all tonight. I almost started to relax, but the vamp who held my attention was slightly better than the rest and had just landed a rather nasty spinning back fist to my face, making blood start to trickle down from my nose and a sharp pain lance across my skull. The son of a bitch had probably broken it. So much for making a good impression on my teacher. Nero no doubt still looked like he'd just stepped out of the shower and into cleanly pressed clothes. Mine had rips and now blood splatters and it was only going to get worse, because don't noses just love to bleed when they've been hit? I swiped my arm across my mouth, catching the blood, but avoiding making contact with the now most sensitive part of my entire friggin' body.

I cranked my neck to the side and rolled my shoulders and then flew at the mofo, executing a beautiful side kick to his torso, following it up with flying punch to his face and what do you know? Blood started pouring out of his nose too. Payback is a bitch. Before he had a chance to swipe at it I sunk my stake in the sweet spot and put him out of his misery.

I was feeling a sense of pride at that move when I knew something was wrong. The sound of fighting; that hard core wrenching of a fist on flesh, air being pounded out of a body in a grunt, the splat of a face-plant to concrete, the stomp of a boot on the ground, the metal clang of a sword on sword or dagger, all of it had vanished. There was nothing but stillness in the air. I spun around and every living being in that square was still, suspended in the night air like grotesque mannequins in the shop window of *Smith and Caugheys*. It was surreal. It was unnatural. It was scary as fuck.

I knew, before I found her, that she had decided to say hello. I sensed her oozing out of the shadows, like something thick and viscous. She peeled away from the dark at the edge of my vision and began to slide across the ground towards me. I could still move, I could still fight, I could have run away, but I didn't. I stood there terrified by what slunk towards me, not human, not animal, just a dense black void of goo pouring across the pavers. She began to solidify a little, the closer she got, as though she couldn't help herself, she needed me to see her. I caught a glimpse of a beautiful face, but then it would be, if she was a goddess like Nut. I thought it looked familiar, but I couldn't place it. Maybe she looked like Nut, maybe that was it, maybe she was the evil twin or something, but I didn't know. I just knew she was evil, that she seemed familiar, but I couldn't tell if it was the feel of her evil or the look of her face that felt so familiar to me.

Just as she came to a stop in front of me and reached

out a hand, she blurred in my vision, so I couldn't get a decent look. But I knew she was growing stronger and no longer just a shape of black, but becoming a person, a goddess. And even though I wanted to see her face, to know who this evil was, I was glad I couldn't. I felt relieved, but I also knew she was going to kill me and I wasn't doing a damn thing to stop her.

I wanted to lift my stake and strike her through the heart. I knew she had one, I could feel it beating. I knew she had taken on a corporeal form even though I could no longer see anything other than a blur.

I watched in slow motion as her hands raised up and a dark black shape began to form at the tip of her fingers, building, getting bigger, stronger, taking on more form and more substance. Kind of like my Light does when I'm about to thrust it out as a weapon. Oh shit.

This was it then and I stood by like a stupid untrained fool. Paralysed.

I'm sorry, Michel. I'm so sorry.

Suddenly, I felt a shift beside me, but it couldn't be any of the vampires, they were all wax models right now, but it was something, someone. I turned my head in time to see the glint of a stake in the light of the moon and the bright white linen of Nero's Egyptian clothing, as he shot out in front of my body, stretching out his arms and torso to cover mine, whilst throwing out his stake at the evil. And I watched in horror as his body took the full frontal force of her Dark striking out from the end of her fingers.

She flickered and wavered and poofed into thin air with a loud crack, the vampires and Amisi all around me falling to the ground with groans and moans and shouts and curses. And Nero landed on the ground at my feet in a crumpled heap of blood. So much blood pouring out of everywhere.

I was in shock, I was alive, I was crying even before I reached for him, because I knew what I would find. He was still breathing, he was still Dream Walking, he was still with me, but he was bad. His arm was barely attached at the right shoulder, his femoral artery had been severed on both legs. His neck had been sliced open and his chest - oh God, his chest - was a ruined mincemeat of red bloody flesh.

"Nero," I whispered as I fell to my knees and tried to find a space to touch him. Everywhere looked painful, everywhere looked red and raw and bloody. I didn't want to hurt him, I didn't want to touch him, I didn't want to know it was real and if I touched him and got bloody then it was.

It was his hand on his left side which grabbed mine. I felt the blood well up between my fingers, there was just so much red, so much warm liquid, but he was pale and getting colder.

"Go back." I think that's what I said, it sounded kind of weird, a little off. "Go back and let Nafrini heal you."

He shook his head and gurgled something, I leant down to try to catch his words, my hair falling into his chest and all that blood. So much blood. I didn't care, his grip was growing weak, his eyes, those beautiful cinnamon and copper and coffee coloured eyes, the windows to his most gorgeous soul, were fluttering, but he still tried to say something. The words lost in amongst the blood pooling in his mouth. He leaned over painfully and spat it out and then tried again.

471

"Just shut up and go," I begged. I was really crying now. Great big heaves of sobs. I had no idea what was happening around me, I could sense a presence, a lot of presences, but all I could hear, all I could care about, was the man in front of me who was dying. I knew he was and the stubborn prick was not returning to his body, where Nafrini could be healing him. He was clinging to me and trying to say something I could not understand.

He kept trying, right up until I felt his essence go. Right up until his hand vanished from mine and I knew without a doubt that he had died. He kept trying to tell me something, something obviously so important to him, that he stayed with me, in a Dream, right up to the end.

I don't know what it was he was trying to say. I couldn't understand him.

But I do know what my last words were to my beloved teacher and friend.

"Just shut up and go."

Epilogue

The realisation that Nero had died protecting me, saving my life, came minutes after he had vanished. Amisi was on her cellphone wailing, confirmation of his death and that Nafrini had burst into dust next to him, coming down the line. Nafrini Al-Suyuti, Master of Cairo City for the past six hundred years, was no more. And neither was her kindred Nosferatin, my beautiful, intense, compassionate friend, Nero.

I thought Amisi would hate me. I had caused the death of her mentor and her Queen. But, when I staggered over to comfort her, with no one getting in my way, she dropped her cellphone and threw herself in my arms. We clung to each other crying and crying and crying and aching for our loss.

It was Michel's arms that came around me, only making me cry more because he had crossed the borders of the city and could now incite war with Gregor because of me.

Be still, ma douce. It is all right, Gregor has invited me in.

I was vaguely aware it was Erika who helped Amisi to a car, that Gregor's vampires formed a sort of honour guard as we were almost carried away from the scene. Michel told me later, it was because we had fought so well beside them and had sacrificed something precious on their soil.

Michel and I accompanied Amisi back to Cairo and stayed for the funeral and *Elysium* service held for Nafrini. It took three days of celebrations, a carnival like atmosphere, a happy remembrance of life. Nafrini had a good second, who was more than capable of taking over the reins. The line would not be without a Master. Nero's Nosferatin community assured a place in their world. We paid our respects to the newly appointed Master. Awan Hamadi seemed a nice vampire, as far as vampires go. Amisi knew him well and it was with his blessing that she returned to New Zealand with us, probably for good.

I hadn't expected her to come back. I thought it would be too painful, that she would need her family now more than ever. She said she would miss them, but her job was now helping me. I think that's what hurt the most. That she had been pulled into the war so completely now, as my new side-kick. I couldn't turn her away though, she knew things about being a Nosferatin that I didn't. She was no Nero, but she brought a chest full of scrolls and various other paraphernalia relating to the Prophesy with her. She had decided to educate herself and to take over where Nero had left off. She wasn't the Herald, but the Herald had done his job, we just needed someone to interpret the signs and head us in the right direction.

I knew Amisi needed to do that, I knew she needed to keep busy, to honour Nero's death, but the hours she spent pouring over those scrolls for the next two weeks was painful to watch. She immersed herself in the Prophesy and we lost our shining Light, our Amisi. She became fixated and nothing would tear her away. Erika tried, I tried, even Michel tried. But she was glued to them and would not let anyone else touch them. It was her responsibility. And hers alone.

I decided all I could give her was time and I ended up being the one to make pancakes and bake blueberry muffins and force feed my friend. Out of desperation, when we hit the two week mark, I called Gregor. His human vigilante problem had been fixed, there didn't seem to be any of them left alive. So, now I really was an orphan. Other than my Aunt and Uncle, who are really the only ones who count anyway, I have no relatives. Well, none that I'm aware of. I still have questions about my father, about what happened on that South Island road when they were killed, but I have no one to ask. My Aunt and Uncle wouldn't know. They didn't even know I was a half breed supernatural, how would they know about my heritage at all?

With Michel's permission I invited Gregor to Auckland. I was grasping at straws, but Amisi had promised she would take on the role of Nosferatin in Wellington once the war had been won, despite the fact that she didn't accompany me when I went there once a week, to hunt. Gregor and I had developed a kind of easy relationship. He'd still flirt, but he rarely touched. I think he had finally got the message when it was only Michel who could calm me after Nero died. Apparently Gregor had tried, to no avail. That's why he had allowed Michel to enter his city. He couldn't bear to watch me so distraught.

Gregor turned up on a stormy Spring night and I left him to Amisi and the house and took a walk along the beach under the solemn gaze of the moon. I asked Nut if the pain would ever leave me, if I could accept what had happened to my friend. She didn't answer, but the wind died down and just caressed, no longer battering me with sea spray, but warming me with a soft touch here and a gentle sweep there. I felt desolate, but not alone and I knew Nero was with her, with our Nut. And that she was taking good care of him until I arrived and could apologise for the final words I never managed to say. That I loved him, maybe not the way he had wanted, but in a way that meant more to me than just a friend.

I hadn't been able to tell he was there, I was on a beach and he always smells of fresh sea salt spray to me, so his scent had been covered by nature, but the fresh smell of clean cut grass did cross my mind briefly. It wasn't until he stepped out in front of me though, hands in his black trousers, open neck black shirt rolled up his beautifully sculptured arms, his lovely long near-black hair blowing in the gentle breeze, that I noticed him at all. He smiled and took my breath away, as he always does. As he has always done.

"I thought you might like some company, *ma douce*."

"I'd love some."

He came and wrapped an arm around my shoulders, kissed my forehead and starting walking slowly with me in the sand. No one else was around, just us, the waves, the odd seagull taking a late night dip and the moon.

"Do you think Gregor can reach her?"

"I don't know. I hope so," I replied, leaning my body against the length of his. "At this point I'm prepared to bring in anyone if it will make a difference. He is going to be her Master of the City and I get the impression, there's something more there too."

"Ah." He laughed quietly. "You are hoping for a trigger other than work, to flip our Amisi back to life. I do hope you are right, *ma douce*. For many reasons."

I could just imagine what other reasons Michel would have. If Gregor showed a romantic interest in Amisi, wouldn't it just make Michel's day?

"I do still care for him, *ma douce*. It is not all business."

Yeah, right.

He squeezed my shoulders at that come back.

We walked on silently for a while. Enjoying the setting, enjoying each other.

"We should do this more often. I do not think we stop to breathe enough, you and I."

"It's a bit hard, Michel, with a war and crazy shape shifters and idiotic humans and a Dark goddess who isn't dead, but just biding her time before she can take another shot at me."

He stopped me and turned me towards himself, wrapping both arms around my shoulders and lying his forehead against mine. This is one of his favourite positions, head to head as it were. He likes it, I think, because he can smell me, can feel my breath against his skin, where it hits his throat just below his chin. He brought one hand back around to tip my chin up and studied my face for a moment, taking all of me in. The colour of his eyes was hard to ascertain in the moon light, I was guessing still a deep blue, nothing else, but when he whispered against my lips, "We should make time." Then gently brushed his own mouth against mine and slipped his tongue inside, I was guessing a little indigo, maybe amethyst was starting to build there, in the depths, changing the deep blue to something altogether different and just as beautiful.

We kissed slowly at first, then more deeply. He pulled my body against his, moulding me with his own, wrapping me up in his arms in a beautiful blanket of Michel, something beyond intimate, beyond perfect and all mine. His hands drifted lower, down my spine, into the dip at the base of my back, cupping both my buttocks, lifting me off the ground and forcing my legs to wrap around him. I could feel his response to me then, hard and firm and long, straining against his trousers, pleading to be released.

I thought he might very well take this further, right here, right now. You know how he is with public displays of affection and you couldn't get more public than the beach, despite it being after midnight. And he was still very much on the claiming wagon, no changes there, despite the fact that we were spending every day together and practically every night. How the claiming had not yet been satisfied, I do not know, but I guess I was still holding something back, I just wish I knew what it was. Michel never complained though, he just took what he could get and kept giving in return. And was I really that upset about being claimed? Not a chance, this is Michel. I could never say no, even at the beginning and definitely not now.

He had walked us over to a low stone wall that surrounds the beach and propped me up on it, still kissing, still touching, still rubbing that beautiful length of his against me. Teasing, letting me know exactly what he was planning to do. I was giving everything I had back too.

Just when I thought he couldn't hold out any further I felt it. At first I thought it was my *seeking* ability, some sort of call from a vampire in the CBD. They still didn't seem to want to meet me out in St. Helier's Bay, it was always a knock on the metaphysical door and off to the city I went. I think that's why Michel was stalling on my apartment, he liked me having that warning. I didn't really complain.

Where would I fit Amisi, a chest full of scrolls, Erika, who was equally part of my home life and Michel's gym in my one bedroom apartment? I think he may well have won the move-in-with-me argument. Even if it wasn't *Sensations* it was still his home.

But, it wasn't my *Prohibitum Bibere* powers that called right now, it was something else altogether. It was another bright light, they always are, they always start that way. I knew it was a power, I'd received a few by now, I knew what they felt like. And I knew Michel was aware too, still in my thoughts, still with me. How many more powers, though, could there be? Wasn't I done already? Hadn't I got my cup full of mojo by now? It seemed not.

Rather than fight it, as I had done so in the past, I just let it wash all over me. I was vaguely aware of a shot of light shooting straight up to the stars, kind of like those huge search lights they have on tall buildings in the city at New Years Eve, strobing across the galaxy, blinding aliens in the Milky Way. I think Michel might have said something, something that sounded pretty much like, "*Merde!*" But I couldn't do anything about it, I was at its beck and call, not the other way around. Kind of familiar. Nut always gives me powers that I have absolutely no control over for at least the first few weeks, why should his one be any different?

When it finally subsided, I don't know how long it took, but it felt like a week, I collapsed against Michel's chest, his firm arms holding me tight and we both held our breaths to see what monster would peek out from behind a closed door. When nothing happened for at least ten minutes we began to relax, incrementally, slowly, uncertainly. Still nothing went boo!

"Wow. That was anti-climactic," I said into the still night air.

"With you, *ma douce*, nothing is anti-climactic."

"What do you think it is?"

He brushed my hair out of my eyes, returned his head to his favourite position and inhaled deeply.

"No matter what it is, my love, we will face it together."

And I knew he was right. We would. It wouldn't be easy, it wouldn't nice, this Prophesy was no picnic, no slow walk in the park. It was not about comfort, but I knew I would have him beside me and that's all that mattered.

Right now, that's all that mattered to me.

Made in the USA
San Bernardino, CA
31 October 2017